THE HIGHWAYMAN

Kendra Chase awoke with a massive headache. Her brother Jason couldn't be serious. After her disastrous interview with the Duke of Lechmere, he'd laid down the law: she would be wed by summer's end.

Riding in the fresh country air was helping her headache clear, but just thinking about that weasel Lechmere made her shiver. And the rest of her prospects weren't much better.

The Earl of Shrewsbury came complete with a meddling mother for which the "shrew" in her name was an all-too-fitting description. The Marquess of Rochford was kind enough, but his hair was completely gray—no doubt from dealing with his seven unruly children. Viscount Davenport didn't talk—he whined. The Duke of Lancashire lived in—well, Lancashire—which was entirely too far from her family. The Earl of Morely was wealthy and wise—but nearing fifty. Lord Rosslyn was young, handsome, and fun loving, but lacking somewhat in brains. She wondered if he could read.

Jason couldn't be serious.

Coming out of her thoughts, she slowed to a stop. She hadn't realized how far she'd ridden. In fact, she noticed with a start, she was at the same spot where she'd seen the highwayman yesterday.

Also by Lauren Royal

Amethyst
Emerald
"Forevermore" in *In Praise of Younger Men*

AMBER

Lauren Royal

A SIGNET BOOK

SIGNET
Published by New American Library, a division of
Penguin Putnam Inc., 375 Hudson Street,
New York, New York 10014, U.S.A.
Penguin Books Ltd, 27 Wrights Lane,
London W8 5TZ, England
Penguin Books Australia Ltd, Ringwood,
Victoria, Australia
Penguin Books Canada Ltd, 10 Alcorn Avenue,
Toronto, Ontario, Canada M4V 3B2
Penguin Books (N.Z.) Ltd, 182–190 Wairau Road,
Auckland 10, New Zealand

Penguin Books Ltd, Registered Offices:
Harmondsworth, Middlesex, England

First published by Signet, an imprint of New American Library,
a division of Penguin Putnam Inc.

First Printing, July 2001
10 9 8 7 6 5 4 3 2 1

PUBLISHER'S NOTE
This is a work of fiction. Names, characters, places, and incidents either
are the product of the author's imagination or are used fictitiously,
and any resemblance to actual persons, living or dead, business
establishments, events, or locales is entirely coincidental.

For my children,
Brent, Blake, and Devonie,
who have eaten too much McDonald's
so that Mom could write

With love and thanks
for enabling me to see the world
again through a child's eyes,
and for always being there
to remind me what's really important

Acknowledgments

I wish to thank:

My editor, Audrey LaFehr, for always knowing how to make my stories better; my agent, Elaine Koster, for being so supportive; my critique partner, Terri Castoro, for her willingness to read it again no matter how many times I decide to Change Everything; my husband, Jack, for encouraging this all-consuming career, even though he thought he was marrying a jeweler, not a writer; my son, Brent, for keeping up my Web site without too much nagging; Ian Archibald, Project Manager for the Burntisland Heritage Trust, for information regarding the search for the King Charles I shipwreck; seventeenth-century poets George Herbert, Robert Herrick, Richard Lovelace, and Samuel Rowley, for inspiring Trick's poetry (and generously—if unwittingly—allowing him to borrow a line or two for period flavor); my official First Readers—Alison Bellach, Taire Martyn, and Karen Nesbitt—for lots of laughs and invaluable feedback; Herb, Joan, Ken, and Dawn Royal, for reading and commenting on the sort-of-spiffed-up version (and, as always, for being willing to make fools of themselves promoting their daughter's/sister's/sister-in-law's books); Libby

Graham and Andrew Metz, for touring me through the used bookstores on Charing Cross Road and sending hard-to-find research material from the UK; my fearless and intrepid Publicity Team—Debbie Alexander, Dick Alexander, Jane Armstrong, Robin Ashcroft, Joyce Basch, Alison Bellach, Caroline Bellach, Diana Brandmeyer, Carol Carter, Terri Castoro, Vicki Crum, Elaine Ecuyer, Shirley Feit, Dale Gordon, Darren Holmquist, Lori Howell, Irm Jawor, Taire Martyn, Cindy Meyer, Lynne Miller, Amanda Murphy, Karen Nesbitt, DeeDee Perkins, Nancy Phillips, Jack Poole, Stacey Royal, Wendi Royal, Sandy Shniderson, Diena Simmons, Connie Story, Stacy Volpe, and Julie Walker—for enthusiastically going above and beyond . . . and, as always, all the readers who have taken the time to write and tell me how you feel about my stories, for being my inspiration. Thanks to each and every one of you—you're what keeps me writing.

AMBER

Chapter One

Sussex, England
June 1668

"Jason is right, Kendra. You're twenty-three years old, and 'tis high time you married."

Kendra Chase slanted a glance at the plainly dressed stranger sharing the public coach, then glared at her twin, Ford, across the shabby interior. "Not to the Duke of Lechmere," she said, exasperated. "I'll not be 'Your Graced' for the rest of my life."

"And what, pray tell," Jason, their oldest brother, drawled in an annoyed tone, "would be wrong with that?" Crammed onto the bench seat between Kendra and his wife, Caithren, Jason tried unsuccessfully to stretch his long legs. "I am only attempting to see that you live a life of comfort. Would you prefer to travel like this all the time?"

As if to drive home her brother's point, the springless vehicle lurched in and out of a rut, rattling Kendra's teeth. She gritted them. Though Jason was careful with money, he was, after all, a marquess, and they did own a rather luxurious carriage. But one of its wheels had broken on their way out of

London, and they'd been forced to take public transport—or else risk missing an urgent appointment
back home at Cainewood Castle.

An appointment to introduce Kendra to the latest
"suitable" man her brothers planned to foist upon
her.

"My comfort isn't the issue here—"

"This is your last chance to make your own
choice," Jason interrupted her, gathering the cards
from the hand of piquet they'd just played. "If you
won't marry Lechmere, you will have to select one
of the other men who have offered for you. Or I will
do the selecting."

"The other men." Kendra tossed her head of dark-
red curls, not believing her brother's ultimatum for
a moment. The wretched day had put him in a bad
mood, but he was generally the most reasonable man
she knew. "Old but well-off, or widowed and settled
with children, or young but just plain *boring*. Stable,
wealthy men in the good graces of King Charles,
every last one of them."

Her brother's green eyes flashed. "Yes, perfectly
acceptable, every last one of them."

"As it should be," Ford put in.

Mournfully shaking her head, Kendra sent Caithren
an imploring glance. "They will never understand."

Cait's eyes filled with sympathy and a bit of shared
exasperation. She laid a hand on her husband's arm.
"I've told ye before, Kendra wants to marry for love,
not—"

With an unnerving suddenness, the coach ground
to a halt. "Stand and deliver!" a deep voice demanded from outside. Stopped in mid-sentence,

Cait's mouth gaped, and Kendra's stomach clenched in fear.

Ford leaned forward and pushed open the door. A man on horseback poked in his head.

The most compelling head Kendra had ever seen.

"You?" Jason and Ford said together.

They knew this man? Since Kendra hadn't heard of either of her brothers being hurt—or even robbed, come to think of it—most of her fear dissipated, and her heart lifted with excitement instead. Nothing like this had ever happened to her!

Looking slightly disconcerted, the highwayman dismounted. "Aye, 'tis me," he said slowly, and, beneath the mask that concealed the upper half of his face, a grin emerged. An engaging slash of perfect white.

Well, not precisely perfect. One of his front teeth had a small chip, but she found that tiny imperfection endearing. And he was dashing, not to mention forbidden. If any of her hopeful suitors had been like this man, she'd have married him in a trice.

She wanted to say something, to make him notice her. But for the first time in her memory, her mouth refused to work.

His gaze swept the coach's dim interior as though she weren't even there. "You," he said succinctly, motioning to the whey-faced businessman seated next to Ford. "Get out."

"There be five of us in here, three of them men, likely with pistols," the man said stiffly. From his haircut, plain clothes, and the short, boxy jacket beneath his cloak, Kendra knew he was a Puritan. "Perhaps thee had better think again."

"Oh, 'tis violence you threaten, aye?" The highwayman's voice was deep and a little husky, with, curiously, the barest hint of an accent. "My friends," he drawled, gesturing toward the hill behind him, "would make certain you cease to exist within the minute. Get out. Now."

Kendra looked out the door and up. Sure enough, there were a dozen or so men at the top of the hill, their guns trained on the coach.

The Puritan must have recognized the threat, for he reluctantly climbed down. Kendra shifted within the coach, the better to see out. The victim was a good foot shorter than the robber, who looked impossibly tall and elegant in a jet-black velvet surcoat. Close-faced and resigned, the Puritan emptied his pockets and handed over his money, then turned to reenter the coach.

"Not so fast." The highwayman reached to grab the victim's sleeve. Visibly shaken, the smaller man froze, but said nothing. "Surely a . . . man of business, such as yourself, will be carrying more gold on his person than this. Where is it? Sewn into your cloak? Hidden in your luggage?"

The Puritan turned back boldly, though Kendra could see the rise and fall of his agitated breathing. "Surely *thee* has no need of it," he spat out, tugging his sleeve from the bigger man's grasp while eyeing his groomed appearance and expensive, tailored suit. "A . . . *gentleman* such as thyself."

The highwayman's eyes were amber, edged in a deeper hue—bronze, Kendra decided—that now spread in toward the center as his expression hardened. "Your luggage *and* your cloak, then—since you won't cooperate." He swung his pistol in the coachman's direction. The driver scrambled down and fumbled with the ropes securing the passengers' belongings. A shove sent the Puritan's trunk to the rutted road with a decisive *thunk*.

"Your cloak." The highwayman held out his free hand, almost as if he was bored, while his victim struggled out of his plain mantle.

"What about *them*?" he sputtered, handing it over. His gaze swung toward the Chases.

The highwayman glanced inside and flashed Kendra's brothers a conspiratorial smile before answering. "They're friends. Good day."

"Good day? *Good day?*" The poor man was as red as a squalling newborn, and Kendra almost felt sorry for him—until she reminded herself that 'twas his ilk who had killed her parents during the Civil War. Had it been anyone else, she was sure her brothers would have jumped to his defense. But because of men like this one, Jason had been left to raise his orphaned siblings, all of them forced to spend the Commonwealth years in poverty and exile.

She turned to watch the amber man remount and make his way down the road and up the hill toward his cohorts.

He'd been superb. Magnificent. Romantic, she thought on a sigh.

Amber. His clean-shaven, suntanned complexion. His eyes, a gold the color of the finest liquor. The black plume on his cavalier's hat fluttered as he rode, and beneath it he wore a long, crimped brown periwig that rather reminded her of her twin Ford's hair. But she was certain the highwayman's real hair wasn't brown. Though many men had shaven heads under their periwigs, he wouldn't. His own hair would be cut short, but not *off*, certainly—she shuddered at the thought—and it would be reddish gold. Amber.

"Are thee going to let him get away with this?" the Puritan demanded, clambering up and glaring at her brothers, both of them armed with swords and knives and God knew what else.

One of Jason's black eyebrows rose, and he spoke for them both. "I expect so."

The coach lurched and they continued on, but the atmosphere was decidedly strained, and the Puritan got off at the next stop.

Kendra moved to sit in the now-vacant spot beside Ford. "A highwayman," she breathed as soon as the carriage resumed moving.

"Why did he not rob us?" Caithren asked. "How is it you know him? He called you a friend."

"He uses the term lightly." Jason flashed an enigmatic smile. "We've run into him before. But he's never robbed us."

"He didn't look like he needed to rob anybody," Kendra said. "His suit was nicer than yours." He'd looked nicer than Jason all around, she mused. Not that Jason wasn't good-looking, but he had the general dark look of her family, a look she was inured to, to say the least. This man, on the other hand, had looked . . . exotic. All golden and dressed in black— black suit, black shirt, black boots, black mask—not the look of your typical scruffy felon, that was for sure.

Jason shrugged, absently running a hand through his wife's straight, dark-blond hair. "Almost anyone can afford one nice suit of clothes, if he makes it his priority. You cannot judge a man by his looks, Kendra."

But of course she had. Judged him, and liked what she saw.

Restless, Jason sighed and stretched his legs, then raised Cait's hand and brushed his lips over her knuckles, earning a soft smile in return. "Perhaps we should turn him in," he suggested playfully. "This is getting to be somewhat of a nuisance."

"You wouldn't dare!" Kendra burst out. "He's . . . well . . . He'd fit in at Court. And he only robbed the Puritan. I'd wager he's a Royalist."

"There could be a reward for him. And Lakefield House is in sad shape," Viscount Lakefield, otherwise known as Ford, lamented half-seriously. "I cannot live with Jason forever."

"Oh, yes, you can," Kendra said heatedly.

Jason turned to face her. "Is it that important to you, then? I didn't realize your Royalist loyalty ran so deep."

"Well . . . it does," she declared, thinking about the highwayman's broad shoulders tapering to slim hips.

"Well, then." Ford's deep-blue eyes gleamed with mischief. "I suppose we'll have to leave him be. At least it provides him with a stake for the card games."

Jason glared at his brother.

"What?" Kendra slanted him a suspicious glance. "What card games?"

"All highwaymen play cards," Jason said firmly. He picked up their own deck and shuffled it expertly, then dealt out new hands. Kendra's mind wasn't on the game, though, and she arranged her cards slowly.

She remembered the highwayman's voice. He'd spoken a bit cautiously, as if he were considering each word.

Not like her family. The Chases, as a rule, blurted everything that came into their heads, generally at the tops of their lungs.

"What was his accent?" she asked. "Did you hear it?"

"Scots, aye?" Cait said, exaggerating the burr she was born to. "Though he sounds as if he's not been home for many a year. I'm surprised ye even noticed."

Jason looked up sharply, but Kendra studied her fan of cards. He frowned back down at his own hand. "Why do you want to know?"

Why? She could scarcely comprehend such a stupid question. She wanted to know everything about the mysterious highwayman. "Just curious," she said lightly, leading with a jack of hearts. "Your turn."

The Duke of Lechmere turned out to be everything Kendra had feared, and then some. He was the epitome of what she was *not* looking for in a husband.

His skin looked like it had never seen the sun. Only God knew what color his hair was, since it was hidden beneath a periwig dusted with enough powder to choke a horse. She suspected he was bald underneath, anyway. His eyes were a pale, lifeless gray.

Not that looks were paramount, but his suit was peacock satin, adorned with so much dangling ribbon and lace that it seemed to quiver when he breathed. No matter the current fashion, Kendra wasn't drawn to men who dressed prettier than she. A simple, dark velvet suit—like those her brothers favored—was far more to her taste. Not to mention the expense of Lechmere's apparel could probably fund an orphanage for a month.

Having been orphaned herself at the age of seven, she would much rather have seen the money spent there.

And he was a *duke*.

"Kendra plays the harpsichord like an angel," Jason said, sending her into a coughing fit. While 'twas true she was a competent musician, she couldn't ever remember hearing her name and the word "angel" in the same sentence. Not from her oldest brother, anyway, who had seen her through more than a few rebellious stages.

"An admirable accomplishment." The duke waved a hand bedecked with gaudy rings. "I should like to hear her play later."

"And she's a brilliant conversationalist," Ford added. If Kendra wasn't mistaken, she caught a gleam in his blue eyes before he focused pointedly on the carved wooden ceiling. Interesting description, brilliant conversationalist, given that her brothers normally spent much of their time telling her to hush up. She would have to call Ford on that later.

After she figured out how to get rid of this mulli-puff.

"Though she seems rather tongue-tied now," Jason put in dryly. "First time in my memory."

Sitting beside Jason in a salmon velvet armchair, 'twas all she could do to resist kicking him. Maybe she should. Perhaps bad manners would put the duke off. But no, she needed something more drastic. Failproof.

"In such a circumstance as this, a bout of speech-lessness is only to be expected," Lechmere quipped in a haughty tone. "And I assure you, my dear, I am not looking for conversation." His cold gray gaze seemed to heat as it swept her from head to toe. "I admire a quiet, biddable woman."

Dear God. She'd better think of something quick. When Jason asked her to pour the wine, she rose quickly, deliberately tripping on the edge of the patterned black-and-salmon carpet.

"Watch yourself," Jason warned under his breath. He smiled at the duke, who was holding out his goblet in one limp-wristed hand.

"Oh, I'm so clumsy," she said, though nothing could be further from the truth. At her brother's glare, she only giggled, prompting a frown. Kendra never giggled.

With exaggerated force, she pulled the stopper from the decanter, then giggled again when it went flying across the room and hit a portrait of one of her solemn ancestors square on his painted forehead.

Her great-great grandfather. She looked to his image for help, but no advice was forthcoming.

"Quite all right, my dear." Lechmere raised his chin. " 'Tis natural to be nervous when meeting a man of my stature. When you're a duchess—"

"When I'm a duchess, I shall open lots of orphanages," she babbled. "There are so many disadvantaged children who would blossom with a proper education in a loving environment. And speaking of blossoms, have you extensive gardens, Your Grace? Because I've theories on crossbreeding flowers—"

"I told you she's a good conversationalist," Ford interrupted.

"Here, Your Grace, let me just take this goblet." She grabbed it from his hand, cringing when her fingers met his cold, clammy ones. "My, what a lovely ruby." Unbelievably, the ring she was speaking of was lodged on his thumb. Apparently his fingers were not numerous enough to properly display his wealth. "Amy would adore seeing it, I'm sure."

"Amy?"

"My sister-in-law—my brother Colin's wife. She's a jeweler." Kendra set the goblet on the table with a bang that made everyone jump.

"Your brother's wife is a jeweler?"

The duke looked positively scandalized, and Kendra could hardly control a grin. She giggled again instead. "Oh, yes. Colin found her on the streets of London." Which was true, in a sense, since he'd rescued her from the Great Fire two years past, but more than a tad misleading. Though her family had been commoners, Amy was educated and wealthy in her own right. "Of course, she's a countess now as well, but a jeweler all the same."

"Hmmph," the duke sniffed.

"Yes, Your Grace. Well, let me just pour, then."

And she did—right into his lap.

He jumped up, watching in horror as a red stain spread on the turquoise satin in a very embarrassing place. "I think I've had enough, my lady, of both the wine and yourself. If you'll excuse me." With his pointy nose in the air, he strode awkwardly from the room.

"Crossbreeding flowers?" Her twin's eyes met her own, and they both burst out laughing.

But Jason was not amused. "Very charming, Kendra." Deliberately he placed his elbows on the arms of his chair, then steepled his fingers, pinning her with exasperated green eyes. "That's one prospect off your list. Need I remind you who is left? I will expect a decision after the weekend, and you will be wed by the end of the summer."

Kendra awoke the next morning with a massive headache. Jason couldn't be serious.

He and Ford and Colin were off to a monthly house party they attended—no women allowed—and, as usual, she and Caithren would be joined by their sister-in-law, Amy, and her baby daughter, Jewel, for the weekend. Usually they had something of a house party of their own, playing with the babe and gossiping away the long hours until the men returned.

But this time, they'd be expecting to hear whom she'd decided to marry.

She stared up at the underside of the mint-green canopy she'd begged for in her youth. Although their parents had depleted the family fortune financing the King in the Civil War, Jason had always seen to it that she'd never wanted for anything. To the best of his abilities, he'd indulged her every whim. He wouldn't force her to marry now.

Would he?

With a huff, she rose and pulled on her new hunter-green satin riding habit. Amy would be here within the hour, but she needed to think. Alone.

She ran a comb through her hair, not bothering to call her maid in to curl and pin it, and in no time at all, she was mounted on Pandora, her mare, galloping across the Sussex Downs. Her brothers would be mightily vexed if they knew she was riding unescorted, but the three of them could go hang for all she cared right now.

Besides, they were away all weekend and would never know.

The fresh country air was helping her headache clear, but just thinking about that weasel Lechmere made her shiver. And the rest of her prospects weren't much better.

The Earl of Shrewsbury came complete with a meddling mother—the "shrew" in her name was all too fitting. The Marquess of Rochford was a widower and kind enough, but his hair was completely gray—no doubt from dealing with his seven unruly children. Viscount Davenport didn't talk, he whined. The Duke of Lancashire lived in—well, Lancashire—which was entirely too far from her family. The Earl of Morely was wealthy and wise—but nearing fifty. Lord Rosslyn was young, handsome, and fun loving, but lacking somewhat in brains. She wondered if he could read.

Jason couldn't be serious.

Coming out of her thoughts, she slowed to a stop. She hadn't realized how far she'd ridden. In fact, she noticed with a start, she was at the same spot where they'd seen the highwayman yesterday.

His friends had been atop that hill, lying on their stomachs, training an impressive assortment of pistols on the hapless Puritan. Waiting patiently, their hats pulled down to conceal their faces.

This morning, the hill was deserted, the highwayman nowhere in sight. Kendra glanced at the sky in an attempt to judge the time, but all was clouded over. 'Twas turning into a beastly day. Not cold, but muggy, with a definite threat of rain. With no sun to confirm it, she guessed the time to be about ten o'clock. Perhaps highwaymen slept in.

Plainly, highway robbery was not a full-time occupation. Not that she had any idea of what she'd have done if he *had* been here. Run for her life, in all probability. But she drifted into a vague fantasy of herself riding down the road at breakneck speed, her long, dark-red hair floating on the breeze, impressing the hell out of him with her horsemanship and her grace. He staring after her, openmouthed with surprise and appreciation. Struck temporarily dumb by a bolt of . . . love at first sight. Well, second sight, actually—but he hadn't paid any attention to her before, so the first time didn't count.

Then she would turn around, ride back, stop in the middle of the road, right in front of him, and slide off Pandora slowly . . . so slowly. He'd close his mouth and come forward, reaching her in two or three of his long strides, his large hands spanning her waist as he eased her to the ground. And then . . .

She had no idea. Inexperience didn't make for detailed fantasies. And she certainly wouldn't have anything to do with a highwayman, anyway. Her fantasy was not only boring, it was absurd.

But instead of turning back, she rode along the crest of the hill a spell, then turned away from the lane. And there, perhaps a hundred feet distant, was a very mysterious mound.

It was not sculpted by nature, Kendra realized immediately. Its shape was angular, its surface dirt, not grass.

A grave. A fresh grave.

Her hands tightened on the reins as she approached the tomb. Was it the highwayman? A victim of his? Either one was unthinkable. She bit the inside of her cheek, worrying the soft flesh with her teeth.

A single raindrop fell on one of her clenched fists, and a gust of wind whooshed as she reached the mound. From her perch high atop Pandora, she saw the loose dirt blow across it, revealing a sheet of canvas underneath. Her heart hammered at the sight. Was the man not buried properly, then—just covered with a spot of fabric?

She slid off Pandora, leading her forward to investigate. She leaned down, took a corner of the canvas, just a corner, in two shaking fingers. Lifted it . . .

If her brothers had been here, they'd have told her, as usual, not to jump to conclusions. And this time, they'd have been right. Her shout of laughter rang across the Downs she threw back the canvas.

Twelve blocks of wood. Twelve narrow pipes of various gauges. Twelve hats with different-colored plumes and a variety of hatbands.

She set a hat on a block of wood with a pipe sticking out from under it. When she stepped back, it looked for all the world like a man lying on his stomach, pointing a gun at her.

He was clever, this man. Very clever.

"What do you think you're doing?"

She froze. She hadn't heard anyone approach, and for the barest second she thought the voice was in her head. But he was standing next to her, not three feet away.

"I'm . . . I'm . . ."

"You're letting my hat get wet."

"Oh." Kendra put a hand to her head, feeling the mass of her hair curling with dampness. She hadn't noticed the increasing drizzle. " 'Tis raining."

"Very observant of you."

She turned then and looked up at him, and he was exactly the way she had known he would be. His hair *was* golden—thick, silky, and straight. 'Twas cut short, not chin-length like a Puritan's, nor cropped like a wig-wearing Royalist's, but somewhere in between, and the front was hanging in his eyes. She wanted to reach out and sweep it off his forehead, but she seemed rooted in place, and she wouldn't have dared to touch him, anyway.

His snug black breeches were wool, not velvet, and his shirt was white, not black. He wasn't here for business, then.

"I've come to put away my props. Will you help me, seeing as you're here?"

Help him? She ought to be bolting for Pandora at this very moment. "Of course."

Had she said that? She knew she shouldn't have. He snatched up the three props, then turned and strode back to the rest of them. Windblown, his golden hair bounced in time with his steps as she followed.

She concentrated on his broad back, watching the play of muscles beneath his thin shirt as he flipped over the canvas and piled the hats on top, bundled them up, and tied the four corners in a neat knot to make a parcel. He hefted it, testing its weight, then turned to her. "You can carry this, aye? Before you, on your horse?" He didn't sound angry, but more as if he was simply resolved to complete his task in the most efficient manner possible. Kendra was somewhat relieved, but she moved in a haze of unreality.

She managed to find her voice, however. "If you'll hand it up to me, yes, I'm sure I can carry it. Where are we taking it?"

"A cottage over the next hill, not too far." He gathered the pipes under one arm and lifted the bundle by its knot. "Let us be off, before it starts raining in earnest."

His horse was tied nearby—amber, of course, his glossy coat a tawny tan color. Pandora's hide was a deep brown, and Kendra thought they made a handsome pair.

'Twas difficult to see over the bundle in front of her, but it was a short ride.

The cottage was unlocked, and the highwayman made short work of tethering their horses before depositing the pipes inside and returning for the bundle. After handing it to him, Kendra slid off Pandora slowly . . . so slowly . . . and a second later he was back, and his large hands were spanning her waist as he eased her to the ground.

His fingers rested on her waist a little longer than necessary, and she felt their warmth through her satin habit. She looked up at him. He had a wide mouth, the full lower lip perfectly straight across the center bottom edge. She wanted to touch him, just there.

Her eyes locked on his, and her breath caught in her throat.

A crash of thunder rent the air, and big raindrops started pelting to the earth. He jumped back, motioning her to follow him inside.

She should leave. Now. But it was pouring . . .

The cottage looked more like a well-appointed

hunting lodge, warm and cozy and very masculine. He shut the door behind them and wandered to a leather-upholstered couch, throwing his long form onto it with a surprising grace. "Close, no? Five more minutes, and my hats would have been ruined. I thank you for your help."

"You're welcome," Kendra said from just inside the door where she still stood in a daze. She couldn't believe she was in a hunting lodge with this dangerous man. 'Twas incredible—and, all of a sudden, incredibly scary. She couldn't remember ever having been alone with a man, save her brothers. And she didn't know the first thing about this one—except that he was a criminal.

Her sudden fear must have shown on her face, because he sat up, patting the cushion next to him. "Come here—I don't bite. You'll stay 'til it stops raining, aye?"

"Aye—I mean, yes." Criminal or not, she loved the way he talked, the words slow and melodic. Though her heart was pounding, she screwed up her courage and moved to sit gingerly beside him. "I'm Kendra. Kendra Chase."

"Trick Caldwell."

"Trick?" she echoed, startled. She turned to him, forgetting for a moment that he was supposed to be frightening. "What kind of name is Trick?"

"Ahh, and that's a story." He smiled at her, a wide smile that lit up the cottage and belied the dreary day. Leaning forward, he reached out a hand and placed it on her wrist, just lightly, but a tingle raced up her arm and throughout her body, warming her in the strangest way. Something snapped inside her, and the sense of unreality was gone. She was here, really here, with the amber highwayman—no, Trick, she corrected herself—alone, and he wasn't scary at all.

Well, not very.

Chapter Two

"**A**re you hungry?" Trick asked suddenly.

She shook her head, wondering if he really had food here. He didn't own the cottage, did he? Well, maybe he knew where the owner kept stores, and she shouldn't be surprised he would use them. He was a thief, after all.

"Thirsty, then? Aye, a spot of wine would do you. You look tense."

Tense didn't begin to describe how Kendra felt. She glanced down at his long, strong fingers ringed lightly around her wrist. He pulled back his hand, and she bit the inside of her cheek. "A . . . spot of wine would be nice, thank you."

He rose with a leonine grace, sauntering over to a cabinet without hesitation, as though he knew every nook and cranny of the place. Crystal goblets and a matching decanter were hidden behind the doors, and he filled two glasses. She took one, hoping he didn't see her hand shake.

"I'll just settle the horses and be right back, aye?"

"Where . . . ?"

"There's a small stable behind." He set his goblet on the mantel. Taking a heavy cloak that dangled from a peg on the wall, he shrugged into it and was out the door with a whoosh of wind.

She sat on the couch, listening to the rain on the roof and sipping the sweetish Madeira. Though she wasn't cold, she shivered. Standing up, she looked around, wondering how he could describe this as a cottage. The cottages in Cainewood were generally tiny and dark, with rough plastered walls and trodden earth floors.

This cottage was impeccably clean. The dark wooden walls and floors were polished, and a lovely Oriental carpet covered the floor. Besides the couch, there were two chairs and several small tables, two marquetry cabinets, and a desk in the corner. She walked over to it and ran a hand along the smooth, rich wood. Everything on top was neatly arranged.

With an uneasy glance over her shoulder, she set down her goblet and slid open the top drawer to find a stack of paper and bottles of ink. Her hand went to the bottom drawer and tugged, but 'twas stuck closed or locked. She frowned at it, then turned to survey the rest of the room.

A beautiful carved dining table and chairs rested on another patterned carpet, both obviously imported from lands far away. A peek through an archway revealed a spotless, quite modern kitchen, the shelves heavily stocked with victuals. Another archway opened on a corridor, which apparently led to several more rooms.

Some cottage, Kendra thought, poised to explore whatever lay off the corridor. All furnished, food, drink . . . Trick seemed quite at home, she realized suddenly. Maybe he lived here after all. She'd never really thought about where a highwayman would live, but she hadn't expected it would be a hunting lodge, or cottage, or whatever he wanted to call it—she'd assumed they slept in inns or the like. But then, he didn't seem like a typical highwayman, even though many had a reputation for being gentlemanly.

When the door opened and Trick walked in and swept off his cloak, she rushed back to the desk and reclaimed her goblet.

" 'Tis not letting up," he announced, stomping the rain off his boots. She was relieved that he didn't seem to care she'd been nosing around.

"Is this . . . yours?" she blurted, making her way to sit on the couch. "I mean, do you live here?"

"Umm . . . close enough."

Kendra felt her face heat. She really shouldn't be so curious. 'Twas none of her business whom the cottage belonged to, and now she'd put Trick on the spot. Of course he didn't own it—men of property didn't turn to the roads for sustenance.

He didn't look embarrassed, though, but more like he was amused. He swiped his wine off the mantel and sat beside her. The room was quiet but for the soft pit-pat of rain. She sipped from her own goblet, peeking at him over the rim. He stared at her through the ends of his damp golden hair, and she saw his eyes darken, but surely he had no reason to be angry.

No, 'twas something else.

Her heart sped up, and of its own accord her hand rose to sweep clear his forehead. Horrified at herself, she snatched it back just in time.

With a sudden grin, he gave a toss of his head that flung the hair from his eyes. "We were speaking of my name," he reminded her—or himself.

She took another gulp of wine. "What is your name, really?"

"Patrick Iain Caldwell." He settled back slowly. "But my father was away when I was born—Father was always away—so my mother named me. Scots-Irish, she was. In any case, he was appalled when he finally ventured home to meet me. Said she'd tricked him good, giving his English son two barbarian names."

Kendra grinned. "Trick . . . since she'd tricked him?"

"And short for Patrick, though he'd never admit it. They hated each other, they did. 'Twas an arranged marriage."

"Why?"

"Damned if I know." He drained his goblet and stared at it pensively, twirling it by the stubby stem. "Neither of them would talk of the other long enough for me to find out."

"How sad," she murmured, the sincere tone of her voice drawing his gaze.

Trick looked up to see Kendra shaking her beautiful head. Sweet Mary, she was lovely. And regardless of the dreary, rainy day, she smelled of sunshine and lavender. 'Twas all he could do to keep from leaning close and burying his nose in her burgundy curls.

Damn . . . why could she not be a bloody serving maid? It had been a long time since he'd bedded a woman—a long time since he'd felt attracted to one—but Cainewood's sister was not the woman on whom to slake his pent-up lust. He shouldn't even have encouraged her to stay. Jason would have his head if he knew she was here, unescorted. But with the rain and all, it had seemed the gentlemanly thing to do.

And he hadn't seemed able to help himself.

Still, the last thing he needed was her sympathy regarding the childhood he'd just as soon forget. "Not so sad," he said, pulling his gaze from her face, only to have it land on her chest. Pert breasts were molded within her riding habit's collarless jacket, in perfect proportion to her small stature. His eyes moved down to her waist, and his palms itched as he remembered his hands spanning it. He forced himself to look out the window. A raindrop trailed in a slow, crooked line. "Arranged marriages are common enough."

"For some, perhaps. The nobility are often compelled to wed for alliance."

God's blood, she thought he was a commoner. She really had no idea who he was. Trick smiled to himself, then sobered. If she knew nothing of him, her brothers were even more protective than he'd thought.

He rose to set his empty goblet on the mantel, then turned and leaned back against it, crossing his arms and ankles. "Your folks were different, then?"

"Oh, yes. They had a perfect, romantic marriage and loved each other very much. Too much, according to one of my brothers. He says they loved each other and the monarchy, and there was nothing left for us."

"But you don't agree."

A statement, not a question. He watched her eyes as she considered it, noting the bright intelligence within their depths. "No," she stated finally. "I never knew them well, because they left to fight in the War when I was yet a babe. But I always felt they loved me."

"Love." Once he would have said the word with derision, but now, twenty-eight years old and wiser, he managed to say it with only dispassion.

Still, she caught his ambivalence. "Do you not believe in love?"

"No."

"Do you not love anyone? Nobody loves you? Not anyone?" Her light-green eyes looked incredulous; then she colored suddenly and stood up. "I'm sorry," she mumbled. "I'm . . . we don't know one another, and I shouldn't ask such questions."

He watched her walk to the window, her steps sure, not the mincing progress that passed for walking among the tittering Court ladies. No, he couldn't picture her whispering behind a fan, though he was sure she attended balls and the like, and probably had a wonderful time. Not a social animal himself, he shuddered at the thought, his eyes following her graceful hand as she traced the path of a raindrop with one finger.

"Ask away," he assured her. "I've nothing to hide." 'Twas not the truth—'twas not even close to the truth—but it sounded nice. "No, I don't love anyone."

He saw her watching his reflection in the window-pane. "Your parents . . . ?"

"Made my life miserable."

She turned to face him, concern shadowing her pretty eyes. "Brothers or sisters?"

"Ha! Not a chance. I reckon my folks came together once, and once only—and lived to regret it, I'm sure."

At his frank words, a becoming pink bathed her skin. He wanted to make her flush again, with the pink glow of passion. But Cainewood's stern face hovered in his mind, along with those of his formidable brothers, and Trick knew 'twould never be. She didn't deserve to be used, and he had no wish to bear the consequences.

"You love someone, then?" he asked.

"Oh, yes." The sunshiny smile was back. "My brothers, all three of them. And my new sisters—my sisters-in-law, actually—and my niece. When I first held her tiny body in my arms and she looked into my eyes . . . 'Twas love at first sight." Her gaze focused on him and darkened. "I guess you don't believe in love at first sight, either?"

He shifted uncomfortably. "I don't believe in love at all. Mayhap I did once . . . but not anymore. 'Tis only an illusion."

Her mouth dropped open, then closed. It looked soft. " 'Tis no illusion," she stated in a tone that brooked no argument.

He grinned, enjoying her naïve confidence. "Love for a babe in arms, well . . . perhaps. Love between adults . . . not bloody likely."

"You have no plans to marry, then? Not ever?"

"Of course I do." Lifting his goblet, he crossed to the cabinet to pour himself another drink. "But that day will come far in the future. And love will have naught to do with it."

"Someday," she said, "someone will change your mind."

She seemed more sure of herself than ever, smug even. "You make it sound like a promise," he said.

"Then you can take it that way. And a Chase

promise is never given lightly." He seemed to remember hearing one of her brothers use those words. "Someday you will fall in love," she repeated.

He laughed. "Hell, lassie, I hope you're right. But I'm not going to lay money on it. Would you care for more wine?" He indicated her goblet.

With a glance out the window at the pounding rain, she nodded and came forward. He poured, set down the decanter, handed her the glass. Their fingers met—his warm, hers cool.

Between them the goblet slipped to the floor.

Kendra gasped, staring as a dark stain spread on the cream background color of the patterned carpet. She dropped to her knees to collect the broken crystal and dab at the blot with the inside of the hem of her riding habit.

Trick stared down at her bright head. "Stop," he pleaded, hard put to keep from laughing at her panic. "You'll ruin your skirt."

"I'll ruin my *skirt*?" Worried green eyes glanced up at him. "Then will the stain not come out of the carpet, either?"

"I haven't the slightest idea," he mused. Surely one of the servants would know how to remove it. If not, he could always bring another rug from his London warehouse.

"But . . . I'm not usually clumsy." She gazed at the stain, then sat back and wrapped her arms around her bent knees. "And I've gotten you in trouble, then."

"In trouble?" he repeated stupidly.

"The crystal and the carpet . . ." She bit her lip, then her eyes cleared. "Tell the owner I'll pay for it. 'Twill not be a problem."

Tell the owner . . . Oh, she was a precious one. She thought he was a criminal, yet she worried about his carpet and problems with his supposed landlord. She'd be more on target worrying about her maidenhead, he thought wryly, reaching out a hand to help her rise.

At her full height, the top of her head came just to his chin. She tilted her face and fastened her gaze on his. Their hands seemed fused together, and he could hear her slightly uneven breathing over the patter of rain on the roof. Slowly, her free hand came up to sweep the hair from his eyes.

"I'm sorry," she whispered, then she touched one fingertip to his lower lip, exactly in the center, so lightly he wondered if he imagined it. His body quickened anyway.

He stared at her soft mouth. "Dinna ye worry," he said low.

She blinked and pulled her hand from his.

He almost made a grab for her, but reminded himself who she was. Damn, but it had better stop raining soon. "Come, there's water in the bedchamber. We'll rinse the stain on your skirt before it can set."

He swiveled and headed for the corridor, knowing she would follow. Composing himself, he poured water into the washbowl and set it on the low table by the bed, then turned to beckon her near and hand her a towel.

She wetted it and leaned down to dab daintily at her hem. Frowning, she dipped again and dabbed harder. Finally, she sat on the bed, rucking her skirts up about her knees so she could plunge the offending stain into the bowl. She stared into space, holding it there with one hand.

Trick sat beside her and grinned. "You're going to sit there 'til it comes out?"

She turned to look at him. " 'Twill not take long this way."

He watched the water soaking her skirt, a dark circle growing to encompass much more than the stain, but she seemed not to notice. Her gaze was riveted on his face, and when he met her eyes, the green darkened. She swallowed and licked her lips. Despite his best intentions, he moved closer, then closer still when he caught a whiff of her sun-fresh skin and flowery hair.

From the main part of the cottage, he heard the door fly open and bang against the wall, but he thought it must be the wind. One of his arms stole around Kendra's waist, and he bent his head to hers, toward that soft, tempting mouth.

"Trick?" a male voice yelled, but his mind was on the woman in his arms. She stared at him, swaying closer and raising her face. Her breath came sweet and warm between her parted lips.

"Trick, we need your help to find our . . ." Jason Chase arrived in the doorway, his brothers Colin and Ford close on his heels. ". . . sister," he finished weakly.

Kendra and Trick jumped up and apart, taking the porcelain bowl with them. It fell to the polished floor with a loud crash.

"Not again . . ." Kendra groaned. "I never drop things."

"This isn't what it looks like," Trick hurried to say.

"No?" A muscle in Jason's jaw twitched. "You mean to say I didn't see you on a bed with your arms around my sister and her skirts pulled up around her waist?"

"My knees," Kendra corrected.

Jason just glared at her.

"What were you doing, then?" Colin asked.

"Rinsing a stain from her skirt." Trick wondered why he felt so uneasy.

Ford rolled his blue eyes. "You expect us to believe that?" He turned on Kendra. "What the devil are you doing here?"

"I was . . . riding. And it started raining, and Trick came along—"

"Trick, is it?" Colin's eyes bore into hers, and Trick saw her flinch. These two had been at it before, he sensed. "Just how well do you know this man?"

"For God's sake, Colin—we just met."

"And you let him put his hands beneath your gown."

Trick leapt to her defense. "Hell, no, Greystone—I told you, we were rinsing out a stain."

"A bloodstain, would that be?"

Trick watched Kendra's eyes narrow with puzzlement. "No," she said.

"How can you think such a thing?" he asked.

"How could we not?"

"Trick." Jason stepped closer. "I'm very disappointed in you. Kendra has never acted particularly wisely, but she has been very sheltered and you ought to know better." He looked toward Trick with doleful eyes. "At least tell me you didn't know who she was."

"Of course I knew who she was!" Trick exploded. "I saw her in your bloody carriage."

Beside him, Kendra gave a surprised gasp.

"Ah, yes," Jason responded, looking resigned. "That will have to stop, you know."

"What the hell are you talking about?"

"The highway robbery. You don't need the money, and Kendra doesn't need to see her husband strung up at Tyburn."

"Her husband?" Trick's heart pounded. Her brothers knew not the truth—oh, they knew he wasn't posing as a highwayman for the money, but they weren't likely to find out the real reason anytime soon. He'd given his word to King Charles.

And now they thought . . . "You think I slept with your sister? You must be mad!"

"They *are* mad!" Kendra railed. She turned to Jason. "You have to listen." And to Colin. "It was only a wine stain." And to Ford. "You're always telling me *I* jump to conclusions—"

Ford's hand snaked out to grasp his twin's upper arm. "Come along, Kendra." With a murderous look at Trick, he pulled her from the room.

"We'll call on you when the banns have been posted," Jason ground out.

"No," Colin said. " 'Twill have to be by special license."

"Bloody hell, you're right." Jason rubbed the back of his neck. "She could be pregnant."

Pregnant! Trick couldn't believe what he was hearing. One minute he was washing out a wine stain, the next he was accused of fathering a child.

With a woman he had never even kissed. But he wanted to . . . with a desire stronger than anything he'd ever felt.

Chapter Three

Water streamed from Kendra's hair into her already tear-blurred eyes. She was soaked to the skin, but she'd have ripped her own tongue out before asking her stubborn brothers for one of their cloaks. Riding behind them, she heard the murmurs of a deeply involved discussion but couldn't make out what they were saying.

She gripped Pandora's reins tighter and took slow, fortifying breaths, forcing herself to concentrate on the clip-clop of their horses' hooves and the patter of the rain. Anything to help contain her fury.

She couldn't let them make her go through with this. But surely they didn't intend for her to actually wed a highwayman.

At long last, Jason sent the others ahead, then halted until she caught up.

Riding silently beside him, Kendra kept glancing at her brother while she waited for him to say something. It seemed forever before he turned to her. "I cannot believe you did that, Kendra."

"It was raining. All I did was come in from the rain."

"That's not the way it looked to us," he said as if that were the end of the discussion.

If she were to be honest with herself, that wasn't the way it had felt, either. She knew full well Trick had been about to kiss her, and the fact was, she'd been about to cooperate.

Thrilled to cooperate, truth be told.

But it hadn't happened. Not to mention a kiss didn't warrant a forced marriage.

But, dear God, Trick had been even more wonderful than in her fantasy. She'd melted just looking at him, and when he'd taken her into his arms, her whole body had felt on fire. She'd been dying for that kiss.

And she had never kissed anyone. She'd been kissed, of course—after all, she was twenty-three and not unattractive—but she'd never kissed anyone back. The fault of those brothers of hers—every time a gentleman managed to pull her into an alcove or onto a balcony and press his lips to hers, one of her brothers would materialize, staring daggers into the unfortunate swain's eyes. And until now, she'd not been enamored of any man enough to make an issue of it.

Why did her brothers always have to show up and ruin it all?

And why were they letting her marry him? Demanding it, as a matter of fact? She stared at Jason's determined profile. A highwayman . . . her brother was letting—no, *making*—her wed a highwayman. Regardless of whether Jason thought she'd lost her virtue to the man, the fact that he'd as good as pledged her to a robber was beyond belief.

Her stare turned to a glare that drew his gaze. He blinked. "What were you thinking, riding out alone?"

Ignoring that, she drew breath. "I cannot believe

you expect me to marry a highwayman," she railed. "You, who wouldn't let Lord Harrison near me because he was naught but a baron!"

Jason stared at her. His lips quirked into a smile; then he threw back his head and laughed. Incredulous, Kendra watched, wishing the rain pouring into his mouth would drown him.

"You—you—you know not who he is, do you?" he choked out.

"Trick Caldwell. Patrick Iain Caldwell," Kendra returned through clenched teeth. "Do you think you would have found me in a man's bedchamber—never mind that nothing happened there—if I knew not even his name?"

Jason just laughed harder. "Patrick Iain Caldwell *What*?"

"What? What do you mean, what? That's not his name?" Kendra bit the inside of her cheek. "I should have guessed he'd lie to me," she muttered, more to herself than Jason. "He's a bloody highwayman, after all."

"You know not who he is." Apparently not noticing her unladylike language, Jason actually snorted. "You *really* know not who he is." With another shout of laughter, he dug in his heels and raced up to meet their brothers. Even through the distance and the driving rain, Kendra heard their loud guffaws.

She rode behind them for another few minutes, listening to their whoops of laughter, hoping they'd expire from lack of air. A buzzard circled lazily overhead. Not exactly Ares's bird, the vulture, but close enough. A fury was rising in her that would do Ares, the God of War, proud.

Finally, she couldn't stand it. She raced up to meet

her brothers, nosing Pandora between Jason's and Ford's mounts.

"He's titled, isn't he?" she demanded. "Or you wouldn't even be joking about this marriage. Who is he?"

Ford looked at her, his blue eyes all innocence. "Who?"

"That man you just betrothed me to! What's his name, damn it?"

"Oh, you mean Trick? Trick Caldwell?"

"All right. Enough is enough." She glared at them one by one. "I did nothing wrong. No matter what you think it looked like, we were washing a stain from my skirt. There is no reason for me to marry him."

The brothers stared at her and then at each other over her head. Individually they nodded; then Jason spoke for them all.

"Did you choose another of your suitors to marry, then?"

"That again? I don't believe this. None of my 'suitors' are at all suitable, and I won't marry any of them. You are finished ordering me around."

"You're right about that," he said. "I am finished. 'Tis long past time you were wed, and Trick's as good a man as any."

"But he's a highwayman," she wailed.

"Not for long," Jason snapped. The men closed ranks, and nothing else was said for the rest of the ride home.

Riveted to the spot in disbelief, Trick stood in the cottage for a good fifteen minutes, wondering how a simple jaunt to save his props from the rain had ended in such disaster. Finally, he rode home to dismiss the rest of his houseguests.

Compton, his butler, met him at the door. "Good afternoon, Your Grace."

"Is it?" Trick handed him his drenched cloak. "What happened while I was gone?"

Compton frowned, one of his habitual expressions. "Lords Cainewood, Greystone, and Lakefield have taken their leave. A messenger arrived with word that their sister had disappeared. They went off to find you, to enlist your help—"

"They succeeded." And turned his life upside down in the process. Leaving the butler midsentence, Trick stalked into his card room.

"I'm sorry, gentlemen, but the party's over." Peeved, he waved a hand in a fruitless attempt to clear the smoky air. The four remaining guests, all aristocrats from neighboring estates, had apparently passed the time by smoking up Trick's small hoard of expensive Virginia cheroots, literally worth their weight in silver.

He coughed and waved some more. "It seems I'm to be wed soon, and I'm in no mood for cards. Besides which, the Chase brothers won't be back, so we've not enough for two tables—"

"Wed? As in married?" David Fielding interrupted in a puff of tobacco, blinking his brown eyes, which always looked a little crossed. "You cannot be serious."

"Aye, as in married." Trick smiled grimly. "And I assure you, I've never been more serious in my life."

The only one without a cheroot twixt his lips, John Garrick heaved his paunchy form from his chair. "Amberley, I . . . I don't know what to say."

Garrick, speechless. Imagine that. In general, the man never shut up, lecturing his hapless companions on the folly of their swearing, drinking, whoring, or any other of a number of activities he considered morally reprehensible, an annoyingly superior smile on his flabby lips. He flapped those lips now, rather ineffectively, Trick thought. "I . . . I just don't know what to say."

"Then don't say anything," Trick suggested. Striding across the room, he plucked a half-smoked cheroot from Fielding's lips, then did the same with Robert Faraday and Thomas Milner. They sat there, their mouths in little Os where the brown cheroots used to be.

He stubbed out the burning tobacco in one of the crystal dishes he kept on the card tables for that purpose. "I will send up some servants to help you pack," he informed them. "And someone else will have to host next month as there'll be a woman here."

"But . . . Amberley." Robert Faraday finally found his voice. He skimmed the long brown hair from his face and rubbed his stubbled chin. "No surcoats, no shaving, no periwigs, no women. You laid down the rules when you set up the card club. And you said then that you'd marry the day the devil settled in heaven."

"He's arrived, gentlemen." At Trick's sardonic pronouncement, Garrick narrowed his eyes. The other men rose, and they all drifted toward the door, presumably to collect their things. "Who will host?" Trick pressed. "I've no intention of spending all my weekends at home. Faraday, Milner? Damn, you both have wives. Garrick?"

"I . . . I'm remodeling. No space at present."

Trick frowned; the man lived in a fifty-room manor house. Old, yes, and in definite need of renovations, but surely there was an area they could use to play cards and enough bedrooms in sufficient shape to accommodate seven guests.

"We'll ask Cainewood," Milner suggested. "His wife can go stay with her sister-in-law. I'll drop by there later this—"

"They've that sister," Fielding interrupted. "Er . . . Lady Kendra, that's it."

"Oh, damn. You're right. They'd have to send her to Greystone, too."

"Nay, gentlemen. Lady Kendra will be here. Though you'll address her as Her Grace, the Duchess of Amberley." The men's mouths dropped open again, and Trick shot them a wry smile. "Aye, the Chases will host—'tis the least they can do. 'Til next month, then?"

Before they could ask any questions he'd rather not answer, Trick grabbed a fresh cheroot and left to closet himself in his study.

Shaking his head, he went straight to the carved walnut cabinet and poured himself a shot of strong Scotch whisky. Kendra. He knew not whether he wanted to kiss her or kill her brothers. Both, mayhap, although it probably wasn't a good idea to threaten the Chases. Colin, especially. From what he'd heard, the man was deadly with a sword.

Trick sighed and dropped into his favorite worn leather chair. In the six months since King Charles had insisted he take up residence in his father's ridiculously overblown house, this was the only room he'd redecorated to his own tastes—classic, familiar, comfortable. Lifting a heavy silver candlestick, he lit the cheroot and stuck it between his teeth, then sat back, rolling the glass between his palms and watching the candlelight glint off the faceted crystal.

What was he going to do? What *could* he do? What did he *want* to do?

The answer came to him, as clear as the expensive crystal cupped between his hands. He wanted to marry her. He'd wanted to bed her the moment he'd glimpsed her in the shadows of Cainewood's carriage. Then he'd thought it impossible—Cainewood's sister, of all people . . . Cainewood, the last bastion of respectability in a society where morals were meaningless. No one at King Charles II's court was virtuous; no one, that was, except Kendra. The Chase men had sheltered her for all of her twenty-three years, even Trick knew that, although he made it a point to keep as far from Court as humanly possible.

Having her had been unimaginable, but now it was imminent. Of course, he would have to marry her in order to bed her, but his wedding day might as well come now as later—he had to sire an heir. And Lady Kendra Chase would make as fine a wife as any. She was of suitable aristocratic birth, and Lord knew she set his blood on fire. While 'twas likely she had no dowry to speak of—Cainewood was as cash-strapped as most of the Royalist nobility—the fact was, Trick didn't need anyone else's money. He had more of his own than he knew what to do with.

He blew out a perfect smoke ring and watched it rise to the carved oak ceiling. His vision blurred, the Amberley crests somehow transforming themselves until he could almost see Kendra's expressive face. Hers was a refreshing, wholesome beauty, and though of course he didn't love her, he wanted her. He supposed he was lucky to find that in a wife.

Aye, he would marry her. Smiling at the thought, he stubbed out the cheroot, threw back his head, and downed the whisky. The warmth of the liquor curled in his stomach. Down lower, his body stirred as he imagined her in his bed. The more he thought about it, the more pleased he was at the idea.

But that didn't mean he wasn't mad as hell at the situation.

"Pardon the interruption, Your Grace."

Trick jerked around, still uneasy with the formal address, never mind that he'd held the title for three years. God knew he'd never wanted it; he'd never wanted anything that came from his father. But the damnable cur had died, and now people—most especially his father's old retainers like stuffy Compton, the butler—insisted on addressing Trick formally.

Trick gazed at the middle-aged man, wondering if he'd been born with a pike for a spine. Compton's receding gray hair was combed straight back from his forehead, and his jowls shook when he spoke, making Trick want to laugh.

"Aye, Compton?"

"The Earl of Greystone is here to see you, Your Grace."

Already? Could this family not leave him in peace for one evening? Trick sighed expansively, causing Compton's nostrils to flare in disapproval of such a show of emotion. "Bring him in," Trick muttered, rising to pour himself another shot.

"Congratulations, Amberley," Colin Chase said from behind him. "Shall we drink to your wedding tomorrow afternoon?"

Trick paused, then silently set about filling another glass. "Tomorrow, is it?" He turned to hand the man his drink, looking into his eyes, deeper green than Kendra's but just as lively and intelligent. "Bloody hell, can you not give a man time to get used to the idea?"

Colin sipped before answering, regarding Trick over the rim. "Jason can pull strings if he wants to. And time is of the essence . . . your heir may be on his way already."

"I didn't bed your—"

"I'm not judging you, Amberley." Colin flashed him a crooked grin. "My own daughter came a month early."

Trick's gaze went to the hilt of Colin's ever-present sword. His reply was slow and measured. "I told you, I didn't bed your sister."

"You know, Kendra kept claiming much the same thing on the way home. Did her fighting best to convince us of it, too."

He'd bet she did. "You didn't believe her?"

"Jason doesn't know what to believe. Frankly, I don't think he cares. Kendra's been a noose around his neck for years. She's absolutely refused to consider anyone suitable, so as far as he's concerned, this circumstance is a dream come true. God knows she would never have looked at you twice if she'd known you're a duke. A stubborn one, Kendra is."

"And now that she knows?"

"She doesn't." Colin laughed. "Thinks you're an impoverished minor aristocrat forced to highway robbery, and she's mad as hell at us for condoning the match. To our faces, that is. I suspect that, privately, she's walking on air. The lady's in love."

"Love?" Trick rolled his eyes. He'd forgotten about her naïve ideas on love. "Don't tell me you're another believer in love at first sight?"

"It seems to be the Chase way," Colin mused, thinking of his wife, Amethyst, who'd captured his heart with a single glance across a jewelry counter.

" 'Tis insane," Trick declared, throwing back the rest of his whisky. "You're all insane. This is absolutely outrageous."

"You're angry, then?"

Trick considered that for a moment. "Not exactly," he said slowly. "I think your strong-arm tactics are abhorrent, but as to the outcome . . . I suppose I must wed, and Kendra's as good a choice as any." Before long, he hoped, he'd be back at the London docks, where he could better oversee his burgeoning shipping empire. Just as soon as he'd satisfied the King's demand. Having Kendra here in the countryside, raising his children and awaiting his attentions, was not an unpleasing thought. "I haven't the stomach for courtship, so a business arrangement suits my purposes just fine."

"Business arrangement? I know what a man looks like when he wants a woman. I saw that look in your eyes earlier. You'd better be careful with my sister, Amberley."

"Careful? *I'm* not the one forcing her into this marriage."

Colin looked astonished at that accusation. "There is no way she'd be forced into any marriage—this one included—if we weren't one hundred percent certain she'd be happy. If that weren't our primary concern, she'd have been off our hands years ago— you'd need only see her list of rejected suitors to be convinced of that." He met Trick's gaze. "She wants this."

Trick had to consciously close his gaping mouth. "What do you mean?"

The other man sighed. "Pride will keep her from admitting it. But you're the first suitor she hasn't outright refused, whether she realizes it or not. And maybe not all that much happened today, but there's something between you two, Amberley—you cannot deny it."

While Trick reeled under that onslaught, Colin drew breath, and his lips parted in a wide smile. "I'm sure it will work out all around." He raised his glass. "To the groom."

Trick looked at his own empty glass, then shrugged and went to refill it. He might as well get foxed on his last night as a free man. "To the groom," he echoed wryly, then tossed the liquor down in one gulp.

Colin finished his own drink and set it on a table. "Well, I'd best get home to Amy and our precious Jewel. Big day tomorrow for all of us, eh?"

Trick nodded.

Nodding in return, Colin stuck out his hand. " 'Til tomorrow, then. Let me just send the messenger back to Cainewood. Jason will be relieved to hear you've agreed."

"Agreed?" Incredulous, Trick pulled his hand from Colin's grasp. "I thought I had no choice."

"Of course you had a choice. What kind of people do you take us for?"

"But—"

"Did you think I came here to run you through if you failed to cooperate?"

"The thought crossed my mind," Trick said dryly.

"You said yourself 'twas a sound decision. Coercion was the last thing in our heads. We're not looking to gain an enemy for an in-law. We want Kendra to be happy." He pivoted on a heel, heading for the door. "And you, of course."

"But you made it sound—"

"Good evening, Trick. Sleep well."

And for the second time that day, Trick found himself rooted to the spot, wondering what had happened.

He was embarking on a new life, his ship about to sail for ports unknown. For a man accustomed to being in charge, this was not an auspicious start.

Chapter Four

"Thank you, Jane." Kendra smiled at her kindly, plain-faced maid and put a hand to her carefully coiffed hair. "You did a lovely job." Even if it was for nothing, she added silently. As Jane left, she turned with a sigh to stare out her bedchamber window. In the quadrangle below, her "betrothed" chatted with her three brothers and a clergyman—or someone dressed like one, anyway.

"No, poppet." Amy Chase disentangled her eleven-month-old's hands from her black tresses and set the baby on her unsteady feet. "Kendra. They're waiting."

"I can see that." Letting the curtain drop, she focused on her sisters-in-law. "But what they're waiting for, I can only imagine. To laugh their heads off at me, I'm thinking."

"Laugh?" Coming close in a rustle of dusky rose satin, Caithren tweaked one of Kendra's long curls into place. "Why would they laugh?"

"This has to be a joke. Very well done, I must admit, but there's not a chance they'll make me go through with it."

"No, Jewel, don't eat that." Amy took an ivory comb from her daughter's mouth and set it back on the dressing table. "I'm not too sure they'd joke about this." She and Cait exchanged a puzzled glance.

Kendra brushed at the silver-tissue underskirt that gleamed from beneath the split front of the blue-silk gown she had dressed in for her "wedding." " 'Tis just like them to make me get all ready, is it not? Their idea of justice, having found me in a seemingly compromising position. But they're not going to actually let me wed a highwayman . . ."

"I dinna think he is just a highwayman, Kendra." Cait's hazel eyes looked hazy, concerned. "He must be suitable. Jason seemed dead serious to me."

"He's serious about scaring me, making me come to a decision. This will be called off at the last minute, at which point Jason will expect me to happily choose one of the other men who has offered. As for Trick being 'just' a highwayman, I couldn't say. I know not the first thing about him."

"But ye like him, aye?"

"He's . . . interesting." A vast understatement. Kendra only hoped her sisters-in-law wouldn't ask for elaboration.

"I like the way you say 'interesting.' " Amy's grin was too knowing for Kendra's comfort. "Sometimes we find love in unexpected places." Her fine features softened as she no doubt considered her own unconventional marriage, that of a shopgirl and a nobleman.

"Aye, she's right." Cait nodded her agreement. "If you'd told me I'd ever be in love with a man and living in *England*"— despite her love for both Jason and their home, she still pronounced the word with a mild distaste—"I'd have said ye were *sodie-heid* for certain." Her gaze narrowed at the puzzled look on Amy's face. "Featherbrained," she added in translation.

Inwardly, Kendra sighed. While 'twas true she yearned for the kind of happiness both her sisters-in-law had found, she didn't think she would find it in a sham marriage to a highwayman. No matter how much she burned for his kiss or fancied herself in love.

"Up," Jewel demanded, providing a welcome distraction as she toddled over to her mother.

Amy perched her on one violet-taffeta-clad hip. "Did you know Colin visited Trick last night? He offered him a chance to back out of this arrangement, but the man turned it down."

"Or so Colin told you." Could the amber highwayman actually want her? She didn't think so, and she knew for sure that the little leap of excitement she felt at the thought was all wrong. "If Colin actually did visit him, I'm sure it was to make plans for this absurd, elaborate ruse. Colin is nothing if not the ultimate prankster."

"Mayhap you're right, and this wedding is naught but a joke. But just in case"—Cait held out a silver coin—"you'll want to put this in your shoe."

"There she goes with her superstitions." An indulgent smile curving her lips, Kendra took the coin and tucked it into one high-heeled satin slipper. "What other old wives' tales might you be worrying about?"

"I've never said I believe it, mind ye, but ye ken what they say. Something old, something new, something borrowed, something blue . . ."

"Your gown fills three of those requirements. Old, borrowed, and blue." There'd been no time to have a wedding dress made, so Kendra was wearing Cait's. She brushed again at the shimmering silk skirts. "I always wanted to wear green for my wedding."

"I've told ye, ye wouldn't want to do that," Cait admonished. "Green is the choice of the fairies." As if that explained anything.

"And as for something new . . ." Amy moved closer, trying to maneuver an object out of her pocket.

"I'll take her," Caithren offered, reaching for Jewel. She cuddled her niece rather wistfully, Kendra thought. After nearly a year of Cait's marriage, there was yet no sign of a babe.

Amy finally extricated a bracelet from her pocket— smooth-polished ovals of amber set in heavy gold links. "A wedding gift," she said, "from your future husband. Colin asked me to pass it on to you." Studded with sparkling diamonds, the bracelet glittered in her hand.

"This is not a real wedding. And as for new, it doesn't look it."

"It isn't," Amy said in the confident tones of a skilled jeweler. "I can tell from the cut of the diamonds that 'tis actually very old. But new to you. And it cannot hurt to wear it." The golden stones seemed to glow from within, secrets of past centuries locked inside their translucent depths. "When Colin handed it to me, he said it would be quite fitting."

Amy looked curious, but Kendra wasn't about to admit she thought of her "betrothed" as the amber highwayman. How had Colin known? Had she said something inadvertently? She was usually careful about such things.

"I cannot believe the lengths your husband will go to in planning his practical jokes." She reluctantly held out her wrist. "It *is* beautiful." After Amy fastened the clasp, Kendra turned her wrist, watching the diamonds catch the light. Surely it wasn't really Trick's, which meant she could make her brothers let her keep it after this farce of a wedding was called off. For putting her through this, they owed her that much at least. It would remind her of the amber man, of the passion she'd felt ever so briefly in his arms.

It would remind her not to settle for less—not to be pressured into a loveless marriage, no matter what lengths her brothers went to.

She touched the amber pensively—warm, it somehow seemed—and drifted over to her dressing table. Watching herself in the mirror, she settled a gossamer-lace veil over her hair and drew it down, tucking the ends into the sides of her neckline to secure it. Her brothers wanted her to play the part of a blushing bride, and a blushing bride they would get. She leaned closer. Pale, too. Which was ridiculous—this was but a game.

"No, poppet," Amy said, reattaching one of the tabs on Caithren's stomacher where Jewel's pudgy fingers had managed to unfasten it.

"Shall we get this little drama over with?" Kendra asked, turning to the door.

"Nervous, man?"

"Hell, no." Trick shot Ford a smile—a confident one, he hoped. The shaking in his legs must be a leftover symptom of last night's overindulgence. He clenched his fists to keep his hands from giving him away, then shoved them into the pockets of his midnight-blue velvet surcoat. More fitted than the current style, he'd last worn the suit a few years ago at Versailles, for one of those blasted social occasions his father insisted he attend to further the "business." A time in his life that Trick would rather not remember, but he had only one other formal suit at his home in the countryside, and he'd be damned if he'd wed in his highwayman clothes.

His gaze swept over the groomed lawn of Cainewood Castle's quadrangle, then darted away when he spotted the parson, his robe billowing in the light wind, hands clasped behind his back. He seemed a kind enough sort, but Trick's stomach lurched at his mere presence. Ford . . . nay, he'd as not look at Ford, either, Kendra's twin and most certainly the man who knew her best.

He looked instead to the ancient keep, the worn stone a comforting reminder of the strength of Kendra's line. Four hundred years the Chases had lived here, save during the Commonwealth. Unlike himself, Kendra knew who she was, what she had come from. Aye, their children would surely benefit from that sort of security. Lord knew he had nothing of the kind to offer. He'd always thought of himself as a mongrel. A mangy one.

Distracted by the bang of a thick oak door, he turned to see Kendra descending Cainewood's front steps.

A vision in a sky-blue gown, she glided his way. The shimmering silk overskirt opened down the front to reveal an underskirt of costly silver tissue—he knew the expense, having bolts of the very fabric stacked in his London warehouse. The sleeves were double-puffed with a spill of silver lace at the wrists—which had made its way from Italy, if he didn't miss his guess. Swathed within the lace, her hands looked small . . . in fact, everything about her looked small. He hadn't noticed that before.

He hadn't had time to notice much of anything, he told himself, attempting to rouse his anger once again. But he had trouble maintaining the emotion when he watched the blush creep up from her low, scooped neckline and then looked into her eyes. Light green, nervous, and wary, but as they locked with his, a hint of interest—even desire?—seemed to kindle in their depths.

Answering warmth stole up his neck, and he knew he was turning a dusky red. Deliberately looking away, Kendra walked toward the family's small private chapel, Jason and Colin at her sides. Their wives trailed behind, a tiny, pink-dressed girl holding their hands, tripping along and giggling between them.

In no time at all, Trick found himself mounting the church's stone steps. Inside, sunshine streamed through brilliant-colored windows to cast the sanctuary in rainbow hues. Squaring his shoulders, he went to face the kindly parson. Jason and Colin kissed their sister, and then Ford walked her to join Trick at the front, delivering her into his care with a kiss and a hug and something whispered into her ear that Trick wished he could hear. Kendra shook her head and rolled her eyes as she pulled away.

Every inch of Trick was aware of her proximity. Just standing beside her, his body heated. Her fiery hair was covered by a fine lace veil that framed her face, the ends tucked into her neckline. Trick reached for her hand, feeling it cold and clammy in his.

"Wait," he said, and pulled her to the side of the

church, ignoring the questioning looks on her siblings' faces.

"You do not have to go through with this," he told her.

She looked even more at a loss than before. "I . . . I don't think—"

"I'll be asked to take my vows first. When the time comes, if you wish to call this off, just shake your head 'no' and I'll not say 'I will.'" Lifting her hand, he ran his fingers over the bracelet's amber stones, feeling slightly disoriented at the sight of the family heirloom on her wrist. It made this all so real, yet unreal, at the same time. He looked up. "I don't expect they can actually force us to marry," he added, thinking of Colin's sword and hoping he was right.

She peeked around at her brothers, then lifted her chin. "If you're willing, then I am, too."

He had his reasons to be willing . . . he just wondered what hers were. What was wrong with her, then, that she thought she couldn't do better than a robber for a husband? He wasn't really one, of course, but he was aware that she didn't know it— doubly aware, since her brothers had made a point of keeping his identity from her, to the extent of asking this afternoon if it would be acceptable for his title to be left out of the proceedings.

She had a problem with dukes, they'd said, and since he didn't care for the title either, he hardly thought it mattered. Married was married.

"All right, then." He nodded, and they went back to the altar.

The clergyman began the ceremony, and Kendra kept looking around, as if she expected something unforeseen to happen. Not that Trick could blame her. He found this more than a little disconcerting himself.

The preliminaries went entirely too quickly. Nobody showed just cause why they could not be lawfully joined together, and before Trick knew it, the parson was reciting the vows.

"Patrick Iain Caldwell, wilt thou have this woman to thy wedded wife, to live together after God's ordinance in the holy estate of Matrimony? Wilt thou love her, comfort her, honor, and keep her in sickness and in health; and, forsaking all others, keep thee only unto her, so long as ye both shall live?"

Kendra stiffened beside him. He slanted her a glance, but she didn't shake her head.

"I will," Trick said, and his heart flip-flopped with the enormity of the step he was taking, but also with a sudden realization. His arms itched to hold her; his lips ached to touch hers. And thanks to her scheming brothers, she had no idea he was a duke. Whatever her reasons might be, she was not marrying him for his title or his money. She didn't know he had either.

She wasn't marrying the Duke of Amberley. She was marrying Trick Caldwell. Despite the bizarre circumstances, the thought lit a hidden place in his heart.

A few more words, a simple gold band slid onto Kendra's finger, and Trick's arms slipped around her waist, just as they had yesterday. He bent his head toward hers, toward those soft lips that had been tempting him since he'd first laid eyes on her.

As his mouth met hers, she melted against him, her lavender scent surrounding him like an invisible cloud. Every bit as responsive as he'd hoped, she kissed him back, untutored but amazingly eager.

And so far as she knew, she was kissing plain Trick Caldwell.

Her brothers cleared their throats, and he reluctantly pulled away. He couldn't wait to see what pleasures lay in store when he brought her to the cottage tonight.

She wouldn't discover until tomorrow that she was a duchess.

An impromptu wedding feast was set out on the mahogany table, and Kendra sat beside her new husband in the dining room, her head still spinning with disbelief. She'd been shocked speechless when the priest concluded the ceremony, shook hands all around, and walked through the front door of the chapel, all without her brothers bursting into laughter. Just yesterday she'd been an innocent girl, fantasizing about a man she barely knew, and now it looked like tonight she would be his woman, body and soul.

But this couldn't be what it looked like. Apparently the script called for this farce to go on a little longer, but she was willing to wager that before night fell, her brothers would be dragging her off to her old bedchamber, congratulating themselves on the success of their joke.

"Are you not going to cut the cake, Kendra?"

Startled, she looked to Amy. Her sister-in-law was grinning widely and holding out a knife. Dominating the center of the table, the bride cake was double-frosted, first with an almond icing and then with a covering layer of sugar. Despite her churning stomach, Kendra's mouth watered; she loved sweets. Very well . . . if her brothers wished to continue the charade, she could play her part a little longer.

Taking the knife, she reached to cut the confection and felt Trick's hand envelop hers.

She turned her head, raising astonished eyes to find him leaning over her, bracing himself with one hand on the table. "We've yet to feast, *leannan*." He nodded toward the servants still carrying in platters.

"Ah, Trick," Jason said, a trace of laughter in his voice. " 'Tis obvious you do not know your wife. She always eats dessert first."

Colin nodded. "And she's taught Amy her unfortunate habit."

"Cake!" Jewel crowed gleefully, banging her spoon on the table.

"Second word she learned," Colin informed them dryly. "Right after Mama and before Papa."

Trick's eyes narrowed beneath his touseled hair, and Ford snorted. "We've other nasty habits, I'm afraid. Perhaps you moved too quickly in aligning yourself with the Chases, my friend."

One of Trick's eyebrows raised in censure. "*I* moved too quickly?" His hand was still on Kendra's, and she froze under it at his words. He seemed to be taking this seriously. Could it be he wasn't in on the joke? Or . . .

Could it be this was no joke?

Suddenly unsure, she looked around the table at her brothers' faces. Their expressions told her nothing. When she saw Colin with Amy and Jewel, and Jason together with Cait, she couldn't help but wish for a family of her own like those her brothers were creating. A whole family, like the one she'd been cheated of growing up in the Civil War and Commonwealth years without her parents. But to expect a romantic marriage with any of the suitors her brothers had presented would be like throwing snowballs against bullets.

This was her *life* they were toying with. She bit the inside of her cheek, then glanced away when Caithren caught her gaze and returned it with heart-wrenching sympathy.

Trick moved to pull back the knife, but she held steady, and he laughed suddenly, then shot her a rakish smile. So clean and white . . . Noticing the tiny chip on his front tooth, she licked her lips, wishing her tongue were tasting that beautiful mouth instead. And she stopped breathing, shocked at her thoughts.

She had never put her tongue in a man's mouth— wherever had that idea come from? Besides, he'd probably bite it off. If this was no joke, he was due a pound of Chase flesh, and she knew it.

But instead of turning the knife on her, he slipped her a wink. "Come, we'll cut it together."

The man was an enigma, to be sure. Kendra's heart steadied as they sliced the cake, his hand warm over hers. She placed a piece on Amy's plate, then one on her own.

All the while, Trick was still standing beside her. She could feel his gaze, feel him shifting, but before she had time to react, he'd reached and plucked the veil from her head.

"What!" She turned and snatched it from his hands.

"I wanted to see your . . . hair," he finished lamely, blinking at her in seeming bemusement. "What the hell did you do to it?"

"Do to it?"

"The . . ." He waved a finger, drawing spirals in the air. "The . . ."

"Curls?" Kendra supplied helpfully. She couldn't help but grin at his expression. "Jane worked on it for an hour. Do you like it?"

"No," he said flatly. "I liked it before." He leaned close, whispering so no one else could hear him. "Wild, streaming down your back."

"Oh." She felt a blush heat her face. "After this, I'll take it down."

"After this, *I'll* take it down."

The wispy lace fluttered from her fingers to the soft blue Oriental carpet. Feeling more confused by the moment, she plopped back into her chair.

"Mmm . . . porcupine," Trick said, reseating himself with a satisfied grin. "At least I've married into a family that knows how to eat." The "porcupine" was actually a stuffed breast of veal, larded all over and studded with small strips of ham, bacon, and pickled cucumber. Trick smacked his lips and added a healthy portion to his already-loaded plate.

"Leave room—we've a surprise as well," Colin warned. Spearing a bite of cake, Kendra looked up as a servant set the dish called surprise on the table. A stuffed calf's head served up in its original shape, it had bunches of myrtle stuck into its eyes and looked very surprised indeed.

The steam rose off it in tantalizing swirls . . . and it bellowed.

Kendra screamed, and a piece of cake went flying off Amy's fork, splattering on one of the diamond-paned leaded windows. Ford jumped up, his lattice-backed chair clunking to the floor behind him. Trick and Jason froze.

When it bellowed again, Kendra rushed from her chair to take shelter in the door frame with Cait, both poised for flight. Stopping only to snatch up baby Jewel, Amy joined them. The women all clung together, staring. Squished between their bodies, Jewel let out a wail.

The calf's head bellowed once more . . .

No, it croaked. With a half-amused, half-disgusted groan, Trick dropped his fork, reached to pry the calf's mouth open wider, then lifted its heavy pink tongue. A toad hopped out and looked around, blinking its bulbous eyes, then leapt off the table and toward the door. Weak-kneed with the release of tension, Kendra broke apart from the others to let it pass between them.

Amongst gales of laughter from the men, she thwacked Colin on the head as she returned to her seat. "For the love of God, Colin! Have you no sense of propriety?"

"A question of propriety from *your* lips, little sister?" Colin rubbed his head good-naturedly. "Was it not just yesterday we found you—"

"Hush, Colin." Amy dumped their sobbing daughter on her husband's lap. "Here. You made her cry, she's yours." She seated herself and picked up her fork, but not before sending her husband a tolerant smile.

Jewel quieted when Colin bounced her on his knee, holding her with one arm while reaching about her to eat with the other. "Well, you've seen us at our worst now," he said to Trick around a mouthful of dressed artichoke bottoms. "Welcome to the family."

Trick shrugged noncommittally. Watching him scan the group around the table, Kendra tried to imagine what he was thinking. It couldn't be good.

It was time to bring this charade to an end.

"How will you get along without me here to direct the household?" she asked Jason.

"We'll manage," her brother said blithely, wrapping an arm around his competent wife. His fingertips played idly in her dark-blond hair. "I set Jane to packing your things."

"Jane is your maid, I presume?" Trick inquired. "She can follow tomorrow. You'll send her along, Cainewood?"

"Certainly."

"But—" Kendra started.

Trick cut her off. "Tomorrow," he repeated.

At the look in his eyes—the keen hunger—Kendra's spoon clattered to her plate. He was acting as if they were really married, talking of maids and spending the night together. Did highwaymen even have servants? She certainly hadn't seen any at the cottage. Fingering the bracelet around her wrist, she recalled what little she knew of him. It wasn't much, and it wasn't good.

"But you're—" Something in his warm eyes made her falter. "—a highwayman," she finished weakly.

Jason reached for the bread. "Yes, we need to talk about that."

Trick tore his gaze from Kendra. "Aye?"

"It has got to stop."

Trick chewed thoughtfully, picked up his goblet, drank some wine, and set it down. The silence stretched between him and Jason, almost as though it were a palpable barrier.

"I mean it, Trick. You don't need the money."

Trick only raised an arched eyebrow at that. "Aye? You think not?" One corner of his wide mouth turned up, and Kendra would swear he was about to start laughing. Did he really not need the money? Had he enough put aside, then? Highway robbery couldn't be *that* lucrative . . . There was something missing here. But she couldn't seem to think straight in his presence; it had been that way since she'd first laid eyes on him. She felt all hot and bothered, and her brain refused to work.

"Why do you do it?" Ford asked.

With a shake of his head, Trick tossed the hair from his eyes and looked straight at her twin. "Mayhap it amuses me."

"You're finished, Trick." Jason's voice brooked no nonsense. He set down his fork with a distinct sense of finality. "Find your pleasure somewhere else."

The golden eyes settled on Kendra again and burned into hers. "Aye," Trick said slowly, softly. "That I will."

Chapter Five

The sun was setting, painting the sky in muted tones as they made their way to Trick's home in the impressive two-seater caleche he'd driven to Cainewood. Borrowed, most likely, Kendra thought, along with the matched bay horses . . . at least she fervently hoped he hadn't stolen them. A furtive glance to the rear convinced her they weren't being followed—she wasn't being rescued—by any of her brothers.

"I cannot believe it," she said.

Trick gave her a long, considered look before responding in that characteristic slow way of his. "You cannot believe what?"

"I cannot believe I am wed. It happened so fast."

He raked a hand back through his shining hair. "Why did you go through with it?"

"I never thought it was real. Even now, I am half-expecting one of my brothers to ride up laughing at their masterful joke."

"They're not coming," Trick said.

She slumped in her seat. "I know." And she knew as well that some tiny part of her had wondered if it might be real all along, and even—maybe—hoped that it was. He was the only man with whom she'd ever felt a sort of magic. But that didn't stop her from wanting to sink her claws into her too-clever brothers.

How dared they scheme like this, marrying her to a known criminal? He could be a murderer, for all she knew! The hard length of his rapier rode in the sword belt on his right. Of course, her brothers carried weapons as well, but they didn't draw and use them on a daily basis.

Her teeth ached from clenching them. Consciously relaxing her jaw, she took a deep breath. "I know they're not coming. But I still cannot believe it. All along, I assumed this was a prank." That desperate conviction had helped her cope all the day, and it was frightening to let go of it. "I thought they were trying to teach me a lesson."

Trick turned to her at that, a hint of a smile on his wide mouth. "Are you due to be taught a lesson?"

She glared at him through the growing dark, then faced forward and crossed her arms. "I'm so furious with them, I swear I won't speak to them for weeks. Do you know they wouldn't even tell me your title?"

He shrugged. "Mayhap they had their reasons for not wanting you to know."

He was as obstinate as her brothers. Whatever had made her believe, even for a fleeting second, that the magic she'd felt in his arms could be enough to sustain a relationship? "I can vow not to talk to you as well, you know."

"What makes you think I'm interested in talking tonight?"

The question was uttered in a voice so silky smooth, it robbed her of breath.

But not for long. "You were manipulated into this

as much as I was," she said, hugging herself to hide the attack of nerves. "Are you angry?"

"Aye, a bit perhaps." He guided the caleche off the main road, onto a less-traveled path. "But not overmuch. And not at you. I know this situation is not your fault." When she offered him a tremulous smile, he grinned back in response. " 'Tis not such a bad bargain I've made, ye ken?"

Kendra blushed wildly, thankful for the cover of darkness. A fair bargain, was she? She couldn't think of anything to say in return to such a statement, so she remained silent, tightening her arms around her middle. Perhaps thinking she was cold, Trick wrapped an arm around her shoulders.

She should be terrified, she thought vaguely. She knew nothing of men in an intimate way, and he was a virtual stranger. But his warmth was oddly comforting.

She scooted closer, and when his long fingers rubbed up and down her arm, she melted against him, thinking about when she first saw him and how she'd wanted him to notice her. Remembering yesterday in the cottage and how much she'd craved his kiss.

And then today, their first kiss in the church. Spellbinding it was, his mouth gentle and demanding at the same time. That single indelible kiss had been everything she'd imagined and more. It had ignited a fire in her blood, making her wonder what might come next.

She'd barely become accustomed to his nearness when the caleche bumped off the path and over a grassy knoll, following a faint trail that led to the cottage. Windows glowed in the distance, the lamps inside already lit. The cottage looked warm and welcoming, but as they rolled to a stop, she tensed. Too soon he would expect her to become his wife in more than just name, and, despite her curiosity, she wasn't sure she could go through with it.

He helped her down and guided her inside with a hand at the small of her back, touching her where she wasn't used to being touched. Shutting the door behind them, he eased her back against it. Close. Entirely too close, his eyes locked on hers, his warmth penetrating the small space between them. She could smell the soap-fresh masculine scent of him—sandalwood, if she wasn't mistaken. She wouldn't expect a highwayman to use imported soap, but then, little about this situation had matched her expectations.

Just when she thought she might panic, he turned away. "I'm going to settle the horses, aye?" The last time he'd said those words they hadn't been man and wife, but now the expression in his whisky-gold eyes left Kendra in no doubt as to his plans for the evening. Before she could react, the door shut behind him.

How could this be happening to her?

Her fashionable high Louis-heeled shoes made a loud, unnerving sound as she walked around the main room, picking things up and putting them down at random. She tried the bottom drawer of the desk again, but it was still stuck tight.

What had she expected? She'd first tried it only yesterday.

'Twas incredible.

Too soon, Trick blew through the doorway with a smile of anticipation that made her breath catch in her throat. He strolled straight to the cabinet and poured them each a goblet of wine. Yesterday's cups were gone, the broken shards of glass picked up, the stain nonexistent, as though the spill had never happened.

But it *had* happened, and because of it, she was married to Trick Caldwell.

"Here," he said, handing her a glass. He tapped his against it, the resulting tinkle of expensive crystal sounding pure and loud in the silence that stretched between them. *"Slàinte mhór."* Kendra watched his throat muscles work as he drank deeply. Perhaps he wasn't as cavalier about the proceedings as he made himself out to be.

Her head spinning even without the wine, she took a cautious sip. *"Sl . . .* what?"

With a gentle smile, he set down his glass and moved to her, slipping his arms about her waist. "Good health—a toast," he translated quietly. "And don't be too impressed. 'Tis all the Gaelic I can remember."

"I . . . I'm . . ." Feeling dizzy, her heart pounding, Kendra placed one hand on his broad chest and leaned into him, knowing she was giving him the wrong idea but unable to help herself. She felt abandoned and confused, and he was her only anchor. "I'm not impressed."

"Oh, aren't you now?" he drawled, taking the goblet from her other hand. He bent to set it beside his on the table, and when he came back up, his mouth descended on hers.

Hot. Hot and soft. That was all Kendra could think. Then hard and urgent. His lips opened, coaxing hers to do the same. Then his tongue was in her mouth, slick and tender. Though the mere thought of such a thing had been foreign until this evening, she wasn't surprised to find her instincts had been right. Tentatively she touched her own tongue to that tiny chip on his front tooth, just the way she had imagined.

'Twas a catalyst. Her body responded with a tingling flush of pleasure, and her arms clenched around him, lest she drop to her knees. She felt a low, pleased chuckle rumble from his chest into hers—from his mouth into hers, too—vibrating within her. His hands moved to her waist, to keep her from falling, and he broke the kiss. She fought to catch her breath.

"Still not impressed, lassie?"

Her answer was a low moan as she reached to pull his head back down to hers, twining her fingers in his silky hair. She was trembling again, but not with fear; instead with a need she found thrilling. Their tongues fenced, and Kendra tasted wine and Trick, sweet and tart and so exciting, she thought she might die from the pleasure.

Not one to do anything halfway, she reached inside his blue velvet surcoat to pull at his shirt. It seemed impossibly long—to his knees, she'd swear— but it finally came loose, and she slipped her hands up under it, to feel the warm contours of his torso.

He jumped and pulled back, almost as though he hadn't been aware of what she'd been doing. Kendra's chest heaved as his eyes, darkened to bronze, burned into her own.

"Sweet Mary. You're so . . ." He gave a shaky laugh. "I almost dragged you to the floor."

Kendra blushed to realize she would have gone right down on the floor with him, no doubt about it. Maybe this wedding night would be easier than she'd thought. He drew a steadying breath and ran a hand back through his hair, and she watched, mesmerized, as the front flopped back down into place.

"Why do you not cut it?" she asked.

"Hmmm?" His darkened gaze still held hers.

"Your hair, where it hangs down in your eyes."

"Mayhap I'm just lazy," he suggested.

"You're hiding," she countered.

"Not tonight." He moved close again and ran his warm hands lightly over her back. "Shall we repair to the bedchamber?"

Kendra didn't think her face could get any hotter, but it did as he took her by the hand and led her down the corridor. The bedchamber had been cleaned up, too; no trace remained of the broken washbowl or its spilled contents. A new one stood in its place.

And, of course, there was the bed. Her gaze locked on it, anticipation and apprehension warring somewhere in her stomach.

"Second thoughts?" At the same time, his jaw clenched and a pained half-smile touched his lips. "I offered you a way out of the wedding," he said with a sigh. "I can also offer you a way out of the wedding night." Sincere though it might be, she couldn't help but notice that the "offer" was uttered in a voice laced with frustration. "I hope to sire an heir, but it doesn't have to be tonight. I know this has been quick."

A tempting offer, indeed. But his eyes seemed to plead with her. And her own body was begging as well, her heart still racing in response to his enthralling kisses. She found herself caught in that imploring gaze as he silently lifted her hand and started working the clasp on the amber bracelet.

" 'Tis lovely," she sighed, feeling tingles as his fingers brushed her wrist. "Was it really from you, then?"

"Aye." Slowly he drew it off, hefting the weight in one hand. " 'Twas my grandmother's, and her mother's before her."

"Then why does your mother not have it?"

"My father never considered her worthy."

Worthy. He barely knew her, yet he considered *her* worthy. She tried to wrap her mind around the significance of that, but found herself distracted when he raised her now-bare wrist and placed a warm kiss to the inside, where her blood ran near the surface. The gesture seemed more intimate than a kiss on the mouth.

She shivered as he moved to set the amber bracelet on the night table. The little metallic *click* made her jump. "Sit," he said, dropping into the room's only chair.

There was no other place to sit but the bed.

A big bed, very big for a "cottage," and big especially for this small chamber. Somehow yesterday that had failed to register. 'Twas a feather bed, too, not straw or wool. The bed-hangings, of palest ice-blue silk, were free of fussy frills and looked very costly and eminently tasteful.

The counterpane was already folded back. She gingerly pushed aside an embroidered coverlet and lowered herself to sit on smooth, luxurious sheets, watching Trick unknot his cravat, loosen the laces on his shirt, remove his boots and stockings.

He knelt at her feet and pulled off her shoes, then

reached beneath her skirts, feeling for the ribbons that tied her garters.

No man had ever touched her legs. "I—" she started, but she knew not what to say. She had no cause to protest—he was her husband. And he'd offered her an out. Twice.

"Does your maid not do this?"

"Well, yes." She felt one garter come loose, and his fingers traced down her legs, rolling the stocking off in a way that made little darts of pleasure shimmer through her. "But . . . with Jane it doesn't feel like this," she managed.

"I would hope not." He raised a brow, making short work of the second garter, then held it up, all lace and satin ribbon. "A lovely little French confection, aye?"

"Madame Beaumont imports them. How did you know?"

He shrugged. "Lucky guess."

She wondered how many other French garters he'd removed over the years. He certainly seemed rather good at it.

Her second stocking came off in a whisper of silk, and he stood, bringing her up with him. He pressed his lips to her forehead, a warm kiss that melted her inside, then gathered her close, resting his chin on her crown. "Your hair smells like lavender fields, *leannan.*"

His low, throaty voice went right through her. She'd wondered what being with a man was all about, and now she had a husband of her own.

Determined to calm her quivering nerves, to project an inner confidence she didn't feel, she slipped her arms beneath his coat and leaned back to look up at him. "I thought that toast was the only Gaelic you knew."

"Pardon?"

"What does that mean, *leannan*?"

"I . . . I know not." His brow creased. "It just slipped out. My mother used to call me that, I think."

"Maybe it means 'misbehaving young man.' "

His laughter filled the small chamber. "I think not." Still smiling, he moved to detach her stomacher. "Does your maid do this?" He set it on a chest at the foot of the bed. "And this?" His long fingers loosened her laces.

"Yes," she whispered, watching as he worked the gown over her shoulders and down to pool in a shimmer at her feet. The silver underskirt glistened in the firelight. When . . . how had it been lit? Kendra wondered vaguely. But Trick's hot mouth was on her neck, doing strange things to the pit of her stomach, and she couldn't seem to think straight.

He lifted his head and gazed down at her. From her vantage point below him, she saw his eyes darken beneath the golden fringe. Then he stepped back, and his gaze traveled the length of her chemise-clad form.

In return, she boldly perused him. But the shirt, which did reach his knees, hung from beneath his velvet surcoat, quite effectively concealing him from her view.

She stepped from the folds of her gown to come forward and tug off his coat. The shirt went next, over his head to join the clothes on the floor. At the sight of his bare torso, her knees went weak. A light sprinkling of blond hair glimmered in the firelight, and she reached to touch him, her palms flat against his chest, caressing, learning the indentations, the sleekness of his skin over the tautness underneath, the springiness of the crisp golden curls. Her breath hitched as his muscles twitched beneath her questing fingers.

"Jesus," Trick breathed. "You're no simpering miss now, are you? Are you sure you've never—"

"I'm sure." Kendra's cheeks heated. " 'Tis just . . . you feel . . ." She hid her flaming face against his chest, certain he would think her wanton. But those thoughts didn't stop her hands from continuing their exploration, moving around him to feel the hard, smooth planes of his back. His chest hair tickled her nose, and without thinking, her tongue flicked out to taste his skin, warm and just the tiniest bit salty. She licked again and inhaled his scent, sandalwood and Trick, musky and exciting. "Goodness, I want to eat you up," she whispered under her breath.

A low chuckle rumbled through Trick's chest. "Be my guest." His voice came rough as his hands moved to pull the pins from her hair. "This marriage seems more suitable by the minute. I never dreamed—what is this?" He jerked back, holding up a long red curl, his eyes registering utter disbelief.

" 'Tis a false curl. To make my hair plumper."

"Plumper? Who the hell needs plump hair?" He raked his fingers through her tresses, coming out with two more curls and . . . "Wires? Why wires?"

"To make the curls stand out." Kendra shifted on her feet, suddenly feeling like Medusa. She tugged her own hands through her hair, plucking out several more wires and three additional curls. "That's six? I think that's all."

"Where do you get these? Wait—I'd rather not

know." He tossed away the curls in disgust. "Wires and curls." Combing the tangles from her hair with his fingers, he shuddered. "Have you any more surprises for me, then? Is your pretty nose your own? Mayhap some false hips are hiding beneath that lovely chemise?"

"No." Her hands went to her hips. "These are mine. You don't . . . They're too wide, you think?"

"Nothing about you is wide." He settled her hair over her shoulders, a curtain down her back. "Except perhaps your smile, and that hair, but we'll not see that again, will we? Or should I have thrown those curls into the fireplace?" He laughed as his hands covered hers, his thumbs tracing her hipbones. "Ah, the better to bear my children, no?"

"Trick, the things you say . . ."

"Ah . . ." He leaned over her. "The things I say are nothing compared to the things I will do." His hands moved to cup her face, and he bent her back for a long, deep kiss.

Her knees buckled. Trick caught her, laughing low, and swung her into his arms to deposit her on the bed. She felt dwarfed in its middle, the bedposts and ice-blue damask towering around her, but when Trick came down next to her, the bed was the last thing on her mind.

"Does your maid do this?" he asked, working the gossamer chemise up her legs.

"N-no. At least, not like that," she breathed, feeling his fingers skim the sensitive insides of her thighs. "No one has ever done—" She gasped.

" 'Tis glad I am to hear it." Refocusing his attentions, he moved up to tease her breasts, and she watched her nipples pucker beneath the filmy fabric.

'Twas scandalous, but wonderful all the same. He drew the garment off her shoulders, then bent his head and fastened his lips on one rosy peak.

Kendra shuddered. Hot and wet, his mouth elicited a melting sweetness within her. She arched with pleasure, tangling her fingers into his hair. A low hum of satisfaction vibrated from his throat into her body, and she arched again when he licked his way to her other breast and lavished it with little kisses and gentle bites whose mild sting he suckled away. Her senses spun, and an ache started building, deep inside her.

When she thought she couldn't take any more, he sat up and helped her out of her chemise. Sucking in a breath, he stared down at her, then broke into a grin that had her heart lurching.

Far beyond embarrassment, she only reached for him, desperate to feel him again. With a strangled laugh, he dodged her grasp and hurried out of his breeches.

She froze at the sight. Dear God, he was beautiful.

But there was no way he could fit.

"Leannan." Clearly unaware of her distress, he lowered himself to the bed and molded his body to hers, drawing up the coverlet to lock in their warmth.

"Trick—"

A smile curved his lips before his mouth descended to meet hers. And then he was kissing her, skimming her body with worshipful fingers, driving every coherent thought—and worry—from her brain.

Almost. She froze again when he reached to part her legs. "You're wet," he whispered.

She was. And his touch felt exquisite. For long minutes he skillfully teased her to pleasure, until she writhed against him with a strange, marvelous feeling so urgent she wondered how she could bear it. Her hands dug into his shoulders, her nails raked his back, her fingers clawed at his hair. And all the while he kissed her, his mouth fused to hers, hot and tasting of the forbidden.

She felt melted inside, too weak to protest when he shifted over her. *"Leannan,"* he breathed, pushing into her, slowly at first. Then harder when he seemed to hit a barrier—a quick thrust that seemed to tear her apart.

The melting feeling died instantly, and she stiffened, every nerve in her body screaming with fiery pain.

"Oh, my God! Get off of me, Trick." She'd known he wouldn't fit. "Stop it! Now!"

"Just wait, *lea*—"

"No!" She pushed at his chest, biting her lip to stop the tears that flooded her eyes.

"Hearts wounds, Kendra. Just wait—'twill go away—"

"No," she sobbed out. "Please, just get out of me." She twisted under him. "Please."

He shifted off her body. "Hell, I don't believe this." He lay there, breathing heavily for a minute, then rolled to the edge of the bed and sat up, rubbing his face with his hands. "I just do not believe this."

She didn't believe it, either.

He dropped his hands and turned to her, reaching for her face. "Sweet Jesus, I'm sorry," he murmured, caressing one tear-stained cheek. "I should have been slower, more gentle. I thought you were ready. You were so passionate. So wet . . ."

"You don't fit."

"What?" His fingertips stilled on her chin.

"You don't fit. We should not have been married." Sniffling, she pushed away his hand and swiped the wetness from her cheeks. "Just leave me alone."

"Kendra—"

"Leave me alone."

She lay stiff as a sugar stick while he rose and drew a dressing gown from the wardrobe, tying it at his waist with a jerky motion borne of frustration. He left the room without saying another word.

She sat up, shaking, and threw off the coverlet, staring between her spread legs. Dear God, she was bleeding. Did people actually like to do this?

No wonder her brothers had married her off without telling her what would happen. She'd have run in the other direction as fast as her legs would carry her, and well they knew it.

Trembling, she made her way to the washbasin and cleaned up, then climbed back into the bed and lay waiting. There was nothing else she could do. For better or worse, she was wed to Trick Caldwell.

It certainly couldn't get worse.

'Twas not long before he came back into the room and stood over her. His golden hair gleamed in the firelight. A muscle twitched in his clenched jaw.

Her own jaw set in response. "I told you to leave me alone."

"You're my wife."

She flinched under his steadfast gaze; then her spine stiffened. "I'm bleeding, Trick. You hurt me. For God's sake, you cannot expect me to do that again."

He stared at her, incredulous. "Hurt you?" he repeated slowly. "I know some women feel pain the first time, but—" He broke off, looking to the ceiling—for patience, she supposed. "Sweet Mary, I've never seen a woman so responsive, until—"

"That's because I didn't know what it was leading to," she muttered miserably. "Did you not hear what I told you? I'm bleeding."

He dropped onto the mattress. "Did you come to this marriage a complete innocent? Did your brothers not tell you anything? Anything at all?"

"My brothers always stuttered when I brought up anything of the sort. I believe they each think one of the others took care of that matter."

He shook his head, clearly sympathizing with her brothers' predicament. Then his voice gentled. "Know you nothing of mating, then, my virgin bride?"

"Of course I know something! I've lived in the countryside most of my life. I've seen animals in the fields—" She sat up suddenly. "Why did you not go from behind?" she accused. "The animals never seem to feel pain—"

"From behind?" In a complete reversal of mood, Trick collapsed into a heap on the bed and laughed until tears leaked from his eyes. " 'Tis possible, and I suppose we'll get around to trying it eventually, but I don't think—" Pushing himself up, he caught her gaze and put a hand on her arm. "Look, 'tis sorry I am that you weren't prepared, and even more sorry I didn't take our . . . courtship . . . more slowly. I knew I should have, or I would never have offered to wait, never mind that I didn't really want to. But 'twill not hurt the next time, I promise."

She jerked back her arm, trembling all over again. "You're right. Because there won't be a next time."

"You think not?" He ran a hand back through his hair.

As it flopped back into place, she licked her lips. "I know not, Trick. I mean it. I won't let you."

He stared at her for a good long while; she was sure he could hear her heart pounding in the stillness. Then his gaze lit with determination. He took a deep breath and blew it out before leaning close.

"You'll let me, lass." He trailed one finger, achingly slow, from her forehead along the bridge of her nose, past her lips, her chin, her neck, and all the way between her breasts, dragging the covers down as he went. He tossed the hair from his eyes and captured her in his gaze, his finger trailing lower, dipping into her navel and stopping there, pressing lightly.

"Ye'll not only let me," he said, his voice low, his accent so thick she had to strain to catch the words, "ye'll beg me."

He paused for so long, so still, that Kendra wondered if he'd ceased breathing. Then he drew away and turned over, leaving her staring at his back and quivering from head to toe.

Chapter Six

The next morning, Kendra was more than relieved when Trick awakened her with a breakfast tray and told her he had "things to take care of" and would return late in the afternoon. She guessed he'd gone out to play the highwayman again and didn't quite know how she felt about that. Or him.

She hadn't any idea what to say to the man, never mind that he knew how to make a decent cup of chocolate with plenty of sugar to satisfy her sweet tooth.

It felt a mite ridiculous to put on the wedding dress again, but she had nothing else to wear until her maid arrived with her luggage. She washed up and used Trick's comb to neaten her hair, then clasped on the amber bracelet, pausing for a moment to appreciate how the diamonds caught the light. Though she had little doubt Trick no longer considered her "worthy," the bracelet was beautiful, and she intended to enjoy it.

She munched on bread spread with orange butter as she wandered about the cottage. There were three more rooms off the corridor, but Trick had apparently found no use for them. The few pieces of furniture were covered in sheets, the floors and walls clean but unadorned.

Her work was cut out for her, but at least it would give her something to occupy her time—she was used to caring for an entire estate and found it hard to imagine what she would do with herself here. Looking forward to Jane showing up with her things, she anticipated the two of them spending a pleasant couple of days rearranging furniture and unpacking before she went stark raving mad with inactivity.

She chose a room for Jane and another she thought would suffice for herself, since she didn't plan to share with Trick anymore. The fourth and last room would make a nice nursery, except she had no intention of doing what it would take to fill it.

No wonder Caithren had yet to become pregnant.

Finished with her survey in a depressingly short time, she briefly considered going home to yell at her brothers, but remembered she wasn't speaking to them. She wandered to the bookshelves that lined the corridor. Noticing an abundance of poetry, she chose a book of Shakespeare's sonnets and the first two volumes of Milton's *Paradise Lost*, then sat herself in the main room to await her maid's arrival.

She was bored silly by the time Trick showed up instead.

He'd said he wanted to give her a "tour of the countryside," as if she hadn't lived in the countryside half her life. He'd brought an elaborate supper for them to share in the caleche on the way, though she couldn't imagine where he'd obtained it.

They'd driven through miles of rich farmland and a country town called Amberley that bustled with prosperity. All the while, he'd kept up an entertaining travelogue, but raised no personal subjects. Nor had he responded to her discreet probing, skillfully turning the topic back to the scenery instead. Three hours later she knew nothing more about him than she had when she said her vows. And after all his threats of last night—*"ye'll beg me"* echoed in her head—he hadn't even touched her.

Not that she wasn't relieved, but nothing about this man added up, and that in itself was disquieting.

The sun was low in the sky when she dropped her napkin into the picnic basket and licked roast chicken off her fingers. "What if Jane and my trunks arrive and we're not home to meet her?"

"Relax, *leannan*. We'll be there soon." He put his hand on her knee, then looked down and snatched it back, flexing it before gripping the caleche's reins.

Her knee tingled where his fingers had lain. "But—"

"Don't worry," he said. "We're almost there now."

"No, we're not." She had an excellent sense of direction, and they were nowhere near the cottage. " 'Tis—"

"There." He inclined his head as he guided the caleche off the road and onto a well-groomed drive. A very long drive. Tall trees lined the way, and an enormous mansion stood at the end. Built of russet brick with more windows and chimneys than she could count, it had to be the size of Cainewood Castle, at the very least. Except Cainewood was mostly ancient, damaged, and closed-up, while this home sparkled with newness.

"There?" She frowned at an ostentatious clock tower atop the building. Eight o'clock. Little more than a day since she'd been wed, and she'd never felt so lost in her life. "Whatever do you mean? What is this?"

"Your new home." His wide mouth quirked in a half-smile. "Do you like it?"

"L-like it?" she sputtered. "I don't understand." Her hands twisted together in her lap, her fingers finding the amber bracelet and worrying the smooth, polished stones. "Do you work here?"

He blinked, then smiled wider. "Why, yes, I do."

"What of the cottage?"

"No, I don't work there. Not usually, in any case. 'Tis more a place to rest, get off by myself for a while—ah, here we are."

Puzzled, Kendra turned from Trick to the house, where the double doors were flung open and a steady stream of crimson-liveried servants poured out and down the wide marble steps.

"Welcome home, Your Grace."

"Our congratulations!"

"Such a lovely bride!"

"Your Grace." A straight-backed, gray-haired man extended one white-gloved hand to Kendra, presumably to help her down.

She paused before putting her hand in his, looking about in utter confusion. "Your Grace?" she repeated under her breath.

"Your Grace," Trick confirmed, helping her to the gravel. Two grooms appeared from nowhere and took the caleche while more servants scurried to join the double line that flanked the tall, carved front doors.

Trick grasped Kendra by the elbow and guided her toward the steps. "May I present my wife, the Duchess of Amberley. I trust you will all do your best to see that she's happy here."

Happy? She nodded and smiled stiffly, all the while planning Trick's murder.

Which would come right after her brothers'.

"You're a *duke*! The Duke of *Amber*ley, no less!" 'Twas unbelievable. No wonder Colin had said that the amber bracelet was fitting. She hooked her fingers through it, barely resisting her urge to rip it off.

"Such venom. God's blood, ye say it as though a duke is the worst sort of knave."

"In this case, he is." Kendra paced the red-velvet-hung bedchamber. "How dare you keep such a secret from me!"

"I don't hold with lying, Kendra. But your brothers asked me not to tell you, and I reckoned 'twas harmless enough, in the scheme of things."

"Harmless! You tricked me! I would never have married you had I known—"

"Rubbish. You were in love with me."

Kendra wanted to slap the smug look off his handsome face. "Love, hah! Why, I don't even know you. Wherever did you get such an absurd idea?"

"Your brothers told me."

"They knew nothing about it." Feeling the red creep into her cheeks, she hastened to add, " 'Twould not matter, anyway. Whatever I may or may not have felt for you was destroyed by your lie, not to mention last night."

"Hearts wounds, not that again." Trick sighed and dropped into a tufted brocade chair. "I told you, 'twas only the first time. 'Twill not hurt again."

She only stared at him, her jaw set.

"And what, pray tell, is so bad about being a duchess? Most women would be thrilled beyond words."

"I am never beyond words."

"Why does that not surprise me?" Trick returned dryly. He crossed his long legs at the ankles. "I really don't understand this, Kendra. How can marrying a duke be such a disastrous occurrence?"

" 'Tis too hard to explain."

"Try." He crossed his arms. "I'm listening."

With a sigh, she sat on the red velvet bed. "I won't pretend I don't enjoy balls and pretty clothes and the other things money can buy as much as the next woman. But I think I know what's important underneath all the trappings. I told my brothers again and again that I care not about titles. I wanted to marry a man I was wildly in love with, but even more, one I could admire. For who he was, not a false honor that society had settled upon him."

"I didn't ask to be a duke—" Trick started.

But she wasn't listening. "During the Commonwealth, my family's title was useless. We were exiled paupers, dragged from Paris, to Cologne, to Brussels, Bruges, Antwerp—wherever King Charles and his court wandered. And 'twas then I learned 'tis what's inside a person that counts. Some people were kind to us, and some were not. And their rank had nothing to do with it."

He swept the hair from his face, his expression clearing. "That is why your brothers asked me to marry you under my given name only," he murmured. "Because you would have refused."

"Probably," she conceded. "Oh, I knew this would

be impossible to explain." With a huff of impatience, she parked her hands behind her and threw back her head. Above her loomed the underside of a gathered silk canopy fit for a king. "*Your Grace.* 'Tis not the title itself that sets my teeth on edge, but what it symbolizes. To me. To the world in general. All the good people who weren't lucky enough to—"

Breaking off, she sat straight, but the dazed look in Trick's eyes only frustrated her further. "Just look at this!" She leapt up and gestured wildly at the room: the padded, satin-lined walls, the carved and gilded ceiling, the four-poster bed crowned with garish poufs of red-dyed ostrich feathers. "See what I mean? Who wants to live in a place like this? I swear, it puts Whitehall to shame!"

He gave a short bark of a laugh at what she knew must be a look of utter disgust on her face. "I know women who would kill for—"

"Kill for this? That's the first thing you've said all day that makes any sense."

He looked heavenward. "Come now, 'tis not so bad."

"I would rather live in the cottage."

"Come to think of it, so would I." He stood, pacing contemplatively before the carved stone mantel. "My father built this bloody palace, not I. Let us move to the cottage. I'll alert Cavanaugh to pack my things, and Jane needn't even unpack yours. We'll make haste for the cottage immediately."

She swallowed hard. "Are you sure?"

He turned to her and raised one brow. "Are *you* sure?"

A long silence stretched between them before Kendra sighed. "No," she said, not sure of anything at the moment. "I don't want to live in that little cottage. Well, actually, 'tis a big cottage, but you know what I mean." She dropped to sit on the bed. "I'm accustomed to directing a large household, and I'll do you proud. 'Tis only . . . when I think of all the money it takes to run a place like this—all the servants and goods—for just the two of us . . . can we not close up some of it? Close up most of it? Most of Cainewood is closed up. We could take the money and put it to good use, give it to some charity or other."

Trick sat beside her, smelling of sandalwood soap. He must have come here and bathed, the wretch, while she yawned her way through the day, reading poetry.

He took her hand. "If we close up most of the house, think of the people who will be out of jobs. My father hired them, but I cannot find it in my heart to send them to the streets."

"Oh . . . I hadn't thought of that."

His smile, crooked but genuine, did much to thaw her icy anger. "And as far as charity goes," he added, "I've something to show you tomorrow."

"What?" She leaned closer to his enticing scent, then caught herself and pulled her hand from his grasp. He'd still lied to her, tricked her, and that was hard to forgive. Especially now, with all the years that yawned ahead . . . years and years. She set her jaw. "What do you want to show me?"

"Patience, lass. Let us get you settled first. Tomorrow will be soon enough." His smile faded when she yawned. "Sleepy, are you?"

"Thanks to you." She glared at him, then fell back

to the pillows. "I know 'tis early still, but I'd like to just call it a night."

"Excellent idea. Yesterday was a difficult day." Trick rose, shrugged out of his surcoat, and started unlacing his shirt. "I believe I'll join you."

She leapt from the bed. "Oh! I thought this was *my* chamber."

"It is." The shirt came off over his head, and her palms itched as she remembered how he'd felt against her hands last night. All warm and firm.

She swallowed hard. "Then where is your chamber?"

" 'Tis mine, too." He sat to pull off his boots. "We're married. We're allowed to sleep together. I've a piece of paper to prove it."

"But . . ." She looked around wildly. "This is a suite, is it not? What is through that door?"

"A dressing chamber. Feel free to use it. Your clothes are inside." At her look of astonishment, he added, "Jane has been here all day, arranging your things. I gave her the evening off."

"She's *my* maid."

"I believe she's in my employ, now." His second boot hit the floor with a thud. He started unlacing his breeches.

"You're a duke, for God's sake. Do you not have a valet?"

"Cavanaugh. But I prefer to undress myself, much to the poor man's constant chagrin." He looked up. "Actually, I'd prefer to have you undress me, but . . ." A wry grin revealed that rakish chipped tooth, and the twinkle in his eye was unsettling. "No, I thought not. But I can play your maid again tonight, if you wish."

"No, thank you." She stalked over to the dressing chamber, shutting the door behind her, then had to duck back into the bedchamber for a candle. Gritting her teeth against his laugh, she closeted herself again and began hunting for a night rail.

Every bit as fancy as the bedchamber, the dressing room had a delicate wood table and two upholstered, fringed stools in the center. One wall seemed to be nothing but an enormous gilt-framed mirror, another wall was covered with wardrobe cabinets, and there were two walls of those newfangled chests of drawers. The first one she opened was filled with Trick's folded things, and she slammed it shut. She found her own clothes in the third chest she tried and stripped out of the wedding dress, diving into the thickest, most voluminous night rail she owned. Her fingers fumbled with the clasp of the amber bracelet, but she finally managed to remove it and set it on the little inlaid table.

The bracelet sat there, taunting her. Amber. The Duchess of Amberley . . . Dear God, however had she ended up in this predicament? Exactly where she'd sworn she'd never be.

When she reopened the door, Trick was already in bed, and—from all she could tell—stark naked.

She paced beside the carved gilt monstrosity, hoping he was already asleep.

His hand snaked out to grab hers, stopping her in her tracks. "I will never take you against your will. You needn't worry."

She bit her lip, eyeing his bare arm and shoulders. "Is that so?"

"Aye. You're safe, I assure you."

"Can . . . can I not have another room?"

"Is something wrong with this one?"

"It's . . . too masculine."

"Too masculine?"

"Yes." She accompanied the word with a brazen stare, since nothing could be further from the truth. The red chamber was satin and velvet, feathers and lace—altogether too gaudy for her tastes. It looked like a brothel. Or what she imagined a brothel might look like, in any case. "This was your father's chamber, no? I believe I'd be more comfortable in your mother's chamber. Where is it?"

"In Scotland," he said shortly, patting the mattress beside him. "Come, Kendra, enough of this. I'm sleepy, and you look ready to drop."

With a sigh, she walked around the bed and gingerly lay on top of the covers.

Sounding exasperated, his voice drifted over his shoulder. "Get under the blanket. 'Tis drafty in this gargantuan house."

Giving in, she scooted beneath the coverlet. The feather bed was soft and comfortable. Lying flat on her back, she could feel the rise and fall of Trick's breathing next to her, the warmth of his body even across the space that divided them.

When he rolled close and laid an arm loosely across her middle, she flinched.

"Shh, *leannan*. Rest." He raised himself to kiss the tip of her nose, his lips soft and temptingly damp. His amber eyes burned into hers, making her stomach flutter. Against her will, her arms ached to wrap around his neck and pull his mouth to meet hers.

But she knew what that would lead to.

"Aye, you're right." His whisper was husky with

meaning . . . Had he read her mind? His mouth brushed hers; his tongue came out to trace her bottom lip. Despite her reservations, her body melted beneath his.

He chuckled low. "Aye, soon enough," he said, then turned away to blow out the candle.

Shaking, from vexation or unwelcome lust—for the life of her, she wasn't sure which—Kendra stared into the darkness and wondered if she'd ever get any sleep while she was married to Trick Caldwell.

"Wake up, milady. I mean, Your Grace." Kendra forced open her eyes to see Jane standing over her. "I've brought you some breakfast, or should I say dinner?" The maid set a loaded tray on the bed. "'Tis late, and His Grace is waiting to take you somewhere. A surprise, he said."

"A surprise?" Struggling into a sitting position, Kendra reached for a cup of chocolate. "He said he had something to show me today, but—"

"A surprise, yes." Jane's tall, thin figure disappeared into the dressing room. "He suggested you wear your simplest gown."

The sound of wardrobes opening and closing came through the open door. "Why would that be?" Kendra asked.

"Well, if you're not knowing, then how could I?" The maid came in with a peach velvet gown. Other than a narrow edging of lace around the neckline and some wider matching lace that spilled from the wrists, the dress was plain. No overskirt, no jewels or embroidery on the stomacher. "Do you suppose this will do?"

"I'm sure 'tis fine."

She slapped a slab of cheese on a slice of bread while Jane ducked into the dressing room again. Her sweet voice drifted back out. "Brown shoes rather than gold, I'm thinking."

Kendra chewed and swallowed, not thinking at all. Her brain was now fuzzy from too much sleep.

"And a chemise, and . . . lud, would you look at this lovely bracelet? Where'd this come from, milady? I mean, Your Grace?"

"Milady will more than do," Kendra grumbled. "And leave the bracelet there."

Jane appeared in the open doorway, her plain face marred by a puzzled frown. Winking in the noon sun that streamed through the window, the amber bracelet dangled from her fingers. "Was this a gift from your husband?"

"A wedding gift, yes."

"Then for certain he'd want you to wear it."

Setting down the bread, Kendra caught a glimpse of the gold ringing her finger. Enough of a reminder that she was married to a lying duke.

"I don't care for it, Jane."

Her maid's mouth hung open. "But 'tis so beautiful. And His Grace is so handsome and kind—do you not want to please him?"

Of course Jane would think Trick was kind—he'd given her half a day off. And he hadn't lied to her, either. "I really don't care for it," Kendra repeated. "Put it away for me, will you? I expect His Grace will forget all about it—you know how men are."

"Very well." A doubtful look in her gray eyes, Jane disappeared back into the dressing room, then came out carrying the shoes and chemise.

She set them on the foot of the bed. "Are you happy here, milady?"

"Of course I'm happy." Gesturing at the rich, garish chamber, Kendra forced a smile. "How could one not be happy here?"

Chapter Seven

"Mr. Caldwell!" A dozen children bounded down the steps of the sprawling Tudor manor house and clustered around Trick. Laughing, he reached to squeeze shoulders and pat heads, leaving no child untouched.

Kendra stared in utter disbelief. "Mr. Caldwell?"

"Part of your surprise." He shot her a sheepish grin, then turned back to the young ones, who had focused their attention on Kendra, gaping at her with frank curiosity. Trick waved a hand in her direction. "This is my new wife. Er . . . Mrs. Caldwell."

"Please, just call me Kendra," she rushed to say. She smoothed the skirt of the peach gown. Goodness, but this was hard to get used to. 'Twas downright strange. She didn't feel like a duchess, but neither did she feel like Mrs. Caldwell.

"I'm glad of your acquaintance, Mrs. Kendra." A tall, skinny, dark-haired lad held his hand out to her, but looked toward Trick for approval. At her husband's nod, the boy reached to grasp Kendra's hand, kissing the back of it fervently.

"Ahem. Andrew." Plowing his fingers through his hair, Trick frowned. The boy looked chagrined, and Trick came to ruffle his stick-straight hair. "Not to worry. A man can't help but admire a pretty lady, aye?"

"Oh, yes," Andrew said reverently, and Kendra watched Trick bite his lip to keep from laughing.

"Mrs. Jackson, there you are." He waded through the sea of children, making his way toward a matronly woman with gray curls and a pleasant if nondescript face. He fished a black pouch from his surcoat pocket and handed it over. "Here you go. I apologize for being late. I've been . . . busy."

"I can see that." The woman smiled at Kendra.

"Mrs. Jackson, may I present my wife—"

"Mrs. Kendra," Andrew supplied in a worshipful tone.

Kendra didn't have the heart to correct him. "I'm glad of your acquaintance, Mrs. Jackson." She executed a tiny bow, for all the world as though they were in Whitehall Palace.

Mrs. Jackson's plump cheeks flushed with pleasure. "Likewise, Your Gr—Mrs. Kendra." The metallic clink of coins sounded as the woman sifted through the pouch. "So generous, Mr. Caldwell! The children are grateful."

"The orphans of Sussex will not starve so long as it is within my power to help them."

"Starve?" Mrs. Jackson's belly jiggled under her apron as her laughter rang through the heavy summer air. "They be better fed than half the parish. Why, I daresay some villagers pray nightly to be orphaned and find themselves at Caldwell House."

Caldwell House? Did Trick finance this entire operation, then? Kendra looked toward her husband, his golden hair glinting in the late-afternoon sun, and her heart melted a little.

He laughed. "Let us hope not. A hearty meal is a sad substitute for loving parents. How is little Susanna?"

"Much better. Her fever is down and she's sitting down, and taking milk. I trust she'll be up and about in a day or two."

"I'm pleased to hear it. Mayhap I should pay her a visit."

"By all means. She'll be cheered to see you."

"Kendra? If you'll excuse me." Without waiting for her agreement, Trick took the six steps in three strides and disappeared though the front door. Dressed in only breeches and a shirt, no cravat and no coat, he looked decidedly unduke-ish.

Through that battered oak door passed a man who had accomplished her own dream—opening an orphanage. Stunned, Kendra stared after him while the children scattered through the garden, picking up balls and hoops.

Two girls tugged shyly on her skirts. "Will you play with us, Mrs. Kendra?"

She smiled down at them. "What would you care to play?"

They settled on blindman's buff, and the game went on for a while, other children joining in the fun. When an impish lad named Thomas stole the blindfold and ran away laughing, the others raced after him. Kendra tried to follow but got halfway around the house and stopped. Thanks to her high Louis heels, the merry chase had far outstripped her ability to keep up.

Trick had been right to suggest a plain gown— next time she'd wear flat shoes, too. Wondering what was taking him so long, she made her way over to where Mrs. Jackson was hanging laundry.

"Know you where my h-husband"—her tongue tripped over the word—"might have gotten himself off to?"

"Of course," the older woman said, tossing a nightshirt back into the basket. "I'll show you the way to the sickroom." She led her around the corner of the house and up the front steps. "I bless your husband nightly for saving these children."

"Bless you for caring for them," Kendra returned, looking around the entry. Though the house and its furnishings had clearly seen better days, it was clean and cheerful. "Are the children receiving an education?"

"Mercy, yes. His Grace has seen to it that tutors attend to that. All but the youngest can figure and read and write—"

"Girls, too?"

"Yes, indeed. Your husband has some odd ideas."

They skirted a few wooden toys on the floor as Mrs. Jackson led her down a corridor. "Are they instructed in the classics? Latin and—"

"Nay, not as yet. I cannot imagine what children like this would be needing with that. But with the new duke directing things, you never know what will happen next at Caldwell House." The woman's ample bosom quivered with a good-natured if slightly befuddled chuckle. "Here we are."

In the room Mrs. Jackson indicated, a young girl, perhaps four or so, sat propped among pillows in a four-poster bed that looked as if it had rested on the same spot for a century or more. Kendra paused in the doorway.

"They're busy," Mrs. Jackson whispered. Trick sat in a straight-backed chair by the bed, an open book in his lap. The girl leaned forward, apparently engrossed in whatever he was reading. Feeling like an eavesdropper, Kendra listened as well.

" 'Then have I gained a right good man this day,' quoth jolly Robin," came Trick's throaty voice. " 'What name goest thou by, good fellow?' "

"And what did he say?" the child asked.

"The stranger answered, 'Men call me John Little whence I came.' "

The girl's blond curls bounced as she shook her head. "No, 'tis Little John!" she corrected, her brown eyes wide with delight.

Trick glanced up from the leather-bound book. "Aye, but that was Will Stutely's doing. He loved a good jest and said"—he looked back down at the book—" 'Nay, fair little stranger. I like not thy name and fain would I have it otherwise. Little art thou, indeed, and small of bone and sinew; therefore shalt thou be christened Little John, and I will be thy godfather.' Then Robin Hood and all his band laughed aloud until the stranger began to grow angry . . .' "

Kendra could only gape. She felt like one of the Graiae, three sisters who had but one eye between them. What was she seeing? A highwayman, telling a story to a sick orphan? Or a duke? Right now, he looked like neither. She backed from the doorway. She knew not this man, not in the least.

"Robin Hood," Kendra said on their way home, in that forthright way of hers that never failed to make Trick smile. " 'Twas fitting, I'll credit you that."

"Oh?" The caleche's wheels crunched on the dusty

road as he wound the horses through the gentle hills toward Amberley House. "Whatever makes you think so?"

"Don't jest with me. 'Tis obvious!"

"Aye?" He looked over at her, but she was gazing straight ahead. Her bright hair glistened in the slanting late-afternoon sunshine.

"I do believe I'm beginning to understand you."

"Pray, enlighten me," he said dryly. "I've been trying to understand myself for years."

She snorted. "*You* are playing Robin Hood," she said with that same cocksure confidence that had drawn him to her the first time they'd spoken. Sweet Mary, was that only three days ago? "Only instead of stealing from the rich," she continued, "you're robbing the Roundheads, who are no doubt responsible for making most of those children orphans, anyway." She sighed. "I do believe I could love you for this."

'Twas his turn to snort. "The man you think you see, sweetheart, isn't me at all. I wish I could be that man," he added under his breath.

"Balderdash. 'Tis well done of you, Trick."

"Nonsense. My father wanted to build himself a bloody monument, so he spent every shilling he'd ever made on the mansion and then abandoned that perfectly good manor house. I wanted to see it put to use. Filled with children, as it might have been had he ever made something of his marriage."

She turned to him, her heart in her eyes. "That's why you play the highwayman, then, isn't it? To pay for the children, since your father spent all his money on the mansion and left you without funds."

"Not precisely." He was about to add that he'd

turned his father's illicit enterprise into a prosperous legitimate shipping company, but thought better of it. Not that he wanted to hide things from her, but damn it, his hands were tied. 'Twas no fault of his he was stuck in this situation. He'd been wracking his brain for a believable excuse to continue playing the highwayman, and she'd just dropped one in his lap.

Never mind that he could finance Caldwell House ten times over. She didn't have to know that. Not right now.

"When I tell my brothers—"

"Don't. Don't tell them anything. I promised them I would stop the highway robbery."

"No, you didn't. You ducked that issue cleverly." She was entirely too perceptive for his comfort. "And if you stopped, the children would suffer, and I couldn't bear to be responsible for that. I was an orphan, myself."

"Yes, well, any feeling human being would be sympathetic to their plight." Trick's mind raced, searching for a way to avoid these secrets and lies. But he saw no choice. He'd promised King Charles he'd not breathe a word of the real activity the highwayman ruse was designed to hide.

He snuck Kendra a guilty glance. She twisted her hands in her lap, and the imported lace fell back from her wrist, leaving it bare. "Why are you not wearing the amber bracelet?"

"It doesn't go with this plain gown."

He wondered why he found her flip answer so disturbing. "Are you still mad at me for being a duke?"

"I'm not sure what I feel. I don't like being lied

to." Though she directed those words to the sky, she soon looked back to him. "Did you feel abandoned, as a child?"

"In a sense," he said slowly, wishing he could go back in time and start this marriage right. He didn't want it to end up like his own parents'. "My father took me from my mother when I was ten. I'd seen him but a few times over the years, and I'd never been more than a dozen miles from our home in Scotland." The caleche bumped over a particularly rocky stretch of the path, and he reached to steady Kendra. "He took me to France . . . A cold man, was my father. He wanted me only to further his business dealings."

"His business dealings?" She subtly shifted away from his touch. "He was a duke, was he not?"

"An impoverished one. He lost everything, including Amberley, financing the war. Upon the Restoration, King Charles returned his title and land to him, but believe me, Father could never have abandoned the old manor house and built that mansion without the enterprise that sustained him through the Commonwealth years. He was ruthless, underhanded— not a man one would want to claim as a relation."

"What was this enterprise?"

"He traded in spirits, among other things. Madeira was his ticket to riches. Every bottle that graced the tables of the Courts—French and English alike— passed through his hands." He hesitated, then decided to come out with it. After only three days of marriage, enough secrets lay between the two of them already. "He was a smuggler."

"A smuggler?" she gasped.

"Yes. One doesn't amass a fortune paying import

taxes—at least not on the scale that he managed. You can see now why I elected not to continue his business, no matter that it was highly lucrative." And since that half-truth caused him no small discomfort, he added, "And as I was only a pawn in his game, you can see as well why it is I felt orphaned as a child." Some small measure of honesty, at least.

"But your mother—"

"She let me go," he said, the words calm and unemotional though he ached with an inner pain that would never go away. "Any warmth or love she showed me was naught but a facade. Elspeth Caldwell is a wicked woman. A Covenanter, plotting against King and country." Crickets chirped as they drove beneath a canopy of trees silhouetted against the cerulean sky. "And a loose woman, besides."

"How would you know all that? You were ten when you left."

"In eighteen years, she never once tried to reclaim me, or even make contact. In all that time, I haven't seen so much as one letter. Blackguard that my father was, I believe what he told me where she was concerned." The details were hazy; no matter how much he'd pressed, his father had refused to discuss his marriage. But Trick had pieced enough of the man's rantings together to figure the gist was true.

Still, he'd never approved of the way his father hadn't tried to make something of the union. Even when Trick was young, his parents had lived totally separate lives. And sadly, he could see all too easily how such a thing could happen. "Tomorrow I need to go to London," he said.

Her eyes danced. "I love London. Have you a house in town?"

"Aye. And I'm sure you'll find it every bit as disgustingly opulent as Amberley House." He smiled on the outside, but cringed internally. "I'll be going alone this time, though."

"Oh." The light in her eyes died. "Why?"

He had to leave—he'd actually, before this whirlwind of a wedding had come up, been planning to leave today. His shipping company needed his attention. The shipping company that he'd decided to keep secret from her for the time being, lest she figure out he could well afford to support the orphanage without resorting to robbery. "I had arranged it," he said dismissively, "before we met."

As he guided the caleche onto Amberley's long approach, he ran a hand through his hair and shot her an appraising glance. Her expression had turned contemplative, and he could almost see the wheels turning in her pretty red head. "Perhaps we can put aside some money and invest," she said. "In the future, with careful planning, playing the highwayman might become unnecessary. God willing, before you ever get caught and"—her voice dropped—"strung up at Tyburn." She turned on the bench seat to face him. "I'll help you."

"You will not! I'll not have you endangering yourself—"

Her laughter rang through the deepening shadows. "I didn't mean with the robberies, but with the investing. I've quite a knack with finances—you can ask Jason."

"He lets you invest his money?"

She stiffened beside him. "Not independently, but I've helped him make decisions, yes."

"Whoa, there." He put a hand on her arm, pleased

when she didn't pull away. The scent of lavender wafted on the breeze to his nose. "I wasn't disapproving, just asking."

"All right, then." Her expression softened. " 'Tis only that I know you not, and—"

"I know you not, either."

"True enough." After a considered pause, an unmistakable glimmer lit her pale-green eyes. "As for the highway robbery, I have a good aim—"

He pulled up before Amberley House and tugged on the reins with more force than was necessary before taking her by the shoulders. "Ye won't." He heard his own accent broadening and winced; what was it about this woman that could drive him to such emotion? He brought his eyes to within an inch of hers. "I mean it, Kendra."

"I was jesting," she whispered, her grin sweet. Something melted in his gut. 'Twas such a small space to bring his lips to hers; he did it without thinking. Her mouth was soft and yielding, and he felt her breath quicken, her pulse race beneath his fingers on her neck. Their lips clung for a long, sweet minute; then he deliberately pulled away.

"Oh," she whispered. "I cannot keep my head when you do that."

"Aye?" He couldn't help but grin as he handed the reins to a groom and hopped down from the caleche. Perhaps he would enjoy this marriage after all.

Chapter Eight

Seated at Trick's desk, Kendra frowned at the ledger in front of her. "So you've been living here at Amberley for six months?"

"Right. And I fired Rankill after two." Trick took a sip of bracing whisky, then set the glass on the table beside his favorite leather armchair. He'd come home from seeing to his London interests to hear his wife had spent the past week examining his books and inspecting his property. After recovering from the shock, he'd decided he was pleased. Even if he still rarely touched her.

Now that he was back home, he would work on that. He'd made progress before he left—he was sure of it. Though he'd as soon strangle her brothers for being right, he had to admit he and Kendra were a damn good match . . . the rest would come in time.

"Were my suspicions about Rankill's dishonestly on target, then?" he asked her, feeling more than awkward requesting his wife's opinion of his own estate business. But between the King's mission and the demands of his shipping enterprise, he had precious little time left to see to Amberley. "Was I right to let him go?"

"You should have done it earlier." She glanced up.

"Your father died three years ago. What brought you back now?"

He couldn't tell her he'd moved home at King Charles's request to track down a problem in the region. Or that he'd agreed to do so in exchange for a pardon from old smuggling charges. The threat of losing Amberley and the title had been veiled and, truth be told, unnecessary. Caring little for that legacy from his father, Trick would have agreed to the mission out of patriotism and friendship alone.

But, no, he couldn't tell Kendra any of that.

"I decided Amberley was in need of my attention," he said instead.

"Well, you haven't paid it much," she countered with a dark glare.

He looked away and noticed she still wasn't wearing his bracelet.

He sighed and sipped again, feigning nonchalance. "What evidence is there that Rankill embezzled?"

"Look here." She waved him over. "Amberley's northwest quarter is capable of producing many more bushels than are recorded. And in the east"— she startled when he leaned over her—"this land will support more sheep than are shown in the records." Slowly she shifted, turning to meet his eyes.

Enjoying her lavender scent, he braced himself with one hand on the desk and held her gaze with his. "Is that so?"

"Y-yes." She drew a deep breath and looked back down. "As a matter of fact, I counted fifty more head than are noted in the ledger. And you should purchase yet more. You are not maximizing your profits in this area."

"Our profits." They were in this together. He

didn't think he'd quite realized that 'til now, or how much of a relief it was to find himself "saddled" with a wife who had turned out to be so competent.

If only he could convince her to let him show her, physically, how grateful he was, life would be almost perfect.

"Thank you." He leaned closer, pressing his lips to the top of her head.

She froze, drawing air in a soft, swift gasp. "You're welcome. You can sit back down now."

Her apparent discomfort was heartening. He didn't sit back down.

A long silence stretched between them before she continued. "The point is, Amberley is quite a bit more profitable than Rankill led you to believe. Run properly, with no one siphoning income, it should be self-supporting and then some. I realize you have a standard of living to maintain—"

"*We* have a standard of living." With his free hand, he skimmed his knuckles along her cheek.

A pink flush rose where his fingers had touched. "Well, yes. But, thankfully, it shouldn't be long at all until this mess is resolved and Amberley can support both you—us—and the orphanage." She paused for a breath. "So you can stop the robberies now, except . . ."

"Yes?"

"There are some matters that need attending. Depending on whether you think they or the children should come first."

"What sort of matters?"

"Repairs and the like. Rankill took money regardless of whether you could afford it. Your people are working with broken equipment, one of the barns needs roofing—"

"You have a list?" He ran a finger down her nose and stopped with it on her lips.

"Y-yes," she whispered against it. She pulled back, her elbow knocking a quill to the carpet.

"I'll take care of it all." He bent down to retrieve it and tickled the feather under her chin, grinning at her discomposure. "I think I can survive another few highwayman masquerades." And hopefully, that would be all it would take. He'd amassed much of the King's evidence already.

"When 'tis your safety against the children's welfare—"

"I'll be fine."

"I hope so," she said. She really hoped so.

In less than two weeks of being married to the Duke of Amberley, she'd surprised herself by discovering she liked life here. Although she adored Jason's wife, she hadn't realized the tension she'd felt at Cainewood—how difficult it had been for her to cede responsibility when Caithren had arrived. Here, the responsibility was her own. The house, the land, the people. And like the extra layer of marzipan on her bride cake, she had her orphanage, too.

"Speaking of the children . . ."

"Aye?" Finally, Trick dropped the quill on the desk and went back to sit down and reclaim his drink. Watching him, she realized this was the one chamber in Amberley House where he actually seemed at ease. Comfortable rather than opulent, it was furnished with the same classic eye to design as the cottage. Polish glinted from the deep grooves of the serviceable walnut desk where she sat, and the shelves behind Trick were stocked with well-read tomes.

"What about the children?" he asked.

"You'll remember, before you left, that I said I wanted to teach them some classical myths." She fiddled with the quill in her hands. "They're excellent learners, all of them."

One sandy brow quirked. "Even Thomas?"

"Well, maybe not Thomas." She smiled, thinking of the mischievous towhead and all the other children, all the fun she'd been having with them. "In any case, we're almost finished with the Greek stories, and before we start in on the Romans, I was thinking I'd like to throw an Olympian party."

Trick looked completely nonplussed. "A what?"

"An Olympian party. I know money is tight, but I've been pondering this, and I really don't think it will be too expensive. The children can all dress up as their favorite god or goddess—I came across plenty of unused dress lengths in storage that they can wrap toga-style. And decorations needn't be too costly. Phillips has agreed to help me make columns—"

"You've talked to the servants about this?"

"They think it's a fine idea. We'll eat ambrosia and drink nectar, and the children can each retell their favorite myth . . . 'Twould be such a treat for them, do you not think? And reinforce what they learned, so they'll be even more eager for the next—"

"It sounds brilliant."

" 'Twill not cost much—"

"Kendra." He set down his glass. "Have your party with my blessings."

"Really?" The Duke of Lechmere would never have allowed it.

Neither would he have allowed her a hand in the finances, which Trick had accepted with an easy grace. Hang her brothers' method of pushing them together, but she had to admit she and Trick really were well matched, other than the physical problem. Even though he'd refused to tell her why he'd gone to London and declined to take her along.

Well, not refused precisely, just dodged the question as skillfully as he did most of her others. Of course she could hardly expect him to tell her the truth, since she'd decided he must be hiding a mistress in London. "A man has needs," she'd heard her brothers say, and she knew full well she wasn't fulfilling Trick's. Best all around if he filled those needs elsewhere, then, even if the thought did rankle. This way, she could have Amberley and her orphanage and Trick's companionship, without worrying about the other.

Marriage was better all around than she'd anticipated. She couldn't imagine why she'd fought it so long.

Life was almost perfect.

A week later, Kendra waved to the children gathered on the steps of Caldwell House. "Good-bye! Take care, Mrs. Jackson!"

"Good-bye, Mrs. Kendra!" they called. "Good-bye, Mr. Caldwell!"

Yawning, she wheeled Pandora around to join Trick, mounted on his favorite horse, Chaucer. "They're excited about the party," he said as they started down the lane.

"Two days. I can hardly wait. But there is still much to arrange."

"You're very organized. With everything else you find to do, I cannot believe you threw this together so quickly."

She shrugged. Planning the party had been the easiest part of her week. It had been much harder to resist her husband.

His offhand touches and occasional fleeting kisses never failed to weaken her knees, igniting her curiosity and desire for more. Yet she knew that more would only lead to disaster again, since they simply did not fit properly. She presumed he understood that too, as he never touched her in bed. Though he insisted on sharing, he left her alone, which, in its own way, she found every bit as frustrating. He was still sleeping naked, and though she refused to so much as take a peek, she was still as aware of his body beside hers as she'd been from the first.

She hadn't found much sleep since he'd been home.

"I think we should check on the barn," he said. "See how the roof is coming along."

She yawned again, then shook herself awake. "I'll race you."

He was off without another word, and she kicked Pandora into a gallop after him. His tawny gelding had a head start, but she slowly gained on him until they were neck and neck. She took gulps of the rushing air, feeling it revive her, enjoying the pace, the wind in her hair, the thrill of competition. When Pandora passed the barn first, ahead of Chaucer by a nose, she laughed triumphantly.

"Good girl, Pandora," she cooed, patting the mare's deep-brown neck.

"You won," Trick conceded with a grin. He slid off his horse, coming close. "Why did you name her Pandora?"

"Simple." Craftily Kendra dismounted on the far side. "Like the Greek goddess opening her box of problems, she leads me into trouble."

She started toward the barn, but he rounded Pandora and easily caught up to her. "Leads you into trouble, does she?"

"All the time. She led me to you, did she not?" With his hand on her arm, Kendra had little choice but to stop. She turned to meet his eyes. "Trouble."

"That was her fault, aye?"

"Yes, it must have been. I certainly didn't head for Amberley on purpose."

"And are you sorry?"

Trapped in his golden gaze, she shook her head. "No," she whispered.

"Neither am I."

Kendra's heart beat double-time when he took her face between his hands. His fingers were warm, and so was his breath as he leaned close, bringing his mouth down to hers.

"Amberley!"

Trick's hands dropped from her cheeks, and they both looked up to see a carriage approaching. A florid man stuck his head out the open window. "We've come to pay our respects," the man called. "To you and your lovely bride."

"Garrick," Trick muttered under his breath. "And Fielding, Faraday, and Milner, I'm guessing." The carriage rolled to a stop, and sure enough, four men climbed out.

Kendra recognized them all—minor aristocrats who lived in the vicinity, not important enough to ever have been on her brothers' list of potential husbands. But country life was insular, and she'd met them at various entertainments over the years. Just last summer she'd danced with Fielding and Milner at Jason and Cait's wedding-celebration ball. She'd found Fielding rather charming in a bumbling sort of way, but Milner's breath had smelled like over-aged cheese.

"Good day, gentlemen," Trick said. "Welcome."

He didn't sound like he meant it.

Garrick walked over to pump Trick's hand. "Congratulations, congratulations." He had a big round head and a belly to match. Apparently he needed to fill it, because when he took out his pocket watch and flipped it open, his flabby lips broke into a grin. "We're just in time for supper, are we not?"

"Trick?" Kendra murmured, awakened by the soft sounds of her husband moving about the bedchamber. Her eyes fluttered open to glimpse his gold hair haloed by the morning sun that streamed through the window. Turning, he smiled and came close, leaning down to brush a delicate kiss across her lips.

"You fell asleep on me last night," he accused, straightening and disappearing into the dressing room.

"Did I?" She stretched under the covers. "I remember not a thing past supper," she mused.

"You nodded into your chicken cullis." His voice sounded muffled, then stronger as he strode back into the room, carrying a pair of boots and a surcoat. "And I'd thought you were enjoying our impromptu party."

"And the cullis was so good," she recalled.

He grinned. "You only liked it so much because it was sweet."

"I don't expect I made a good impression. Are those men really your friends?"

"Your brothers' friends, too." He sat on a tufted velvet chair to pull on the boots. "We all play whist once a month."

"The mysterious weekend house parties." More secrets. This man was so evasive, she wondered if she'd ever truly come to know him. "Why do men have to be so secretive?" she said, more darkly than she intended.

But he didn't seem to notice. "Harmless games," he answered with a shrug. "Did you not like the fellows?"

"Faraday is a terrible flirt, especially given he's married. Fielding is agreeable enough, but never quite seems to know what he's about. Garrick is a strange sort, is he not? He couldn't seem to stay seated, always seemed to be poking around. I wonder what he could have been looking for? And Milner wears entirely too much scent. He should think about taking a bath, instead."

His gaze on her, Trick rose. "You're very astute. I couldn't have summed them up so succinctly, and I've socialized with them for months. You were with them naught but a couple of hours."

" 'Twas enough." She watched him shrug into the surcoat. "What do you see in those men?"

"Money. They always lose." He grinned as he slid

his sword into his belt, then took a pistol from atop the dressing table, hefting it before arming himself with it as well. "I'll see you this afternoon." He came to her, bending for one more kiss, soft and lingering. His tongue traced the seam of her lips, then he straightened once again. "Rest up, *leannan*."

The door closed behind him with a muted click, and she listened to his footsteps retreat down the corridor. 'Twas not until a few minutes later, when she replayed his words—and his kisses—in her mind, that she realized he'd been wearing all black.

Chapter Nine

He was getting close. With any luck, this would be the last time.

He'd pulled two robberies this week while Kendra was reading to the children at Caldwell House. He wished he'd escaped unseen today, but she'd lain abed late and it had been necessary to leave. He'd seen a pattern occurring, every third day mid-morning, and today was day number three. Hopefully his wife had been sleepy enough that she'd not noticed what he'd been about.

She'd been losing sleep. Over him? The thought made him smile.

He was making subtle progress, in more areas than one.

Her pulse pounding, Kendra dismounted and tethered Pandora to a tree, then made her way on foot to the hill. As she neared the crest, she dropped to her knees. One hand snaked out and snatched a hat, a handsome brown one with a bright yellow plume. She perched it on her head and slithered forward on her belly, tossing the wooden block behind her and lying low, hopefully at the same level as the other hats. Maneuvering a pipe before her, she propped her chin on it and peeked to the road below.

Oh, God, Trick had someone already. Mounted on Chaucer, he aimed his pistol into the gaping blackness of an open coach door. Her heart thundered in her chest as a gray-garbed man emerged and climbed reluctantly to the road.

"Oh, aye?" Trick's drawl floated up to her. "You may want to reconsider. My *friends* would think it great sport to put a bullet through your chest. Or a dozen, mayhap. Ah, a contest. Target practice on your sorry hide."

The man would have been quaking in his boots, except he was wearing ugly thick shoes with dull silver buckles. His eyes flicked nervously up toward Kendra, and she held her breath when Trick's gaze followed. It took every ounce of her will to keep from flinching or ducking as her husband squinted in her direction.

The victim's own eyes narrowed. In seeming slow motion, Kendra watched as the man backed away, one hand deliberately rising. He stared at Trick with a tight expression that made a cold knot form in Kendra's stomach. But her husband's concentration remained fixed on the place where she hid.

Oh, God, why had she come? Recognition lit Trick's eyes along with clear displeasure, and she knew he would kill her—if he didn't die first. As the stranger's hand inched beneath his coat, her fingers clenched on the pipe, vainly searching for the fake gun's nonexistent trigger. Why was Trick not taking heed?

And why was the Puritan not afraid of Trick's "friends"? In her peripheral vision, she could see the hats and pipes lined up in a soldierlike array. An explicit threat to anyone below. But the stranger's edginess was obvious, his gaze glued on Trick, who in turn was still focused on her. The man wasn't thinking clearly, Kendra realized—distracted as he was, he couldn't be counted on to act rationally. He was dangerous. As his hand delved even deeper, she found it increasingly hard to hold still, and Trick, damn him, wasn't paying attention.

Silver flashed—a pistol or a knife? It happened so fast, Kendra couldn't be sure. Her heart seemed to stop, and her mouth opened to cry out a warning. But before it could pass her lips, her husband burst into action.

A blur of flying arms and legs, Trick leapt from his horse. Her breath caught in a short gasp as he landed and twisted the Puritan's hand up behind him, all in one smooth motion. The next thing she knew, a gun had thudded to the ground, and the man was facedown in the dirt with a knee in the small of his back.

Her heart stuttered and restarted. Where the hell had Trick learned to do that? The men she knew trained with pistols and swords, and quite a few were proficient in boxing, besides. But that was a gentleman's sport—nothing like the skills Trick had demonstrated here. She'd never seen such lightning-quick reactions.

Neither had the Puritan, apparently. Fear was etched on his face, and she could see his legs shaking when Trick finally allowed him to rise, still holding one arm twisted back and high.

Relief singing through her veins, she collapsed flat

on her belly. The hat fell off, rolling a foot before it slipped over the edge and tumbled to the road below with a muted *plop* that made her grimace.

But her husband didn't spare it—or her—a glance. At his bidding, the man managed to empty both pockets with his one free hand, defeat evident as he hurried to comply. When Trick demanded his coat as well, he relinquished it without argument.

After a short glimpse into the cabin and a circuit around the coach seemed to convince Trick no more booty was forthcoming, he released the stranger and shoved him inside. Motionless, he held Chaucer's reins while the coach rumbled off down the road.

Dust puffed in its wake, settling slowly to earth as the carriage disappeared into the distance. Naught but the calls of blackbirds filled the air when Trick finally turned to the hill.

His voice wafted to Kendra, calm, but no less dangerous for it. "What the hell do you think you're doing up there?"

He led Chaucer forward, stopping to retrieve the victim's gun and the fallen hat before walking around and up the hill. He removed his mask as he went, then stood gazing down at her. She dropped her head to the grass. Though her face was mashed into the springy blades, she felt his eyes boring into her back.

"Well?"

"I was spying on you," she squeaked.

His breath huffed out. "Sit up, Kendra. I cannot talk to you like this."

She pushed up and sat, her gaze on her hands clenched in her lap. Her pale yellow gown was damp, the area around the knees stained bright grass-green.

"Look at me," he said, unmistakably exasperated. "This is not like you to hide. Not how I envision you at all." As she glanced up, he flicked the long, crimped brown periwig hair over his shoulders.

"I came because I was afraid you'd get hurt," she said.

"What made you think I'd get hurt?" His eyes narrowed, appearing naked without the mask and their usual veil of blond hair. "Do you . . . care?" he asked slowly.

"Of course I care!" She couldn't remember ever having been more frightened in her life. "I saw him pull the pistol. He could have had a knife, too."

"He did." He drew a long, lethal blade from the coat and dropped both to the grass, moving closer. "But I can handle myself, aye? So long as you don't show up and interfere."

"I didn't—"

"Your very presence broke my concentration. And had he seen you up here . . . do you imagine he'd be put off by a pack of women?"

"Were it women with guns, I'd hope so!" she shot back.

Blinking, he reached a hand to help her rise. She was surprised to find her knees trembling.

His eyes searched hers. "Do not ever, ever do that again," he said very quietly. He moved closer still, and his breath whispered over her face. "You could have gotten me killed."

Tears sprang to her eyes.

"Never." She saw a muscle twitch in his jaw. "You understand, aye? Never."

"Oh, Trick." Her arms came up and wrapped around his neck, of their own volition, it seemed. She buried her face in his shoulder, chagrined at her tears. For what? A man she barely knew, never mind that they were married? A man who kept secrets and mistresses? A man who lied to her? It made no sense.

"Shh, lassie." His own arms stole around her, held her tight. " 'Tis all right. No harm done." He kissed her hair. "You care, no?"

"I don't want you to do it again, Trick. But the children—the children will suffer . . ."

His grip tightened. "I've yet to be hurt—"

"You've been lucky. And luck can change."

"Not luck." He pulled back and fixed her with a calculated grin. "Talent."

Having seen that talent demonstrated, she had to offer him a shaky smile.

"Mayhap just a few more times," he said, "and then—"

"There will be enough to invest. And you can stop?"

"Something like that," he murmured. His eyes searched hers, their amber depths holding her hostage. Summer sun glinted off the roughness of his unshaven cheeks. Her breath caught as his mouth came down on hers.

Warm and tender, his kiss was a silent apology for the harsh words, and a promise for their future. His tongue traced her lips, then plunged inside. None too solid already, her knees turned to pudding as his mouth demanded a response she seemed helpless to deny him. When he broke off, her breath came loud and ragged.

"Yes," she whispered.

"Yes, what, *leannan*?" His smile caught her off guard.

"Yes, I mean, no, I . . . won't come here again."

"Thank you." He nodded solemnly and kissed her again, a light brush of the lips that left her wanting more. She leaned closer.

"Hell, lassie, you tempt a man to go back on his word." He waggled his eyebrows suggestively. "Unless you've changed your mind?"

"N-no." She took a step back, almost tumbling down the hill.

He caught her, laughing. "Let's get you out of here."

"Are you finished?"

"It would seem so," he said wryly, gathering the hats. He tossed them onto the canvas spread nearby. "Come to the cottage, and we'll see what we got."

"Not very much." Kendra frowned at the few coins spread on the carved dining table.

Trick laughed. "A greedy thief, are you? 'Tis mostly gold, not silver."

"True." She lifted one. "How about in his coat? Anything there?"

He dug into the pockets, felt the collar, the seams, the hem . . .

"Ahh."

"Was he hiding something?"

With a quick flick of his knife, he slit the stitches. One by one, more bright gold coins dropped to the table with satisfying little clunks. Clunk. Clunk. Clunk. *Clink.*

"I'll be damned." Trick scooped up the latest addition. He walked to the window, held it to the light, bit into it. "Eureka," he said softly, then rushed back to the table and opened the rest of the hem, flicking the coins to the surface. Clunk. Clunk. *Clink.* Clunk. *Clink. Clink. Clink. Clink.* Clunk. *Clink.*

"They're larger denominations," Kendra pointed out.

"Aye."

Clink. Clunk. *Clink. Clink.* Clunk.

"Good?"

"No." He pulled the last one from the ragged hem, then sorted them swiftly on the tabletop. "They're counterfeit."

"Counterfeit?" she huffed. "Why, that's criminal!"

He pinned her with a pointed look.

"Oh . . ." Heat rushed to her cheeks.

He moved to her and took her chin. "You're not guilty," he said.

"You're not, either," she countered loyally. "They're Roundhead scum. They deserve it, and 'tis for a good cause."

"The end justifies the means?" Trick walked to the hearth. "I think not, *leannan.*" He reached up, sank his fingers into a crack in the mortar, and coaxed out a small key. "Now, can you tell me what the man looked like? Whatever you remember."

"What he looked like?" Kendra watched as he opened the desk's top drawer and slipped the key into a hidden lock. The bottom drawer—the one she'd been unable to open—sprang free. "He was shorter than you, by a good six inches, I'd say." She shut her eyes, trying to remember. "Thin, pale, pale eyes I think, too, though I was at a distance."

She opened her eyes as Trick pulled a sheet of paper from the top drawer.

"Hair?" A bottle of ink and a quill came out next.

"His hat covered most of it, but his hair was brown, was it not? Gray-brown."

"Just as I remember." He scribbled it all down. "His clothing?"

"Gray, all gray. Plain—well, he was a Puritan. Nothing to distinguish him there. Oh, his shoes had very ugly dull buckles. Square. Pewter, I'm guessing." She frowned as he wrote. "What does all this matter?"

"Wait." He held up a hand, still writing. "Any scars?"

"Too far to see."

"I think he had a healing cut on his chin. And a wart alongside his nose." The quill scratched some more, then Trick ended with a flourish. "There. Job well done. You really are quite observant." He shoved the page into the bottom drawer and slammed it closed.

"Trick?"

"Aye?" He returned to the mantel and reached to replace the key.

"Will . . . will you stop doing this? For me?"

He whirled to face her. "I cannot promise that, Kendra."

"We can find another way to support the orphans. I'll speak to my brothers—"

"I cannot stop." He came close and put his hands on her shoulders. "Soon, but not yet."

"It frightens me." Her voice came out a whisper.

"You do have a way of melting a man's heart."

He tilted her chin, looked into her eyes. "I'll be careful," he said softly.

"Promise?"

"Cross my heart."

She smiled faintly and touched him lightly on the chest. "This one?"

"That one exactly." He placed his hand over hers and bent to take her lips in a slow kiss. She leaned against him, sighing into his mouth.

When he finally pulled back, it was with a chuckle. Playfully, he tugged on her hand, pulling her toward the corridor. "Shall we try the bed again, do you think?"

She stood her ground. "Not on your life. You think your kisses are good enough to tempt me to try *that* again?"

"I'm betting on it." He scooped up the coins and stuffed them into his surcoat pocket. "And I'm not a losing man."

They rode across the Downs, taking a leisurely route to enjoy the warm day. Trick felt better than he had in months. Odds were he had enough information now—he would send a message to the contact the King had provided, meet with the man, and hopefully be done. Premature though it might be, relief flowed through him in heady waves.

His gaze drifted over to Kendra, her hair bright in the midday sun. A grass stain on her knee brought a smile to his lips. She was a challenge, but he found it impossible to stay angry with her. She was the helpmate he had never thought to have. As soon as word came that his mission was done, they could start anew.

Their marriage was suspended on a fragile web, but without this secret between them, he could begin to spin it stronger.

"Trick?"

"Hmm?"

"Why did you want a description of that man?"

He shrugged uncomfortably, suddenly questioning the wisdom of allowing her to have seen him do that. But he'd always made his notes immediately, while the vision was still fresh in his mind. "To send to the authorities," he said in an offhand manner. "Anonymously of course, so they can identify the blackguard without my being involved."

"Why do you suppose he is counterfeiting?"

"To get rich, I imagine."

"I imagine there's another reason. Something tied in with his being a Puritan." Her eyes unfocused, she stared right through him, clearly lost in contemplation. "I don't think he's acting alone," she said.

"What makes you say that?"

"He didn't seem bright enough." Not as bright as she was, that was for sure. "I'm thinking he's part of a bigger operation, and if the members are Puritans, perhaps in league with some other Parliamentarians, they might be acting against the King's interests. Passing worthless currency in an attempt to undermine the economy and the people's confidence in the monarchy. An attempt to regain the power they once had, that died along with Cromwell."

She stole his breath. Both the strength of her reasoning and the fact that she'd hit it on the mark— the very suspicions that Charles had put forth and Trick himself was in the process of attempting to prove. He'd never considered that his beautiful young wife might understand the intricate linkage of economics and political power.

But 'twas dangerous, this line of reasoning. She might have a sharp head and atypical interests, but he couldn't allow her to go spreading this idea around, risking the chance the perpetrators might hear and discover someone was on to them.

"Mayhap," he said lightly, keeping his face and tone nonchalant. "But I expect he's just trying to get rich."

She stared over at him, her hands tightening on Pandora's reins. "How easily you dismiss my ideas. Are you still angry that I followed you earlier?"

"No," he said, relieved to be on a different subject. "No harm was done." They turned up Amberley's drive, the trees on either side throwing cool shadows across the pathway. "I think you'll find me more forgiving than most. The only thing I won't stand for is infidelity, and I've nothing to worry about on that account, have I? Yet." Someday soon he would initiate her into the joys of physical love . . . and then, mayhap, he would have something to worry about.

"Infidelity?" A challenge in her voice, Kendra jostled Pandora closer to Chaucer's side. "Most men expect fidelity only from their mistresses."

Most men had not found their betrothed wife in bed with another man. "You will learn, *leannan*, that I am not like most men."

She shot him an arch look. "And what if I am not like most women? What if I expect the same fidelity from you?"

"Turning the tables, are you?" He risked leaning from the saddle to chuck her under the chin. "You surely know how to try a man's patience."

Her green eyes flashed. "That was no sort of answer."

He sighed. "I wouldn't ask something of you if I weren't willing to offer it myself."

Her expression said louder than words that she didn't believe him. But she dropped the topic, her gaze drifting to Amberley's impressive facade. "My brother Ford will want to go up the tower and see how the clock works."

"He already has."

Her pretty brow creased in a puzzled frown.

"The house parties, remember? He seems much taken with clocks. Stayed up there half an afternoon, while we twiddled our thumbs waiting to play cards. Here we are." Trick slid to the gravel and handed his reins to a groom. With a gentle hand at her back, he urged Kendra up the steps of Amberley House.

"Dinner," he said as Compton opened the door. "I'm fair starving. And then—"

"A letter, Your Grace." The butler proffered a silver tray. "It arrived while you were out."

Frowning, Trick snatched it up. Wrinkled and grubby, it looked as if it had traveled quite a distance. "Thank you, Compton. We'll just take it to the study. Let us know when dinner is ready."

"Certainly." Compton's jowls wobbled with the nod of his head. He took himself off to the kitchens, and Trick ushered Kendra into the study, tossing the letter on the marquetry table that sat between two leather chairs.

She dropped into one of them while he poured himself a shot of whisky. He took a seat in the other chair and threw back a gulp of his drink, then set the glass on the table between them and lifted the letter.

Kendra watched him worry the seal with his long fingers. "Open it," she suggested.

"Not just yet." He turned it over and stared at his name written on the back.

"What is it?" Wondering why he seemed so pensive, she hitched herself forward and frowned at the parchment. "Do you know who it's from?"

He looked up at her, his face set in unfamiliar lines. Not teasing, not angry, not thoughtful, not seductive—not any emotion she'd seen there before. Not even evasive—another all-too-common mood she was learning to distinguish.

" 'Tis from my mother," he said softly. "After all these years, I still recognize her hand." He blinked, then suddenly thrust the letter at Kendra. "Here. You read it."

She almost dropped it, but caught it in time. "No," she protested. " 'Tis addressed to you."

"I'll listen. Then I winna hear her voice, but yours." Her heart ached at the pain in his tone, and the telltale Scottish word that had slipped into his careful English speech. "Read it, please." He slumped down in the chair and took a long sip of spirits, then leaned back his head and closed his eyes.

She smoothed the parchment against her skirt, then slipped a fingernail under the seal. It lifted off with a little snapping sound, and Trick winced.

"Go ahead," he said huskily.

The paper crackled as she opened it and held it to catch the light from the window. "Her writing is beautiful," she said.

He said nothing.

She took a deep breath. "My dear Patrick Iain," she read, "My heart is heavy with sorrow for all the years we've been apart. Now I am dying, and it is my fondest wish to gaze upon your beloved face once more. Though I know you're a man grown, my bonnie lad you'll always be. Come to me, Patrick, come make an old woman smile as she greets the next world. With all the love in my heart. Mam."

Silence. Kendra took one long breath, two . . . three.

Trick opened his eyes and sipped slowly from his glass.

"Can I go with you?" she asked.

"Where?" He shifted to face her. "You don't think I will go to her, do you?"

"You must!"

"She cannot ignore me for eighteen years and then expect me to jump to her command."

"She's dying, Trick."

He shrugged.

"You must make your peace. 'Tis your only chance."

"I don't care to give her the satisfaction."

" 'Tis your own satisfaction at stake here. If you fail to go now, you will always wonder. Always. Go to her and find your answers, before it is too late. Close your heart if you must, but go. Say good-bye."

"You think yourself wise for your years." He drained the glass and rolled it between his palms.

"I didn't get to say good-bye." The letter crackled as she folded it and set it on the table. "In my dreams, awake and sleeping, I've accused my parents of leaving me and I've told them I loved them. I've been angry at them, and sad. But face-to-face, I never got to say anything."

He took a deep breath, and the crystal stilled between his hands.

"Go, Trick. Now. Tonight." She'd have to postpone the children's party, but so be it. "I'll come with you."

"No," he said slowly. "I'll go alone. Tomorrow."

Chapter Ten

After supper, Kendra found herself mounted on Pandora, heading toward the cottage for the second time that day. She slanted a glance at Trick riding beside her. She'd tried halfheartedly to talk him into taking her along to Scotland, but he was absolutely set against it. Besides, perhaps it would be a relief to be free from him for a while.

Free from those rare kisses that made her lose her head. Free to catch up on her sleep. Free to think about whether she wanted to try again, because the agony of that first night was becoming harder and harder to remember clearly.

Still, part of her was reluctant to see him go, so she'd clung to him like a sticky bun all the afternoon, while he completed the tasks that stood in the way of his leaving.

The full moon reflected off the cottage windows as they approached. "I had no idea of the extent of your responsibilities," she said through a yawn.

"I just want to drop off some papers."

Her eyes felt gritty. "And after that . . . ?"

Trick slid from Chaucer and reached to help her down. "I still have much to do before I can sleep."

She tethered Pandora and followed him inside.

"You're pushing yourself." She closed the door and leaned against it, watching while he lit a single candle. "I know you must be worried for your mother—"

"I'm not particularly worried." Finished, he felt for the key above the fireplace.

"She's dying!"

He shot her a look as he unlocked the desk. "You said yourself her writing is beautiful. A woman on her deathbed would have a shaky hand, or dictate to someone else." He pulled a sheaf of papers from his surcoat and slid them into the bottom drawer.

"Perhaps she did dictate it."

" 'Twas her own hand—I'd bet my life on that. Aye, she's up to something, all right." He shut the drawer and relocked it. "I'll play along with her game, just in case I'm wrong, but she's a conniving—"

"You cannot know that, Trick. Not after all these years."

In the act of replacing the key, he cast an assessing glance over his shoulder. "Time will tell which of us is right. In the meantime, I'll not live in hope that she has changed." He shoved the key into place and began to blow out the flame, then suddenly stopped. "Damn, the hats and pipes. I wonder what else I'm forgetting? Wait here—I'll be back." He set the candle on the mantel, and before she knew it, the door had slammed behind him.

She stood still for a moment in guilty indecision, then walked slowly to the fireplace. Teetering on her toes, she reached for the key, finding Trick had placed it too high for her reach. She dragged over the desk chair and climbed atop it, nudged the key from its hiding place, then jumped down and rushed to the window.

Moonlight illuminated the grounds, and Trick was nowhere in sight. Seconds later she had the bottom drawer open and was pawing through its contents.

On top were the notes he'd just dropped off and those he'd concealed there earlier today. Not to keep them from her, obviously—he'd made no secret of the drawer. Surely he wouldn't care if she looked.

Or so she told herself.

Realizing she was chewing up the inside of her cheek, she stopped and ran her tongue over her dry lips. She swept the candle off the mantel to examine more pages of descriptions like the one she'd helped Trick make of the Puritan today. She smiled at his writing: very bold, the letters clear but plain, obviously written in haste.

Carefully she set the candlestick on the desktop, then put the papers back in the drawer and looked beneath them. An accounting of some sort. A record of his takings? Quite detailed, including descriptions of specific coins. Today hadn't been the first time he'd run across counterfeits.

Underneath that . . . She pulled out another stack of papers, some of them older and yellowed. Written by the same man, but more carefully, the words painstakingly formed, neat and even. They reminded Kendra of the letters she used to send to her parents as a child, letters written and rewritten, then a final, perfect draft carefully copied.

Choosing one at random, she read.

Pain and sorrow forevermore dwell
Inside the deepest bowels of hell.
Betrayal has yet took from me
What love and trust had once set free.

Poetry. Kendra sat abruptly on the edge of the desk. Trick, a poet? She never would have thought it; in fact, had someone suggested such, she would have laughed herself silly.

She didn't know her husband at all.

He'd been hurt by someone, terribly. Her heart clenched as she suddenly understood his words: *I don't believe in love at all. Mayhap I did once . . . but not anymore. 'Tis only an illusion.*

Who had done what to him to make him feel this way? Was he never happy? The paper seemed brittle when she set it down—as brittle as the words upon it. But the words on the sheet underneath did nothing to soothe her sympathetic ache.

Twixt fathers and tyrants a difference is known:
Fathers seek their sons' good, tyrants their own.

With a sinking heart, she riffled through the pages, pausing to read here and there. The touching verses hinted obliquely at events in Trick's life that had shaped him into the man she saw today. Pain, anger, disillusionment . . . ah, there it was. Love, happiness. His hand was lighter here; the words fairly leapt off the page in their exuberance.

Sweet day, happy, calm and bright
Love has brought me to this light
The sun that sits in yonder sky
Today can shine not more than I
And if tomorrow it should rain
Her smile will make sun shine again

She bit her lip. Was this written of the same love

that had later turned to betrayal? Could this carefree Trick live somewhere beneath the cynical man who shared her home? If trust had been shattered by one woman, could another restore it?

Hoofbeats. Oh, God, he was on his way back. She stuffed the poems beneath the other papers and locked the drawer, then jumped to the chair to replace the key. She was just pushing the chair back to the desk when the door flew open and Trick sauntered inside with the bundle of hats under one arm, the pipes under the other.

He dropped it all in a corner. "Ready to go?"

His crooked grin made her heart leap; he was so unsuspecting. She flushed, unbearably guilty just looking at him after reading his private compositions.

"I suppose," she said. "Though I was hoping we could talk."

"Now? About what?"

"Life. Yours." She met his gaze, willing him to share some of his past. "And mine, of course. All the years that led to now. The people who loved us—"

"None."

"—and hurt us."

He only shrugged. "None worth talking about."

"And what we like . . . for instance, do you like to write? I keep a journal, and sometimes I've written poems."

"Poems?" His gaze flickered down to the drawer. "No, I don't like to write." He leaned past her to blow out the candle, then turned and went to the door, holding it open. "Come along, will you? I've much to do."

Crushed that he refused to even consider confiding

in her, Kendra pushed by him and outside. Before she could mount Pandora, he caught her by the arm.

"I know you mean well," he said softly.

Silent, she searched his eyes, gray in the darkness. They went darker still. "I'm sorry you're so unhappy," he said.

"I'm not unhappy. Just confused. I'm worried for your life, and I don't like keeping the truth from my brothers about what it is you're doing. There are parts of you I admire—your compassion for the children. And more parts I don't understand—parts I think you've locked away. And now you're leaving."

"I'll be back." The words were a low, husky promise. "Mayhap you'll miss me while I'm gone." His hand slid down her arm until his fingers were laced with hers, and he leaned to press a soft kiss to her mouth. When he pulled back, she stared at him helplessly. Her lips tingled.

She heard his low chuckle before he turned away to lock the cottage, and it drove her to a decision. Once, in jest, she had promised he'd find love, and a Chase promise was never given lightly. She would bring back to life what another woman had killed; she would make him believe in love once again.

Accomplishing it while avoiding his bed was not going to be easy.

But then, worthwhile things rarely were.

Trick eased through the bedchamber door and closed it quietly behind him. He carried the candle to the bedside and set it on the table by Kendra's head, where it would illuminate her face. She looked angelic in sleep, her long, dark lashes feathery against her sun-pinked cheeks, her bright hair tumbled on the pillow, glistening in the candlelight. He bent and kissed her on the forehead, and a faint smile curved her lips, then faded away.

Something softened in his gut. She was more compassionate and forthright than he'd expected, this new wife of his. And distressed. Responsibility for that fell squarely on his shoulders, sparking his guilt along with tender feelings he'd long since learned to suppress. But he had much to hide, and good reasons for doing so. At least for now. As soon as the job for King Charles was completed . . .

He felt so close to uncovering the truth. Were it not for this unfortunate delay, he would soon have this behind him, and mayhap, without secrets between them, he and Kendra could begin to establish some sort of trust.

But first things first. He undressed swiftly, checking off the list in his head to make sure he'd taken care of everything before he left for Scotland, a journey that might take a month or more, up and back with time spent there. Letters of instruction to the various people who ran the estate—done. A purse of gold for Compton to see delivered to Mrs. Jackson at Caldwell House—done. A note to King Charles explaining the delay of his mission—done. While his staff had been scurrying about, readying to leave— because a duke, no matter his personal preferences, didn't travel unattended—he'd checked a dozen tasks or more off his private list. Everything, in fact, but the one he'd have found most pleasant . . . teasing his bride into willing submission.

From all evidence, Kendra had been busy as well. Goods for tomorrow's party were stacked neatly against one wall. A pile of colorful folded fabrics would make unique togas and doubtlessly thrill the wee wearers. Small baskets overflowed with sweets and treats that would make the recipients think they had died and gone to heaven. Or Olympia, in this case.

How clever his new wife was.

He blew out the candle and crawled into bed, cuddling against her sleep-heavy form. Slipping an arm about her waist, he pulled her closer, inhaling the faint lavender scent of her freshly bathed skin. Flickering light from the fireplace danced over her face and brought out golden glints in her dark-red hair. Brushing soft curls from her face, he leaned up to kiss her cheek.

She shifted, emitting a tiny moan that brought a smile to his lips.

He kissed her ear.

She stretched beside him like a contented cat, with a low-pitched purr to match.

What time was it? Three in the morning? Four? No matter, he would not waste these last hours with her by sleeping. He rolled her over and kissed her full on the lips.

"Mmmm," she breathed into his mouth. Her arms entwined around his neck, and her lips opened beneath his. He swept his tongue into her mouth. Lord, she tasted so sweet.

He nibbled her lower lip, feeling her truly awaken. Her breathing changed, and her mouth answered his, making his pulse speed, the blood rush faster through his veins. He'd never had a woman affect him so, not even . . .

No, he wouldn't think about her. After all these years, whatever had brought her to mind? She was long out of his life, and Kendra was here instead. Sweet Kendra, writhing beneath him now. He reached to caress her breast through the pristine white night rail she wore—then stopped cold.

He was man enough to be patient, and he'd been patient so far. He'd ruin everything by moving too soon.

Her eyes fluttered open, a question in their fathomless depths. She reached a hesitant finger to touch his bottom lip, the sensation as light as a whisper. And he almost melted.

But he wouldn't go back on his word. Though the thought of weeks apart made him physically ache, he wouldn't risk what little trust he'd built between them. He had a lifetime ahead to touch her, to make love to her—when she was ready. And he had no doubt she'd be ready eventually, mayhap even soon . . . But bloody hell, 'twas so hard to wait.

For long minutes, he just kissed her, instead. His own hands remained still while hers wandered his back, skimmed his sides, frantically tried to wedge themselves between their bodies. His nerves rippled in response, but still he only kissed her. Forever, it seemed, until he felt her straining toward him and a mewling sound of want escaped her lips.

"Trick?" she asked breathlessly, the name warm against his mouth.

"Hmmm?"

"Can you not . . . touch me?"

He pulled back and gazed into glassy light-green eyes. "No, I cannot," he said, though he had to force the words past his lips. "Should I touch you, I may not be able to help doing more. And I promised I would not seduce you in bed." He teased her lips with his. "But you like the kissing, aye?"

Her hands tightened in the hair at his nape. "Oh, heavens, yes. I like it. I just want—"

"Hmmm?" His tongue traced her trembling mouth. Let her ask for it. "What do you want, *leannan*?"

"I . . . I know not," she whispered, burying her face against his neck.

"You know," he said softly. "We both know. Say it, Kendra."

Instead of saying it, she took a ragged breath and released it with a shudder.

" 'Twill not hurt, lass. 'Twas just that first time, I promise. 'Twill not ever hurt again."

Kendra felt the words, the promise, vibrate in his throat. She ached for him—truly she did. But what good were promises from a man she couldn't trust? And even if he was right—even if it wouldn't hurt— how could she share her body with a man who refused to share his life?

She was touching him now, but she wasn't really. Her hands were upon his body, but she had yet to reach him where it counted. A barrier stood between them, and she couldn't bring herself to risk the crossing. He had built it. He would have to be the one to bring it down.

"What do you want?" he asked again.

"I want—" She turned her head away, staring up at the underside of Trick's red silk canopy. Not hers. No matter how many times he insisted that what was his was hers as well, she didn't feel that way in her heart. Not while he kept the most important thing of all from her.

Himself.

"I want to go to sleep," she whispered.

He trailed his fingers lightly across her cheek. "One more kiss?"

"I think . . . no," she said on a sigh. Another kiss would only make her more sad, and the lump in her throat was hard to bear already. She rolled away from him, turning her back. "Good night," she whispered. The words seemed to hover in the heavy air of the still room.

After a moment he snuggled against her, and she could feel the hardness that said without words just how much he wanted her. "D'ye think you might miss me, lassie?"

A groan rose from a place where she ached deep inside, and he went to sleep with a smile on his face.

She knew, because after his breathing evened out in the pattern of slumber, she turned and gazed upon him, filling herself with the sight of him to hold her through the weeks ahead.

It took her longer than ever to drift off that night, and when she awakened, he was gone.

Chapter Eleven

"Mrs. Kendra?"

"Yes, Thomas?" Kneeling in the grass by little Susanna, Kendra squinted up at the impish towhead.

"We're athletes in the Olympic games, am I right?"

"That's the idea."

"Well, then . . ." A gleam came into his sparkling blue eyes as his hands went to the fabric draped over his shoulder. "Should we not be naked?"

"Leave that on, you rapscallion!" She was hard put not to laugh at his pout. "I never said we were strictly authentic."

"Aw, all right." The pout turned into a mischievous grin before he ran off.

"Stand still, Susanna." Kendra tucked the girl's "toga" more tightly, smiling to herself. Luckily her lessons hadn't covered fashion, so her students were ignorant of the fact that the Greeks had worn solid colors, not brightly flowered calico. "There you go."

"My thanks, Mrs. Kendra."

"You're very welcome." She patted Susanna's blond curls and stood, knowing as she sent her off that the girl would be back in a few minutes to be tucked in again. She'd learned that togas weren't the ideal clothing for young children.

That was her only miscalculation, though—the rest of the party had gone brilliantly. The children's retelling of their favorite myths had been riotous. Now they were participating in Olympic "games," and the victory wreaths she had woven from laurel leaves might as well have been solid-gold crowns considering how much they were cherished. Fortunately, she'd brought enough for everyone, and she was not above fixing the contests to make certain each child came out a winner.

The party was a wild success, and they hadn't even feasted yet. Nor had she distributed the favors. Her baskets of goodies were still hiding under a blanket in the caleche, and she couldn't wait to see the children's faces when they received them.

Wrapped in stately blue stripes, young Andrew tugged on her toga. "Who are you, Mrs. Kendra?"

"Why, Hera, of course." She looked down into adoring dark eyes—his crush had not abated over the weeks. "Do you remember who she was?"

"Zeus's wife," he said proudly. "And the protector of marriage."

"Very good," she returned, although, for her, the job description seemed an ill fit at best. Rather than protecting her marriage, she'd sent her husband off alone. She should have argued until he agreed to let her go with him. Surely if she'd put up a fight, he would have relented—her brothers almost always did. But she'd never really tried, thinking of his devastatingly cold response to his mother's letter and knowing how difficult it was for him to go at all.

Andrew shifted on his feet, looking shy. "I memorized one of the poems about her."

"Did you?"

He nodded and began to quote.

Golden-throned Hera, among immortals the queen,
Chief among them in beauty, the glorious lady
All the blessed in high Olympus revere,
Honor even as Zeus, the lord of the thunder.

He finished with an awkward bow that should have brought a smile to Kendra's lips. But in contrast to the Hera of the poem, she was feeling anything but glorious at the moment.

"Mrs. Kendra? Are you all right?"

"I'm fine, Andrew." Amazed at the young man's perception, she forced the smile. "Mrs. Jackson is organizing a chariot race," she said brightly, glancing over to where the buxom woman was lining up four wheelbarrows. "I imagine a tall, strong boy like you, with little Susanna in his chariot, could come out a winner. Run along now—I'm fine."

But despite how well the party was going, she wasn't fine at all.

Trick should have been here. He was supposed to have been Zeus.

He'd created this. Her gaze followed Andrew as he joined the other laughing children, and she knew that without Trick, none of them would be here today, herself included. He'd repeatedly risked his life in order to bring this about.

Hera had always been zealously covetous of Zeus, and God help her, she missed her man.

When Kendra arrived home, she stopped only long enough to switch her toga for a riding habit and grab a key from Trick's desk drawer. Then she ran to the stables, mounted Pandora, and fairly flew over the Downs to the cottage.

Once inside, she could almost smell him. Since this morning when she'd awakened in his home, something—his vibrancy—had been missing. Instead of feeling free, she'd felt bereft. But here in the cottage, she could feel his presence. Unlike Amberley House, this clearly wasn't designed by his father—Trick's personal style was stamped on the walls, the floors, every piece of furniture.

'Twas amazing the loss she felt, given she'd known him only a few weeks. Just when she was beginning to form a fragile bond with him, he'd left. She strode straight to unlock the drawer and dig to the bottom.

The poetry was gone.

She riffled through all the papers to make sure. Gone, all of it. Her knees buckled, and she sank to the floor, her heart sinking along with her. Not only was her one link to him missing, he was clearly intent on keeping her at arm's length. Rushed to begin a long journey to a foreign land, he'd nonetheless taken the time to stop and remove the pages. Remove any possibility that by reading his words, she might discover who he was, deep inside.

She couldn't allow him to isolate himself like that. Not if they were to live a lifetime together.

She should have gone with him.

"He left," Kendra told Caithren late that afternoon. "He had no choice."

"Of course he didn't." Cait stopped beneath an arbor and played with the ends of her dark-blond hair. "But why did ye not go along?"

"He didn't want me." Kendra squinted at her

sister-in-law in the shadows. "Is this not the loveliest garden?" Her gesture encompassed more than the vine-covered walkway. "The head gardener told me 'twas designed by Salaman de Caux himself."

"Salaman who?"

"De Caux. The celebrated Frenchman. Have you not heard of him?"

"Nay. My garden at Leslie was filled with herbs and vegetables." Cait's lips turned up in a self-deprecating smile. "Nary a posy in sight."

Amberley House's gardens were the most extensive Kendra had ever seen. Geometric configurations of flower beds, knots, and borders surrounded a lake where fishes darted beneath the clear water. Avenues lined with painted and gilded stone lions flanked a massive bowling green. Walls of fruit trees divided the charming wilderness garden from those more formal, like the privy garden they were heading toward, where a copper statue graced an elaborate marble fountain.

They strolled from the arbor into the sunshine, and her gaze trailed to the massive mansion that loomed over it all. "I'm afraid Trick's father depleted his entire fortune building this place."

"Has Trick said so?"

"Not in so many words," she said, hesitating to say more. Confiding Trick's financial instability might lead to speculation about his continuing highwayman activities, and she didn't want to get into that.

"Then I wouldn't assume so," Cait said. " 'Tis very impressive, but then, he *is* a duke. And ye are very good at changing the subject."

Kendra flashed her a wry smile. "I was hoping you

wouldn't notice." She reached overhead to pluck off a fragrant flower, worrying its soft petals between her fingers. "Part of me still cannot believe I'm married. Do you know, even as we rode away, I was sure Colin would come riding after us to say it was all an elaborate joke. I'd convinced myself the parson was in on it—that somehow the ceremony wasn't valid."

"But it was."

"I was furious, I can tell you. I still am. I don't feel like talking to my brothers—any of them." Her voice dropped. "Then I found myself alone with Trick, and still I didn't quite believe it."

"How did it go? The first night, I mean."

She looked away. "Not well," she murmured, studying the way the light filtered through the leafy canopy of a yew. "Did it hurt you very much that first time?"

"I suppose it did, but only that first time, of course. And I was in no state to take notice of it overmuch."

"Well, is Jason very . . . big?"

Caithren's eyes widened. "Michty me, what a question! I've nothing to compare him to, ye ken? I can only say that to look at him, he seems too big, but he always seems to fit just fine." Her half-embarrassed laugh rang through the garden; then she focused on Kendra, shading her hazel eyes with one hand. "It went better for ye the second time, I expect. Surely it didn't hurt."

Kendra bit her lip. "There hasn't been a second time."

"What?" If possible, Cait's eyes widened even more. "You've been married almost three weeks!"

"I won't let him. He . . . we don't fit. Not everyone

does, I expect. In fact, I wonder now why it is that men insist on wedding virgins. You'd think they'd want to try the woman out first and make sure it will work."

" 'Twill work, Kendra." Cait bit her own lip, but clearly not in consternation—rather to keep from laughing. "By all the saints, did your brothers not tell ye anything? Jason will hear from me about this."

"Please, no." Kendra felt her face heat. "He'd make fun of me all my days. What is it he failed to tell me?"

"It hurts most women at first. But only the once, ye ken? Only that first time, when your maidenhead—"

"I may have heard that word." Kendra frowned. "But I never knew what it meant."

" 'Tis a membrane, ye ken, inside every woman. Every virgin, that is. Ye could say it guards your entrance. I read once that 'tis properly called a hymen."

"Hymen is the Greek god of the wedding feast."

"Really? How fitting." Caithren cleared her throat. "Now, the first time ye make love it is torn, and ye bleed—"

"I did," Kendra whispered.

"But ye won't next time. And 'twill not hurt, either, because the maidenhead will be gone. And he'll fit, I promise."

Trick had been telling the truth, then. A wave of relief washed over Kendra, tempered by a stab of regret. She should have believed him.

And now she *really* wished she'd gone with him.

In obvious wonder, Cait shook her head. "Almost three weeks."

And another month, Kendra thought, until he'd be

back. Remembering his kisses, the way he'd made her feel last night—the way she'd almost given in—she could barely stifle a groan.

Cait knelt to inspect some bell-shaped flowers. "He must be the most patient man on Earth," she murmured. "Even I could see how he wanted ye. However did ye manage to keep him away?"

Kendra gave an evasive shrug. "We were strangers. We still are."

"Ye will come to know one another. Just give him another chance." She frowned down at the plant. "Ye have dwale growing here!"

"Dwale?"

"Black nightshade. Belladonna. Look." She waited until Kendra knelt beside her, then skimmed a fingertip over one dingy purplish flower with a berry in its base. "D'ye see these dark-green leaves? They are lethal. 'Tis said that Macbeth poisoned a whole army of Danes by calling a false truce and then offering them liquor mixed with an infusion of dwale."

"Then why is it here in the garden?"

"Used properly, the root makes a good liniment. 'Tis the leaves and berries that are poison." When Kendra reached out, Cait held back her hand. "Dinna touch. It is possible to fall ill without even eating it."

"What sort of ill?"

"Shock, fever, slowed breathing, dilated eyes, stomach pain—"

"Enough." She shuddered. In the year since Caithren had arrived, she'd taught Kendra many uses for herbs and plants. But Kendra wouldn't take a chance on misusing this one. "I shall tell the gardener to remove it."

"Make sure he wears gloves." Cait stood and

brushed her hands on her rose-colored skirts. "Now tell me about ye and Trick. Besides the problem in the bedchamber, ye ken."

Kendra met her sister-in-law's gaze. "He's just . . . well, I don't understand him, Cait. We didn't wed under the best of circumstances. For either of us."

"Nay, ye didn't. But Jase is convinced you'll be happy. Or so he claims."

"Does he?" Even though she'd come to accept her life here at Amberley, the anger rushed back. "What possible excuse could he have for deceiving me the way he did? Not even telling me Trick was a duke, for God's sake!"

"I asked him the same thing myself after the whole story came out. He claims ye would never have married Trick if you'd known he was a duke."

She gritted her teeth. "I hate it when he's right."

"He also said catching ye two in a compromising position was a godsend, because Trick would never have consented to court ye even if Jason had suggested it. He claimed not to want a wife."

"Not in the near future," Kendra admitted darkly.

"Jason told me his hand was forced, because he kent ye two suited perfectly."

"Well, there's where he was wrong." Trick might be a good kisser and tolerant of her nontraditional interests, but a man who refused to share of himself would never suit her perfectly. Regardless of whether they might fit in bed.

For a long moment, Caithren was silent. "Ye must give Trick another chance in your bed," she finally said. "And I hope you'll forgive Jase. He loves ye. He's been watching ye. He'd never forgive himself if it turned out ye were unhappy."

Kendra's jaw went slack. She didn't know whether to feel outraged or touched. "What do you mean, he's been watching me?"

"Nothing as sinister as you're imagining." Cait laid a hand on her arm. "He asked Jane to let him know if anything seems awry. And every day, he sends a messenger to check with her." She offered a tentative smile. "He cares, Kendra."

That explained why every day, sure as the sun rose and set, Jane had been asking if she was happy here at Amberley House. Kendra released a long, slow breath. "Were you sent here as a peacemaker?"

"Aye," Cait admitted, a faint pink coloring her cheeks. "More or less. But I wanted to see ye, anyway. I have news, and no one else to share it with."

"News?" Kendra seated herself on a carved stone bench. "What sort of news?"

Cait sat beside her, lacing her fingers protectively over her stomach. "I'm with child."

"Oh, that's wonderful!" Kendra grabbed her hands and squeezed tightly; then her forehead furrowed. "How are you feeling?"

"Fine." Caithren laughed. "Motherhood agrees with me."

"Jason must be thrilled."

"He doesn't know."

"He—*what*?" Kendra dropped Cait's hands. "You haven't told him?"

"Nay, and ye mustn't, either. Not until we've gone and returned from Scotland. I dinna want to miss my visit home, and I'm afraid Jase wouldn't want me to travel."

"You're right," Kendra said slowly, staring at

Caithren's still-flat middle. "But will he not be furious when he finds out?"

"I will tell him I just then discovered it. I've never been pregnant afore, so how should I know the signs?" She flashed a conspiratorial smile. "Ye won't tell him, will ye?"

"Of course not. I'm not speaking to him, remember?" Kendra returned Cait's grin. "When do you leave?"

"Tomorrow. That's another reason I wanted to visit. To say farewell for a while."

"For a month, do you think? Trick said he'd be gone a month, up and back and with time spent there."

Cait nodded. "Aye, for a month." She looked around the enormous, quiet estate. "Mayhap you would like to go stay with Ford? Or with Colin and Amy?"

"I'm not speaking to Ford or Colin, either." Kendra's grin went flat. "Anyway, I've much to learn around here. By the time Trick returns, I expect to have this place running like clockwork. 'Tis been missing a good financial manager, not to mention a woman's touch. Trick said his father built it, and so far as I can tell, there's never been a mistress here at all." She took Cait's hand and rose. "Come, let us have an early supper together. I've taught Mrs. Chauncey some new recipes, and you can help me see how she did with them."

Their footsteps crunched on the gravel as they crossed the privy garden. They went through the back entrance to the house.

"A letter, Your Grace." Just as he'd done for Trick

yesterday, Compton held out a silver tray. "It just arrived for His Grace, but since he is gone . . ."

"Thank you, Compton." She took the letter and turned it in her hands. Trick's name was written on the back, but not in his mother's beautiful writing, or anyone else's she recognized. Well, of course it wouldn't be—she still knew not the first thing about her husband or his acquaintances. Chiding herself, she hurried to the study with Caithren following behind.

" 'Tis probably nothing," Cait said as they dropped into two chairs. "Open it."

" 'Tisn't addressed to me."

"You said yourself he won't be home for a month. It could be important business."

"I suppose you're right." Feeling more than a little uneasy, Kendra slid a fingernail beneath the black seal. "How odd," she said quietly.

"Aye?"

" 'Tis addressed 'Dear Patrick Iain,' rather than by his title." She read further and released a little gasp.

"What does it say?"

"Listen." She drew a deep breath. " 'I know not if you'll remember me, since eighteen years have passed since I've set eyes on your face. But as a dear old friend of your mother's, I feel honor-bound to warn you of possible danger. When Elspeth—' " Kendra paused. "That's Trick's mother," she clarified.

"Go on."

" 'When Elspeth wrote the letter to summon you home, she was in perfect health. In the two days since, she has begun a rapid decline that I find inexplicable and alarming. I beg you, take heed. Yours in friendship, Hamish Munroe.' " She looked up. "What could he mean? Why would she write a letter saying she was dying, were she in perfect health?"

"Mayhap she wanted to reconcile, but didn't believe he would come home for that alone."

"Possibly," Kendra conceded. But her heart was pounding unevenly. "Yet this Mr. Munroe clearly believes that something is afoot. Trick could be in danger."

"I imagine he can defend himself, seeing as he used to be a highwayman."

Although she was tempted to tell Cait that Trick still was a highwayman, Kendra didn't quite understand what was going on herself. And she knew he wouldn't want it discussed. Much as she trusted her sister-in-law, she couldn't risk her brothers finding out that he hadn't stopped robbing Puritans after all.

Surprised to find herself bound to Trick by some form of loyalty, she suppressed the urge to share her concerns. "I think I should go to him," she said.

"Pardon?"

"I think I should go to Trick. He needs to see this letter."

"I dinna think Jason—"

"A pox on Jason! He lost his right to tell me what to do when he married me off to Trick. Now I'm duty-bound to warn my husband of possible danger." And she could also give Trick that second chance Cait had spoken of. In truth, she burned for it, now that she knew it wouldn't hurt.

She rose and began to pace. "I must leave—immediately . . ." Her mind raced with possible plans.

"Is tomorrow soon enough?" Cait asked.

"Probably. He didn't seem in much of a hurry, so

if I rush—" She turned and looked at Cait. "What are you thinking?"

"We're leaving for Scotland tomorrow. Jason and I. Mayhap ye can come along. But you'll have to talk to your brother," she added with a small smile. "You'll have to break this vow of silence."

"I suppose I will," Kendra said grimly. "And Mrs. Chauncey's supper will have to wait."

"How dare you marry me off to a duke!"

Seated at the desk in his study at Cainewood, Jason steepled his fingers atop a leather-bound ledger. "Ah, the return of the formidable Kendra. 'Tis been less than three weeks since your lovely wedding. Leaving your husband already?"

"No, he left me."

Seeing his mouth drop open, Kendra felt a small nudge of satisfaction. "To go to Scotland," she added. "His mother is sick—dying—and she asked to see him. Except she wasn't dying until after she sent the letter. But Trick doesn't know that. I received another letter—"

"Whoa. Slow down." Jason gave a violent shake of his head, then rose from behind the desk and came around it to embrace his sister. "How are you doing?"

"I've been better," she muttered into his chest. "And I hate you, you know."

"I'm sure you do." He pulled back and kissed her on the forehead. "Now sit down and tell me about these letters."

"Ford?" Kendra called softly.

Surrounded by burning candles and a plethora of

ticking clocks, her twin looked up from the gears in his hands, his gaze going to the dawn-lit window. "Is it morning already?"

"It is." She walked closer, reaching a finger to set a pendulum swinging as she went. "We're leaving."

As he stood and stretched, a clock started chiming, and another, and another, a cacophony of discordant tones. Laughing, Kendra wrapped her arms around her brother. "I'll miss you and all your experiments," she said, her gaze sweeping over beakers and magnets, chemicals and microscopes, and the long, impressive telescope she and Colin had given him as a birthday gift two years before.

"I'm going to turn base metal into gold," he said, returning her hug. "And then I'll restore Lakefield House to a glorious standard."

"And fill it with machinery, no doubt."

"Of course." He pulled away, smiling. "Come, I'll walk you down to join the others."

Outside, early-morning sun slanted against Cainewood's ancient stones, bathing the quadrangle in a golden glow. Kendra pressed a kiss to her twin's cheek and swung up to Pandora's saddle.

"I'll miss you, too," he said. "Are you sure you'd rather not stay here with me? Jason can take the letter to your husband—"

"We've been over this already. I'm going."

Her twin looked up at Jason, mounted on his favorite silver gelding. "Impossible, isn't she?" he asked his oldest brother. "I'll wager you're happier than ever she's another man's responsibility now."

"Not yet, it seems." The glint of amusement in Jason's eyes saved Kendra from anger at his sarcastic tone. "But the minute we reach Duncraven, I'll be happy enough to turn her over."

Sitting atop a shiny red-brown mare, Caithren shook her head. "Hush up, you two. Ye dinna mean any of this." She turned to Kendra. "They love ye, the both of them."

"I know," Kendra said with both a huff and a smile. No matter that she had yet to quite forgive them, she knew her brothers would always be there for her. Family. That was what mattered.

Would she ever forge one with her husband?

Not if they didn't get going. Toying with the stones on her amber bracelet, she looked over at the three carriages—one for themselves should they tire of riding, one for their servants, and one for everyone's baggage—and knew this trip would be a torturously slow affair. And her husband traveling ahead, blithely unaware of the danger that might lurk at his childhood home.

"Are we not going to leave?" She lifted Pandora's reins, an impatience in her voice she was helpless to control. "Trick has a whole day on us—let us be off."

Chapter Twelve

Night was falling and Trick was spooning up the last of his soup when his wife blew through the door of the World's End tavern.

'Twas storming outside, and the room was dark, and for the barest moment, he wondered if he were seeing things. God knew he'd thought of little else than Kendra these two weeks past. She'd consumed his thoughts both waking and sleeping.

But she was not a figment of his imagination. She was actually here. Had he conjured up his lovely and exasperating wife, he wouldn't have conjured up her brother and sister-in-law along with her.

He stood, almost knocking over the small square table. "What the devil are you doing in Edinburgh?"

She turned at the sound of his voice, then just stood there, halfway out of her cloak, her mouth hanging open.

"Looking for you," Jason answered for his uncharacteristically speechless sister, striding forward to shake Trick's hand. He removed his dripping wide-brimmed hat. "Although we had no expectations of catching you. We were planning to bring her to Duncraven tomorrow."

Aghast, Trick dropped back onto the hard wooden

bench where he'd been seated. "When did you leave?"

"The day following your own departure. We were already planning a visit to Leslie, and Kendra talked us into tagging along. I can see we made better time than you did. Was your journey unpleasant?"

"It went fine." Though he hadn't dallied, he hadn't been in a particular hurry, either. The closer he got to Duncraven, the less he looked forward to a reunion with his mother. Half of him was afraid to hope for a reconciliation—afraid she'd disappoint him once again. The other half was hoping too much.

"Finding you here is a timely stroke of luck," Jason added.

Perching her wet cloak on a rack beside Kendra's, Caithren aimed a coquettish glance over her shoulder. "Does this mean we get our own room at an inn tonight?"

Jason's green eyes sparkled down at her. "Just like old times, sweet," he said, referring to their own madcap courtship conducted mainly on the road. He waggled a brow, and his wife went on tiptoe to press a kiss to his lips. "Mmm," he said, pulling back with a grin. "I'm going to get us something to eat." He took Cait's hand and drew her toward the bar.

Kendra slid onto the bench next to Trick. "How long have they been married?" he asked, moving close.

She smiled. "Almost a year."

"Newlyweds," he murmured.

"We're newlyweds, too," she reminded him. As though he could have forgotten. He moved closer still, and, unbelievably, she leaned against him.

This wasn't the Kendra he remembered—the one

who always shied away from his advances. To convince himself she really was here, he ran a hand through her dark, rain-soaked hair, but it felt as real as it looked. "I still like it this way best."

She pulled something from her pocket and glanced up at him. "What?"

"Your hair. Wild and streaming down your back. And wet isn't bad, either. In fact, I'd like to see all of you wet."

She blushed, then removed his hand from her head and put a letter into it. "I came all the way to bring you this. Read it."

"What could be so important?" Pushing his soup bowl aside, he spread the paper on the table and dragged a candle near. The letter was wrinkled and the ink a wee bit runny, but still readable. "Dear Patrick Iain," he said under his breath, then scanned the page and whistled.

" 'Tis a good thing I brought it, no?"

He nodded thoughtfully. "It could mean nothing. My mother might have asked him to write it just in case I'd decided not to come. A last-ditch effort, if you will. But 'tis difficult to tell. I am left to wonder what I'll be walking into."

"What *we'll* be walking into."

He nodded again, not at all sure he was happy about that.

Wondering what could have happened to change her attitude, he tentatively laced his fingers with hers, smiling when she didn't pull away. Conversation buzzed around them, mixing with the sounds of eating and drinking. "Do you remember this Mr. Munroe?" she asked.

"Aye. He was a jolly type, always hanging around,

it seemed. A very old friend of my mother's—they grew up together. From what I remember seeing through the eyes of a lad, I wouldn't be surprised to learn he was sweet on her." His other hand gripped his tankard, and underneath the table, he slid his foot against hers.

"Did that not bother your father?"

"He was never home. In any case, I'm sure nothing ever came of it. Of course, Father accused Mother of all sorts of things . . ." Musing, he took a long sip. He didn't like to think of his mother as an adulteress, no matter what his father had said.

Something brushed his boot, and regardless that Edinburgh was teeming with rats, he'd lay odds it wasn't one. It was, incredibly, his wife's shoe. Looking toward her, he gulped at his ale.

A faint smile curved her lips. "Now that your father is dead, what's become of her home, then?"

The question jarred him back to his senses. "Why, it belongs to me," he said, surprised at that sudden realization. For most of his adult life, he'd done his fighting best to banish all thoughts of home from his mind. "The castle was her dowry. So it belonged to my father, and now to me. But I won't be selling it out from under her. She may have been an appalling mother, but I'll not put her out on the streets."

He drained the rest of his ale, wondering whether to be annoyed or pleased that his wife had materialized in Scotland. Experimentally, he tried to draw his hand from hers, feeling his body quicken in response when she held it tight. He was pleased, he decided. A long abstinence did much to sway a man's emotions.

Not to mention the apparent change of heart on Kendra's part. Mystifying, to say the least. But he'd be insane not to take advantage. "Are you hungry?" he asked.

She shook her head. "Only tired." Her gaze flew to Jason and Cait, heads leaned close at another table as they talked while Jason shoveled meat pie into his mouth. "We ate but a couple of hours ago." She yawned, meeting his eyes. "We're too far to go to Duncraven tonight in the darkness, are we not?"

" 'Tis a good day's ride, yes."

With darkened eyes, she held his gaze. "Then will we sleep here?" she asked, the words threaded with husky curiosity.

Sweet Mary, she wanted to sleep with him. He could hear it in her lowered voice, see it in her deep-green glance.

'Twas too good to be true.

"A fine idea," he said, amazed at this new good fortune. He rose, almost stumbling over his own feet. "Shall we go to bed?"

Trick stopped only for a stack of towels before he rushed her to the room he'd rented. When they got inside, he dropped them on the polished wood floor, set the candle he was carrying on a table by the door, and dragged her into his arms.

His mouth on hers was hot and needy, and she responded in kind. She found it amazing how much she'd missed him. How much she'd missed this. His tongue swept into her mouth, meeting hers with a thrilling urgency. Craving his solid warmth, she plastered herself against his body. A long minute later they pulled apart, and she leaned back in his arms, gazing up into his seductive amber eyes.

How could she have put him off so long? Just the

scent of him made her head swim, and she swayed in his grasp.

"Are you too tired?" he asked.

She was exhausted, but, "God, no."

His smile was blinding. "You missed me, aye?" Her heart flip-flopped at the sound of the low, throaty words, and when she nodded, he kissed her all over again, his mouth even more demanding, if that were possible. Her breath was ragged by the time he stepped back. "You're soaking," he said.

Her gaze slid down his now-damp form, and her hands went to her drenched skirts. "I'm sorry."

"I told you, I like you wet." Lazy and persuasive, his grin seemed to touch a place inside her. A warm, melting place. "Come, *leannan*, let us get you out of these clothes."

She only nodded as, with practiced fingers, he detached the tabs on her stomacher and unlaced her bodice. He drew it down to her waist, and his palms reached out and fitted themselves to her breasts. Puckering in response, her nipples strained against the thin fabric of her chemise.

He sucked in a breath. "I've wanted to touch you like this," he said huskily.

A little mewling sound rose from her throat. She'd wanted him to touch her like this, too. He hadn't done so since the night they were wed, and goodness, she'd craved his hands on her body. If only she'd believed him when he'd said it wouldn't hurt.

She licked her lips, and his eyes darkened. He bent his head, taking the peak of one breast in his mouth, suckling through her gossamer chemise. Her breath caught, and she plowed her fingers into his hair, holding him closer still.

"Trick." His name hung in the air, not a protest this time, but an entreaty. He raised his head, measuring her with his gaze and apparently liking what he saw. In the next moment, he dropped to his knees, and one hand found its way beneath her wet skirts. He worked it up, up, and before she knew what was happening, he'd plunged a finger into a place that was wetter still.

Dear God. Her knees felt about as substantial as jellied fruit. Slowly, seductively, he worked his finger in and out, holding her gaze with his. Something was happening to her. She started tingling and shaking all over, but just when she knew she would collapse to the floor, he drew away and rose to his feet. "Let us get you dry."

Her breath came out in a rush. She nodded wordlessly, the only response she could manage, but it seemed to be enough for him.

In no time at all, he had her stripped, her hair wrapped in one towel while he briskly rubbed her with another. The rough strokes sent her blood coursing like a spring flood. When he was finished, her skin was dry and warm and sensitive beyond whatever she could remember. At his lightest touch, she felt pleasure spiraling through her.

He raised one of her limp hands and ran his fingers over the amber stones that circled her wrist. "You're wearing it," he murmured.

"I—it matched my dress."

He cast a glance to the gown on the floor. "Aye. Purple and amber—they go together so well."

She blushed, but he only laughed, a warm sound that rippled right into her.

He started ripping off his own clothes, his gaze on

hers commanding her to watch. She backed away
and sat on the edge of the bed, unwrapping her hair
to towel it dry. Her eyes widened at the sight of him,
tall, rangy and lean, with long, ropy muscles.

When his breeches slid down, her gaze slid down
along with them. He was still as big as ever. Bigger,
even, she would swear.

Her breath caught as a tremor of panic took her
by surprise. What if Cait were wrong? What if it
worked for most people, but in this case . . . what if
he really wouldn't fit? She remembered the pain, and
her lids slid closed.

"Kendra?"

He sounded so concerned. Trying to smile, she
opened her eyes, but despite herself, she couldn't
help where her anxious gaze was fastened.

His own gaze followed. "I promise you, 'twill
not hurt."

"I know. Caithren told me."

His eyes snapped back up to hers. "When?"

"After you left." She bit her lip.

"You didn't believe her, though, did you?"

"Yes." She nodded frantically. "Yes, I did. And I
came here wanting . . ."

"But then . . ." he prompted, waiting expectantly.

When she didn't continue, he sighed. "I knew this
was too good to be true." His eyes slid closed momentarily, then opened and burned into hers. "Listen," he said, reaching to draw her up to stand before
him. "The night before I left, you wanted me to touch
you, aye?"

Like a simpleton, she stood there with her arms
dangling loose by her sides. "Yes, but—"

"I wanted more than that. You know I did. I've

thought of nothing but you since the moment I rode away."

Heat rushed to her cheeks—and other parts of her body. She'd thought of him, too, and how he could make her feel. She wanted to feel that again. This fear was irrational, and she had to overcome it.

But that was easier said than done. "Trick—"

"Look at me."

She did, and he wrapped his arms around her waist. "I've told you I wouldn't take you against your will, and I meant every word. But I'm finished playing games."

Her heart skipped a beat at that, then began racing in her chest. "Trick—"

"No. Hear me out." He tossed his head, clearing the hair from his eyes, and his arms tightened around her middle, arching her back, bringing her hips snug against him. She could feel how much he wanted her. "I am done expecting you to beg. I still want you in my bed, but I can wait until you're ready. In the meantime, there are other ways we can pleasure one another without me entering your body."

She flinched at the frank words, the mental picture. But relief flowed through her veins. And the idea he proposed was intriguing.

"What sorts of ways?"

"I'll show you, lass." His eyes darkened. "Like this."

Her pulse skittered as he moved his hands to her shoulders, then pushed, until she tumbled back on the bed. He came down over her, settling his weight on his elbows. Against her melting softness, his body felt warm and hard as his lips descended to meet hers. Then, with calculated skill, he kissed her breathless. Senseless. Her head seemed to be spinning by the time he rolled to his side and began tracing his fingertips along her heated skin.

"Like this, *leannan*," he murmured huskily. "We can make each other happy like this." And his mouth followed where his fingers had been, over her breasts and down her arms and across her waist in a warm, damp dance. She heard little moans, and they were hers. She reached for his shoulders, tracing her fingers in a way that mimicked his, trying to pull him up so she could touch more of his body.

He raised his head, his breath warm against her belly. "No, lass. Tonight just feel . . . Lie back and feel what I can do for you." As he talked, his hands worked up her sides, caressing. "Then tomorrow . . ." he said, "tomorrow, I'll show you what you can do for me." He flicked his thumbs over her nipples, and a jolt of excitement streaked through her. "This can be good for us both."

Rich as velvet, his voice was a sensuous promise, a heady invitation that made her emotions whirl. And while she was still reacting to that, he lifted her knees and moved between them.

He kissed and licked and bit the tender skin of her inner thighs, and her fists clenched, bunching the sheets in her hands. A little cry escaped her lips when his tongue traced the crease where her legs met her body. Then it plunged into that place that was hot and aching, and she let out a gasp of shock and pleasure. Something was happening to her— something confusing and marvelous. As his tongue continued a rhythmic, sensual assault, every nerve in her body came alight with fiery sensations, sprinting throughout her until she thought she would scream unless something happened—

She exploded, convulsing in wave after wave of pleasure so intense 'twas almost beyond bearing.

It seemed a long while before she could think straight, before Trick made his way up her body to place one last, gentle kiss on her lips. "Tomorrow . . ." she whispered.

"Tomorrow is another day," he said. "And together we can make it a wonderful one."

"Wonderful," she breathed, meaning not tomorrow but tonight. The glory of what had just happened.

"I know." A smile of pure male pride curved his lips. "Now sleep, *leannan*."

She inhaled deep of his distinctive scent, and another scent that was new to her, the seductive fragrance of spent passion. She sniffed again, smiling to herself, wanting nothing more than to lie awake and replay every moment, relive all the incredible new feelings.

But her earlier exhaustion overcame her, and wrapped in his arms, she drifted off.

'Twas pitch-black when she awakened sometime in the night, the candle long since guttered out. In his sleep Trick was hugging her, his arms still wrapped tight. When she tried to wiggle free, they tightened still more, holding her fast against his warm chest. She felt smothered, trapped. But she couldn't fight him, couldn't get away. She was too tired . . . she would try again later, after she got some more sleep. . . .

Dawn was breaking when next she opened her eyes, feeling inexplicably lonely. Squinting in the faint gray light, she looked over to where Trick lay on his back, apart from her, snoring softly, his hands lax by his sides. She scooted close, throwing an arm across his chest, but he snored on, still motionless. A stab of hurt, tiny but deep, took her by surprise. Tamping it down, she rolled to her back and stared at the beamed ceiling overhead, replaying last night in her mind.

Wonderful. Full of wonder. But something had been missing.

Everything he'd done had felt incredible, and she was certain she could do the same for him. But she wanted to be closer. Cait had said it wouldn't hurt. And maybe . . . maybe if she let Trick into her body, he would let her into his heart. Maybe she could start chipping away at the emotional wall he had built.

And beyond those logical reasons, the naked truth was, she wanted him. Craved him. His body joined with hers, her heart joined with his.

"Trick?" she called softly.

He didn't respond.

She poked his shoulder. "Trick?"

"Hmm?" He rolled toward her and flung an arm over her middle without opening his eyes.

Still, she snuggled happily into his warmth. "To-morrow," she said, struggling to keep the tremble from her voice, "tomorrow night, I want to sleep with you."

"Sleeping now," he murmured.

"No. I want . . . I want . . ."

His eyes slid open and stared into hers, so close. "Are you begging, *leannan*?" he whispered, a tentative note of hope in the words.

"I'm begging," she answered simply.

He raised his head to give her a sleepy smile, and she kissed him, running her tongue across the chip in his tooth. When his head dropped back to the pillow, his arms tightened around her, holding her fast against his body.

And she drifted off to sleep again, not feeling smothered at all.

"There's the castle," Trick said after a long day spent on the road. "In the distance, on the top of that hill. Just as I remembered."

Kendra squinted through the half-light of dusk. "It looks . . . forbidding." At the end of a narrow, twisty path, twin square towers rose from the hill, thrusting gray and ugly into the leaden sky. "How old is it? Is there no manor house attached?"

"No, just the two connected keeps. They're large, though—the distance is deceiving. Since the thirteenth century, they've stood atop that hill."

"It must be very cold."

"There are fireplaces."

"I'm not talking about the temperature. It doesn't look a friendly place."

"It isn't," he said shortly.

While two carriages and a luggage cart rolled slowly behind, attended by Trick's servants, they guided their mounts silently past a somber graystone church that stood at the edge of a small village. The simple homes seemed eerily empty, however. Though the rain had stopped, no children had come out to play, no women were hanging out wash, no men were at work. The clip-clop of their horses' hooves sounded loud in the odd stillness.

"Where is everyone?" Kendra asked.

"I'm wondering myself." He looked back up the hill. "Do you hear laughter?"

"Maybe. Far away."

"Up at the castle." As they rode closer, he could hear it better. "They must be holding an entertainment that includes the whole village. Strange . . . I cannot remember anything like that from when I lived here. Mother doesn't strike me as the hospitable type."

"People change in eighteen years."

"I expect you're right." Lost in memories, Trick remained quiet as they made their way to the hill and then started up it. The laughter grew louder. When they crested the rise, they saw athletic events in progress on the lawn that bordered the keeps. Five young men were lining up for a foot race while two other lads executed standing jumps and lassies poked fun at their results.

"Will you test your skills?" Kendra asked as they slid off their horses.

"Mayhap later." Trick gave her a shaky smile, handing his reins to an Amberley outrider. A few curious glances were focused their way, but no one made a move to greet them. Shrugging, Trick instructed his staff to find the stables and settle the horses, then took Kendra's elbow and headed inside. Worn stone steps rose to a landing and a small, arched door that stood open, allowing still more laughter to drift out into the cool early-evening air.

Beyond the door, a passageway led through the twenty-foot-thick wall. Moments later they stepped into the first towering keep. 'Twas every bit as dark and cold as he'd remembered. Iron chandeliers dripped with candles, struggling vainly to brighten the Great Hall, a vaulted chamber of ancient gray stone.

He stood stock still while memories flooded back: having lessons at the old oak desk with his tutor; taking meals at the long trestle table with his mother; playing at her feet while she sat with her embroidery at the far end where flames roared in the immense canopied fireplace, his toy soldiers lined up on the scarred wooden floor. The Cavalier soldiers had always won, of course, since his father had been away fighting among them.

The chamber was teeming with people, and two children chased around him, but he barely took notice even when one bumped his knees. "I remembered it larger," he murmured to Kendra. " 'Tis not nearly the size of Cainewood's Great Hall."

" 'Tis large enough."

"I recall thinking as a child that it was so big and high a man on horseback could turn a spear in it with all the ease imaginable."

She grinned. "He'd have to get through the door first." Indeed, the entrance they'd just ducked through was shorter than himself by a head or more—precisely to stop raiders on horseback from entering. Even on foot, a grown man couldn't enter without stooping, therefore hampering his ability to attack. He remembered asking about that short doorway as a child, over and over, as children were wont to do.

Kendra's lips moved, but he cocked his head, unable to hear her through the din. "You look pale," she repeated loudly.

"Memories." He shrugged, looking around. "I believe there is a painting of Queen Mary of Scots under there," he said, indicating a rectangle draped in black.

"Why is it covered?"

"To prevent the spirit going in the wrong direction."

He blinked, wondering who had answered. "You look oddly familiar," he heard Kendra say, and turned to see whom she was addressing.

He could only stare. Several heartbeats passed while all around them people cheered on their favorite of two men playing jump-the-stick.

"I'm Niall," the blond young man introduced himself, bewilderment clouding his golden eyes. "And I thank ye for attending my dear mother's wake." He paused expectantly and then added, "Whoever ye may be."

"Patrick Caldwell, the Duke of Amberley," Trick replied. "And my wife, the Duchess. And I'm looking for *my* mother."

"Holy Christ." Niall visibly paled. "I should have guessed. She always said we looked like twins." And he launched himself at Trick, wrapping his arms around him and letting loose a deep, shuddering sob. "Ye came," he blubbered. "You're a wee bit late, but ye came, after all. I told her ye would."

At a loss, Trick let the young man hang on his body, wetting his surcoat with heartfelt tears. Hesitantly he placed his hands on the lad's back and gave him a couple of awkward pats. His mind swimming in confusion, he looked to Kendra, sending a silent plea for help.

She tapped Niall on the shoulder. "Who are you?" she asked.

The young man stilled and pulled back a bit, a

frown creasing the forehead above his red-rimmed eyes. He turned to Kendra and blinked hard, then swiped a hand under his nose. "I'm your husband's brother," he said slowly.

Feeling blank-headed, Trick gingerly extricated himself. "I have no brother."

"Aye, ye do." Niall's gaze trailed to the center of the chamber. "And our mother is in that coffin."

Chapter Thirteen

Robbed of breath, Trick woodenly followed Niall to the open coffin. He wanted to protest—in his head, he was screaming this couldn't be his brother, that couldn't be his mother in that box—but words wouldn't come. Words were beyond him just now. Stepping closer, he peered inside.

'Twas her.

She appeared older than he remembered, though her gown looked as though it would befit a younger woman. Her *deid-claes*, he realized—the first duty of a new Scottish wife was to sew the funeral clothes for herself and her husband. She'd obviously followed the custom. Beneath the gown, her legs were encased in the traditional white woolen stockings, and upon her feet were sturdy shoes, symbolic of the thorny path she was about to journey.

He'd traveled all the way here to make his peace with his mother, but that was never to be. His mother was dead.

It seemed impossible.

Her serene appearance sat at odds with the churning in Trick's stomach. Why had she written to him? What would have been said between them had he arrived in time? Questions raced in his head, and he wished mightily that she would open her eyes and answer them. But there were coins on her lids to keep them closed—it was feared that if one looked a corpse in the eye, it would take you as a companion. And he knew that, coins or not, she wouldn't be answering him, anyway.

His mother was dead, and he seemed rooted to the floor.

"Touch her," Niall urged, doing so himself, his fingers gentle on their mother's cheek. "They say 'twill banish the ghosts of her from your mind."

Trick reached out, then pulled back. "I cannot." It had been too long since he'd touched her in life. Eighteen years of loneliness, eighteen years of resentment. This journey had been a pilgrimage of sorts, his chance to mend old wounds, reconcile his past so that he could start life anew with his wife. But inside him, the wounds seemed to gape open fresh. His mother had always failed him, and this time was no different.

He turned and stared into his brother's golden eyes. His own eyes, it seemed. Niall's hair was longer, shoulder-length, but the same shining straight blond as Trick's, and though Niall was quite a bit younger—seventeen, Trick guessed him at—they were of a height.

His brother. He'd never had a sibling. His heart swelling with sudden emotion, Trick gathered Niall close, and Niall hugged him back, hard. Then they pulled apart and looked each other over.

"I have a brother," Trick said, and a small smile ghosted Niall's grief-ravaged face to match the larger smile on Trick's. "Who is your father?" Trick asked.

"Hamish Munroe. His wife died, and he

Mam . . . Well, they'd always . . ." The younger man drew a shuddering breath. "I'll take you to him."

He motioned them to a turret off one corner of the Great Hall.

They followed him single file up a narrow, twisting stone staircase lit by dangerous, old-fashioned torches set at intervals. The rocks looked ancient, and when Kendra put her hand to the wall for balance, she half-expected it to crumble beneath her fingers. But her hand just came away dirty.

She wiped it on her skirts. "I cannot believe people are playing games down there."

" 'Tis the Scots way," Trick told her.

"Folk were somber early in the week," Niall added. "But Mam has been gone six days now. All the tears have been shed, all the stories of her have been told and told again. The feasting, the games and riddles—'tis all in her honor. The wake is a celebration of her life."

They followed him out into a spacious sitting room that seemed lacking in furniture. Though the windows were small and set back in incredibly thick walls, the stone was whitewashed here and reflected the candlelight, making this chamber much lighter than the one downstairs. A large tapestry hung on one side, looking like it could use a good cleaning, and across from it, four faded red chairs were arranged to face a fireplace.

"Still and all," Niall continued, "this is nothing like Calum MacKinnon's wake last year. They propped up the dearly departed and put a pipe in his mouth, then took turns throwing boiled turnips at him to try to knock it from his lips. I dinna think Mam would appreciate that."

"I would expect not!" Kendra exclaimed.

"Da is in here." Niall pushed open a door. "Come along."

The room was sizable as bedchambers went, with substantial oak furnishings lining the walls and a large four-poster bed in the center. A tall, gaunt man lay beneath the coverlet, snoring softly, and a middle-aged couple sat nearby on two chairs. They began to rise, but Niall waved at them to stay seated.

"Da." He reached out to jiggle the man's shoulder. "Someone is here to see ye."

Hamish Munroe started and opened his eyes, then blinked and looked again. "Patrick? Is that ye?"

"Aye, sir, it is."

To Trick's apparent dismay, the older man's eyes flooded with tears. "Come here, lad." He held out a hand. "Let me touch ye." With seeming reluctance, Trick gripped his fingers. "Elspeth said ye would come. I didn't believe her."

"I received your letter," Trick said, slowly re-claiming his hand. "Or rather, my wife did, and came after me to deliver it." He wrapped an arm around Kendra's shoulders and drew her forward. "My wife, the Duchess of Amberley."

"I'm glad of your acquaintance," she said, reaching for the man's outstretched hand. It trembled in her grasp. "Please, just call me Kendra."

The man's fingers weakly squeezed hers, feeling hot and dry. "Then ye must call me Hamish. 'Tis pleased I am to meet ye." Dropping her hand, he rolled his head on the pillow, indicating the other couple. "These are my oldest friends, Rhona and Gregor Haig."

"Your Grace." Rhona rose and curtseyed, first to Trick and then to Kendra. "Your Grace."

Kendra hated the formal address as much as she'd always thought she would. She smiled at the pale woman, wishing she could set her at ease. "I'm glad of your acquaintance," she said.

"Pleased to meet ye," Rhona returned softly, not quite meeting Kendra's eyes with her shy blue ones.

Gregor bowed. "Your Graces." Blue-eyed and silver-haired as well, he resembled his wife in the way that long-married couples often did. Kendra wondered if she and Trick might end up like that some day, but casting his golden countenance a glance, decided not.

"Sit," Hamish said before turning back to Trick. "They've been keeping me company." He paused and grimaced in pain, then blew out a breath. "I've fallen ill with the same plague that killed Elspeth, ye see, and Rhona here is a fine healer."

His friend shook her head. "My possets and infusions dinna seem to—"

"Hush, woman. I ken you've done your best."

Wiping her hands on the skirts of her cranberry-red gown, Kendra stepped closer. "Your letter said that Elspeth's illness was inexplicable and alarming—"

"I thought so, at first," Hamish said. "But 'twas only that it was such a coincidence, ye ken, her sending that letter and then . . ."

His voice faded, and Niall took over. "It seemed such a coincidence that she should claim she was ill and then suddenly succumb. When Da fell ill as well, the doctor came to visit and"—tears flooded the young man's eyes—"and said they were suffering from a bilious fever. Nothing inexplicable."

"Did he say it was fatal?" Trick asked.

Niall crossed his arms, his familiar eyes radiating a mixture of grief and denial. "That doctor is a bampot if ever I met one. Da is stronger than Mam was. He is not going to die."

Gregor shook his head mournfully. "Last night, a coal in the shape of a coffin jumped from the fire to the hearth. Right there." He indicated the fireplace across from the bed.

"Old beggar-woman tales." Clearly agitated, Niall went to the hearth and grabbed a poker. "I dinna believe such nonsense."

As if to contradict his son's opinion, Hamish's face contorted with another pain, and he bent over double in the bed. Rhona rushed to his side and pressed a cup filled with vile-looking green liquid to his lips. "Drink, Hamish." One tear rolled down her wrinkled cheek. "Have a sip for me, will ye?"

He did, and then his eyes closed and he seemed to fall asleep. Niall stabbed angrily at the fire, as if daring another coffin-shaped coal to jump out.

Trick moved closer and took Kendra's hand. "Only at Duncraven," he muttered under his breath, "is it cold enough in the middle of summer to keep a fire burning day and night."

" 'Tis cold within Cainewood's thick stone walls as well," she whispered back. But that was one of few similarities between the two castles. Though both were centuries old, the parts of Cainewood that had been restored were modern and clean, while this place looked aged and worn out. The white paint was chipping off the walls, and cobwebs lurked in the corners.

As the estate's mistress, she would never stand for

such slipshod housekeeping. But Elspeth had been ill these weeks past—perhaps that explained the neglect.

"Come along," Trick said. "Let us leave him to sleep."

"Patrick. Wait. I wish to talk to ye." Hamish forced open his eyes. They looked black, until she realized they were light brown but seriously dilated. The older man's voice wheezed through paper-dry lips. "About . . . about your . . . your mother's letter."

"You're weary, Da." Niall dropped the poker and crossed to his father, brushing the straggly gray-blond hair off his forehead. "You're always better in the morning. Ye can talk with Patrick then."

"Elspeth's burial is in the morning," Rhona reminded him in a strangled whisper.

"Oh, aye." The young man closed his eyes for a moment while he recovered his composure. "Then after," he said when he opened them. "Or the next day. Ye dinna have the strength now." When his father nodded and rolled to his side with a grimace and a groan, Niall ushered Trick and Kendra from the room.

Back downstairs, Niall beckoned to his newfound brother. "Come, ye should sit. This must be quite a shock to ye both."

Trick allowed himself to be led through the crowd of reveling mourners. Servants passed among them, offering plates of oatcakes and shortbread. Goblets filled with spirits sat waiting on a sideboard, and he snatched one as he walked by, drinking deeply.

Beside the Great Hall's magnificent canopied fireplace, Niall pushed him into a seat niched into the wall. Trick drank again, then looked around him and leapt to his feet.

"Nay, ye belong in the sedile now," the younger man said, gently easing him back down to the fur that draped the stone bench.

Kendra joined Trick there and silently took his hand, and he gave her a grateful half-smile. Just as he felt uncomfortable in his father's mansion, neither did he feel that he belonged in the sedile—the seat of honor for the master of the house. Against his back, the stone felt too cold, too solemn.

But he did belong here now—that much was the truth. No matter how uncomfortably that truth rode on his shoulders.

Heat rolled out of the fireplace beside them, and torchlight glinted off the armor scattered around the perimeter of the chamber, a reminder of days gone past. Curious glances were slanted in Trick's direction, and people seemed to be edging their way over.

Oblivious to it all, his mother lay in a box in the center of the room.

Sipping again, he looked away, up to Niall. "I cannot believe she is dead."

"I share your disbelief." Niall paused, then seemed to come to some sort of decision. "And unlike Da, I am not entirely sure there is no evil force at work. I intend to get to the bottom of it." His suddenly narrowed gaze hinted at bravery beyond his years. "Will ye help me?"

"I wasn't planning to remain here," Trick said. "I came at my mother's request, and now she is dead." He had pressing matters back home. The King's mission was waiting to be completed. And a trusting relationship with Kendra was waiting to begin.

"Who is this?" a woman asked, stepping close. Her dull chestnut hair was pulled back into a severe bun, and she looked to be near Trick's own age.

"Ah, Annag." Niall's smile failed to reach his eyes. "May I present the Duke of Amberley, my mother's eldest son. Patrick, my half-sister, Annag."

"Pleased to meet ye," Annag said, although she clearly wasn't. Her dark-brown eyes flashed with some emotion Trick couldn't put a name to. But 'twas plain enough she didn't like him. Or didn't like him here.

"And Duncan," Niall continued as a man joined their little gathering. Another of Hamish's grown children, from the looks of him. He and Annag bore a marked resemblance to each other, the most obvious being their matching expressions of distaste.

Raising the tankard in his hand, Duncan took a deep swallow. "When are ye going home?" he asked, skipping the preliminaries.

Wondering why he felt surrounded by the enemy, Trick rolled his shoulders and changed his mind about leaving so quickly. "When I'm good and ready. I've only just met my brother, and—"

"Oh, *him*," Annag interrupted, shooting Niall a look that was every bit as deadly as the one she'd given Trick. "High and mighty Lord Niall."

Apparently Niall had been passed off as the duke's son, and Hamish's other children resented him for it. But the young man only gave a good-natured shrug. "If ye cannot be civil, Annag, I will ask ye to leave my home."

Duncan took another gulp of spirits. " 'Tis *his* home now," he said, indicating Trick with a smarmy, pleased gleam in his eye.

Niall flinched, but recovered swiftly. "And so it is, I suppose."

"I'll not be throwing you out," Trick assured him.

"I wouldn't trust him," Annag told Niall, as though Trick were not even there. "He may have been born here, but he's turned English." When Niall just glared at her, she continued. "Well, listen to the man speak. English through and through. He's forgotten his Scottish roots, and even ye, gowk that ye are, ought to know better than to trust a Sassenach."

"Dinna the women need help in the kitchen?" Niall asked his sister. "And what are your bairns up to? And Duncan, have ye sat some time with Da this day? Rhona and Gregor could use a break. They're good friends, but you're his son." After that brave speech, he looked down at his scuffed black boots. "Give us some peace, will ye? Our mother just died."

"And good riddance," one of them muttered as they shambled away. Trick wasn't sure which, but it didn't seem to matter. So far as he could tell, they both hated him equally. The fact that they'd hated his mother as well came as no surprise.

From what he knew of her, she, at least, had not deserved their love or admiration. His father had made no secret of all her faults, and already one had been proven true this night: His mother had been a whore. Perhaps Hamish's wife had been dead when Niall was conceived, but Elspeth's husband had not.

He slumped in the stone niche and extricated his hand from Kendra's, belatedly realizing she'd been holding it in an iron grip. "Welcome to Scotland," he said, flexing it ruefully.

Chapter Fourteen

Though it had grown late, the castle was still over-
run with people. Apparently, after his years away
had made it clear to Elspeth that her husband was
never returning, she'd invited Hamish to live with
her and Niall. Since her death, Hamish's older children and his grandchildren had been staying here to
keep him company. One big, happy family, as the
saying went.

Somehow, Kendra didn't think it applied in this case.

"Are ye sure ye dinna want the master's chamber?" Niall asked.

Trick shook his head. "I wouldn't dream of moving your father. There must be a spare bed here
somewhere."

And that was how Trick and Kendra came to follow Niall up what seemed like miles of winding
stone stairs, until finally they stepped into a huge,
deserted chamber. Their footfalls echoed off the
wooden floor as they entered. A few torches on the
walls did little in the way of brightening the place,
and the room gave off a musty scent that spoke of
long disuse.

Kendra stared up at the gloomy vaulted stone ceiling. " 'Tis spooky."

Niall gave her a wan smile. "Cromwell garrisoned his soldiers here when he commandeered it during the War. One hundred of them, lying foot-to-head on the floor, with a second hundred on another level that rested on those posts that protrude from the wall." He pressed a key into Trick's hand. "Your staff has moved your things up here already. Shall I have them sent up to attend ye? You've a valet, do ye not, and a ladies' maid?"

"Aye, my man goes by Cavanaugh, and Jane sees to Her Grace." Trick's gaze met Kendra's. "But I think we can fend for ourselves tonight."

Though she didn't know if he'd intended to remind her, Kendra's skin prickled as she recalled what she'd promised would happen this evening. Then he looked away, pensively moving off, and she knew that he was no more thinking of such things than she had been. After all the upheaval today, last night seemed so very long ago.

"Good night, then," Niall said.

"Good night," she returned softly.

Listening to the young man's footsteps fade, she shivered. The candle in her hand wavered, throwing shadows on the gray stone walls. "I dislike to think of Cromwell visiting this house, let alone using it as a headquarters." Oliver Cromwell had been indirectly responsible for the deaths of her parents and her own exile that followed.

" 'Twas against my father's wishes, to say the least. He was a Royalist, through and through." Trick wandered to one of the deep-set windows, and his voice echoed back out from it. "My mother talked him into leaving."

"Did she, really?" Squeezing into the niche, Kendra joined him at the window. In the small space he felt warm and near, and yet cold and distant, too. By moonlight, she could barely make out the village below, surrounded by acres of wild pasture and tended fields. "This was her family's ancestral home, was it not? Why would she willingly surrender it?"

"She was a Covenanter," he said shortly, stepping back into the room. "Come, our chamber is this way."

He ducked through an arch in the wall and pushed open a thick oak door. On her way inside, she shot one last look at the empty vaulted chamber. The garrison. She wondered if it was haunted by ghosts of dead soldiers.

Not that she believed in anything like that.

The bedchamber was enormous. A four-poster bed in its center looked dwarfed, and after the din of the wake below, the room seemed deathly quiet.

She moved to set the candle on a bedside table, the dull wooden floor sounding gritty under her shoes. A fire burned on the hearth, and she wondered who had built it. Jane or Cavanaugh? One of Duncraven's servants? "Are we the only ones up here?"

"Aye. The towers are mirror images. One great room and one bedchamber on each top level." With a rueful smile, he locked the door behind them. "As a child, I was terrified to come up here alone."

"I'm rather terrified now," Kendra admitted. She sat gingerly on the edge of the bed. "After you left, how long was it before you returned?"

"Until now." Trick shrugged out of his surcoat, folding it over the back of a chair that sat before an immense carved oak desk. "My father settled my mother with relatives and spirited me away to

France. I was ten." Abruptly he dropped to the chair. "I never saw my mother again. And now I never will."

His voice cracked, and Kendra rose to wind her arms around his neck from behind. "Surely she knows that you cared, that you came for her."

"Mayhap." Sighing, he absently slid open the top desk drawer and riffled through some papers. Dust flew out, tickling her nose. She felt him stiffen. "Sweet Mary, would you look at this."

She straightened. "What is it?"

"A letter. From Oliver Cromwell himself."

A chill ran up her spine. "We were just talking about him. How odd." Irrationally afraid to touch the evil man's writings, she kept her distance while Trick scanned the page. "When was it written?"

"Eighteenth November, 1650."

"So long ago. Almost eighteen years."

"Other than my father, I rarely remember anyone coming up here." His gaze swept the chamber. "Nothing's changed in the interim. The same bed, the same desk. It probably sat here all this time."

"What does it say?"

He looked back down to the yellowed parchment. " 'I thought fit to send this trumpet to you, to let you know that, if you please to walk away with your company, and deliver the house to such as I shall send to receive it, you shall have liberty to carry off your arms and goods, and such other necessaries as you have. You have harbored such parties in your house as have basely and inhumanly murdered our men; if you necessitate me to bend my cannon against you, you may expect what I doubt you will not be pleased with. I expect your present answer, and rest your servant, O. Cromwell.' "

"Dear God." Kendra let out the breath she hadn't realized she'd been holding. "Words from the devil himself. Can you blame your mother for wanting to walk away?"

He shrugged uncomfortably. "Father refused at first. He'd fought well and bravely in support of Charles, but when Cromwell opened fire . . . well, I was inside." He drew a sharp, shuddering breath, obviously remembering.

Kendra was horrified. "He opened fire with a child inside?"

"Aye. The bombardment destroyed the east parapet and tore a large cavity in the stonework—did you not see it as we walked in?"

"I wasn't looking."

"At my mother's behest, Father sent word to the Lord Protector that he saw the point, and he walked away, taking me with him and never looking back."

She folded the bed's simple white coverlet back and lowered herself to the plain sheets below. "She wanted to save you."

"She wanted to save her family's castle." He turned in the chair to face her. "If she'd cared for me, she would have come along with us."

"Maybe your father wouldn't allow her."

"Mayhap," Trick conceded. "He was certainly mum on the subject." He shoved the paper into the desk and slammed the drawer. "And I wouldn't blame him if he did leave her that coldly. She was no mother or wife to be proud of. Besides being a Covenanter, she was an adulteress, and—"

"You judge her harshly."

A momentary look of self-doubt crossed his face, then disappeared so fast, she wondered if she'd imagined it. "I've told you how I feel about infidelity."

She'd told him how she felt about infidelity as well, but knew better than to bring that up. Living with three brothers had taught her how to deal with men's moods. Gingerly. "Do you remember her as being that terrible?"

"No, but I was naught but a child."

Kendra glanced down and smoothed her cranberry-colored skirts, then lifted her head to meet his gaze. "If your father and she were at odds, why do you believe everything he told you about her?"

"For the longest time, I didn't want to," he admitted. "But then so much time passed and she never, ever came for me . . ."

"There are two sides to every story, Trick."

If his sudden silence wasn't agreement, at least he was man enough to consider she had a point. The only sound in the chamber was that of the flames that danced in the fireplace, until at last he said, "But I'll never hear her side of it, will I?"

The pain radiated off him in waves, but she knew that now was not the time to talk about that. 'Twas too fresh. "What is a Covenanter?" she asked instead. "I know English history by rote, and Greek and Roman, but I'm afraid I was never taught much of Scotland's past."

"I cannot say that I am surprised," Trick said dryly, but the remark didn't sound at all disparaging, only resigned. He leaned back in the chair, starting to untie his cravat. "Many men, including my mother's father, signed a document known as the National Covenant. When the Civil War broke out, the Covenanters sided with the English Parliament against the King in return for Cromwell's promise of a religious reformation in England and Ireland, based on the Scottish Kirk."

"And Cromwell never followed through."

"Nay, he did not. But it took a long time for the Scots to realize they'd been duped."

"They'd thrown their lot in with the devil."

Nodding, he slowly drew off the cravat. "I'm afraid this castle was instrumental in Cromwell's victory. My father never forgave my mother for that."

With a flick of his wrist, the cravat landed on the desk in a flurry of frothy white. She stared at it. He was undressing. Whether or not he'd spent the whole day thinking about it, she was sure that he expected to make love with her tonight. A little ball of anxiety lodged in her middle.

She tore her gaze from the lace-trimmed linen. "My father fought with King Charles, too. And died, along with my mother. He would have sympathized with your father's stance."

His expression hardened. "Father was no saint, believe me. I liked him no more than I did my mother. I am well rid of them both."

"Trick—" She bit her tongue. Disparaging her husband's feelings was no way to fortify their shaky relationship. She forced a gentle smile. "How does it feel having a brother?"

He smiled in return—perhaps the first smile she'd seen from him that wasn't tainted with a touch of cynicism. "He's quite nice, is he not?" His eyes softened as his fingers worked to loosen the laces on his shirt. "I find it hard to believe he came from my mother, and—and that man."

She wasn't surprised to find he didn't care for Hamish, either. "Niall looks just like you."

"I know. 'Tis bloody amazing." Leaning forward, he pulled off a boot. "I wish I could stay longer and get to know him. Mayhap he'll come visit us at Amberley."

"That would be nice." The more of Trick's clothes that came off, the more her stomach quaked at the thought of what she'd promised last night. Too nervous to just sit there and watch, she stood and wandered over to a small arched door. "Where does this lead?"

"To another staircase, if I remember right." In stockinged feet, he padded over and unlatched the iron bar that secured the door, poking his head into the darkness beyond. His voice echoed back. "Aye, another winding stairwell. To the roof above. Prisoner's Leap."

"Prisoner's what?"

"Prisoner's Leap." He turned to her, the stairwell gaping blackly behind him. "In the old days, prisoners were brought up from the dungeons once a year and allowed a chance to gain their freedom by successfully jumping from one tower to the other. Twelve feet, with their hands tied behind their backs and a hundred-foot drop to the bottom. And no running start."

"My God. Did any of them make it?"

"I expect not." His lips turned up in a half-smile. "Mayhap that's why the villagers were practicing their long jumps today."

A little shiver ran through her. "I'm not sure I like this place, Trick."

"Why? Because I had barbaric ancestors?" Although reserved, his grin did seem to lighten the room somewhat. "There is no one in the dungeons today, so far as I know."

"So far as—"

"I'm jesting." He shut the door to the stairwell, and she relaxed a little. "Come here."

"Not until you bar that door."

With a strangled laugh, he did so. "There, we're safe. Come here, Kendra. I need you tonight."

No one had ever said anything like that to her, ever before, and surely they were words to melt a woman's heart. Frightened as she was, she walked into his arms.

When his mouth met hers, her reservations faded away. If her head didn't remember what had made her decide she wanted him last night, her body certainly did. She knew what he could make her feel now, and she wanted that again, and more. Much more. The tinge of fear in her stomach turned to a rush of anticipation.

She wrapped her arms around his neck and threaded her fingers in his short, silky hair. Her mouth opened beneath his, and his tongue swept inside, soft and sweet, flavored with the faintest trace of the whisky he'd sipped downstairs.

He eased back to plant little kisses on her cheeks, her nose, her forehead, and finally the sensitive hollow of her neck. He lingered there, suckling gently while his hands went to work on the front of her gown. Her own hands streaked between their bodies to tug the bottom of his shirt from his breeches.

Her stomacher dropped to the floor as she worked the shirt up his torso, his bare flesh warm against her questing palms. She yanked the shirt over his

head, and he gave a frustrated laugh when his arms
tangled in the full-blown sleeves.

Soon their clothes were gone, and she plastered
herself against him. Ah, the give and the take, the
heat and the scent, the pure pleasure of his skin
touching hers. He bent his head to take her mouth,
running his hands down her sides and around to cup
her bottom and pull her closer still. At the intimate
contact, she felt a jolt, a flood of excitement that at
the same time made her feel heavy and lethargic. Her
body trembled. He smelled of soap and sandalwood,
and she couldn't tell where he stopped and she
started. If he wasn't holding her up, she would melt
to the floor in a puddle of sensation.

Slowly he backed her up and eased her onto the
bed, coming down beside her. He hesitated, levering
up on an elbow, his head hovering above hers. Beneath his shining gold hair, his eyes caught and held
her gaze. The faint blond stubble on his chin glistened in the candlelight. Her heart pounded, and her
breath came ragged and uneven. Every fiber of her
being ached for his touch, screamed for release. She
turned, reaching to pull him close.

The air was rent by a strangled groan.

"I cannot do this," he gritted out, then rolled away.
"I cannot do this. I cannot do this with my mother
lying in a box downstairs."

She felt an instant of stunned disappointment before her head cleared and her arms went around him
anyway. She squeezed tight. " 'Tis all right. I understand."

"I'm sorry," he whispered. "I just cannot—"

"Hush," she said. Slowly she drew air into her

lungs, to give herself time to adjust, time for her body to recover. "There is nothing to be sorry for."

She sat and pulled the coverlet over them both, then lay back down. With a regretful sigh, he turned to face her and gathered her close, his hand warm against her bare back, his head heavy against her shoulder. "I'm sorry," he whispered once more.

And long minutes later, when her heart had calmed, for the second night in a row, she fell asleep in his arms.

Still wide awake an hour later, Trick eased away from Kendra and slid from the bed. Quietly he drew on his breeches and pulled his shirt back over his head, then lit a candle and slipped from the bedchamber, softly closing the door behind him.

The stone steps felt cold and rough beneath his bare feet as he trod carefully down them. A low murmur of voices drifted up the stairs. Arriving on the lower level, he stopped and stared.

Annag and Niall sat before his mother's coffin. Behind it, Duncan hid, manipulating a clever arrangement of twine and twigs. A deep, unearthly "Oooooooh" issued from his throat as he twisted his hands. Elspeth's body jumped and twitched, and Annag jumped and screeched. Rising to his feet, Duncan burst into laughter, lifting a glass of whisky in a clearly drunken toast.

Trick couldn't believe his eyes.

Niall caught his gaze and offered a small smile. He rose and came to meet him at the bottom of the stairs. "Could ye not sleep?"

"I kept thinking of her lying down here. Cold, in a box." Trick ran a shaky hand back through his hair.

"It seems so unreal. I thought I could just sneak down here and . . . convince myself, mayhap. Sit here a while."

Niall nodded slowly, then turned to his half-siblings and raised his voice. "Give us peace, will ye? Go on to bed. We'll sit with Mam alone." Still laughing, they staggered out, taking a bottle of spirits and their glasses along with them.

The candles surrounding Elspeth's casket flickered in their wake. "Why were they sitting with her?" Trick asked after they'd stumbled out of earshot. " 'Tis plain as anything they held her in no esteem."

"Da wouldn't like to hear they've been shirking their duty. Mam must never be left alone—they say that a corpse left alone will find the road to hell."

Knowing his mother's history, Trick imagined Hamish and Niall *would* worry about her finding the road to hell. He went to the coffin and set the candle he was carrying beside the others, averting his gaze from his mother's waxen face. "I feel like I should be able to talk to her. I came all the way from England to talk to her."

"Ye can."

He sighed, wishing he had some of his brother's calm confidence—wishing he knew where to start. Owing to Duncan's prank, Elspeth's hands were no longer neatly crossed on her chest. Wincing at the sight of the twine still attached, he began to reach, then stopped. "Fix her, will you?" he asked in a voice rough with frustration. "Get that off her."

While Niall gently did as he asked, Trick dropped into a chair, staring blindly ahead. "I would think you'd rather sit by yourself than with those two. Especially considering they accord her no respect. I cannot believe what I saw when I walked in here."

"I cannot sit alone—there must always be two on guard." Niall took the seat next to him. "And a good prank at a wake is often enjoyed, even encouraged. Ye dinna ken our ways here, Patrick. Even though ye were born within these walls."

"You've the right of it there," Trick sighed. He'd never felt very English, but he didn't feel Scottish, either. He only felt confused.

"What did ye want to say to her?" Niall asked. "Ye can say it, ye ken. Out loud, or in your head. Either way, she will hear ye."

"Think you so?" He turned to stare at his brother. "You are young yet, but wise. Did you know that?"

Niall broke into a grin—straight, white, and as familiar as the one Trick saw in the mirror when he was shaving, except none of his brother's teeth were chipped. "I dinna think Annag would agree."

"Nay, I expect she wouldn't. How do you put up with those two?"

The younger man gave a sheepish shrug. "They're not as bad as they seem. I grew up with them, ye ken? It takes two to fight."

"And you refuse to participate."

"More or less. Of course, once in a while . . ." The engaging grin reappeared before he sobered. "Annag . . . well, her husband's dead these two years past. And her with three bairns on her own . . . She wasn't always so bitter."

He hadn't realized she was widowed. "And Duncan?"

"He's never wed—no sane woman would have the bastard." Niall scrubbed his hands hard over his face, then blinked and looked at Trick. "The three days of keening have passed, but if you've no words for Mam, perhaps the traditional ones would help."

Trick knew little of this land's traditions. "I'm listening."

Now that the rowdy mourners had gone home to bed, the Great Hall seemed larger, yawning huge and dark, much more like Trick had remembered. Niall took a deep breath, then his voice rose in song—not the mournful, haunting wail that Trick had imagined a keening would be, but a heartfelt, melodic lament that echoed off the vaulted stone ceiling. "Oh, Mother, ye have left us! *Ochone!*"

He paused and looked at Trick, his golden eyes expectant.

"*Ochone?* Is that some pagan god?"

"Nay, 'tis Gaelic. Nothing more than an expression of sorrow or regret."

"*Ochone,*" Trick said softly, expecting to feel silly. But he didn't. Sharing the sitting duty with his brother, keening their mother together, felt right.

"Why did ye leave us? *Ochone!* What did we do to ye? *Ochone!* That ye went away from us?"

"*Ochone!*" Trick sang for him.

" 'Tis ye that had plenty!"

"*Ochone!*"

"And why did ye leave us?"

"*Ochone! Ochone! Ochone!*" The ancient syllables slipped through Trick's lips, and some of the pain along with them.

Chapter Fifteen

When dawn had broken, Trick made his way upstairs to find a woman in his room, her back to him as she stoked the fire on the ancient, blackened stone hearth. At the sound of him entering, she slowly straightened and turned.

He gasped. "Mrs. Ross?"

"Aye, it be me," the tiny woman said in a reedy voice, coming closer. She was shorter than he remembered, but of course he'd last seen her through the eyes of a child. Her face was even more wrinkled, if that were possible, her blue eyes faded but glittering the same as they always had. "Why, I'd recognize ye anywhere, even after all these years. Patrick, dear, how fare ye?"

"I am well." The door banged louder than he would have liked when he shut it behind him, and in the bed, Kendra stirred. "How are *you*?" he asked Mrs. Ross. Sweet Mary, the woman must be eighty years old.

"No complaints. But your mam . . ." The blue eyes flooded with tears. "I dinna ken what happened. 'Twas so fast . . ."

"Trick?" Kendra blinked herself awake. At the sight of a stranger in the room, she clutched the blanket over her naked shoulders and tucked it under her chin.

"My wife, the Duchess of Amberley," Trick introduced her. Smiling to himself, he walked over to smooth her sleep-mussed hair. "Good morning, *leannan*. No need to blush—'tis only Mrs. Ross, my old nurse."

"And his mam's before him," the older woman added.

"I haven't thought of her as Mam in eighteen years," he murmured. "She's Mother to me now."

Mrs. Ross's thin, bluish lips straightened into a disapproving line. "She was never Mother to ye, and well ye know it. She was much warmer than that. And why did ye not write her, aye?" Her expression hardening, the bird-like woman came near and whacked him on the shoulder, although not without a modicum of affection. "Eighteen years and ye never once answered one of that poor woman's letters."

Trick rubbed his shoulder. "What the hell are you talking about? She never sent me a letter."

"The devil she didn't. She cried for weeks after your father dragged ye away, then she started writin' the letters—"

"I never received any letters," Trick insisted.

But Mrs. Ross wasn't listening. "—every week at first, then every month, and then, when she never heard back, once a year. Until finally she gave up. Ye broke her heart, Patrick Iain. I kent ye were a bairn yet, but I thought I'd taught ye better—"

"Mrs. Ross!"

The woman jumped and started twittering, and Kendra clapped her hands over her ears, her eyes wide as round portholes. He waited until his old nurse quieted before continuing. "I never received her letters. Did you hear me, Mrs. Ross? I *never* received her letters. Not one."

She froze, studying him for a long moment. "Did he keep them from ye, then?" she whispered and burst into tears.

He gathered her fragile frame into his arms. "There, Mrs. Ross. I know you miss her." Patting her on the back, he silently cursed his father—the blackguard—for hiding the mail. And himself, for never considering the possibility. "Mother wouldn't want you to be sad."

"Your mam was like a daughter to me." She raised her tear-stained face. "A woman isna supposed to outlive her children."

He pulled back and nodded, and they gazed at each other until Kendra shifted on the bed and cleared her throat. "What was she like, Mrs. Ross?"

The old nurse dashed the tears from her wrinkled cheeks and sat herself down. The bulky oak armchair dwarfed her. "She was good. A good woman, Elspeth. She had no easy life."

Kendra slanted Trick a glance, knowing he didn't want to hear this, but also knowing he should. "How is it she came to marry the duke?"

"*Him.*" The woman looked like she wanted to spit. "King Charles—the first one—arranged the match. Part of his plan to Anglicize Scotland." She twisted her bony fingers in lap, her voice going softer, as though it were coming from far away. "And my poor Elspeth was so in love with . . . But her father had never liked Hamish Munroe. Too common for his tastes. A third son, and a businessman besides, buying flax for the weaving and then selling the cloth. He made a fine living, but Elspeth's father was the laird, ye ken, and he expected better for his daughter. The Stuarts had made him an earl, but that didn't make him English."

"Of course not," Kendra said gently, noting that Trick seemed to be studying his bare toes. "My husband told me his grandfather signed the Covenant."

"Aye, the old earl was a bit of a rebel. 'Tis in the blood. But still and all, he was happy enough when the King matched his daughter with a duke. He forced poor Elspeth into it."

Thinking of her own forced marriage, Kendra bit the inside of her cheek. "How?"

"Ye dinna want to know." The nurse's lips pressed tight, and Kendra knew that her brothers' matchmaking had been nothing like Trick's grandfather's. Unlike Elspeth, deep down she knew that a tiny part of her had *wanted* to wed Trick. And she also knew that her brothers wouldn't have pushed her into the marriage if that hadn't been so.

"She was unhappy all her days," Mrs. Ross continued. "Even after the duke left her alone to reclaim her lost love, she never recovered from the loss of her son." She brushed at her gray skirts and stood. "Well, I'd best be off about my duties. Welcome to Duncraven, Duchess."

"My pleasure. I hope we can talk more later."

"Aye, we can. After we bury my Elspeth." With a long, miserable sniff and a swish of her skirts, she sailed from the room.

Kendra waited until the door clicked closed behind her, then released a heartfelt sigh. "Oh, how terribly romantic. Does it not give you the shivers?"

"Does what not give me the shivers?" Trick opened a cabinet and started pulling out clean clothes.

"Thinking about Elspeth and Hamish, in love all those years. And finally getting to be together." While his back was safely turned, she slid from between the sheets and hurried into her chemise. Relieved, she made her way over to look for a suitable gown to wear to a burial. She wondered what would be an appropriate way to wear her hair. She would have to send for Jane to come up and style it. "Now that I've heard your mother and Hamish's story, I'm so glad she invited him to live with her here. Maybe they found a bit of happiness, after all."

"Mayhap my mother sent me letters. But that didn't make her a good woman." He shook out a shirt, then stripped off the one he was wearing, a long pull of his muscles as he drew it over his head. Kendra watched, enjoying the view more than she'd be willing to admit. "She was still an adulteress, and a Covenanter, and she betrayed—"

"Did you not hear a word your nurse said about what happened between her and Hamish?" Pulling out a forest-green dress, she sighed and held it up. "This is the darkest thing I brought. Do you suppose I'll be scorned for not wearing black?" She turned it around and frowned at the low, scooped neckline. "What will Hamish think? I noticed yesterday that the women here wear more on top."

He blinked at her. "Your top looks fine to me. Niall knows you didn't come here expecting to attend a funeral. And I cannot imagine why you'd care what anyone else thinks. Hamish, especially." He put on the clean shirt, then began to unlace his breeches. "I feel sorry for the old man, but that doesn't mean I like him. He lived in sin with my mother—"

"I suppose, then, that you've never bedded a woman without the benefit of wedlock."

His long fingers fumbled on the laces. "Will you stop interrupting me every time I try to make a point?"

Ignoring that request, she stared at him a long moment, until he lifted his head to meet her gaze. "Well?" she pushed.

"You know very well I was experienced when I took you to my bed." Clearly fuming, he remained silent while he hopped on one foot and then the other to remove the breeches. Half-annoyed, half-amused, her gaze followed the breeches down, but his long shirt covered the interesting parts. She blushed when he caught her looking, but he only crossed his arms and leveled her with a glare so fierce that, had he been a Gorgon, she would surely have turned to stone. "I've already told you I don't hold with infidelity. I've never slept with a married woman."

"Congratulations. You're probably the only male member of Charles's Court who can say so." She dropped the green gown over her head and wiggled it into place. "Hamish and your mother were victims, Trick. They shared a love that lasted decades—a love the thought of which melts me inside. A perfect love, like my own parents'." Threading the laces across her bodice, she looked up. "How can you think to deny them what little happiness they found?"

" 'Tis not up to me to deny or allow it, is it? What's done is done. That doesn't mean I have to like it. Or them." A knock came at the door, and she yanked her laces tight and reached for her stomacher while he stomped over to answer it. "What now?"

Dressed in a red kilt, Niall took a startled step back. He turned to leave, taking with him an armful of matching plaid wool.

Trick reached to grab his elbow. "Forgive me, Niall. I thought you were Mrs. Ross. Not that I should have been barking at her, either." He blew out a breath before turning to face Kendra. "And I'm sorry I was so short-tempered with you."

"I understand," she said softly. The stomacher safely attached, she smoothed her skirts and put a hand to her disheveled hair.

Niall didn't seem to notice it, however. "Patrick didn't get any sleep," he told her.

"Did you not?" She cocked her head at her husband speculatively. "Any at all?"

"Nay. Niall and I stayed up with Mam." Kendra thought she caught a look of surprise when he heard his own use of the name. "We did some keening."

"Did you?" She couldn't imagine.

"Ochone!" Trick sang, the word vibrating up to the beamed ceiling, and Niall laughed, breaking the tension. "Come in," her husband said, closing the door behind his brother.

Niall aimed a glance at Trick's bare legs and then held out the length of red tartan. "I've brought ye this."

Trick made no move to take it.

"I thought mayhap ye would like to wear it to the burial."

"My father wasn't Scottish."

"Your mother was." Niall pushed the woolen fabric into Trick's arms, along with a wide leather belt.

"Wear it in her honor. Just this once. She'd have been proud to see ye in it."

A long silence stretched between them while Trick shifted the cloth in his hands, a range of conflicting emotions playing across his face. "I know not how to wear it," he said finally.

His brother's smile managed to look sad, pleased, and relieved, all at the same time. "That I can help ye with." He placed the belt on the floor and crouched beside it, his own kilt skimming the wooden planks as he folded the plaid into pleats and arranged it on top of the leather. "Lie down on this," he instructed.

Trick's lips quirked. "You're jesting."

"Nay. The only way to get it on properly is to lie down."

Kendra squelched a laugh as her husband looked askance at his brother, then sighed and lowered his big frame to the floor.

"Nay, move up," Niall said. "The belt must be at your waist." After Trick scooted higher, his brother went about wrapping the pleated material around him and belting it securely. "Now ye can stand," he said, offering him a hand up.

Trick flexed his knees experimentally while Niall took the large expanse of fabric above the belt and tucked it into the front, crisscrossing it to make what was essentially two big pockets. Then he drew up the extra cloth in back and draped it over Trick's shoulders.

Trick took a few steps, watching the kilt sway around his knees.

"Feels odd," he said. "What is worn underneath?"

Niall glanced down at his own kilt. "Nothing is

worn. Everything underneath is in good working order." He looked up with an engaging grin.

Kendra's gaze drifted over to her husband, who looked mildly scandalized. He also looked devastatingly handsome. Better even than he had in his black highwayman garb, or maybe it was just knowing there was nothing underneath. The very thought of that brought heat to her cheeks.

"Well?" Niall asked, and she glanced up to find both men's eyes on her. "How does he look?"

She felt her cheeks burn even hotter. "F-fine," she managed.

"I cannot wait to get it off," Trick grumbled.

Neither could she.

Led by a piper with a black pennant tied to his pipes, Trick and Niall headed the eight bearers carrying their mother's coffin from the castle down to the little kirk. Behind them, family, friends, and castle staff followed along in a rather informal procession.

"Why are there not more women?" Kendra asked in a low voice from where she walked beside Trick, modestly wrapped in a homely brown shawl she'd borrowed from Mrs. Ross. Her hair was constrained in a braided bun.

"Most of the women usually remain at the home," Niall explained. "They'll be preparing for the return of the mourners. And keeping my father company. 'Tis not customary for a husband to attend his wife's burial."

"And she was his wife in his heart, I'm sure of it." Her romantic sigh put Trick's teeth on edge. "Hamish couldn't have come along, anyway. Not in his state of health."

"Well, 'tis nice to know his illness isn't keeping him from something he'd regret missing later." Keeping her eyes on the piper's fluttering banner, she leaned close to Trick. "Hardly anyone is wearing black," she observed beneath her breath.

" 'Tis unnecessary to wear black in order to pay your respects," Niall said, obviously overhearing her. "Not everyone can afford special clothes for mourning."

After that, she kept quiet. The bagpipe music was loud, the notes sad and lingering. All too soon they were gathered in the small graveyard, and the solemn tune came to an end. The single wreath of heather was removed from atop the oak coffin, and the lid lifted for one last time.

Stepping closer, Trick peered inside, trying to memorize his mother's features and reconcile them with his faded childhood memories. Had she been the warm woman he sometimes saw in his dreams, or the cold one his father had told him about? What had they said, those letters he'd never been able to read? Had they been written out of duty, or had the pages been spattered with her tears?

Knowing this was his last chance, he reached to touch her.

Her body felt cold and unreal, and touching it did nothing to banish the ghosts of her from his mind, as Niall had said it was meant to do. A shiver ran through him. Their rocky past would always stand between him and what should be happy memories.

Others came forward to pay their respects and touch his mother, then two men moved to replace the lid. Trick bent down with it as it was lowered into place, catching a final glimpse of her face.

"Good-bye," he whispered, and Kendra squeezed

his hand. He hadn't even realized she'd been holding it.

A short service was read, but he never heard what was spoken. His mind was numb, the words filtered through a haze. He shuffled his feet on the soft green grass, his gaze wandering over the gentle mounds that marked where bodies lay, many of their headstones rendered smooth and unreadable by the ravages of weather and time. A bell was rung; then the mourners filed past the tree where it hung, dropping coins into the plate below as they went. Burial silver. For form's sake, he imagined—surely the Dowager Duchess of Amberley wouldn't need help to defray her funeral expenses.

Or would she? He admittedly knew nothing of his parents' financial arrangements. Upon his father's death, he'd clearly failed in his duty as a son. And now it was too late. He cursed himself roundly, if silently.

The mournful whine of the bagpipes rose again, and people began drifting out of the little cemetery. As he turned to leave, Kendra came around to face him and took both his hands. "I'm sorry," she whispered.

He shrugged. " 'Tis not that I'll miss her, precisely."

"But you'll miss what could have been."

She was wise, his new wife. Her fingers tightened on his; then she dropped his hands and turned to Niall. Without hesitation, Trick's brother walked into her arms and stayed there, his shoulders hitching while she murmured words of comfort. She was not only wise, Trick amended, but compassionate. She would make a good mother for their children. If only he could gain her trust.

But secrets stood between them, and 'twas not yet time for the truth.

At long last Niall pulled away and gave Kendra a shaky smile. "Thank ye."

"I'm your sister now," she said kindly. "And you've no one here, Niall. Your mother is gone, your father is ill, and your sister and brother—" She broke off. "I'm here for you."

"I'm here for you, too," Trick put in, surprised how good it felt to say that. To be needed by someone, and to need him, as well. He hadn't had that in eighteen years, and he'd never thought he'd have it again.

Despite all his father's tales of his mother's treason and treachery, he looked at the stoic backs of the people walking toward Duncraven and knew that once upon a time he'd felt happy in this place. Even living in that forbidding gray keep at the top of the hill.

And now here was a brother, needing him. And a wife, if only he could break down the barriers between them.

Clouds were gathering again, and the air held that elusive scent that meant wet weather was on the way. He pulled the wool tartan around his shoulders as they started following the others. "What happens now back at the castle?" Kendra asked.

"A *draidgie*," Niall said. "Entertainment, dancing, drinking, eating. Some tears and some merriment."

"More merriment?" She looked incredulous.

"To celebrate the life of the one who passed on. A

time to wish the departed spirit a safe landing on the other side."

She nodded, apparently accepting what Trick was coming to realize: Things were different here. Not bad or wrong, just different.

Still, they were both surprised at Niall's next words to Trick.

"Are ye ready for a good fight?"

Chapter Sixteen

Niall stomped into the Great Hall, stuck two fingers in his mouth, and let loose a loud, piercing whistle that had every head snapping in his direction. The jabbering tapered to an expectant silence.

He drew a deep breath and raised his voice. " 'Tis a sad day when my mother is put into the ground and not even one blow is struck at her funeral!" And without another word, he turned and slapped the nearest man.

Instantly, the chamber erupted in a free-for-all. Colorful tartans whirled in a blur. Food and drink went flying; trestle tables were overturned and chairs tossed aside. Along with the other women, Kendra backed against a wall, not caring that it was rough and probably grungy. She clutched Mrs. Ross's shawl to her chest, unable to believe her eyes. No fists were used, but the sounds of open-handed slaps rang in her ears as family and friends went at each other with enthusiasm.

She watched as Trick delivered a stinging slap to Duncan, who retaliated with a blow across the mouth that had her husband backhanding blood from his lips. But he flashed her a chipped-tooth grin, then pivoted on a heel and slapped a perfect stranger.

He looked to be enjoying himself immensely.

"Men," she muttered under her breath.

The woman beside her shook her head, her gray-brown braids swishing along with it. "I will never understand them."

"Ye want mine?" another one asked.

A good ten minutes went by before Niall decided enough violence had been done to pay the proper respect to his mother, and finally called for a truce.

Still grinning, Trick made his way over to Kendra. "Could you believe that?"

"No," she said flatly.

"Me, neither. I've never seen anything like it. But it felt good, ye ken?" He paused for a satisfying breath. "I was angry. I've been angry since I got here. I didn't want to come in the first place, then my mother was dead—"

"But you discovered a brother."

He rolled right over that. "It felt good to whack some people. Cleansing."

With a wry smile, she shook her head, and he smiled back, then winced and put a hand to his mouth. "Are you hurting?" she asked.

"Not enough to care." As if to prove it, he dragged her close and pressed his lips to hers. She tasted the faint coppery tang of blood, and then, as he opened his mouth, the warm, sweet slickness that she was learning to think of as Trick. Her hands went around him, sliding beneath the folds of his plaid to feel the planes of his back under his fine lawn shirt. He leaned into her, and she felt the clear evidence of his arousal through her skirts and the kilt. The kilt with nothing underneath.

The thought turned her legs to pudding, and she

sagged in his arms. "Is something amiss?" he asked
with a grin, setting her away. Her braided bun was
beginning to unravel, and he tucked a rogue strand
of hair behind her ear.

Mrs. Ross's shawl slipped from her shoulders to
the floor. "Goodness." She pressed her hand to her
racing heart as her gaze traced down his body. The
red kilt seemed rather primitive apparel, and it awakened a matching primitiveness inside her. She'd
never imagined a man's bare knees could be so
exciting.

She knelt to reclaim the shawl, sneaking a peek
beneath the tartan as she came back up, but 'twas
too dark under there to see anything. On this cloudy
day, the dozens of candles in the chandeliers overhead were all but useless against Duncraven's gloom.

Trick's lips quirked in a knowing smile as he took
the shawl from her and settled it back in place. "I
asked Niall what *leannan* means," he said.

"And?" She reached down, her fingers skimming
the kilt's hem.

"Sweetheart." He rubbed a gentle thumb beneath
her chin, then bent to brush a soft kiss across her
lips. "It means sweetheart."

Something went melty inside her. "I want to reach
under here," she whispered.

"Is that so?" Leaning closer to shield her from
view, he traced a finger down her throat and into
the low neckline of her very English dress. "We'll
have to accommodate you, then. But not here."

At the word "here," his expression sobered, as
though he'd just remembered what had happened
here today. He dropped his hand and smoothed
down the front of his kilt. "Sweet Mary, I'm tired."

"You didn't get any sleep."

He looked around the gathering. A few thoughtful souls were helping tidy the worst of the brawl's aftermath, but most folk were back to eating and downing spirits. Their chatter seemed to grow louder in proportion to the drink they consumed. "I think mayhap I'll lie down a spell."

"Shall I come with you?"

"Nay." He scrubbed his palms over his face, avoiding her gaze. "I'm really tired."

She tried to ignore the rush of disappointment. "Perhaps I'll go sit with Hamish a while."

"You do that. 'Tis a difficult day for him."

He started to leave, but she snagged him by the sleeve. " 'Tis a difficult day for you, too, Trick." When he shrugged and pulled away, she let him go.

"How is he doing, dearie?"

Startling from a doze when Rhona came into the room, Kendra bolted upright on her chair. "He slept the whole hour I was here." For the hundredth time since she'd entered the chamber, her gaze darted to the bed and she was relieved to see Hamish still breathing.

Rhona touched a hand to her shoulder. "I thank ye for the break. 'Twas a welcome respite."

"I can stay longer."

"Nay, ye run along now. Down at the *draidgie*, all the young people are telling ghost stories." The older woman took the second chair and settled to her embroidery.

Kendra slowly rose. "If you're sure, then."

At Rhona's nod, she slipped out the door and closed it quietly behind her. She didn't want to hear ghost stories—this bleak castle gave her shivers as it was. Deciding to check on her husband, she made her way up the dozens of winding stone stairs.

He wasn't in their chamber.

Someone had made their bed after they'd left, and 'twas clearly undisturbed. He hadn't come up to rest at all. Disappointed that he'd apparently fibbed to get away from her, she wandered to the room's only window, deep in an alcove set into the wall. Resting her palms on the cold stone sill, she leaned out and looked up at the sky.

Gray, to match her mood. The clouds were moving swiftly; rain was on the way. A blackbird fluttered from the heavens and down to the garden below, spreading its wings to make a graceful landing on a stone bench.

Right next to a figure clad in a bright red kilt.

He was hunched over something in his lap. Something white. Paper. The man who'd told her he never wrote anything was outside scribbling up a storm.

She hurried downstairs, huffing and puffing by the time she reached the bottom, and headed for the door.

Niall caught her on her way out. "Why such a rush, lass? Is something amiss?"

"N-no." Of course nothing was amiss—in the midst of catching her breath, Kendra wondered for a moment just exactly what she'd been rushing out to do. Yell at Trick for not taking a nap? Or for pouring his heart out on paper? He was a grown man, entitled to do as he pleased, especially on a disturbing day like this one.

She forced a smile for her brother-in-law. "Nothing

is wrong. I thought I'd just go out and take some air."

The bagpiper was warming up discordantly, and a fiddler was busy tuning. "The dancing is about to begin," Niall told her.

She looked around, noticing the tables and chairs had been pushed against the walls. "There is really going to be dancing?"

"Aye, there is. Mam would have expected us to celebrate her life rather than the death that ended it." The musicians launched into a jaunty tune, and Niall made an incongruously solemn bow. "Are ye dancin'?"

She could see that he was trying very hard to keep what he considered to be the proper *draidgie* outlook, although she was sure he ached deep inside. Her heart went out to him. No matter that dancing today seemed wrong to her, she dropped a curtsy and gave him the answer he was expecting.

"Are you asking?"

With a low laugh that reminded her of Trick's, he twirled her into the center of the room.

The dance was performed by four couples in a circle, and it took all of Kendra's concentration to follow it. Halfway through the complicated pattern, she was already breathless and realized she had little time to think on her troubles, and neither did Niall. Perhaps dancing on a day like this wasn't such a bad idea, after all.

When the tune ended, he took her by the elbow to draw her from the floor. "My father wants to talk to ye and your husband," he said conversationally.

Surprised she hadn't lost it, she resettled the shawl on her shoulders. "He's sleeping."

"Patrick?"

"No, Hamish. Trick is out in the garden."

"Ah, then 'twas him ye were rushing out to see." The music started again, and couples began forming a double line down the middle of the chamber. "Why d'ye call him Trick?" Niall asked.

"A childhood name. His father called him that."

"But Mam didn't." He sighed. "So much I dinna know about my brother."

"He doesn't know you, either. But he'd like to, I'm sure."

He gave her a sad, gentle smile. "He won't be staying long enough to get to know me."

"Not this time. But he'll be back. I'll make certain of it."

"Now, that I dinna doubt." The low laugh rang out again. "I saw ye two kissing earlier, and I'd wager ye could make him do anything."

She felt her face heat. She'd never thought of herself as a woman who could persuade with kisses. With words, yes—having been raised a Chase, she could argue with the best of them. But she'd never been much of a flirt, let alone a seductress.

Pleased at the thought, she grinned. "Thank you for the dance, Niall."

"My pleasure." The second dance was ending, but another would start soon. "Will you do me the honor again?"

"Maybe later. I've a man to meet in the garden." And hopefully persuade to open up and share himself with her . . . with kisses, if necessary.

"Trick."

Her voice was gentle, but he still startled, quickly

flipping the paper facedown on the bench beside him. He'd been so entrenched in his thoughts, he hadn't even heard her approach.

Her soft sigh belied her smile. "You shouldn't chew on your quill."

He swept it from his mouth. "I know," he agreed shortly, helpless to stop the annoyance he felt at being caught writing—something he'd hidden all his life. He took a calming breath. " 'Tis how I chipped my tooth. What are you doing out here?"

"What are *you* doing out here?"

"Nothing." Fiddling with the quill in his hands, he looked up at the sky. "I couldn't sleep."

"Did you try to sleep?"

He was silent a few beats before dropping his gaze to meet hers. "Not really. I . . . I was writing." Silly that it seemed hard to admit, but there was no point in lying, seeing as she'd found him in the act.

Her expression seemed wary, reserved; then her gaze went to his kilt and she licked her lips. Remembering her earlier words, he bit back a smile as she met his eyes. Her cheeks flushed a delicate pink. "May I read some of what you wrote?"

His hand moved protectively to the thin stack of paper. "Why would you want to?"

"What you write is part of you, Trick." True, but not the best part. What spilled out onto paper was often the parts of him he didn't like. "Is it poetry?" she asked.

"Aye. It's just poetry. Pretty words that sound good together. Meaningless."

" 'Twould not be meaningless to me."

Hurt dulled her eyes, and he looked away, wishing he had it in him to give her what she wanted. Rolling the sheets into a narrow tube, he tucked it into the pocketed front of his kilt. "Come, let us walk. The garden is quite whimsical."

He took her down a path where dozens of tiny model castles nestled in the shrubbery on either side. "The castle garden," she said with a smile, brightening with a determination that didn't fool him. "How very clever."

" 'Twas my mother's doing. When I was a lad, she spent hours out here every summer. And when winter kept her inside, she designed and built the little castles. Sometimes she let me help." Their footsteps crunched on the gravel path. "Of course, Father thought it a waste of time."

"What did he want her to be doing instead?"

"I know not." He'd never wanted to know; it had felt safer not to. "I was but a child, and I never did understand them or the way they were together."

"Was he a difficult man to live with, your father?"

"Difficult" didn't even begin to describe the late Duke of Amberley, but Trick didn't have the energy to go into it. Or the will. "I cannot say what living with him was like for her, but for me, 'twas a living hell."

She slipped her hand into his. "He had high expectations for you, did he?"

"No. At least not in the way you're thinking." He felt as tired as he knew his voice sounded, drained and numb. "I was naught but a means to an end. A pawn in his game. 'Tis safer to send a child to do the dangerous work, you see. Nobody would expect a child to be smuggling goods in his clothing. Nor would they see a child alone on a hill with a lantern, night after long, cold night, and suspect he was there to signal in ships."

"He had you do those things?"

"Those are the tamer examples." Her question sounded so innocent, the sympathy in her eyes so acute, he couldn't bring himself to burst her naïve bubble with any details.

"And when you were older?"

"He found different ways of using me." He stopped on the path. There were some things best unremembered. "Must we talk about this now?"

There was a long pause while she seemed to come to a decision. "No, of course not," she said with a smile he suspected was forced. "Your mother's castle garden is charming. 'Tis quite secluded back here, is it not?"

"Aye, it is that." The trees made a leafy avenue, shielding them from prying eyes. "No one has ventured back here for an hour or more."

"Hmm . . ." she said speculatively, the smile turning real.

"Hmm? What have you in mind?"

"Only this." And she backed him against a poplar, leaning up on her toes to crush her mouth to his.

After a stunned moment, he responded, gathering her into his arms, letting her lips and body comfort him the way words never could. She'd rejected him for so long that he found himself wallowing in her sudden acceptance. Her soft fragrance surrounded him, more potent than aged whisky.

A long, intense minute later, he drew his head to the side, still holding her close. "You've never kissed me first before. What's gotten into you, *leannan*?"

Silent save for the uneven sound of her breathing,

she searched his eyes. The wind came up, sending the poplar's white-bottomed leaves into a silvery dance, and she leaned back in his arms. " 'Tis this kilt, Trick. It drives me wild."

Though he was sure 'twas something more than that, he grinned and tucked a loose curl behind her ear. "I will have to ask Niall if I can keep it."

"The idea is not displeasing."

"But only if you kiss me again," he added, then lowered his mouth to hers before she had a chance.

This new passion of hers made him desperate and demanding. His tongue swept her mouth again and again, as though he were trying to lose himself in it. She leaned against his chest, slipping her hands under the plaid to rest against his shirt. Beneath her fingertips, he knew the beat of his heart matched hers that he could feel through her gown. Frantic.

Pulling away, he leaned his forehead hard against hers. "Is this wrong?" he asked in a whisper. A strangled whisper, because he knew the answer.

Another gust of wind sent the brown shawl flying, but she let it go. "No, of course it's not wrong." Mere inches away, her eyes looked confused. "We're married, Trick."

"That was not what I meant." How the hell could he keep her at arm's length for the sake of respect, when after all these weeks she'd finally come around? He wanted her to understand. He wanted to understand, himself. "I buried my mother today. And now I want . . . I want only to be with you. To have you. As though her death, her life, didn't matter."

"Of course it mattered." Her fingers clenched on his shoulders; her eyes cleared of the confusion and filled with concern instead. " 'Tis natural, Trick. To want to reach out, reconnect. With people, with living. Like the *draidgie*, don't you see? Niall said it was to celebrate your mother's life, rather than dwelling on the death that ended it. It cannot be wrong."

She made a sort of sense, and he wanted to be convinced. Powerless to resist, when she touched her lips to his, his shoulders relaxed under her fingertips. The kiss turned from sweet to devouring, and for a long, euphoric minute, Kendra was the center of his world. The only person, it seemed, who had ever really cared.

"I dinna deserve you," he whispered, wondering when this would end. Because everything good in his life always did.

A soft smile on her lips, she went on tiptoe to kiss him again.

"Patrick! Kendra!" Niall's voice slashed through the leaves overhead.

Trick tightened his hold around her waist. "What does he want?" he muttered against her mouth. When his brother appeared on the tree-lined path, he dropped his arms and groaned.

"Da is awake," Niall said. "And this seems to be one of his good days. He wants to talk to ye both."

"Elspeth wasn't dying," Hamish said, still in bed, but sitting up for the first time since Kendra had met him. "When she wrote that letter, she was in perfect health."

His voice was strong and sure, and Kendra hoped that meant he was getting better. "Perhaps she was already ill but didn't want to tell you."

"Nay, lass. Elspeth and I kept no secrets."

A look of disbelief crossed Trick's face. Seated in the chair beside him, she took his hand and squeezed, feeling tension coursing through him. He didn't want to be here, talking about this. He wanted to be back in the garden. He'd grumbled as much to her three times on their long trek up the stairs.

"Why, then?" he demanded. "Why would she have written saying she was dying if she wasn't?"

"She wanted to see you," Hamish said simply. "She was hoping the thought of her death would bring ye here to Duncraven, even though you'd never answered any of her other letters."

Trick set down the goblet of whisky he'd snatched in the Great Hall and brought along with him upstairs. "I never received any of her other letters."

"So Mrs. Ross informed me quite tearfully this morning."

"But you didn't believe her."

Hamish blinked. "Of course I believed her. What makes ye imagine I'd think the worst of ye, Patrick? If ye say ye never received the letters, I take ye at your word."

A faint pink stained Trick's neck. "My father must have intercepted them."

"Your father . . ." Hamish's fingers tapped an irritated tattoo on the coverlet. "I wouldn't put it past him, I can tell ye that."

"I assure you, sir, I didn't hold him in any higher esteem than you did."

Sitting on the bed beside his father, Niall sipped from his own glass of spirits. "Da, d'ye not think ye should tell Patrick why Mam summoned him?"

Trick's gaze snapped to his brother's. "Did she not

just want to see me, then? Had she a specific reason?''

"Aye," Hamish said, "and 'tis a long story. A story about the first King Charles and his ill-fated visit here to Scotland."

"What could that have to do with—"

"Just listen." Looking toward the closed door to ensure their privacy, Hamish settled back against his pillows for the telling. "Charles was born here, ye ken, but left when he was yet a bairn, and we Scots heard tell he rather fancied himself an Englishman." He took a small sip of the green concoction Rhona had left him, then grimaced and held out a hand for Niall's drink. "Still and all, Charles was our king—a Scottish king. The nobles insisted on a second corona-tion, on Scottish land with the Scottish crown jewels. Thirty-five years ago, in the eighth year of his reign, he finally assented to the visit."

Intrigued, Kendra leaned forward. "Had he not been home in all that time?"

"He didn't think of it as home, as you will soon see." Hamish drank, closing his eyes for a moment in contentment as the whisky slipped down his throat. "Excitement was rampant," he said after smacking his lips. "Everyone threw themselves into the prepa-rations. Roads were fixed and bridges were repaired. Thatched roofs were replaced with shingles, lest the King should think us poor. All in all, a great deal of money was paid out to improve and decorate the Royal route and show we were as good as the En-glish. We hoped to appeal to his Scottishness, so he'd let up on us and allow us to live as we saw fit."

He paused for another sip. "But it soon became clear that he wanted to forget his origins. He arrived here for a month-long tour with a baggage train two miles long. Fifty wagons, two bishops, dozens of courtiers. Along the way, they stopped to lodge with our Scottish nobles, bankrupting them one by one. On a whim, Charles would change his itinerary, bypassing the places that had been so carefully prepared and making it clear he wasn't impressed with the preparations anyway. He treated us like lessers when we hoped he'd relate to us as the Scot he was by birth."

Trick's thumb kept teasing the palm of Kendra's hand, and his lips quirked when she shivered in response. He didn't seem to be paying attention at all. Although Niall's eyes sparkled with amusement, thankfully Hamish wasn't watching.

"When the coronation finally took place, 'twas not the traditional Scots one that had been planned, but an elaborate religious ceremony instead. A Church of England ritual, and the people were aghast to learn such Popishness and blasphemy had taken place in one of our own kirks."

Apparently listening more than she'd guessed, Trick grimaced. "I expect they were angry as hell."

The older man nodded. "His actions started a rebellion that eventually led to his end. But I get ahead of myself." He wetted his papery lips. "After the coronation, his last scheduled stop was at nearby Falkland Palace. All the local nobles were invited, and your mother went, of course, along with her family. Every able-bodied commoner was drafted to help with the elaborate banquet, myself among them, although I was not even Niall's age as yet. We all thought the banquet a roaring success, the entertainment more impressive than ever we had seen. But by then Charles had tired of Scotland—no doubt as much as we had tired of him—and at three the next morning, he woke the household and announced that he'd decided to leave immediately. Everyone at Falkland scrambled to ready his belongings for travel."

"What sorts of belongings?" Kendra asked, pulling her fingers from Trick's. She folded her hands, but Trick reached over and untangled them, moving one to rest on his lap and trapping it there with his own hand on top. Scandalized, she glanced at Niall, but he was studiously looking elsewhere.

She couldn't help thinking what was beneath that fabric under her hand. Nothing.

"Ye wouldn't have believed what he'd brought along," Hamish was saying, his gaze glazed with memory. "My eyes boggled, they did. Besides clothing and furnishings fit for a palace—he slept in his own Royal bed—King Charles traveled with his household goods, personal treasures, jewelry, and his entire kitchen, including the Royal plate. Half a ton of silver and gold. Not for him to be eating off plain Scottish dishes or drinking from plain Scottish cups. Nay . . . he and his courtiers dined on the Royal plate, and 'twas this we were ordered to help pack up for his return to London."

Beneath Kendra's hand, Trick stirred, and her palm tingled. "It must have taken you all night."

"The smells of the banquet still hung in the air, and we had but a few hours. Charles couldn't wait to leave. At first light, he set out as quickly as he could. On the journey up they had crossed the River Forth by the bridge at Stirling, but this day the King was too impatient to take the long way around. His men found three boats to cross the firth from Burntisland to Leith and loaded two of them with as much as they possibly could. When it wouldn't all fit, Charles insisted the rest be loaded anyway, 'til everything was aboard and the ferries rode low in the water."

Trick frowned and shifted, draping an arm across Kendra's shoulders. "Were you there to see it?"

"Nay, but stories have been told. 'Twas storming something awful, that I do remember. The wind blew stronger and stronger as they piled the treasure aboard, the waves tossing it to and fro. King Charles was rowed to the third ship while his domestics and servants went with his goods. Twenty-five people on one of those boats . . . and only two lived to tell what had happened."

"What happened?" Kendra wondered, knowing the answer couldn't be good.

"The rest of them went to the bottom of the Firth of Forth, along with the treasure. Safe aboard the other ship, Charles could see the ferry founder and sink, but there was nothing he could do to stop it."

A chilling vision. Despite her resolve and Niall's knowing gaze, Kendra leaned against Trick's side. He was so very warm. "Charles must have been furious."

"Aye, that he was. Folk claimed the sinking was an act of God to avenge his religious misdeeds, but he decided that witches were responsible. And he rounded up people to punish. 'Twas injustice of this sort that led to our siding with the Roundheads in the Civil War, wrong though we were to do so."

Trick's fingers traced lazy circles on her shoulder, and her free hand fisted in her lap. The one on *his* lap felt hot against the wool. Keeping her face passive, she nodded at Hamish. "Were the goods ever recovered?"

"Nay, lass, for the Forth is cold and deep. The chests lie there in its bottom to this day." He drew a long breath, briefly closing his eyes. Eyes that looked familiar, Kendra thought suddenly, wondering why.

"But the treasure," the man said in a tone both deep and significant, "is not in those chests."

Trick's hand stilled on her shoulder. "Pardon?" Beneath his golden hair, his brow knitted. He reached for the goblet beside him.

"The people were angry, ye ken, even before the witch hunt. Your mother stole from her chamber that night and met me in the storeroom along with Rhona and Gregor—the four of us were best of friends, even then. The Yeoman of the Buttery had been charged with packing the kitchen, which included the Royal plate. John Ferries was his name. Shorthanded, he was, and willing to accept whatever help he could find. So we helped."

He fell silent.

Niall put a hand over his father's atop the coverlet. "Tell them how ye helped, Da."

Hamish sighed. "First we helped get John Ferries drunk. Then we helped pack the chests, but not with gold and silver plate . . ." He drew a long breath, a dramatic pause. "With rocks."

Trick choked on a sip of his spirits. "Rocks?" he repeated incredulously.

"Aye." Shifting in the bed, Hamish looked less than proud of what he'd done. "The treasure we spirited away. It all remains hidden to this day."

"Where?" Kendra breathed.

"If you're willing, I will send Niall to show ye. First thing tomorrow."

Trick failed to see the point. Intriguing as the story might be, he was planning to leave for home tomorrow to finish the King's mission. And to make a fresh start with Kendra. He gave her hand in his lap an experimental squeeze, smiling to himself when the pulse at her wrist sped up. Sweet Mary, she set his blood on fire.

His goblet hit the table beside him with more force than he had intended. " 'Tis an interesting tale, but what does this have to do with my mother's summons?"

"She hoped—we hoped—that you'd return the treasure to its rightful owner. King Charles II."

Disappointment scraped a raw place inside him. His mother hadn't been wishing for a reconciliation. Like his father, she'd only wanted to use him for her own ends.

"They haven't so much as sold one piece," Niall put in, a transparent attempt to make light of his parents' wrongdoing. " 'Tis been locked in twenty-three chests for thirty-five years."

Hamish nodded. "We're a poor country. If anything so rich as that treasure had ever shown up in Scotland, questions would have been raised. But ye must believe me, we didn't take it to gain wealth. 'Twas a prank, an act of revenge. We were young enough—angry enough—to risk such folly. And although we were fortunate that our rocks sank and were never discovered, and poor John Ferries's body washed up on shore sometime later, the episode has preyed on our minds ever since."

It would, Trick supposed. But the fate of his mother's soul was in God's hands now, and he wasn't responsible for relieving this old man's conscience. Without Hamish's influence, perhaps Elspeth would have come to love her husband, or at least learned to live with him, and Trick would have had a family.

He owed this old man nothing.

Hamish took a long, bracing sip. "Charles was beheaded—he paid for his actions. His son is a better man, a better king. We dinna really want the treasure—we never did. But your mother feared that if we returned it, we'd face arrest. So she was hoping you'd do it for us. King Charles admires and trusts ye—"

"How would you know that?"

"D'ye think your own mother wouldn't keep watch on ye the best she could? We—she hired people to report to her. If ever you'd really needed her, Patrick, she'd have been there."

He *had* really needed her. The times he'd been left alone in a school in France, and the other times, the endless years he'd worked as little more than a slave for his father's illicit business.

But that was past and done. He'd long ago accepted the hand he'd been dealt, and the heaviness in his chest was naught but a moment's weakness. There were matters that needed his attention.

King Charles deserved the Royal treasure—God knew he needed it. The poor man was reduced to selling titles to make expenses. Even now, his ambassadors were roaming the country with blank forms to be filled out by anyone wanting and willing to pay for a baronetcy. Regardless of whether this old man deserved his loyalty, Trick couldn't argue that his monarch did.

Charles. His life these days seemed to be reduced to serving Charles.

"I'll do it," he said with a resigned sigh. "Show me the chests tomorrow, and I'll make plans to get them home."

Chapter Seventeen

They barely got out of Hamish's room before Trick started muttering. "If I'm going to lug this treasure home," he grumbled on the way down the stairs, "I need to make plans."

All the sensual feelings between them seemed to have vanished into thin air. Behind him in the dark, narrow turret, Kendra put a hand on his shoulder. "What is it you have to do? Maybe I can help."

"I must see these twenty-three chests and decide how many extra vehicles will be needed to transport them, how many additional guards I must hire. And what am I going to do with it all during overnight stops? We'll attract attention traveling through the country with an entourage worthy of royalty. 'Twill have to be protected around the clock."

"We'll work it out," she soothed. "Let us see the treasure first—then we'll deal with the logistics."

"My head aches just thinking about it."

"Perhaps 'twould be best to dispatch a messenger to Charles. He could send a contingent of soldiers to escort the goods."

"And wait here, twiddling my thumbs, for three weeks or more until the soldiers arrive? I think not."

They arrived downstairs to find that the dancing

had ended and the trestle tables were back in place. Torches had been lit on the walls to augment the light from the iron chandeliers, and women bustled about, setting out all the dishes they'd brought for the *draidgie* supper.

Trick handed Kendra a trencher from a stack on one end of a table, then took one for himself. The food smelled delicious, but he was in a devil of a mood, and the offerings he piled on his platter didn't seem to help any. Odd, he was, for a man. She thought about that as she chose a piece of spice cake and a wedge of lemon tart. Her brothers had never failed to be cheered by a hearty plate of food.

Niall waved them over to join him at an empty table, filling two more goblets with ale from a pitcher. They'd no sooner settled themselves than Annag and Duncan dragged her young ones over to take the remaining seats.

"What did Da want with ye?" Annag demanded, waving a girl into a chair and plopping a runny-nosed toddler beside her.

Niall scooped up a spoonful of carrots. "Nothing of your concern."

Duncan sat, lowering his trencher to the table with a thud. "Did he not tell ye of a new will, then?" he asked in a voice pitched to sound casual.

"No," Trick said flatly. He cut a hunk of mutton with more vigor than was strictly necessary.

"Here, Alastair." Annag shoved a dish of hoch-poch in front of another of her children, a boy who seemed to have a sneer to match hers. "Are ye certain there was no mention of a will?"

"Aye." Niall reached for some bread. "And Da seems to be gaining strength. So whatever it is you're hoping to gain from his will, ye shouldn't be expecting it anytime soon."

Kendra thought Annag's affronted look was less than convincing. "I'm not wanting Da to die, ye eejit."

"But now that *he's* shown up, a duke and all"— Duncan slanted a none-too-friendly glance at Trick before focusing back on Niall—"you'll not be needing any of Da's paltry holdings. With a new brother to provide for ye."

Niall's mouth opened and closed like a salmon out of water.

Kendra saw Trick's jaw set before he pointed his knife at Duncan. "What makes you so certain I'm willing to provide for Niall? I'd lay odds your father didn't jump to such a conclusion."

Duncan sipped from his ever-present whisky, glaring over the rim. "What know ye of our father?"

"Enough to suspect he'd not readily cut his youngest son out of his will." Trick met Duncan's glare with one of his own. "His *favorite* son."

Sensing violence about to erupt, Kendra bit the inside of her cheek. "Can we not all just be civil?"

Annag turned with a huff, her gaze narrowing with disdain on Kendra's low neckline. "Ye stay out of this."

"You will address my wife with respect," Trick said through gritted teeth. If Annag had been a man, he'd have been on her, Kendra thought, drawing the shawl tighter to cover the front of her gown. As it was, she could feel he was barely holding himself in check.

When Annag's son started crying, Duncan's face turned red to match. "Who needs this trouble?" he barked at Niall, half-rising out of his chair. "Ever since they've gotten here, I cannot have a word with ye without them sticking in their noses. Keep them out of our family business, or else—"

"Or else what?" Niall stood, his fists clenched at his sides. "I'm grown now, ye ken? Ye cannot beat me up anymore. I'll floor ye in a minute." 'Twas no idle threat. Niall topped the older man by a good four inches, and his youthful frame was hard and honed, while Duncan's was softened by sloth and drink.

Apparently not as dim-witted as he was surly, Duncan sat back down. "Just keep them away," he growled. "Both of them."

"They're family as much as ye," Niall shot back. "*My* family."

Annag aimed a pointed look at Duncan. "Blood will tell."

"Blood will run if ye dinna back off," Trick said darkly. His knife clattered to his trencher, his chair scraped back, and as he stood, his hand went to the hilt of his sword.

Clutching the shawl closed in front, Kendra rose. "Have we not seen enough violence here tonight?" Evidence still remained of the earlier brawl. "Come, Trick. I know where I'm not wanted." She curtsied to Niall but ignored his siblings as she took Trick by his sword hand and led him away. He let himself be dragged, although not before fixing Hamish's older children with a murderous glare.

That was exactly what Kendra was afraid of—murder. Trick was a highwayman, after all, accustomed to violence of a sort, and she'd never seen him this angry. Wanting to get as far from Annag and Duncan as possible, she led him out the door and around to the garden. The whole long way he said not a word, but as they stepped into his mother's wonderland of tiny model castles, she felt him begin to relax.

Night had almost fallen, and the branches overhead were black silhouettes against the dark, gray sky. In silence they walked up the long avenue of trees and back, up then back again. The crunch of their footsteps on the gravel seemed lost within the sounds of rushing wind and rustling leaves. Trick's grip softened on her hand, and his breathing settled; his gait became looser. A light mist began to fall, and in mute agreement, they headed back inside.

The door shut behind them, blocking the rain and the noisy wind. In the tunnel that led through the thick stone wall, Trick stopped and put his hands on her shoulders. Illuminated by the torches that lit the entry, his eyes searched her face. Kendra stared back, wondering what it was he was looking for.

"I don't like those two," she said quietly. "I wouldn't put anything past them. I know not what Hamish has to bequeath to his children, but I suspect they would go to any lengths necessary to make sure it ends up in their hands. All of it."

Trick shrugged, moving closer, backing her up until she felt the wall against her spine. He ran a hand through his hair and sighed. "They're powerless, and they know it. They speak from desperation." He reached to skim his knuckles across her cheek. "Don't worry your pretty head about them, *leannan.*"

Leannan. It sounded different now that she knew what it meant. "My head is more than pretty," she retorted, not immune to his scent and the sudden spark that lit his eyes.

He nodded slowly. "Aye, that it is." The wind had blown much of her hair loose from the bun, and he tucked it behind her ears, one side and then the other. He glanced into the Great Hall, sending a quelling glare to some poor soul who dared to look their way. Then, shielding her body from view with his larger one, he lowered his lips to hers.

The kiss was long and soft, reawakening the stirrings in her belly that had started in Hamish's chamber. Her hands moved to clasp him by the hips; then her fingers worked down to the kilt's hem and edged underneath.

"Hmmm." With a low laugh, he swept both her hands into one of his, then raised them above her head as he pressed her against the chilly stone. In comparison, his body felt so warm along the length of hers. And his mouth this time was harder and hot, hungry, his tongue demanding. She itched to touch him, but his hand tightened and she couldn't, and 'twas strange what she felt, the twinge of frustration mixed with the heady thrill of the kiss.

He pulled back and cocked a brow. "That'll teach you to take advantage of a man in a skirt."

"Will it?" she asked. Nervously intrigued, she glanced up to their three hands.

His own gaze followed, and his laugh this time was short and amused as he released her wrists. "Seeing as it's taken you five weeks to come to my bed, I reckon I'll give you a few years before I go hunting for a way to keep those hands tied up and both of mine free."

"Tied up?" she wondered breathlessly. He was always so outrageous.

"Scarves, a pair of cravats"—he glanced down—"mayhap a tartan sash?" His expression going from playful to meditative, he met her eyes. "Later, *lean-nan*. Much later for that, I think."

She blushed furiously, not at all as put off by that mental image as she thought she should be. Then his mouth claimed hers again, gentle once more, and she wrapped her arms around him, no longer thinking of that or anything while she gloried in his kiss.

As he drew back, a delicious shudder rippled through her. She knew for sure it would happen tonight.

"Are you cold, lass?"

"Maybe a bit." Nervous and excited and backed against the cold stone wall. But those stones were more than cold. "There's something about this place . . ."

He put a palm to the wall and leaned his weight on it. "What?"

"I . . . well, I'm just not comfortable here." She tried to look away, but he captured her chin in his free hand, forcing her gaze to his. "Throughout my entire childhood," she said, "marooned in exile on the Continent, parentless with no home to call my own, I never felt as out of place as I do here in this castle."

One of his fingers traced a lazy line on her jaw. "Then you'll understand why I was not in a hurry to return."

Her skin tingling under his fingertips, she nodded. But 'twas not only this place, these people, that contributed to her sense of unease. Although she was physically drawn to her husband, more so by the moment, he was still emotionally distant. Still a stranger, keeping the essence of himself far from her grasp.

Her hands rubbed up and down the plaid wool, and she swallowed hard, imagining the bareness beneath. He'd made a start, confiding a little bit about his childhood. If she trusted him with her body, would he perhaps return the favor by trusting her with his heart?

There was only one way to find out.

"Come upstairs," she whispered.

Chapter Eighteen

"Good evening, dearies." When they stepped into their chamber, Mrs. Ross came forward, two goblets in her hands. "I thought ye might be wantin' a wee sack posset to put ye to sleep."

Kendra knew that going to sleep now was the last thing on Trick's mind. Or hers, truth be told. She took one of the cups and sipped the thick, warm liquid, sweet and fragrant with the scents of wine and cream. Gazing at Trick over the rim, she watched as he removed the roll of papers from the front of his kilt and tucked it into his trunk.

"We thank you." He nodded and smiled at the woman. "And we wish you a good night," he added pointedly.

Kendra sagged against the door after he closed it. "How strange that she would be waiting here for us."

"She was my old nurse." He unbuckled his sword belt and tossed it on the desk. "I imagine she saw us together earlier and figured it wouldn't be long until we were for bed." When she blushed, he pulled her close. "I don't want to be thinking about Mrs. Ross now."

His eyes burned into hers, and she felt the heat

pooling in her middle again. She sipped some more of the posset, hoping the wine would bring her strength. And courage. She still wasn't sure he would fit. The thought made her heart skitter and brought a rush of warmth low in her belly.

Without another word, Trick pried the cup from her fingers and set it down beside his own. He pulled the shawl from her shoulders, balled it up, and tossed it into a corner. Lowering his head, he teased his lips over her cleavage. "I much prefer these delightful English dresses," he murmured.

The words felt warm against her skin. Until today, she'd never thought twice about wearing the revealing necklines that had been in fashion since King Charles was restored to the throne. Since trends were driven by Charles's love for everything French, she'd worn gowns like this all her life, even as a young girl exiled on the Continent.

But, thanks to her exasperating, overprotective brothers, never before had anyone taken advantage of all the skin to which it allowed access. A shame, she thought now, enjoying the sensation of his mouth against her flesh.

"I like this dress, too," she said breathlessly.

"I'd like it even better on the floor." He licked a shivery line up her throat, all the way to her lips. Just as she'd fantasized all day, she reached beneath the hem of his kilt, her hand making contact with the warmth of his legs, the springy softness of the hair that covered them. So different from her own, so very, very male. Feeling very daring, she reached up, up, until her fingers wrapped around steel encased in warm velvet.

God, she hoped he would fit.

She moved her hand experimentally. He stiffened, then sighed, and a thrill raced through her, that she could affect him so much with a simple touch.

"Aye," he murmured. "I will definitely have to ask Niall if I can keep this kilt." Then his hands went to work undressing her while he kissed the very breath out of her body.

She pulled her hand from under the kilt and reached for his shoulders, pushing the wool tartan off and behind. Then, under the draped front, feeling for the buckle on the thick leather belt, working it loose with frantic fingers. Finally the kilt fell off, all of it, just dropping to the wooden planks around his feet, the heavy buckle landing with a satisfying *thunk*.

He spread her bodice and worked the gown down her body, to pool on the floor as well. And there was nothing left between them except his thin lawn shirt and her even thinner chemise.

His hands came around her back, and she leaned in, pressing her breasts against his hard chest, her hips to where he was even harder below. A hot rush of desire weakened her knees, and her arms wrapped around him to hold herself up, wantonly reaching beneath the tail of his shirt to clutch his buttocks and press herself even closer.

"Sweet Mary," he breathed, clearly liking it. But for her, it was still not nearly close enough.

At a noise on the stairs, she stilled. Her heart beating double-time, and not only from the mounting feelings she was experiencing, she dropped her hands from his body. "Do you hear something?"

Reaching behind himself, Trick fished for her hands and plastered them back where they'd been.

With a sigh of contentment, he nuzzled her neck. "Something like what?"

"Like footsteps." His muscles tightened under her fingers, striking a spark of hungry desire. She arched in pleasure, then froze again. "In the stairwell—can you not hear it?"

"No." He raised his head. "Wait. Mayhap I can." The sound was faint, muffled, so soft the beat of her heart and her heavy, uneven breaths almost drowned it out.

Almost.

She bit her lip. "There are people in there, I tell you."

"Dinna worry about it." Trick hooked a finger in the top of her chemise and drew it down, fitting his palms to her breasts. Her nipples puckered in response and sent a hot streak of sensation down lower. His lips grazed hers, then his tongue flicked out and teased the seam where they met, slick and sweet with the flavor of creamy sack posset. "It must be the ghosts of men going up to Prisoner's Leap," he murmured against her mouth, and she couldn't tell if he was jesting or not. "No one that would bother us in here."

"D-do you believe in ghosts?"

His shrug was a mixture of amusement and frustration. "Right now I believe I want to finish what we've started."

She twisted away from his kiss. "What if it isn't ghosts on those stairs, but someone much more real and frightening?"

With a strangled groan, he stepped from the kilt at his feet, then bodily picked her up. He walked to the bed and plopped down, sitting her on his lap. "Like who?"

Fear mingled with bawdy thoughts of what she felt against her thigh. "Mrs. Ross, maybe? What if she only used the sack posset as an excuse, and she was really up here as part of a plot, but we surprised her—"

"A plot?" He shook his head decisively. "Mrs. Ross wouldn't hurt a midge." He reached to the bed-side for his goblet of sack posset, taking a healthy gulp as if to prove he was sure it wasn't poisoned. "She cared for me as a bairn. Why would she want to do me harm?"

"She cared for your mother more, and she's less than happy with the way you ignored her all those years."

"She was, true enough. But she knows now that 'twas not my fault. I cannot believe she still holds a grudge."

"How about Annag and Duncan? They surely do."

Trick's clever fingers pulled the pins from what remained of her bun. "I seriously doubt Annag and Duncan are hovering behind that door." The gray day had delivered on its promise, and rain slashed against the small window set deep into the wall. " 'Tis the storm you're hearing, *leannan*."

"Niall, then? He's been passed off as the duke's younger son. If something were to happen to you, he'd inherit it all. The dukedom, Amberley, Duncraven . . ."

In the midst of combing his fingers through her loosened hair, Trick stopped and just stared at her, his jaw slack with disbelief.

"No, I don't believe it, either," she admitted with a sigh.

A flash of lightning brightened the window, and he smiled. "Listen." His gaze captured hers as the answering thunder rumbled. " 'Tis naught but the storm. And a storm I'm feeling inside, right now."

He claimed her mouth once again, and in seconds she forgot the mysterious footsteps, caught up in a storm herself.

His lips opened, his tongue meeting hers, circling hers in a way that drove her wild. She tasted the tiny chip on his tooth, then sucked his tongue back into her mouth, wanting to return to him all the passion he was showing her. Her hands went to the sides of his face, her fingers reached to tangle in his hair. One of his hands cradled the back of her neck while the other crept under her chemise, caressing her legs with a skill that sent a shudder ricocheting through her.

He worked the chemise out from under her, and she wiggled farther onto his lap, loving the feel of his skin against hers, reveling in the heat of the hard length of him beneath her bottom. She shoved a hand into the placket of his shirt, gripping his shoulder, and the warm skin felt good, but she wanted more. One-handed, she loosened the laces, then broke their kiss to pull the shirt over his head, blowing out a long, audible breath as she smoothed a palm across his bare chest.

He groaned in return, urging her legs apart with his fingers. One hand delved between them and found its mark while his other arm curved around her shoulders so he could cup a breast. Above and below, he played her body, his fingers doing an intimate dance that made her quiver and squirm on his lap. Closing her eyes, she threw back her head, surrendering herself to the feelings.

She wanted more, more. A finger worked its way inside, teasing her to madness, and still it wasn't enough.

"Now," she whispered. "I want you now."

"Look at me, lass."

When her eyes fluttered open to meet his gaze, she knew she'd never seen anything so intense and compelling in her life. "I want you," she breathed again.

He ripped the chemise over her head and, in one smooth motion, twisted her off his lap and onto the mattress. Then he was lying atop her, skin to skin, heavy and warm and exciting beyond anything she'd ever imagined. Instinctively, her legs came up to cradle his hips, and he raised himself, poised to enter her body. She felt him there, against her, and let out a little mewling sound of need.

"Now?" he asked.

"Now." She held her breath, still uncertain yet wanting him more than she'd ever wanted anything. As he slid home, she braced for the pain.

Nothing.

Well, not nothing exactly. She felt stretched, and filled, and where their bodies were joined was a feeling so urgent that a whimper escaped her throat. She arched against him, wanting more, needing more.

It seemed an age before he began to move, while she held her breath, her eyes sliding closed once again. Then slowly he began to shift in and out. Little by little, the tension built, until her entire world was centered on Trick and what he was making her feel.

A glorious whirl of exquisite sensation, and still it wasn't enough.

"Faster," she whispered, and he plunged into her faster and deeper, again and again, until she couldn't breathe and her body erupted and the world turned upside down.

She heard his groan and felt the hot flood of his release, and the tremors still wracked her body. Finally, spent, he collapsed against her, kissing her neck and cheeks and whispering her name over and over.

"Dear God." She struggled to catch her breath. "I just—"

"What?" Trick asked, his voice husky against her mouth. "What is it, *leannan*?"

She sighed, a sound of regret from the deepest place in her heart. "I cannot believe I deprived myself of five weeks of *that*."

His reply was a strangled laugh, and another groan, but he clutched her close and kissed her all over again.

She felt languid and drained, and 'twas a long time before her heart slowed and her breathing quieted. A long time before she noticed the phantom footsteps again.

"'Tis the rain," Trick reminded her when she flinched. His voice sounded low and lazy, satisfied, content. It thrilled her to know she had made him that way. "We're alone here at the top. It cannot be anything else."

"Annag and Duncan . . ."

Taking her with him, he turned over and cuddled her against his chest. "Do you honestly think they've climbed up on the roof to come down these stairs in hopes of doing murder? On this stormy night?"

She shrugged. "I wouldn't put anything past those two. 'Tis obvious enough they don't like you . . . or me."

"They're bitter. Odds are Niall has always been favored as the duke's son—a lord and all when they weren't. Then their father left them to move in here—although they were grown, that had to hurt."

"And now you've returned to claim that father—"

"A bit of his attention, mayhap, but I've no claim on the man."

Rain pounded on the roof above them, loud needles of it striking the small window. Silently she met his eyes, remembering other eyes that had looked familiar. Beneath his shining hair, his brow furrowed in puzzlement. Suddenly she pictured Hamish, that same expression on his face, and it all fell into place.

She reached a hand to graze his cheek, the faint whiskers scratchy against her fingers. So very male. "Do you not see, Trick, how much you are like him?"

"Niall? Aye, I've said how uncanny—"

"Not Niall. Well, yes, Niall, but you must know there's a reason for that, for why you're so very alike." He needed to hear this; he couldn't deny the evidence any longer. " 'Tis because you share not only the same mother, but the same father as well."

"Think you so?" Some of the puzzlement cleared, and his amber eyes filled with a hesitant hope instead. "I suppose the timing makes it possible. Father was last here when I was ten, and Niall was born the next year . . . I wouldn't have thought he and Mam would share a bed again, but then I wouldn't put rape past the man, either. Mayhap Niall *is* my full brother." His voice managed to sound bitter and elated at the same time. "Would that not be something?" he added before he suddenly frowned. "But why, then, would he say he is Hamish's son?"

"Because he is," she said gently. "And so are you."

The breath left his body in a rush. "That cannot be."

"It is." Her eyes searched his; then she scooted up to sit against the headboard beside him, taking the coverlet with her. "No, I haven't asked him about it, nor did he come to me. But I've eyes in my head, Trick, and I'm not so close to the situation as you are. You share Hamish's features, I'm telling you, and his manner, and then there's the way he looks at you. With longing, and pride . . . Were you another man's son—a child gotten on his love by another—would he not look on you with resentment, instead? He's your father, I'm sure of it."

He couldn't find the words to disagree, mostly because he wasn't sure whether he disagreed or not.

"Is it not wonderful?" Kendra pressed. She took their goblets from the bedside table and handed him his. "I know you don't hold him in much affection, but that will come, do you not think? Deep down, I believe he's a good man."

" 'Tis much to absorb," he admitted. "Finding a new brother, and now mayhap a father, too."

"We found a new brother last year," Kendra said, looking down to the goblet in her hands. As she talked, she moved the bracelet back and forth on her wrist. "Jason had a run-in with a man who turned out to be our half-brother, the spawn of our father before his marriage. Only our brother turned out to be wicked. A murderer, nothing like Niall." She glanced up. " 'Twas a horrible thing to accept."

For a few moments he remained quiet, imagining. "That must have been very hard."

"It was. Although I don't expect accepting Niall and Hamish is easy, either." The amber stones of her bracelet glimmered in the firelight as she slid them with a finger. "An instant family, as it were."

"Niall felt like my brother right off. 'Tis hard to explain." He stared at the bracelet, remembering when he first saw her play with it like this, before their wedding in the chapel. It had looked strange on her then, but tonight it looked like it had belonged there all along. Just the way he felt with Niall. "But Hamish . . ." He met her gaze. "I feel nothing there. I hear what you're telling me, and it makes sense, but I'm not at all sure I believe it."

"Just think about it." Kendra drained the sack posset in her goblet, cold now, he was sure. The rain coming down sounded cold, too, but she felt warm wedged beside him. He wondered how she managed to smell like sunshine on a blustery night like this. "There is no need to rush into acceptance," she said softly.

"He could be dying." Trick downed the last of his own drink, cold, yes, but still thick and bracing. He took her cup and set them both on the table at his side.

"He could," she conceded. "But he seems to be getting better."

"This may have just been a good day."

"Morning will tell." She yawned, then leaned over for a kiss, the sweet milkiness of the posset mingling on their tongues. With a soft smile, she lay down and curled tightly against him, like precious cargo carefully nestled in a ship's hold.

She felt good there, a perfect fit. " 'Tis odd," he said, his voice low, his breath fluttering the downy hairs on her neck where she'd swept aside her tresses. "They know me not, really, and yet they seemed to accept me from the first."

"They're family," she said simply. "They love you, Trick. Unconditionally."

And now she was family, too. Unconditional love. The idea was so alien to him that he thought about it far into the night as he watched her sleep.

Chapter Nineteen

"Wake up, ye gaberlunzie." Mrs. Ross poked Trick's shoulder, and he moaned and rolled over. "Lord Niall is downstairs, pacin' and waitin' to take the two of ye off somewhere, ye ken? So get yer bones out of that bed."

"I'll make sure he gets ready," Kendra told her, sitting down in a chair to pull on a stocking. She watched his old nurse bustle around the room on her morning duties. "Can you send Jane up to fix my hair?"

"Aye. That I can do." With a smile, the wiry woman gathered the empty goblets they'd left on the night table. "Did ye enjoy this, then?"

"Very much." Kendra silently scolded herself for thinking it might have been poisoned. Trick was right; though she sometimes had a brusque manner about her, the old nurse wouldn't hurt a midge. "Do you know, Mrs. Ross, where that corner staircase leads?"

The woman swiped her dust cloth over the table— not that it helped very much. The dirt just flew up and settled right back down. "That turret comes from the dungeons, lass. And goes to the roof above."

"Oh." Just as Trick had said. Kendra glanced at her

slumbering husband. Although they'd come upstairs early last eve, he slept like the dead. Like he'd spent another wakeful night before succumbing in exhaustion. She, on the other hand, had slept like a newborn babe, dreaming dreams that made her cheeks burn to remember them.

Mrs. Ross was watching her, a question in her faded blue eyes. Kendra put a cooling hand to her face. "Though Trick insisted 'twas surely the rain, I thought I heard footfalls on those steps last night."

The woman's gray head nodded sagely. " 'Tis been said to happen."

"People go up on the roof?"

"Not people, lass."

"Ghosts, then?" Kendra's breath caught. "The ghosts of prisoners?"

"Not that I've heard." She blushed as the woman bent to retrieve yesterday's clothes from the floor. Cavanaugh and Jane ought to be doing that—not that she and Trick should have left their garments on the floor in the first place. What could Mrs. Ross be thinking?

But apparently she was still thinking about the stairwell. "Other ghosts," she clarified, shaking out Trick's discarded kilt. "One in particular, a young servant girl who was said to have borne an illegitimate Duncraven son in this room some two hundred years past. Potential threats to the title, they were, and both swiftly put to the sword by an anonymous knight."

Kendra swallowed. "Anonymous?"

"Well, now, ye cannot very well tell who's in a suit of armor now, can ye? But word has it 'twas Lord Duncraven himself. A heartless man, to hear the legends." She smoothed the folded tartan over one arm. "The girl still wanders the spiral staircase, looking for her bairn. Some say they've seen her in this room, watching at the foot of the bed, where a cradle may have once rested," she added, laying the red fabric right where Kendra imagined the poor murdered girl might stare. "Dinna ye worry now, lass. She doesn't do any harm."

Had she heard the ill-fated servant girl, then? Kendra wondered. Or was Mrs. Ross only inventing this story to cover her own wanderings? Or had Annag or Duncan been trodding the stone stairs?

Or had it truly been the storm, mixed with her own imagination?

Her musings were interrupted when Mrs. Ross bustled over to Trick. "Wake up, ye lazybones." She thwacked him with her dust cloth. "Lord Niall is waitin'."

Halfway downstairs, Trick's feet dragged to a halt on the landing. "Stop."

On the step below him, Kendra turned and looked up. She tightened Mrs. Ross's shawl across the bodice of her lemon gown. "Niall is waiting to take us to the treasure chests."

"Then he'll wait." She looked so pretty this morning, all cheerful yellow against the dingy stone staircase, her mouth slightly swollen from his morning kisses. He bent down to give her another one, wishing he could just take her back to bed. Their lips clung for a long, sweet minute; then he straightened with a sigh and stepped from the turret, crossing the sitting room to knock on the master bedchamber door.

"Enter," came a muffled voice.

A voice not unlike his own? Trick hesitated, his hand on the latch.

Her brow furrowed, Kendra came up beside him. "Did you not want to go inside?"

He took a deep breath and pushed open the door. Beyond it, Hamish sat against the sturdy oak headboard, his long, skinny legs looking like stilts under the coverlet. Trick stared at him, a burning question inside him—a question only this old man could answer.

But he couldn't seem to make himself cross the threshold, nor could he force the question past his lips.

Kendra had no such compunctions. She pushed past him and hurried over to Hamish, grasping the old man's hand. "Goodness." With a flounce of her English skirts, she seated herself at his bedside, a bright ray of sunshine in the gloomy room. "Rhona's vile green drink really worked magic, did it not?"

Indeed, Hamish was munching on breakfast and looking much better. Younger. Trick was surprised to realize he wasn't such an old man at all.

"Aye, I expect it did work magic," Hamish agreed. "But although she left a supply, I've not been able to force myself to take it." He made a face. "She'll be at me like a screaming banshee when she sees it. Mayhap I can prevail upon ye to bury it somewhere?"

Kendra laughed. "Where is Rhona, anyway?"

Hamish shrugged. "I'm mending, ye ken, and she has her own life to attend to. There are people here to help me should I need it." His mouth curved in a smile very like Niall's—and his own, Trick grudgingly admitted. "To tell ye the honest truth, 'tis been pleasant to spend a wee bit of time alone. A man gets cranky with people always fussing all over 'im."

"I'm sure he does," Kendra said, slanting a glance at Trick. She rose and went to open the shutters, letting morning light flood the room.

Hamish's gaze shifted to the open doorway, and his forehead creased in a frown. "Come in, lad, will ye?"

Trick did so, slowly, staring at the man that Kendra insisted was his father.

"Have a seat," Hamish said.

He didn't. The question still fought to get out.

The older man blinked. " 'Tis uncanny how much ye look like Niall. I used to catch your mother staring at him with a sad, faraway look in her eyes."

The same sad, faraway look that Hamish was giving him now. The same look Trick suspected was on his own face. Finally, the words stumbled forth. "Niall and I . . . We look so alike because . . . because we have the same father, don't we?"

Before Hamish even answered, Trick knew that Kendra had been right. "Why?" he asked. "Why was I never told? And why did my mother marry another man and then have a child with you?"

Hamish licked his lips, not so papery this morning. " 'Twasn't like that, Patrick. She was already carrying ye when she agreed to the marriage. Her only other choice was to give birth to a bastard child." His light-brown gaze met Trick's own. "Her father threatened to kill me if she refused to marry the duke."

Kendra's gasp split the silence. "He cannot have meant that."

Hamish turned to her. "Can ye blame Elspeth for not testing him, lass?"

"I know not," she admitted. "I cannot even imagine . . ."

"Well, ye didn't ken the man. The threat was not so hard to imagine coming from him."

"Very well, then, mayhap she had a reason." Trick ran a hand back through his hair. "But why keep the truth from me?"

"The duke never kent ye weren't his child. We never meant to keep ye in the dark forever, but ye left here at ten—too young to be told, to understand why it was so important to hide your true parentage from the man you thought was your father. And when ye returned . . ." Hamish's gaze flickered down to his lap, then back up. "The moment ye arrived, I wanted to tell ye, but after all this time, I wasn't sure how you would feel."

Despite a long night spent thinking about just that, Trick wasn't sure how he felt himself. Anyone, even Hamish, was better than the duke had been, but the discovery of a new father left him reeling.

"I'll have to get used to this," he admitted.

Hamish nodded. "I've waited twenty-eight years to acknowledge ye as my son. I can wait a wee bit longer."

The day was sunny, the ride toward the town of Falkland pleasant over rolling hills. It felt so good to be out of the depressing castle that Kendra found herself smiling at nothing more than the light breeze, the purple thistles dotting the hillsides, a pair of blackbirds flying by. She chattered to Niall about anything and everything, enjoying his easy company.

Seeming as grateful as Kendra to be out and about, Pandora felt warm and frisky beneath her.

Trick, however, was brooding.

Two miles into their journey, he finally turned to Niall. "Why did you not tell me?"

"Pardon?" Niall cocked his head, gleaming blond in the sunshine. "Why did I not tell ye what?"

"That our mother's is not the only blood we share."

Niall reined in at that, turning sideways to block the road. His mount danced under him as he stared at Trick. "What are ye trying to say?"

"Did you think I wouldn't want to know we're full brothers?" His jaw tight, Trick studied Niall a moment. "Did you think I wouldn't care to know that Hamish is my father as well as yours?"

The younger man's face went white. "I didn't ken." His amber eyes wide, he swallowed hard. "Are ye sure? I swear to ye, Patrick, I didn't ken. Mam and Da never breathed a word."

Kendra, for one, believed him. Nobody was that good an actor.

But her husband, apparently, was blind. "Why would they not tell you?" he pressed. "What possible reason could they have had?"

"Trick!" she exclaimed in irritation. Not unlike her own brothers, he could be thickheaded beyond bearing. "I expect they thought your parentage was none of Niall's business."

"My mother kent how to hold her tongue," Niall added, his amber eyes darkening to bronze. "And my father is the most loyal man I've ever met. A loyalty I thought we'd share, now that we've found each other." With a jerk of his reins, he turned and trotted off down the road.

Kendra glared at her husband until his face turned red and he looked away. "All right," he shouted after his brother. "I believe you!"

There was no response, and looking at Niall's stiff back, she could sense his pain. Trick dug in his heels, motioning impatiently for Kendra to follow. "You might also say you're sorry," she suggested under her breath as she drew alongside.

He stared at her a moment, then back to Niall. "And I'm sorry!" he called. Maybe not as sincerely as she'd have liked, but the effort was there.

Yet his brother's back remained tight. She saw a muscle twitch in her husband's jaw. "Very well, then, I'm not sorry," he growled.

They caught up to Niall and rode three abreast, the men in an obstinate standoff on either side of Kendra. The blowing of the horses failed to drown out their alternating huffs. She felt like Zeus in the Trojan War, stuck between the battling gods, wanting to stay neutral but suspecting she couldn't.

The gates of Falkland loomed ahead, and still neither of them softened. They were definitely brothers, one as stubborn as the other. As they entered the town, a few people waved to Niall, calling out greetings and condolences. He nodded his acknowledgments without uttering a word.

They rode past Falkland Palace, two long ranges of gray stone with a charming turreted gatehouse and slanting, moss-covered slate roofs. Kendra turned to her brother-in-law and forced a jaunty tone. "From how Hamish described the banquet, I expected the town of Falkland would be larger. Busier."

She'd known he wouldn't ignore her. "At one time 'twas more important," he told her, looking straight ahead. God forbid he should inadvertently meet his brother's eyes. "But Falkland today is naught but a small market town, populated mostly by weavers who keep indoors practicing their craft. Ye can blame the Union of the Crowns for that."

"Why would that make a difference?" she asked brightly. "Trick, you know a lot of history."

"Not of Falkland." She'd never heard him sound quite so peeved, not even when he was fixing to murder Duncan. "For God's sake, I haven't lived here in eighteen years."

As her efforts at conversation ground to a halt, she heaved an internal sigh. The clip-clop of their horses' hooves on the cobblestones seemed loud as thunder against the men's willful silence. As they rounded the market cross, a dray cart coming from the other direction forced them to the side of the narrow street, close by the houses.

"The lintels are all carved," she remarked, prattling on like a featherbrained nincompoop. She pointed to the nearest door, the stone beam above it engraved with letters and numbers. "What do they mean?"

"They're marriage lintels—" Trick started.

"Look there," Niall interrupted. "Two lovers' initials, and 1610 the year they were wed—the year their household was established. And other markings indicate their occupations. See, the crossed mells of a stonemason. And there, a shoemaker's knife."

They rode past a few more, and Kendra started to

make sense of the symbols. "I see a butcher's cleaver. But the big '4' with three little x's . . . what does that mean?"

Niall opened his mouth then clamped it shut when his brother rushed to answer before him. "A merchant—a burgess with trading privileges."

The carvings were lovely, she thought, determined not to let their attitudes affect her appreciation. Lasting memorials to marriages begun in hope, not deception. She turned to her surly husband. "Do you not think these lintels are romantic?"

Trick rolled his eyes, prompting Niall to nod—pleasantly, she would think, if she didn't know it was mainly to make his brother look bad. "There are some going back a hundred years or more. Watch for them as ye ride."

She peeked down the wynds as they went, but soon they were passing through West Port, the gate that marked Falkland's boundary. Dense woodlands loomed ahead. "The trees are so near to the town," she remarked, sounding inane to her own ears.

"Why wouldn't they be?" Trick asked churlishly.

"Actually," Niall said with a smug smile, "though nearly all of Fife was once covered in forest, the only large tracts left are here by Falkland. One of the reasons the Stuarts of old so valued their palace, a place to escape from affairs of state and spend some time hawking and hunting the wild boar."

She half hoped to see a wild boar now—at least such a threat would put an end to this bickering. Here they had to ride single file, weaving through the trees, which looked much the same as trees in England. Finding nothing left to comment on, Kendra chewed the inside of her cheek, wondering why she had bothered trying to get her husband and his brother to talk in the first place. Brothers would be brothers, that she knew—from entirely too much experience with her own.

They were both stubborn as mules, she decided, and they could hate each other for life for all she cared.

Suddenly Niall heaved a sigh and looked back, his gaze reaching past her to Trick. "Full brothers," he said, calm as anything. "Bloody amazing, isn't it?"

"Aye." Aghast to hear Trick's agreement, she twisted in the saddle to see a smile teasing at the corners of his wide mouth. "Bloody amazing."

And just like that, they were best of friends once more. Men. She wanted to spit.

She was still muttering to herself when they came to higher ground, a sparser wooded area that must once have been a clearing. 'Twas peppered with stone ruins so thick and old, they could be of nothing else but a long-ruined castle. Overgrown with clinging plant life, low broken walls seemed to tumble over the uneven land, and the foundations of a round tower stood open to the sky, a few worn steps leading up to nowhere.

"We're here," Niall said.

They dismounted and tethered their horses. Pulling a heavy key from his pocket, Niall stepped into the circle of stone and reached through a layer of dirt and dead branches that seemed stuck to the hard-packed forest floor.

Not by a quirk of nature, though—by design. His fingers found a concealed padlock and fitted the key inside. It opened with a rusty *click*, and he tugged it off, hefting a wooden trapdoor that lay hidden beneath.

"Go ahead," he said. After staring for a moment, Kendra followed Trick down a steep stone staircase, pausing momentarily when the trapdoor thudded shut and plunged the space into blackness. Holding her breath and her husband's hand, she felt her way to the bottom.

'Twas a dungeon, deep in the earth. The only light came from a tiny shaft high on the ceiling, behind an iron grille, and as her eyes adjusted, the sparse illumination revealed gruesome instruments of torture. A musty smell seeped from the packed dirt floor, and she imagined the ground wet and red with the blood of prisoners. Hugging herself, she shivered.

A human cage swung near the center of the chamber, its door hanging drunkenly from ancient hinges. A wooden rack sat in one corner, used to pull the victim apart. On the far wall, four sets of manacles for ankles were anchored near the floor, with matching sets for wrists higher up.

I reckon I'll give you a few years before I go hunting for a way to keep those hands tied up and both of mine free.

She heard the scrape of steel on stone, then the soft hiss of a wick catching fire. "They're gone!" Niall burst out behind her, his voice laced with disbelief. She swung about to see him holding a candle high in the air, his eyes wide in the flickering light. "The treasure chests are gone!"

Trick reached to put a calming hand on his arm. "Where were they?"

"Here, I tell ye. Here, and here, and here." He paced the dim chamber, indicating bare spots where heavy, rectangular objects had once clearly sat. "I saw them but two days ago—the morning of the day ye arrived. They were here, same as always. As they've been since afore I was born."

The dungeon was warm and stuffy. While Trick found another candle and lit it from Niall's, Kendra slipped off her cloak and hung it from one of the manacles on the wall. "Whatever were you doing here?"

Niall hesitated but a moment. "This was Mam's secret retreat. I came . . . to feel closer to her. To escape the clamor of the wake, just for a wee while. How can all that treasure have gone missing since then?" He held out the lock, staring at it. "How did they get it open?"

Trick took it from his hands. " 'Twas not forced or picked."

"How can you tell?"

"There would be marks." He handed it back. "Who else has a key?"

"Only Rhona and Gregor. So far as I ken, nobody else even knows this place exists. It makes no sense. Twenty-three huge chests, all gone." Niall stepped closer to Trick, his face looking sallow and sick in the light from the candle in his hand. "Will ye help me find them?"

Trick blinked. He'd planned to leave for England tomorrow—a search could take days. Weeks. "I must get home. This is not my responsibility. But of course I will bring the news directly to the King."

"What if the thieves start selling the treasure, aye? Gold and silver platters and goblets? Surely someone will figure out whence it came, and then an inquisition would be made, and Mam and Da could be implicated."

"She's dead," he said. "What does it matter now?"

"Hamish isn't," Kendra reminded him. But he didn't want to be reminded. He still didn't know how he felt about his father, and the last thing he wanted was a reason to stick around and find out while the rest of his life remained on hold.

"He could hang, Patrick." The flame wavered, ruffled by Niall's impassioned words. "Or worse. Stealing the Royal plate is treason."

"Treason," Kendra whispered. "Punishable by hanging, drawing, quartering—"

"I know the penalties for treason. But that doesn't change the fact that I must get home. And, hearts wounds, 'tis been thirty-five years since the crime." Surely there would be no evidence left to tie it to his parents now. John Ferries, the only witness, was dead. These fears were groundless. Emotional rather than logical.

"Trick." She came close, capturing his gaze with hers. "Even should the crime continue undiscovered, King Charles would never regain what his father lost."

He hesitated but a moment, realizing she knew him better than he knew himself. Always it came down to what would be best for Charles Stuart. "Very well," he muttered. "I'll spare a day or two to help find it." That was the most he was willing to delay his return to England. "But let us not go off half-cocked. There may be some clue here of who took it or its whereabouts."

Niall's breath rushed out in relief. "Da may have some ideas, as well. Mayhap someone else knew of the treasure or had a key to the lock. And in any case, he will want to hear immediately of its loss."

"Go ahead, then, and speak with him. Kendra and I will remain behind to search for clues."

"Ye ken the direction to Duncraven?"

"Aye. Back through the town, then southwest. Be on your way. We'll meet you later and formulate a plan. God willing, one of us will discover something useful in the interim."

Niall gripped him by the shoulders. "I thank ye."

"Think nothing of it," Trick mumbled. "We're brothers, aye?"

"Brothers." The younger man kissed him on both cheeks and pressed the lock and key into his hand. He gave Kendra his candle and was off, the trapdoor banging closed behind him.

She released a long breath. "That was good of you, Trick."

"He didn't leave me much of a choice." But his voice hitched, and he knew it was the result of this brotherly affection.

Hearing the catch in his words, Kendra moved to her husband. "Why did you hesitate to agree?"

He stepped closer, and his fingers trailed the length of her arm. "After last night, I'm suddenly wanting to get home and start anew with my lovely wife."

She sensed that wasn't the whole truth, but his words caused her heart to race anyway, very aware they were alone deep in the earth. "After we help your family, there will still be time for that."

"You can be sure of it." He kissed the tip of her nose, then took the candlestick from her hand and set it atop the rack, where it bathed the stone chamber with a faint but welcome glow. He set the lock there as well, an unnerving *thunk* of metal on wood. "Shall we see what we can find?"

"I really don't like it down here."

"We'll not be staying long." Another candle blazed to join the two already lit, and Trick set it into a holder and placed it across the chamber. "There now, 'tis not so eerie after all, is it? Rather cozy, do you not think?"

Was it her imagination, or had his voice taken on a seductive tone? "Well, I don't expect it's haunted if it was your mother's secret place. But I cannot say I care for the decor, either."

"Early Torture is not your style?" His easy grin made her feel a little better, but his gaze on the manacles had the opposite effect, even more so when the hot look he shot her made her knees go weak.

Memories flooded: *The things I say are nothing compared to the things I will do . . . There are other ways we can pleasure one another . . . Look at me, lass . . .*

She shook herself from the images playing in her head. Knowing the way his mind worked, whatever he was thinking was most likely wicked, and she had no business being intrigued by that. Her brothers had always warned her that her adventurous nature would lead her to nothing but trouble.

"Kendra?" Her gaze snapped to his. She thought he sounded entirely too pleased with himself as his eyes burned a path down her body. "We'd better start looking."

Maybe she was only imagining it all, but the heat pooling in her center . . . that wasn't her imagination. In a dungeon, for God's sake. She shook herself again. "What are we looking for?"

"Hell if I know. A clue." He slowly traversed one

side of the room while she paced the other. Gingerly touching the cold instruments of torture worked well to dispel inappropriate feelings. The blackened metal felt evil beneath her fingers, the air thick and heavy with age, not to mention horrific tales.

She jumped when he let out a little hoot of discovery. "Footprints."

She joined him, crouching down. "What do these tell us? They could be your mother's, or Hamish's, or even our own. No telling if they're hours old or years."

"But they're concentrated around where a chest once sat, see? As though people were recently here, trying to lift something heavy. And here, this deep line in the dirt. They used a board or something as a lever."

"One set of small prints and three larger ones. Yes, I see." She looked up. "But whose?"

He shrugged. "Just information to bring back to Hamish. Mayhap it will jog an idea. Let us see what else we can find."

Half an hour's careful search revealed more footprints clustered around where other chests had sat, and little else. A scrap of dark fabric that Trick pocketed, a curved shard of cheap broken glass. It could have lain there for centuries, for all they knew.

He sighed. "Let us go up. We may find more clues outdoors."

'Twas a relief to ascend the stairs and see daylight once again.

"More of the same footprints." Breathing deep of the fresh air, Kendra followed the marks. "And wheel tracks," she called. "Here, leading out of the woods. How did we miss this before?"

"We weren't looking." He hurried over to see for himself. "I'll be damned. Multiple tracks from the same vehicle. Many of them. I'm guessing the chests were carted away one at a time."

"Southeast," she agreed. "Around the town. And then where?"

Trick lifted a shoulder. "Shall we go find out?"

They mounted their horses and headed through the woods, following the tracks. Once clear of the ruins, the trees grew dense, providing reason for the chests to have been carted out singly. A larger cart would not have made it through. At the forest's edge, the marks stopped.

"They loaded them on a wagon here," Kendra said.

"Two wagons. No, three, or mayhap four. Look." Wider-set tracks turned south and continued. "Shall we see where they went?"

The tracks were easy enough to follow, leading Trick to believe they'd missed the thieves by not more than hours. Clouds were gathering again, and the trail would soon be washed away. But for now, the air was warm, the day bright as only a Scottish summer afternoon could be. The colors seemed more brilliant here, slopes of blues and purples, the land's harsh contours brought out by shadow and sun. Rabbits scurried in the underbrush, and a flock of swallows soared overhead. Scotland was beautiful, and Trick had missed it in a way he hadn't realized 'til now, stuck in the confines of the dingy gray castle.

"What happened back there?" Kendra asked quietly.

"Hmm?"

"With Niall."

"Oh. That." Warmth crept up his neck, his memories of the incident childish at best. "I'm not sure. But 'twill not happen again."

"It will."

"Nay, it won't. I'm not usually as volatile as you've seen me . . ." His voice trailed off, because he didn't know how to explain it. The longer he stayed at his crumbling childhood home, the more confused he seemed to get.

His early years apparently had not been as he remembered—or as the duke had later caused him to remember. His world had tilted out of control. And though he'd found family, they were too new, too unfamiliar, to possibly lean on yet.

Which left him his wife. He needed her more than he'd like to admit.

Thank God she was here. He gave her a wavery smile, jockeying Chaucer closer so he could lean to touch her glimmering hair. Unbound today, it felt soft against his fingertips. And no wires. The thought widened his grin. "I just need to become accustomed to having a family. 'Twill not happen again."

"It will," she insisted. "He's your brother."

"Exactly, and so he deserves my best. I'll apologize for disbelieving him, and from now on I need to be more patient. He looks a man, but he's yet a lad, and I must remember that."

"No." Her laugh rang over the hillside, and her smile would lift the most morose man's mood. Sweet Mary, he was lucky to have her. "Don't be so hard on yourself, Trick. This is the way brothers are. Families are. We don't give each other our best, I'm afraid, but more often our worst. We slide into comfort and forget ourselves. 'Tis the hugs after the battles that make it worthwhile."

A concept so unfamiliar it bordered on incomprehensible. It had been so very long since he could reliably expect a hug from anyone, let alone someone he had hurt.

Lost in thought, he was caught by surprise when Chaucer balked at the edge of a river. Kendra tugged on Pandora's reins. "Look, the tracks disappear. Shall we cross?"

There was no bridge in sight. The water didn't look too deep—waist high, he guessed, at most—but he eyed her long skirts and the sun overhead. "The day is getting away from us. Let us take what we've found back to Hamish and Niall. They may have an idea where the thieves were headed."

"Oh! I left my cloak in the dungeon."

"We'll follow the tracks back. I'm not certain how to return from here, anyway. Are you?"

"No." She shook her head, her lips curved in a faint smile. He wanted to kiss them.

Hell, he always wanted to kiss them. "Come along. We also forgot to lock up."

Kendra's heart felt light as they rode back. She'd heard a warmth in Trick's voice that made her feel perhaps he was finally opening up. When she smiled over at him, he smiled back, raking her from head to toe with those amber eyes. A glimmer in them assured her that he liked what he saw, and her body reacted immediately. How many more hours until they could sneak back up to their chamber tonight? She'd never thought she'd look forward to anything in that gloomy place, but they had five long weeks to make up for.

Back at the ruins, she tethered Pandora and followed Trick into the dungeon, shivering a bit as she descended the narrow, cold staircase in the slanting light of the open trapdoor.

He turned to her at the bottom. "You're not still frightened, are you?"

"Maybe. A little." She hurried to get her cloak from the manacle on the wall, but he blocked her path and grabbed her around the middle, leaning to give her a kiss. A dizzying cloud of his sandalwood scent surrounded her, permeating the dungeon's mustiness and reminding her of what she'd been thinking earlier in this place. Her senses spun wildly, and before she knew what was happening, he had lifted her by the waist.

"Oof! What are you doing?"

His only answer was a raised brow as he walked forward, then sat her in the open cage, letting her legs dangle out where the door hung loose. He gave the ugly black thing a push to start it swinging.

The metal felt cold beneath her skirts, and the swinging chain made an awful grating noise. Holding tight to the opening, she gave a shaky laugh.

He grinned. "See? 'Tis not scary down here at all. Not with the sunlight and the company. And apparently 'twas not scary to my mother, either, since it was her special place."

Trying to be a good sport, Kendra reached her toes to push off again. The chain moaned a protest. "I can imagine her coming here to think," she told him, swaying to and fro. "The way you go to the cottage at Amberley."

He hesitated, then nodded his head. "Yes, just like that."

Pleased that he'd admitted as much, she pressed for more. "You write there, don't you?"

"Sometimes." He gave the cage another shove, sending the chain to its screeching song.

"I wonder if your mother wrote here?"

"I never saw her write anything other than letters. But I'd lay odds she came here with Hamish when they were younger, and not to write." He pushed her again, flashing a grin or a leer, she wasn't sure which. "Aye, I can picture them here, all right. I bet they came here to secretly make love."

A little tingle started in the pit of her stomach. "Make love? In here?"

" 'Tis private enough." He cocked a brow. "I was conceived here. I can feel it."

"That's ridiculous." But intrigued, she looked around. "There's no bed."

"What makes you think we need a bed?"

"W-we?" Her fingers clenched the iron bars. "You cannot be serious. I cannot imagine—"

With his hands on the bars that flanked her head, he stilled the cage. "Ah, lassie, 'tis not really so hard to imagine." His wicked smile drew her attention to that tiny, charming chip on his tooth, and he took advantage, reaching down to flip up her skirts.

"Trick! What—" He was fumbling with the laces on his breeches. "Oh, my God." Suddenly she had no problem imagining at all. In fact, her imagination was becoming reality. Her breath caught in her throat, and her heart began to hammer in her chest.

"This would be easier in that kilt," he muttered.

Chapter Twenty

Kendra watched, riveted, as he ripped the lacing from its holes and stuffed it into his pocket. The front of his breeches gaped open.

"Oh, my God." She gripped the iron bars even tighter. "You cannot think—"

"Aye, now that you mention it, I *am* having trouble thinking." He stepped close, tossing his hair from his face, a lethal look in his eye and a grin to match. "My head feels a bit light."

"Oh, my—"

Cutting off her words, his mouth came down on hers. Hot and frantic, his tongue delved inside immediately, and all at once, her head felt light, too. His hands spread her knees, and he stepped between them, pressing close. His warmth teased hers, and a shimmer of melting sensation rippled every nerve in her body. Just like that, she wanted him inside. Part of her had been waiting for this from the moment he'd given her that lust-threaded look the first time they were down here.

He kissed her chin, her throat, the broad expanse of her cleavage exposed in the yellow gown's low neckline. Down below, she strained against him. "Oh, my God." She wiggled forward, wanting him, craving him. She needed him to fill her. "Now, Trick. Please."

With a low groan, he shoved his hips closer, and the cage swung away.

Suddenly bereft, she hung there in space—such a loss, the heat of his body. When the cage swung back she released the bars to grip him tightly.

"Hell, *leannan*, this won't work."

"It has to." A fire burned inside her—how instantly it had flamed! She hadn't known it could happen so fast. She wrapped her legs around him, straining closer, a hot ache in the place she wanted him to be. Her hands roamed his back, and she groaned, irked to find so much clothing covering his body. A surcoat, a shirt, a cravat around his neck where her lips wanted to nip. "Your skin," she whispered, nipping his earlobe instead. "I want to touch you." She tugged at the knot about his throat, managing to loosen it, ripping at the laces beneath. But the placket wouldn't allow enough access to make her happy, so she tugged the shirt out of his breeches in the back, slipping her hands up underneath.

"Jesus, lass." He rocked his hips closer again.

And the cage moved right out from under her.

The forward force of her body made him stumble back, but he managed not to drop her or fall. She clung to him, arms and legs wrapped tight.

"Hang on," he grated out. Capturing her mouth in a kiss, he walked forward, every movement an exquisite friction in that small, unclothed area where her body met his. By the time he sat her on the rack, she was gasping for breath. He eased her onto her back and made to climb up—but the ancient, rickety contraption shuddered under them.

At the ominous sound of cracking wood, she twisted and jumped off, having to rip her skirt free of a large splinter. She frantically looked around. Once this space had been filled with nice, solid chests, but nothing was left now to support them.

"The floor is dirt," she moaned.

"Easy, lass." Reaching for her, he raised a devilish brow. "We've no need to lie down." His hands warm on her shoulders, he backed her up until she was flush against the wall.

She couldn't envision how it would work, but she didn't care, so long as they could finish what they'd started. And when he took her mouth in a heated kiss, the thoughts fled her head entirely. As the caress deepened, she raised her arms, intending to wrap them around his neck—and one of her hands hit an unhinged manacle.

At the muted thud, they both looked up, their ragged breathing the only sounds in the deserted dungeon. The expression in his eyes made her heart leap in her chest. Watching his reaction, she wriggled her wrist into the open oval.

"Nay." His hungry gaze went down to her raised breasts, then back up, darting between the manacles on either side of her head. Her own gaze followed.

"Nay," he said again. A more frustrated laugh she'd never heard. "It may be every man's fantasy, but you're not ready for that, *leannan*."

She was burning for him, and never in her life had she imagined herself fulfilling a man's fantasy. "Please," she whispered. She wrapped her free arm around his neck but left her other hand half-cuffed as she went to her toes for another kiss.

His tongue swept her mouth, and she could feel

his heart pounding against her breasts, her own blood rushing to match the wild cadence. "Please," she repeated against his lips.

A soft murmur vibrated from his body into hers, a sound of capitulation mixed with unbridled lust that made her senses spin, her knees threaten to buckle under her.

Lifting his head, he locked his gaze on hers. "Do you trust me, *leannan*?" His amber eyes fluttered closed and then open, burning into hers, the most fervent, forthright gaze she'd ever seen. "D'ye trust me?"

"Oh, yes," she breathed. And she did. No matter that he robbed Puritans and didn't seem to trust *her*, in his own unique way he was the most honorable man she'd ever known. It seemed he always—always—wanted to do the right thing.

She waited, willing him to believe her, until finally he reached up. Cold metal circled her wrist, a grating creak in her ear and a *bang* as the manacle closed. "Oh, my God, Trick."

" 'Tis not locked. Just tell me if you want out." When she didn't cry off, he lifted her, fitting her legs around his middle before he reached for her other arm. "The offer stands—I can have the cuffs open before the words pass your lips." His voice turned hurried, frenzied. "Keep your legs wrapped, *leannan*. I don't want any weight on your hands. I would never, never want to hurt you." *Snap*. Another bracelet around her second wrist, black iron instead of amber. Pressing her against the wall while he reached between their bodies, he tugged up her skirts and tucked the hem behind her shoulders. And with a quick upward thrust, he drove into her.

"Oh, my God." Her eyes shut, she struggled against the restraints, not hurting or frightened—he hadn't locked them, after all—but just frantic with the need to feel him. In her few lessons on love, she'd enjoyed the giving as much as the taking. Although she wanted to gift herself over to him, 'twas so hard to only succumb.

But as his hips initiated the rhythm her body craved, succumb she did. She clenched her fists against that urge to touch, her fingernails digging into her palms. Helpless to participate, she could only feel. Her skin prickled, her heart raced, and her whole world centered where her body met his. 'Twas agony, but sweet, so sweet. As his tempo quickened, she felt a throbbing, and she couldn't tell if it was hers or his. Then it grew, until she knew it belonged to them both. Until she felt him pulsing within her and responded in a burst of exquisite glory.

"Oh. My. God."

"Are you all right, *leannan*?" Panting, he moved to release her wrists. Her legs straightened, reaching for the floor, and she slid down his body, her gown still wrenched up between them. As she stood there on trembling limbs, he brought her wrists to his mouth and kissed them, one and then the other, so cherishingly that she thought her heart might crack at the tender look in his eyes.

"I think mayhap I got carried away there," he confessed in a husky whisper, circling her wrists with his hands. Rubbing. Warm, and so gentle. "Are you all right?"

She gave him a shaky smile. "I don't believe I've ever been better."

His hands stilled, and the beginning of a grin

tipped one corner of his mouth. "Are you sure, *leannan?*"

"Dear God, I've never been more sure in my life."

The ride was hardly short, but Kendra was still glowing with aftereffects when they walked through the tunnel and into the Great Hall. Their hands were joined, and she looked down to her wrist. A bracelet of amber and the faintest pink line, not enough to hurt or even feel, just enough to remind her of the glorious afternoon.

Seated at a trestle table with a hearty meal before him, Hamish's gaze went to their joined hands as well. He smiled, an elaborate sigh escaping his lips. "Ye two put me in mind of my Elspeth, ye do. Happy newlyweds ye are, and glad I am of it."

And 'twas true they were happy. True for Kendra, and as she met Trick's gaze, she knew it was true for him, too. Perhaps the matter of his parentage was disturbing, and perhaps she was still climbing the wall he'd built between them. But they'd turned a corner in that dungeon—they had laid the foundation for trust. A foundation they could build on in the days and weeks to come.

"The first time Da's been downstairs in weeks," Niall told them with a grin. "Join us, will ye? Da has been trying to puzzle out what happened. Did ye find any clues?"

Trick handed him the key. "Not much," he admitted, emptying his pockets. "Just this scrap of cloth"— he gave it to Hamish—"and this piece of glass." He set the shard on the table with an audible *clink*, then seated himself. Kendra took the chair at his side, and plates were set before them. Seeing nothing sweet on the table, she took a wedge of spinach tart while Trick eyed a platter of meat slices swimming in onions and a savory-smelling sauce. "What is this?"

"Mutton," Niall told him. "Scotch collops."

"Sounds good." He transferred a piece to his plate.

"Homespun." Hamish fingered the dark fabric. "It could have belonged to anyone, but most likely a common worker. Certainly not Elspeth or myself. As for this"—he picked up the glass—"it looks to be part of an old bottle. Wine, I'm guessing. We broke our share of them down there over the years."

Feeling her face heat, Kendra exchanged a look and a secret smile with Trick. Maybe he *had* been conceived there. And they could have conceived there themselves, she realized with a start.

He turned back to his father. "We also found a lot of footprints—they looked to be of four different people, clustered around the chests as they lifted. Three larger sets of prints and one smaller." He polished off the mutton and reached for another serving. "So more folk than Niall supposed must have known about the treasure."

"More folk know about it now," Hamish corrected. His mouth straightened into a grim line. "After the original folk enlisted their help in this crime."

"The original folk?"

With a sigh, the older man ran a hand back through his thinning hair, a gesture that reminded Kendra of Trick. "Gregor and Rhona," he practically spat. "My *friends*. Or so I thought."

"Da!" Niall's eyes went wide. "Ye cannot really mean to accuse them?"

"No one else kent of the place. Or the treasure's existence." Hamish's voice sounded bitter, betrayed.

"One small set of footprints—Rhona's. And three larger—Gregor and two men. One of them wearing homespun. Who else could it have been? The thieves had a key."

"Then they borrowed it or stole it—from ye or Rhona and Gregor. Someone could have followed ye there sometime. All those years . . ."

"No one followed. As for all those years . . . There were things that happened in those years, things ye dinna ken."

Looking shaky, Niall took a long sip, then set down his pewter goblet. "Such as?"

"Friends do not always get along. The four of us quarreled from time to time. Bitterly."

The spinach pie had turned out to be sweet after all, swimming in butter with cinnamon and sugar, but the last bite turned sour in Kendra's mouth. "What did you fight about?"

"For years now, Gregor and Rhona have wanted to sell off the treasure. The office of Town Clerk of Falkland does not pay so well, ye ken, at least not well enough for the two of them to live as they supposed they should, their best friend being a duchess. But Elspeth and I—we always argued with them, and we always won."

Niall ran his goblet back and forth on the pitted trestle table. "Ye were afraid if anything were sold, ye would be discovered."

"Aye, that was it in part, although Gregor always talked of carting the goods to London before disposing of them. Among the riches in that great city, he was convinced the treasure would go unnoticed, and in any case, not be connected to anyone back here in Scotland."

Kendra ran a finger around the rim of her own goblet. "But you didn't agree?"

"Royal plate is quite recognizable. But the truth is, we had other reasons for not wanting it sold. We only wanted it returned—off our hands."

Trick helped himself to a hunk of bread. "Could you not convince them?"

"We thought we had. Over and over. But always a few years later they would bring it up again." Hamish cut a piece of mutton. "I can only assume, Patrick, then when ye arrived, they saw their last chance slipping away. So they took it upon themselves to enlist help and make off with the chests before it was too late."

"Gregor and Rhona." Reluctantly, Niall nodded. "I expect that is why they've been absent since after the burial. I thought they needed rest, but come to think of it, 'tis odd they left ye alone, Da. When they spent every day here since Mam fell ill."

Hamish returned the nod.

Trick pushed away his plate. "So you think they're bound for London?"

"I expect so, son."

If Trick noticed the endearment, he didn't react. "We found cart tracks outside the tower, heading southeast around Falkland, and then more tracks from four wagons that went due south. We turned back when they crossed a wee river. Where would they go from there?"

"Down and over to Stirling Bridge," Niall said. " 'Tis the only way across the Forth."

"Unless they were in a hurry." Hamish dabbed at his lips with a napkin. "Then they'd head for Burntisland and the ferry over to Leith. Just as King Charles did all those years ago."

"They're in a hurry," Kendra said.

The three men turned to her. "How do you know?" Trick asked.

"They crossed the river instead of heading up or downstream to a bridge. Although it wasn't overly deep, there had to be some risk involved in traversing the water with such a heavy load."

A new appreciation lit Trick's eyes. "You're right. But still and all, even taking shortcuts they cannot have gotten far, not with a burden like that. The tracks were visible, and that means they left today." His gaze went to one of the deep-set windows. A light mist had begun to fall as they'd headed back to Duncraven. "I imagine the trail is washed away now. And they're making even slower progress."

Niall's chair scooted back with a scrape. "If we ride out immediately, we could make it there before them. And wait." Kendra could hear the excitement in his voice. 'Twas more than a mission for right he envisioned, but adventure as well. He and his new older brother, off to save the world. "I dinna suppose 'twill be too difficult for the likes of we two to dissuade one old man and woman."

"Watch your tongue, lad," Hamish put in, a ghost of a smile transforming his grim face. "Who are ye calling old?"

With a laugh, Trick stood. "I'll get my cloak." He started for the turret steps.

"Wait!" Kendra's chair fell over when she leapt up to go after him. But he was already far ahead of her, his boots disappearing around the tight curve as he took the steep staircase two steps at a time. She could only manage one.

By the time she caught up, he was already inside their chamber, spreading his cloak on the bed. Breathless, she caught him by the arm. "I want to go with you."

He spun to face her. "No. We've been over this before."

"This is not a highwayman raid, Trick. I'll worry—"

"And I'll worry more if you come." He caressed her cheek with the backs of his long fingers, then moved away to root through the clothespress. "Stay with Hamish," he said, pulling out a black shirt and breeches. "He needs people around him."

"He has Duncan and Annag, and his grandchildren."

"Aye?" He tossed the garments on the open cloak. "Then where were they today?"

"Back at their homes," Niall said behind them. They both turned to find him standing in the open doorway, a roll of parchment in one hand. "Packing up their lives. Seems they're moving here for good."

"Good?" Kendra asked incredulously.

"Bad choice of words." In the light from the garrison's torches behind him, he half-grimaced, half-grinned. "But I dinna want to upset Da by questioning this. Not until he's stronger."

"I understand." And she did. But that didn't mean she wanted to stay here with Niall's brother and sister. Left to deal with them alone, she could picture herself tearing her hair out. She'd be bald by the time Trick returned.

Suddenly she realized they were Trick's brother and sister, too. "They're yours," she blurted.

"Pardon?" He buckled on his sword belt.

"Duncan and Annag. They're your brother and sister."

In the act of shoving a pistol into his boot top, he froze, the gun dangling from his fingers. Niall leapt into the room to catch it. "*Half* brother and sister," he corrected.

Trick's face had gone pale, and Kendra wished she could see the expression in his eyes, but his hair hung in the way.

"They're my half siblings, too, and I manage to survive," Niall joked weakly. " 'Tis not all that bad."

"I just hadn't thought of it."

"Then have ye thought about the fact that you're Scottish?" Niall handed over the gun.

Trick stared at it as if he'd never seen one before. "Scottish?" he repeated.

"One-hundred percent Scots," his brother said in an exaggerated burr. "Both your parents."

"I hadn't thought about that, either." Regaining his color, he shook his head as though to clear it, but the hair fell right back into his eyes. "I thought Mam was half Irish?"

Niall shrugged. "I suppose. But either way, you're not English, ye ken?"

A small smile tugged at Trick's lips. "I never did feel very English."

"Well, that's because ye aren't." His brother returned his grin. "But ye up and married a Sassenach, aye?"

"Guess I did, at that." He reached an arm to pull Kendra close, and she relaxed, seeing that he was over the shock. He felt warm against her side, and she wished he wasn't leaving. She looked down, twisting the bracelet on her wrist.

Trick jammed the pistol into his boot top. "Are you ready?" he asked Niall.

"I brought a map." Walking to the desk, his brother unrolled the parchment. "I thought you'd like to see the way."

Trick helped him smooth it on the scarred oak surface. "We're here, are we?"

"Aye, and going here." Leaning over the map, Niall traced a finger southward. "Alongside the mountains and through the hills to the coast. Burntisland is directly opposite from Leith, do ye see?"

"Across the Firth of Forth, aye." Trick's own finger followed the path. "How long should it take to Burntisland?"

"On horseback, not long. Two, three hours. With twenty-three chests of silver and gold, a whole day, maybe longer. Especially in the rain. The way is not flat at all."

"That's in our favor." Trick stood, rerolled the parchment, and stuck it into his belt. "Shall we leave?

"Just give me a minute to fetch my things. I'll meet ye downstairs." Niall left, his footsteps hurrying through the garrison and then echoing as he descended the stairwell.

When the sound faded away, Kendra turned into Trick's arms. "Are you sure I cannot come with you?"

"I'm sure, *leannan*." He bent his head, his lips apologetic on hers. "This shouldn't take long. A few hours to get there, a day to get back with those chests." His lips brushed hers again, then lingered. His tongue teased her mouth, robbing her of breath, making her want to beg him to stay.

But she wouldn't. Rhona and Gregor had to be

stopped. And she wouldn't push any more to go along. She was determined to be better than in the past, the sort of supportive wife he deserved.

"Be safe," she said softly.

"I will." A final kiss only left her wanting more. "I have a plan, so dinna ye worry."

She squeezed him around the middle. "You're talking like a Scot already, you know that? Before much longer, Caithren will be the only one at home who can understand you."

With a laugh, he was gone.

"Sit still, milady." Jane's hands curled and twisted. "You're restless this morning."

Feeling like little Susanna at the orphanage, Kendra sighed. Her gaze went to the bedchamber's window. It had rained all night, but seemed to be letting up now. "I wonder how they're doing. All the night and into the morning."

"I'm sure they're fine, milady." Jane stole a cube of cheese from Kendra's untouched breakfast tray and popped it into her mouth. "They're probably on their way home already."

Kendra fingered the amber around her wrist, a bit sad that the slight pinkness from yesterday was gone. Trick had said he had a plan. She hoped it was a good one. "I didn't say I was worried."

"Of course you're worried." Jane tied a purple ribbon and stepped back. "There you go. He'll be home soon. You're doing well here, are you not?"

Was Jason checking up on her here, too? Kendra wondered. The thought made her warm inside, and although she knew 'twas unlikely, Leslie Castle being as far from here as it was, she also knew that her brother would do so if he could. He cared—just like Jane cared enough to ask the question.

"How are *you* doing here, Jane?"

"Why, fine." Gathering combs, pins, and ribbons, the maid arranged them in her little traveling case. "I've a room to myself bigger than the one I share at Amberley—why should I not be fine?"

"How is that?" Kendra frowned. "I would expect the servants' quarters to be crowded, what with Duncraven's staff and now Amberley's."

"Did you not know, then, milady?"

"Know what?" She rose and wandered to the window. The rain had stopped, and she smiled at the scene below, where a mama rabbit hopped after her baby through Elspeth's garden.

"When His Grace—not your husband, but his father—left all those many years ago, he stopped providing Her Grace's allowance. She had to survive on what Duncraven earns, which I gather isn't much. Most of the servants were dismissed."

"My God." Kendra swung from the window, the room looking suddenly dark. That explained why a nurse companion was doing bedchamber duty. And why the castle was so run-down. "His Grace—my husband—doesn't know of this, Jane. That I can promise."

"Calm yourself, mistress." Jane shut her wooden case. "No one here blames him, and besides, this happened long ago. The remaining staff are just happy to have employment. And since Mr. Munroe moved in, they even get paid." She took her curling iron from the hearth and blew to cool it off. "Shall I sit with you and play some cards? The day might pass more quickly."

"Maybe later. I think I may sit with Hamish a while."

Jane's plain face split in a smile of approval. "Excellent idea. You know where to find me."

"I do. My thanks." Kendra followed her maid out the door and down the winding, torchlit stairs, biting the inside of her cheek. She knew Trick wouldn't stand for his father and brother scrimping to the point they apparently were. Estate management was her strength, and she hoped to get to the bottom of Duncraven's problems before he returned. And find a solution that wouldn't involve him playing the highwayman any longer. Coming into the sitting room, she headed for Hamish's door. Perhaps there were opportunities for income that they had missed.

"Where did they go off to, Kendra?"

She whirled and, finding herself face-to-face with Annag, stifled a groan. "I told you, I don't know." And told her and told her. At least a dozen times last night, before she'd escaped the Great Hall to toss and turn in her lonely bed. She skirted past her sister-in-law, toward the master chamber's closed door. "Why are you so interested, anyway? Have you some stake in the outcome of today's work?"

Annag came around to block her way, fists raised. "Of what are ye accusing me?"

"Go ahead, hit me. I've three brothers, and I can assure you they've schooled me well."

The woman's eyes narrowed, but she dropped her hands. "I'll get Duncan to find out, then." She flounced to the door, opened it, and slipped inside, slamming it behind her. "Dun-cannnn!" her voice came through the thick oak.

So much for consulting with Hamish—the last

thing Kendra needed was another round with Duncan and his sister. So far she still had all her hair, and she preferred to keep it that way. She headed downstairs and outside instead, hoping for some peace to appreciate the whimsical world that Elspeth had created. Once it had calmed Trick; perhaps the castle garden would work the same magic on her.

Though the rain had stopped, the day was blustery, the sky still gray and forbidding. She walked the paths, bending to touch a little castle here and there, smiling at Trick's mother's inventiveness. A blue one with little bits of metal to make it sparkle. A yellow one surrounded by miniature trees. She could almost picture Elspeth working on them, a small blond boy at her side. If he'd "helped" as well as the children at the orphanage did, she imagined it had taken the woman twice as long as necessary to build each one.

There was a fanciful one, painted pink, a green dragon guarding its entrance. It looked so pretty surrounded by bell-shaped purplish flowers.

She froze. Bell-shaped purplish flowers.

Black nightshade. Belladonna. Dwale.

She reached out, then snatched back her hand. *Dinna touch. It is possible to fall ill without even eating it*, Caithren's voice haunted her head. *D'ye see these dark-green leaves? They are lethal.*

Only a few of those dull, dark-green leaves, because most of them had been plucked off.

Like Cait, Rhona had knowledge of plants and herbs. And she'd been feeding a concoction to Hamish. Her "cure" with its dark-green hue. Hamish's symptoms—likely Elspeth's symptoms as well—had been just what Caithren had described: shock, fever, slowed breathing, dilated eyes, stomach pain . . .

Rhona had been poisoning them both.

She ran for the castle and upstairs to her chamber, ripping off her gown in exchange for a riding habit. She threw on her cloak, praying she'd not run into anyone on her way back outside.

Dear God. She had to warn Trick and Niall. Her husband and his brother were all that stood between Rhona and Gregor and that treasure, and if the two of them had been willing to murder twice, they'd be willing to do it again.

Before she even puzzled it all out, she was heading for the stables and Pandora. Tapping a foot, she watched the stable boy lift the saddle to the mare's back. "Hurry, would you?" She'd hung over Trick's shoulder as he and Niall pored over the map yesterday, and she was sure she knew the way.

The stable boy frowned. "Ye cannot go riding alone, Your Grace."

She forced a smile. "At home in England, I ride alone all the time."

"This is Duncraven, not England. Allow me to arrange for an escort."

"I thank you, but no." An escort would see where she was headed and ride right back. Then she'd be caught and kept from going altogether. Hamish would want to send someone else—a messenger or, God forbid, Duncan. And she was not going to sit here worrying while the men in her life were facing murderers. "I really prefer to ride alone. It clears my head."

The stable boy was backing through the doors, clearly going for help. Taking over where he'd left off, she cinched the saddle tight, then swung herself up. "Tell Mr. Hamish I'll be back," she called as she rode off.

'Twas more miles than it had looked on the map, but Pandora was swift. The hours took her over rolling land nestled against a range of green mountains, then finally on a tree-lined road that wound through the hills that shielded the coastline. Cattle grazed in the meadows, and purple thistles sprouted everywhere. A fine mist fell from the sky, and the clouds were growing darker, promising heavier weather to come. When the twisting road crested and she could see the small village of Burntisland tucked into a bay in the distance, the Firth of Forth tossing fitfully beyond it, she started worrying about how she would locate her husband.

As luck would have it—bad luck—she barreled through a sea of cornflowers, rounded a bend, and almost rode right over him.

Chapter Twenty-one

"Grab her!" Rhona yelled.

Trick looked up from the man and the rope in his hands to see Kendra yanked off Pandora. A heartbeat later, Gregor had a blade to her neck. Where the hell had she come from?

Stunned, Trick could barely find breath. Empty-saddled, Pandora reared and galloped up the embankment, his and Niall's mounts bolting after her.

"Damn ye for a dastardly whoreson," Gregor grated through gritted teeth. "Release my man, before your pretty wife's head is rolling down the road."

"Don't listen to him, Trick!" Tears swam in Kendra's eyes. "He'll only kill you. He's murdered once already, almost twice—"

"Now!" Gregor bellowed.

His gaze riveted to Kendra's, Trick dropped the rope and slowly stepped back, the blood pounding in his ears. *I'm sorry*, she mouthed, her heart in her glistening eyes. She raised her clenched knuckles to her teeth while the tears slipped down her cheeks.

"Rhona, get the weapons."

Stalking over to retrieve the pistols Trick had made them drop to the ground mere minutes earlier, Rhona smirked at Kendra. "Thank ye, dearie." She shoved a gun into one of their accomplice's hands. "For a while there, your husband thought he had us fooled." The man Trick had been restraining struggled out of his half-tied bonds, and she handed over another pistol. "Imagine he and his brother thinking they could hold the four of us up."

Atop the rise overhead, Niall shakily stood, the lone real gunman among a dozen hats and pipes they'd arranged around him. He ripped the makeshift mask from his face. "We *did* fool ye," he spat.

"Until your bonnie sister-in-law showed up and we put two and two together." Gregor tightened his hold around Kendra, and she flinched, making Trick's heart leap into his throat. "Drop your gun, lad, lest ye be the next to feel my knife."

"He'll kill you anyway, Niall! I'm telling you—"

Niall's pistol fell to the road with an ominous thud. Steaming—at Kendra, or Gregor and Rhona, or the world in general, he really wasn't sure which—Trick tore off his own mask and tugged the periwig from his head.

"Dinna move!" Gregor growled. A tiny red nick appeared on Kendra's creamy skin, and her whimper took a year off Trick's life. Gregor swung his gaze on one of the other two men, motioning toward Trick with his head. "Kill him first."

"I told you!" Kendra wailed.

"Kill?" Palms forward, his own gun pointed to the sky, the man backed away. A Duncraven villager—Trick had slapped him at the *draidgie.* Now he wished he'd pounded him into the floorboards.

"Nobody said anything about killin', ye ken? We were supposed to move some chests and go home with gold in our pockets. Nobody said anything about killin'."

"I'm with ye, Davie." The second man's pistol dropped to the dirt. "Good day to ye people. I know not what game you're playing, but I'll be heading back to Duncraven now—ye may keep my horse wi' my compliments." Casting a wistful glance to the animal in question, which was hitched to one of the wagons, he started walking.

"Wait!" Rhona's eyes darted back and forth between the retreating men and her husband. "We dinna have to kill." Her voice rose an octave. "I told ye from the first, Gregor, we didn't have to kill!" The men halted and turned back around, apparently reserving judgment. "Damn ye, Gregor, I told ye we didn't have to kill!"

"Aye, and then ye talked me into that milk-livered way of doing it, when we could've been done with the deed and clear to London weeks before *he* showed up." He aimed a deadly glance at Trick.

"Hell mend ye!" the first man said, pivoting away.

"Wait!" Rhona shot her pistol into the air.

Everyone froze. A choked sound came from Kendra's throat.

"We dinna have to kill," Rhona repeated, her jaw tight with fury as she faced her husband. Visibly shaking, she gestured wildly at the four loaded wagons. "We cannot do this alone. We cannot let them walk." Her gaze fell on the rope Trick had dropped to the ground. "We can tie the bastards up, like they were going to do us." He'd never heard such language from a woman's mouth. "We'll be long gone across the Forth before they can follow. The tide will turn, and they'll be stuck here 'til tomorrow."

Other than his labored breathing, Gregor remained silent. Resolute. The two other men exchanged looks and resumed walking.

A crack of lightning rent the air. "Come back," Gregor grated out as thunder rumbled and rain began pelting the earth. "I'll hold this one until ye tie up the others." His breath came in spasmodic jerks. "You!" he shouted to Niall. "Get down here unless ye want to see the inside of your sister-in-law's gullet."

Niall didn't need to be told twice.

Using Trick's own ropes, they tied him and then his brother on the muddy ground, feet together, wrists crossed and bound behind their backs, then lashed to their bodies for good measure. Finally Gregor wrestled Kendra to the ground, and the two men gave her the same treatment.

"Ouch!" she yelled. "Ouch! Ouch! Ouch! *Ouch! OUCH!*" Lying on his side, Trick winced with each tug of the rope, though frankly he couldn't imagine what she found so painful. The entire situation was aggravating as hell, but it didn't hurt so much as to warrant squealing like a pig. His poor wife must have the lowest pain threshold in history, he decided, remembering her reaction on their wedding night. Should she ever give birth, he would do best to keep clear of the house. Of the county, mayhap.

He was jarred from those musings when Gregor came to stand over him, murder in his cold blue eyes. "Ye bleedin' bastard!" A swift kick to Trick's side knocked the breath from his lungs. Gregor's jaw clenched, and he kicked again, a blow so hard Trick heard the sharp crack of a rib. Pain knifed through him, exquisite agony that made the worst of his father's beatings seem insignificant. He shut his eyes, gasping for air, hearing the wagons roll down the road as he waited for the pain to subside.

"Trick? Oh, my God. Trick, are you all right?"

"I'll live." She was too far away to touch, but he opened his eyes and sent her a wan, forced smile. "Are *you* all right?"

"Yes." The tears welled up again. "Oh, God, I'm so sorry. I know you told me not to come, but she was poisoning them, Trick, they were—"

"We'll talk of it later." He was too confused right now, torn between fury that she'd shown up and relief that her throat was intact. The pain was becoming bearable, an insistent throb along his left side. "Niall? You all right, man?"

"Aye. I should have shot him."

"Don't be a horse's arse. 'Twas four against two, and a knife at her throat." His eyes widened when he looked back to Kendra. "What the hell are you doing?"

"Getting out." She gyrated in the mud. "Angus and Davie, they're nice men at heart. I talked to them at the *draidgie*."

"What?"

"I thought if I could convince them they were hurting me, they'd leave the ropes loose." She wiggled free one hand. "It worked."

"Holy Christ," Niall breathed. "She's a bloody genius."

And Trick was a damned idiot.

Her arm was still tied to her body, and it took another few minutes to work it free. Then more long minutes to unravel the rest until only her ankles were bound. She made short work of those bonds and scrambled to her feet, shaking out the kinks, splattering mud to the ground.

"I never thought I'd say this, but thank God 'tis raining." She tilted her head back, letting the downpour run into her mouth and wash down her body.

A wry laugh shot from Trick's throat, shortened by the pain in his ribs. "Untie me, wench."

Minutes later, he was free, hugging her like he never wanted to let go, never mind the ache in his side. He dropped kisses on her mouth, her cheeks, her eyes. "Sweet Mary, *leannan*." He pulled back, running his fingers over the tiny cut on her throat, convincing himself it wasn't serious. "I thought I was going to lose you." Then he kissed her all over again.

Laughing, she drew away. "Don't forget your brother."

He knelt, stifling a groan, and loosened Niall's bonds, grasping his hand to help him up. They embraced hard, then drew back and met each other's eyes. "Shall we go get them?" Trick asked.

"Hell, yes."

The villains were already at the quay in the distance, unloading the wagons into a broad-beamed, single-masted boat. Or rather, the men were unloading. Rhona was wringing her hands, and an agitated ferryman was alternately assisting and barking orders short-tempered enough to cut through the wind and the rain all the way to Trick's ears.

"No more, I tell ye! She canna hold it! And the tide has turned—we must leave, or we willna clear the harbor mouth—"

His words were cut off when Gregor turned a pistol on him. "Faster!" he shouted, shooting a shocked and then furious glance to where Trick and the others thundered closer on their horses. "Faster!"

"Enough!" the ferryman cried. "Take the last two off! 'Twill sink, I tell ye!"

As the tide flooded out, the water level dropped between the two great stone piers that thrust east and west, the hundred-foot gap between them the only exit from Burntisland's harbor. In minutes, 'twould be too shallow and dangerous to navigate.

Trick reached the quay, his wife and brother arriving on Chaucer's heels. In unison they dropped to the dock, throwing their reins over a rail.

Ignoring the warnings, Gregor and the other two men thrust the last chest onboard and shoved off, the boat so laden there was barely room to stand. With a shouted oath, the ferryman jumped to the dock in the last instant, sputtering as the craft pulled away, already taking on water. In mute but panicked agreement, Gregor's helpers abandoned ship as well, leaping into the chilly harbor.

The boat's sails billowed, and it lurched forward, nearing the harbor mouth. Trick untied a smaller boat and scrambled aboard. "You, come!" he shouted to Niall. When Kendra made to follow, he waved her back. "You stay here!"

"A pox on you!" she screamed. With a running leap, she cleared the gap just as the boat pulled away.

Cursing under his breath, he shot a glance at the other boat floundering its way into open water. No time to argue, no time to turn back. "We'll discuss this later, too. Have you not learned anything today?"

Niall grabbed two oars and started rowing. Before long, the ferryman looked like a tiny toy doll back on the quay, pacing and pounding his fists into the air. Another rumble of thunder ripped through the heavens.

"Look!" Kendra gasped.

From the west, a dense black cloud was sweeping down the firth.

"Bloody hell!" Trick had spent enough time aboard ships to know what that meant. Saying a quick prayer for the souls aboard the already-faltering boat, he snatched up the second set of oars to help row toward the laden ship, his ribs throbbing with every stroke. "If we transfer a chest or two aboard," he panted, planning as he went, "mayhap we can lighten the load enough for the ferry to make it back. Niall, help me move them. Kendra, when I pull alongside, take the oars and try to keep her in place."

With the storm bearing down, he hadn't the luxury of being angry with her now. He would use her now, and yell at her later for complicating everything. Damn stubborn woman. Always doing exactly as she pleased. Riding out by herself and getting them trapped into marriage, showing up on a highwayman raid when he'd expressly told her not to, running after him to Scotland, following him to Burntisland. And now this.

A few minutes later, they bumped up against the bucking ferry. "Now!"

He leapt across, his landing painful but safe. Niall followed, dashing to the nearest chest. Damn, it was heavy—not easily loaded by three men, and Trick was one injured man with a lad. But necessity bred strength, and together they wrestled it to the rail. Frantically bailing water, Gregor and Rhona failed to notice them until they'd already half-shoved it into their craft. A scrape and a clunk, and it was aboard—and Gregor rounded on Trick with a vengeance.

Trick took a punch to the gut that glanced off his tender ribs. He doubled over, wheezing in pain before he gathered force and returned the favor, smashing a fist into the older man's face. Niall added his own blow to the midsection, and Gregor stumbled backward, landing hard in a foot of water.

The ferry was pitching and yawing, slashing rain pounding its decks. As Gregor struggled to his feet, the whole vessel tilted. Thrown against the rail, Rhona screamed. One of the chests skidded past her, missing her by inches, and crashed over the side, taking a section of railing and Rhona along with it.

"Rhona!" Gregor scrambled after her, grabbing for her hand as she slid from the deck, their fingertips grazing but failing to grip. Trick leapt to keep Gregor from going overboard, his arms around the man's waist slamming him back into his abused body, while Niall jumped in to save the man's wife.

Tossed on the roiling firth, Niall's head swung wildly in search, but she'd already slipped beneath the waves. He disappeared after her. Bracing between two chests, Trick grimaced and hung on to Gregor, holding his breath until his brother's blond head broke the surface, the woman draped limp on his back. Niall fought his way to the vessel's outer ladder, shoving her aboard before clambering up himself, fighting the wind and the rain.

Gregor wrenched from Trick's grasp and threw himself on his wife while Niall lay on deck, panting, water washing over him and into his open mouth.

"We've got to move another one!" Trick yelled. "She's still taking water!"

Niall nodded and pushed himself up.

"Trick!" Kendra's panicked voice came thready through the storm. " 'Tis slipping!"

He rushed to the other side of the ship. Tossing wildly, the smaller boat had drifted yards away. Though she strained against it with both hands and a shoulder, the chest he'd loaded was inching toward one end, threatening to overbalance the boat.

Threatening to drown Kendra.

Faster than the wind, Niall flew past him and into the water. Priming to follow, Trick found himself smashed to the deck by a huge, roaring wave. He gasped for air, the deck awash, the rush sucking him over the side.

Freezing black water covered his head. He fought his way to the surface, only to be blindsided by a plunging chest. Woozy, he flailed in the lashing surf, battered by waves and debris. Chunks of broken timber, lengths of rigging, thick hunks of rope. He took water into his lungs, and it burned like the fires of hell. His ribs screamed with pain, and he couldn't lift his arms, couldn't swim, couldn't keep his head above the pitching seas that seemed determined to send him to a watery grave.

His last thought was of Kendra, struggling against that chest. Stubborn, willful, beautiful Kendra. Kendra, who put orphans above riches. . . . Kendra, who'd accepted his own family before he did. . . . Kendra, who could make his heart pound with a single glance. . . .

Damn, but he loved her.

Chapter Twenty-two

He was freezing.

He wasn't dead, then. Hell was supposed to be hot. And heaven—not that he expected to go there—was supposed to be like floating on a warm, comfortable cloud. Yet he shivered with a bone-deep cold, so cold it felt as if he would never be warm again. And he was far from comfortable.

A teeth-rattling jounce drove home that last point. Even hell would be better than this, he thought with a groan.

"He's coming around!" The voice was heavenly, the warm lips pressed to his face more heavenly still. "Oh, Trick, I'm so sorry, I'm so sorry . . ."

"Cold," he murmured.

"Just a minute. I'm almost finished."

A tug against his side sent such pain spiraling through him, he decided he must be halfway dead, at least. "Hurts," he grated out.

"I know. This bandage should help."

He forced open his eyes, lifting his head, which felt entirely too heavy, so heavy it dropped back with a skull-jarring bang. But he'd seen her. Kendra. Sweet Kendra. She hadn't drowned, after all. His heart wanted to fly, but the rest of him insisted on staying earthbound. "Bandage?" he wondered.

"My chemise. Or part of it, anyway." A bump sent his body into the air and back down with a wracking jolt. Not earthbound. Wagon-bound. He was in a wagon. And his precious wife was wrapping his ribs in a bandage ripped from her chemise.

His brain struggled to put the pieces together. How had he been hurt, but even more intriguing, how had she torn the bandage from the chemise? He pictured her lifting her skirts, her lovely, shapely legs coming into view as she rent the ivory fabric. Wishing he'd been able to watch that, he realized he must not be half-dead, after all. Parts of him were far from dead, although other parts made him long for that peace. Then she raised her gaze to his, and he was glad, oh, so glad he was still alive.

"He's awake, Niall!" Her hair was a tangled mess, her face smeared with dirt, but her smile enough to brighten the cloudy day. Then her expression fell. "Oh, God, Trick, I'm so sorry." Tears sprang to her eyes, and he wanted to tell her not to cry, but the words were stuck in his throat.

"Brother!" Elated, Niall's voice floated to his ears from somewhere above his head. "How d'ye feel?"

"Throat hurts," he croaked, still staring at his wife. Even red-rimmed, her eyes looked the most beautiful green.

"Ye tossed a heap of water," Niall explained. "Jesus, was it disgusting." Something was passed over Trick's head. A flask. "Kendra, give him this."

She cradled his head in one hand, lifting the flask to his lips with the other. He drank greedily at first, then choked when the liquor burned his raw throat.

"*Usquebagh*," Niall called. "Water of life. Whisky. Take more, it'll do ye good."

He did, gingerly this time, feeling the spirits burn a path to his belly. "Warm," he murmured.

Drawing a shuddering breath, Kendra blinked back her tears. "I'll warm you in a minute." She tied off the makeshift bandage, a blessed tightness that seemed to pull him back together, both his body and his mind. Memory rushed back, and with it some of the anger at her for interfering. But, too, he remembered his thoughts as he'd sunk beneath the water. Thoughts of love, from a man who'd been convinced he didn't believe.

Later. He would think about all this later.

As she struggled to tug down his shirt, he levered up and found himself surrounded by horses. Niall had roped the four dray animals together to pull the wagon, and their own three mounts trotted behind. They were making good time.

His feet were braced against a chest—the single chest they'd wrestled off the doomed ship. One chest saved out of twenty-three. He dropped his head to a makeshift pillow fashioned from his soggy surcoat. The rain had stopped, and the sun was struggling valiantly to peek between broken clouds.

"There." She drew up a blanket to cover him. It felt warm, warmer still when she crawled beneath to cuddle up to his good side, sharing the heat of her body. Heavenly. He was in heaven, after all.

"The ferryman gave it to me," she said.

"Gave you what?"

"The blanket."

"After you puked all over his floor," Niall added.

"Nice of him." He laced his fingers with Kendra's. "Especially considering he lost his boat."

Fresh, warm tears wetted his almost-dry shirt where her head nestled on his shoulder. "We lost them," she said, the words soft and regretful. "Gregor and Rhona and the treasure."

"But we didn't lose each other." He squeezed her hand. "I think, *leannan*, we can thank God for that. And Niall."

"Nay," his brother called back. "Thank her. She's the one who pulled ye from the water."

Stunned, he gasped. "How?" He was twice her weight, at least.

He sensed rather than saw Niall's shrug. "I managed to get to the boat, was dealing with the shifting chest. The next thing I knew she was leaping over my head."

"That wave." Kendra's voice shook with memory. " 'Twas like a mountain. It came down, and you disappeared for a moment. Then I saw you go over the side. As though you were riding a waterfall, it looked. I've never been more frightened in my life."

"I know the feeling," he soothed, remembering the sight of her with a knife at her throat. "Rhona and Gregor? Did you see them, too?"

"No," she said. "We never saw them at all. They were there, them and the boat, and then they were not. By the time I got you aboard, there was nothing where that ship had been but an eerie calm patch on the surface of the water, dotted with bits of debris."

Slowly he nodded, feeling an overwhelming weariness suddenly swamp him. Sweet Mary, she had saved his life. Because she'd disobeyed him—because in spite of his protests she'd flown into that boat like an avenging angel—she'd been there, and she'd saved his life. . . .

"I'm so sorry," she whispered.

But Trick was already asleep.

'Twas nearing midnight by the time they arrived at Duncraven, cold, hungry, and—at least on Kendra's part—exhausted. Trick's long sleep in the wagon bed seemed to have gone an amazing way toward restoring his strength, and Niall clearly found his second wind as they neared the castle, itching to tell his father all about the adventure of a lifetime. But she hadn't slept a wink on the bumpy ride, too caught up in wonder that they were all alive, tempered by a wrenching regret that her own part in the day's events had led to its tragic end.

While Trick and Niall went straight to fill Hamish in, she begged off and dragged herself upstairs, wanting nothing but a hot bath and a good night's sleep.

She'd almost accomplished the first when Trick came in, a platter in one hand and two goblets in the other. Quickly she slid deeper into the water, crossing her arms over her breasts. No matter that he'd seen all of her before—no man had ever seen her bathe. It seemed different. Private somehow. And too intimate, considering what she'd put him through today.

He shouldn't want to see her at all.

"I can take over from here." He nodded a dismissal at Jane, and she left, quietly closing the door behind her. "Hungry?" he asked matter-of-factly.

"Not really." Her eyes filled with tears. "I'm so sorry, Trick, for ruining your plan. If I hadn't arrived and tipped them off as to who you were, none of this would have happened."

"You cannot know that; we cannot know what would have happened." He set the food on the desk, his amber gaze filled with concern. "Mayhap you ruined our plan, but you also saved my life. I thank you for that, lass, from the bottom of my heart."

Her own heart hurt. Oh, if only she could forgive herself as easily as he seemed to forgive her. Then he ran a hand back through his hair, and she blinked, staring, so stunned her own guilt fled her mind.

"You cut it," she breathed. "Your hair."

A wry grin twitched at his lips. "Mrs. Ross cut it. There I was, telling Hamish all about what happened, her fussing over Niall and me both. Moving chairs near the fire so we could warm, pushing hot drinks into our hands. As we talked, she removed Niall's damp coat and ran a comb through his hair. And the next thing I knew she was standing over me with scissors."

"You didn't stop her."

His only answer was a shrug. But he was no longer hiding, not from her. The heart that he'd spoken of thanking her from was right there in his amber eyes.

He came close and knelt by the big wooden tub, setting the goblets on the floor beside him. "No more tears. I hold you blameless for anything that happened today. You must believe that."

When he drew her hands from her body, she forgot to be embarrassed. She squeezed his fingers, staring into those unguarded eyes. "You blame yourself instead, don't you?"

"Aye," he admitted, toying with the amber on her

wrist. "But Hamish—Da"—a fleeting smile curved his mouth—"did his best to set me straight."

"What did he have to say?"

He kissed her fingertips and sighed. "He thinks 'tis just as well that Niall and I didn't manage to keep his friends from drowning, since it saved him the trouble of having them hanged. As for the Royal plate, he believes 'tis fate . . . and only fitting that it ended up where it was thought to be all along."

She heard very little conviction in those words. "You don't agree."

"'Tis difficult to avoid feeling like a failure when you lose an immense fortune and two lives into the bargain. But I'm working on it."

She'd been working on trying to better herself, too. "I wanted to stay here like you told me to—truly I did—but then when I realized they were murderers, and thought of you out there not knowing that . . . your lives at risk . . ." At the very thought, she felt her heart pounding all over again. "I tried to obey, but I'm not made that way, Trick."

"I know." He sighed theatrically, but the tilt of his lips told her 'twas only for show. "I expect I will just have to get used to that."

"I'm so glad you're willing to try." Though she still didn't hold herself blameless, relief flowed through her in heady waves. He was accepting her for who she was. More than anyone ever had in her life. "I was only trying to warn you of their wicked ways, but it all went wrong."

"Your heart was in the right place." His lips brushed her knuckles, and his breath on her hands warmed not only her fingers but somewhere deep inside. "I'm not used to anyone wanting to take care of me," he told her in a deep, husky voice, "but I do appreciate it. And I'm hoping we can make a fresh start, and that some day, I will prove myself deserving of your special sort of loyalty."

Could they really begin anew and learn to trust one another? Her heart soared at the thought. She sent him a tremulous smile, and he dropped her hands, reaching down to raise a goblet. She took it, sipping at the fortifying wine while he walked over to the desk.

"Midnight supper." Carrying the platter, he dragged the chair over to sit by the tub. "Will you have some bread and cheese?"

She nodded, surprised to find herself suddenly ravenous. "I'm worried, Trick. About Hamish and Niall."

"Aye?" Balancing the platter on his knees, he cut a slice of pungent cheddar. "What are you worried about?" he asked, tearing a hunk of bread and handing them to her together.

"Things have not gone well here since your father—the duke—took you away." She nibbled on the bread. "Jane told me he cut off your mother's allowance, and she had to dismiss most of the servants."

Taking a hearty bite of his own, he nodded as he chewed. "I guessed as much, noting the state of this place." He swallowed, washing it down with a gulp of wine. "I asked Niall about it on our long trek to Burntisland."

"And?"

"Hamish does well for himself in the cloth trade. But other than allowing him to make up back pay for the servants, she refused to take his money when he moved in." In three big bites, he polished off a slab of cheese. "Stubborn woman. She may not have been as bad as the duke had convinced me, but she was far from perfect."

"We all are," Kendra reminded him. "Will they be all right here, then, do you think?"

"Aye, with Hamish's help. And Niall is planning to visit Amberley later this year and learn some more progressive farming. Scotland is behindhand, it seems—I thought mayhap you could help him with that."

His steady confidence did much to make her trust in this fresh start of which he'd spoken. And Hamish and Niall would be fine. She sagged with relief, draining the rest of her wine.

"Feel better now?" he asked.

"Immensely." Everything was working out perfectly.

"Good." He rose, taking the goblet from her hands. Was that a gleam she saw in his eyes, she wondered, or was it only that she wasn't used to seeing them so clearly?

She got her answer when he started ripping off his clothes. "Wh-what are you doing?"

"Joining you, *leannan*. I'm grubby as hell."

"B-but . . . together?" She half rose out of the tub.

With a hand on her shoulder, he pushed her back down. "Together."

"You're jesting," she said. "And you're hurt." But as his gaze held hers, his words that first night in Scotland slipped through her thoughts: *I'd like to see all of you wet*. And she knew he wasn't jesting at all.

"Aye, I hurt a bit," he admitted. "But I trust you'll be gentle." Opposite her, he stepped into the water.

"Your bandage!"

"Stop being such a worrywart, lass. 'Tis more comfortable with it on." As he lowered himself, he nodded toward her tattered chemise. "There's another where this one came from."

She sat motionless as his legs slid under her own, then gasped when he grasped her by the waist to bring her up and onto his lap. But his small grunt of pain didn't seem to signal any loss of enthusiasm. His lips went to hers immediately, his tongue plunging into her mouth while he reached back to arrange her legs around his body.

Lulled by his kiss and his hands roaming her wet skin, she pressed closer. Below, her body met his, and a hot stab of desire took her by surprise. Dear God, he was right there, almost inside her.

He smiled against her lips. "Not yet, *leannan*. We haven't washed."

"I've washed already."

He reached for the soap behind her head. "Then you can wash me," he suggested, holding it out.

At the silky tone of his voice, her heart pounded wildly, and when she took the soap, it slipped between her fingers and plunged to the bottom. His knowing smile only flustered her further while she fished for the hard-milled ball in the water. But when she brought it up and its scent wafted to her nose— her lavender fragrance, not his sandalwood—a wicked idea took hold in her mind.

Languidly, she passed the soap back and forth in her hands. "I'll wash you," she told him, "but only if you promise not to move. Not your arms, not your legs, not anything."

"Not even my head?" He lurched forward and stole a kiss.

Her lips tingled as she firmly pushed him back. "Not even. Not even one inch."

Contemplating that, he ran his tongue over the chip in his tooth, and she wished it were her tongue, instead. "Why?" he asked.

"You're injured. You mustn't strain yourself. And besides . . ." Her lips curved in a calculating smile. "I wish to play Poseidon and rule these waters. Because I owe you. For the dungeon."

"Sweet Mary," he breathed as she lathered her hands. Dropping the soap on purpose this time, she smoothed her palms over his shoulders, tracing circles down his back until her fingers met the binding around his ribs. Then up again, slowly, slowly, as his eyes slid shut, his head tilted back.

"Don't move," she reminded him, a little breathless. Feeling even more daring, she ran her hands down his chest, skimming the bandage until they met warm skin below. And down. All the way down.

He moved—more than an inch—before his eyes flew open. "Are you sure I didn't drown?" he husked out.

"Hmm?" She brought one hand out of the water, smiling to herself at the glazed expression in those newly unshielded eyes. Dear God, they were beautiful. Moistening a finger on her tongue, she wet his bottom lip, right there in the center where she always thought of touching it. Thrilling to his soft intake of breath, she licked her finger again and drew it across his lip on the top. So chiseled, and so talented—oh, what that mouth could make her feel. A third time she sucked her finger, then worked it between his lips, rubbing his tongue while she held his gaze with hers. 'Twas heady, the power of seduction, driving her to try things she'd never even imagined.

A dazed smile on his face, his eyes slid shut when she moved her hand beneath the water, leaning forward for a long, melting kiss. "Don't move," she reminded him when she pulled back.

His hands clenched on the edges of the tub. "I know I drowned," he gasped, "because I've died and gone to heaven."

Duncraven seemed lighter the next morning.

When Kendra woke, the chamber seemed brighter, and the walls seemed to hold fewer secrets. Ghosts no longer seemed to be lurking. She found herself almost sorry to leave.

But Trick was in a hurry.

"I want to deliver what's left of the King's treasure. Get it off my hands." He latched his trunk. "And I want to get back to Amberley. Although . . ."

His words trailing off, he watched her look up from tying a garter. "What?"

"It shouldn't be mine." He'd been thinking about that ever since he'd had other obvious facts pointed out to him—that Annag and Duncan were his siblings, and that he wasn't really English at all. "Amberley, and the dukedom. By rights, by blood, they shouldn't belong to me."

And the shock of it was, he found that disturbing. Mere months ago he hadn't wanted Amberley at all, hadn't wanted anything that came from the man he'd thought was his father. His shipping concern had been more than enough to support him, the estate and title just another reminder of the life he'd wanted to forget, another responsibility he hadn't needed.

But he needed them now. He needed them for his wife and the family he'd begun envisioning. No sane man would reject something that so clearly benefitted the people close to him. He would embrace such a thing, instead.

Loving Kendra had changed everything.

"Who would get Amberley if not you?" Always direct, his Kendra.

"I know not. Neither of my parents had siblings . . . some distant cousin, I imagine. Someone I've never met."

"And do you imagine he'd use that dukedom for the same good that you do? Do you imagine he'd shelter orphans in the old manor house?" Always straight through to the heart.

"I know not that, either."

She rose and walked close. "You earned that dukedom, Trick."

"Did I?"

"Yes. With your sweat, and I suspect your blood and your tears." She leaned up to press a soft kiss to his lips. "Legally, 'tis yours, and I see no reason on Earth why it shouldn't stay that way."

Mayhap she was right, and there was no reason he shouldn't be able to keep it. No reason except his monarch's threat hanging over his head if he failed to finish the job he'd started.

He kissed her back, a kiss filled with all the hope he had for their future. "Come, *leannan*, let us traipse down these endless stairs one last time. I am suddenly in a hurry to get home, to get started on our brand-new life."

* * *

Kendra held Hamish's arm, thrilled that he was strong enough now to accompany them outdoors along with Niall. They stopped on the drive where their servants waited. "What will ye tell King Charles?" Hamish asked Trick.

"I'll think of something." Trick looked up to the single chest he'd had lashed to the top of the ducal carriage. "At least nobody will suspect I'm carrying anything of special value." He'd told her that when they stopped for the night at an inn, they would simply bring it with them into their room. They didn't need all the extra guard he'd been envisioning. Four Amberley outriders stood ready, and that should be enough. They planned to travel directly to London.

Her gaze followed his. "I want to see it," she said.

"See what?" Niall asked.

"The Royal plate that brought about all this treachery and heartache. 'Tis beautiful, is it not?"

"I wouldn't know." Her brother-in-law shrugged. "I've never seen it myself."

"In all those years?" She hadn't pegged him as being so uncurious. "I would have begged until my parents let me look."

"Oh, I did. But 'twas pointless. There is no key to the padlock."

Hamish gave her a hard hug. "I tossed all the keys into a loch years before Niall was born. After one of those bitter quarrels. To keep the pieces from disappearing one by one."

So he'd distrusted his friends, even then. Unfortunate that he'd failed to take those feelings to heart—it might have saved Elspeth's life. But as the old French saying Kendra used to hear on the Continent put it, "*L'amitié ferme les yeux.*" Friendship closes its eyes.

Drawing her from those thoughts, Niall stepped forward and planted kisses on both her cheeks. "God willing, I'll see ye soon."

She was surprised to feel tears welling up. "I expect you at Amberley before too long."

He nodded. "After the harvest."

Trick embraced his brother. "I thank you for taking care of that for me."

"We—Da and I—thank ye for allowing us to stay." Niall's gaze flickered over to the castle's open doorway, where Annag and Duncan stood glaring, her children behind them. "And allowing them to stay, too."

Trick shrugged. "They're harmless." And he was right. For all Kendra's wild imaginings, Duncan and Annag had never done anything to hurt either of them. "Besides, they're my siblings. I won't pretend to like them, but if it makes Da happy to give them a home, then I'm happy, too."

Tears welled in Hamish's eyes as he took Trick by both hands. "We dinna deserve ye, lad."

He shook his head. " 'Tis I that don't deserve you—a father and a brother that would do any man proud. Family, after all these years." Blinking back his own tears, he wrapped the older man into his arms and held him a long moment. "We'd best be going."

"Aye, I suppose ye must." Hamish forced a smile as he watched them climb into the carriage.

Trick closed his eyes until they rode away, then opened them and pulled Kendra across the cabin for a soft kiss. "When we get to London, I'm going to ask my solicitor to deed Duncraven over to Hamish, with Niall as his heir."

If she'd had any remaining doubts that her husband was a good man, they vanished then. "That's wonderful, Trick."

"Not wonderful, only decent." He kissed the tip of her nose. "Besides, the last thing I need is an estate in Scotland. My father—the duke," he corrected himself, "left me more than I can deal with as it is."

Maybe he could fool himself into thinking his actions were less than generous, but Kendra knew better.

Chapter Twenty-three

It felt strange to Kendra to be back in London but at Trick's town house instead of the one she'd always known in Lincoln's Inn Fields. And Caldwell House, a dark monstrosity built before the Civil War, was every bit as disgustingly opulent as he'd said. Standing in the master bedchamber, where she was dressing before attending Court, she was reminded of an overdecorated cake.

A blue-and-orange one.

"Ghastly," she said, kicking off her shoes.

"I told you that you would hate it." Trick shrugged out of the surcoat he'd worn for travel. "Feel free to redecorate."

"I imagine I have better things to do that will keep me busy a while." Peeling off her garters and stockings, she frowned at the lavender gown that Jane had selected. Too insipid for her mood. They had sent a messenger ahead to request Kendra's London clothing be moved from the Chases' town house, and she hurriedly flipped through the gowns that had been crammed into the master bedroom's wardrobe. "I wonder how all the children are getting along?"

"Fine, I'm sure," her husband said absently while pulling a fresh shirt over his head.

Cavanaugh had laid a blue velvet suit on the bed. Men had it so easy, Kendra thought with a bit of weariness-induced irritation. Brown or green, velvet or satin. With the exception of varying quantities of braid, lace, and ribbon, everything looked the same. Their shirts and cravats were always white, their shoes—with the exception of some foppish Court dandies—invariably black. High-heeled with fancy buckles for Court, low-heeled and plain for every day. There really was nothing much for them to decide.

She selected a cloth-of-gold gown and held it up. "What do you think?"

His back to her as he reached for his breeches, Trick answered, "Fine." For a moment she stood there, aggravated, until he turned and favored her with one of his blinding white smiles.

He was right. Everything was fine, after all.

In a few short weeks, their relationship had come a long way—longer than she'd thought possible. The journey to London had been almost blissful. Trick had been the most attentive of lovers, but even more important, he'd answered most of her questions without resorting to evasion. The days on the road had gone a long way toward convincing her their future was bright indeed.

Bless her brothers for bringing them together, she thought, then silently laughed at her reversal of feelings.

"Come here, *leannan*," he said, and she did, letting the gown slip to the floor as she walked into his arms. His kiss was everything she hadn't been able to imagine before meeting him, and she was breathless by the time he finished. "I'm sorry to rush you right out of the house when we only just arrived," he murmured regretfully, his gaze lingering on the garish orange-hung bed, "but I just want to finish my business with King Charles and take you home to Amberley."

With a sigh, she pulled from his arms and started detaching her stomacher. "I still wish I could see it."

"See what?" he asked, tugging on the blue velvet breeches.

"The treasure. Will we be bringing it along to Court?"

Trick's gaze wandered to the massive chest against one wall. He wished he didn't have to deal with this. He wished he didn't have to deal with King Charles or his problems at all.

"I think I'll just meet with Charles tonight to explain, then arrange to send it along later."

She wiggled her gown down and off. "I cannot wait to see his reaction."

Sweet Mary, he couldn't let her be there. He had delicate matters to discuss with the King. Looking down as he tucked in his shirt, he made his voice as casual as possible. "I believe Charles will feel this is a matter best settled between men."

He raised his gaze to hers, expecting to see that look in her eyes. The look she'd given him when he'd told her she couldn't come along to Scotland, again when he went off to Burntisland, and yet again when he'd ordered her not to get on the boat.

But instead he saw a different look. Hurt.

He wanted to hit something. Not an hour in London, and the damn deceptions were coming between them already.

Characteristic of her, though, the hurt look was

fleeting, and the one he'd expected came into her eyes, after all. He watched her draw breath, girding for battle. "Charles likes women," she said.

"In his bed, yes."

"No." She caught his gaze and blushed. "Well, yes, but 'twas not what I meant. He listens to women. Really listens, as if he cares what we say. Even about politics."

Lucky him, marrying one of probably three women in England who would think to discuss politics with their monarch. "If I let you see the treasure, will it make you feel better?"

"You cannot do that." She rolled her eyes. "There is no key, and Charles is going to wonder where the lock is if you hack it off."

"Then I won't."

"I knew you wouldn't."

"I mean I won't hack it off."

She glanced at the chest, then back to him, speculation narrowing her pretty green eyes. "Can you pick the lock?"

"You insult me." He swiped his knife off the dressing table, and she followed him to the chest, where he knelt and went to work, delicately probing the keyhole. "There isn't a good smuggler on Earth who doesn't know how to pick a lock."

Wearing nothing but the amber bracelet and a flimsy chemise, she sat on the chest. She crossed her legs right in front of his face, and his knife slipped. "Were you a good smuggler?"

Determinedly, he refocused. "Actually, I was a bad smuggler. My heart was never in it." A satisfying *click* reverberated in the room. "But I can pick a lock."

Removing it, he stood. With a happy gasp, she jumped up and threw open the lid.

"Oh, my God, Trick. Look at this." She hefted a solid gold charger, running her fingers over the delicately engraved rim. " 'Tis beautiful."

"He'll probably melt it down."

"No," she breathed, dropping to kneel before the chest. "He wouldn't." She set the charger on the floor and reached for a silver pitcher in the shape of a swan. "Oh, I just knew I wanted to see this." One by one, she removed pieces, each more impressive than the last. Plates, bowls, goblets, cutlery, serving utensils, platters. "Hamish was right. The first Charles truly did live like a king on his coronation journey."

He smiled as she delved deeper, her lovely, scantily clad bottom lifting as she leaned into the chest. Helpless to resist, he gave her a little pinch.

Laughing, she slapped away his hand. "Oh, what is this?" She drew out an ivory casket inlaid with scrolled gold wire.

He shrugged. "Small items?"

"In a beautiful box like this? And locked?"

Taking it from her, he made short work of that and put it back in her hands.

With a sigh of anticipation, she raised the lid. "Jewels." She lifted an exquisite sapphire-and-diamond necklace. "My God, it looks like pirate's booty! How did jewels get in here?" Replacing the necklace, she slipped a gaudy emerald ring on her finger. "I don't understand this," she said, staring at it. Obviously made for a man, it dangled loose. "I thought Hamish and his friends only packed the kitchen."

"Supposedly." He ran a hand back through his

hair, still surprised to find the front so short. "But then they took the chests out one by one, aye? And emptied them and filled them with rocks. I guess somewhere along the way, someone filched this and slipped it inside."

"Rhona or Gregor, I'm guessing. I wonder if Hamish knows?" She dug around some more and drew out another necklace. "Goodness, will you look at the size of these pearls?"

The biggest round pearls Trick had ever seen, with one huge teardrop-shaped pearl dangling from the center. "Fit for royalty, all right."

She dropped it back into the casket. "Oh, Trick, look at this." Her voice turned wistful. "Amber."

"When did you grow to like amber?" he teased.

She blushed and pulled the jewel out, only to find it was a clasp attached to a gleaming string of smaller pure-white pearls. "Oh, 'tis lovely," she sighed, dropping it over her head.

'Twas so long, he reached to double it, settling the second half around her neck. "Do you not own pearls?"

"Father sold all our jewels to help finance the Civil War." Her fingertips danced on the lustrous strand. "Jason has bought me things over the years, of course. And Colin and Ford. But pearls are terribly expensive."

And immensely popular. All the Court ladies wore pearls, and most of the men, come to that. "You look beautiful in pearls, *leannan.*"

She blushed and took them off. "For the price this trinket could bring, I expect we could feed the orphans for a year."

"A decade, probably." He smiled.

She dropped them in the box. "Help me put this all away, will you? I still need Jane to do my hair, and if we don't get to Whitehall soon, we'll miss the presentations."

"The Duke and Duchess of Amberley!"

Trick shot the puffed-up Court usher an annoyed glare. "I abhor this sort of thing," he muttered under his breath as he and Kendra made their way down the aisle to where King Charles and Queen Catharine sat on the dias, dressed in crimson velvet with a swagged canopy overhead to match. "I really hate this."

"Oh, hush," Kendra chided. "A little pomp and circumstance never hurt anybody. And there will be dancing afterward—"

"I cannot wait."

Under different circumstances, she might be tempted to slap him. As it was, she flashed Queen Catharine a brilliant smile and dropped into a deep curtsy, pressing a kiss to the back of the woman's slim proffered hand. "Your Majesty."

"Lady Kendra," Catharine said in gracious Portuguese-accented syllables, "or have I heard 'tis the Duchess of Amberley now?"

"You've heard right," she said, then leaned closer to her husband. "As long as he behaves himself," she added for his ears only.

Suppressing a laugh, he rose and traded sides with her. King Charles smiled as she kissed his hand. "'Tis glad I was to hear that two of my favorite families are united."

She only just managed to conceal her surprise. "I am happy to have pleased Your Majesty."

He nodded, then looked back to Trick. "We will talk later, yes?"

"Aye. And I've something to give you."

"Do you, now?" The King was not above delighting in gifts. "Did you bring it along?"

"It is rather . . . large. 'Tis at my home, but I can have it delivered—"

"Amberley House or Caldwell House here in London?"

"Here in London, but—"

"I have matters to discuss with you in any case." Charles raised a meaningful brow. "I shall sneak out of my bedchamber this evening and come to you."

"Sneak?" Kendra burst out, then clapped a hand over her mouth.

Charles let loose a booming laugh. "My Master of the Backstairs is quite accustomed to making these arrangements, I assure you." His eyes twinkled, and Kendra blushed. She knew he meant that he usually sneaked out for assignations with his mistresses, but she felt sorry for his long-suffering queen, who was studiously looking elsewhere.

She would never put up with that from her husband, not now that things were right between them in the bedroom. He'd promised her fidelity, and she expected him to give up his mistress. Just let him try to come alone to London again.

With another bow and curtsy, Kendra and Trick moved away so the next courtiers could be presented. "Well, I expect we can leave now," Trick said as soon as they were out of earshot.

"I am not leaving until after we've danced." Kendra flipped open her painted fan.

"Don't tell me you're going to titter behind that thing."

"Me? Titter?" She frantically fanned it at her face. On this late-summer night, the Presence Chamber was hot and close, lit by hundreds of candles in wall sconces and liveried yeomen holding flaming torches. "What did Charles mean, two of his favorite families?"

Trick tucked his tongue in his cheek. "Were you not aware the Chases are favored?"

For the second time this evening, she was tempted to slap him. "You know very well what I mean. I've never seen you at Court—"

"I do my best to avoid it."

"And I don't remember you from the years in exile, either. So how is it you've come to know Charles so well?"

"My father—the duke—was a major supplier of kingly-type luxury items," Trick said dryly. "All through the Commonwealth years, we had, uh . . . dealings."

Kendra stopped fanning. "You're jesting, right? Charles was as poor during those years as we were."

"I'm not jesting. The duke was happy enough to supply him free of charge."

"Out of loyalty?"

He snorted. "Out of greed. Charles promised him the dukedom restored upon his own restoration." He frowned across the chamber, then turned back to her, pulling at his cravat. "If you're not going to fan yourself, you may as well fan me."

"My wrist is tired. I've decided to sweat instead."

His lips quirked, and he leaned forward and gave her a kiss. "Ladies don't sweat. Ladies glow."

"I'm a duchess now, not a lady. I can do as I please." He was staring at a woman across the chamber. "Trick? Who is that?"

"Most people call her Lady Charlotte Waller."

She blew out a breath, her free hand curling into a fist. If this was his London mistress . . . "Most people?" she asked carefully.

"Charlotte, Harlot—what's the difference?"

Despite her distress, she laughed, thinking there were very few women present who didn't deserve such a designation. "And what, pray tell, could this Lady Harlot have done to earn such a title at King Charles's Court?"

"She slept with the Earl of Danforth."

"From what I understand, so have half the women here."

He raised a brow. "Not while they were betrothed to me."

"Oh." Dear God, not a mistress, but the woman from Trick's poem. The reason Kendra had yet to hear a declaration of love from her husband's lips and despaired that she ever would. Following his unfocused gaze, she glared at the simpering blonde across the room.

Harlot. "I hate her."

"Aye. 'Twas clear enough that despite her protests of love, 'twas my title she wanted, not me. Of course, I mightn't have been quite so upset had she not refused more than a kiss from me by claiming herself a virgin. And had I not found them together in said virginal bed."

And Kendra wouldn't have had an uphill battle to

gain her husband's trust. Of course if he'd married the harlot, he wouldn't be her husband at all, but that was beside the point.

No, that was the point entirely . . . he was her husband, not the harlot's. And although not long ago she'd never have believed it, she was very happy about that.

Courtiers were gathering around the dance floor, a rainbow of brilliant colors in the blazing light, jewels glittering on ears, necks, wrists, and hands of men and women alike. She couldn't help but notice that most everyone wore pearls. With a secret smile, she fingered her amber bracelet. Who needed pearls, anyway? Looking down to her hands, she noticed the plain gold band around her finger. So very Trick. She should have realized from the first that he wouldn't be the type of duke she detested.

And she'd found she didn't so much mind being a duchess, either. Together in those roles, they could do much good. Whether 'twas fair or not, people listened to what dukes and duchesses had to say. With whispers in the right ears, they could raise enough money to open a hundred orphanages if they wanted.

And he wouldn't have to play the highwayman anymore. In fact, before they got to Amberley, she would demand he stop. Now. His attention still across the room, she sneaked a glance at her husband. His golden good looks sent her heart to racing, and she knew that she couldn't stand to even think of the possibility that he might be hurt or—God forbid—arrested. She would find some way to keep the children fed and clothed until she could put her new plan into motion.

At the far end of the chamber, musicians were tuning up, and King Charles was leading Queen Catharine through the crowd to begin the dancing.

"Shall we dance?" Kendra asked Trick.

Tearing his gaze from the harlot, he looked down at her. "Am I not supposed to do the asking?" He smiled. "Oh dear, I almost forgot. You're a duchess now and can do as you please."

Laughing, she turned into her husband's arms and let herself be led to the dance floor, where a minuet was playing.

He bowed to her, then did a small plié in a mirror of her own moves. "Do you realize we've never danced?" he said conversationally.

She stepped forward with her right foot, rising on her toes. "I danced with your brother, you know."

"Did you? When?" They both brought their feet together, lowering their heels. "Should I be worried?" Trick asked with a mock-stern frown. "Remember what I told you about fidelity." Though she was sure he didn't intend it, his gaze went to Lady Harlot, who seemed to be pointedly ignoring him.

She repeated the steps with her right foot, her own gaze going to King Charles. "Remember what *I* told *you* about fidelity."

His laugh made her feel a lot better. He dropped her hands so they could both turn. "Niall and I danced at the *draidgie*," she said coquettishly over her shoulder. "When you were outside writing." His hands felt warm when he reached for hers again. "'Twas a wild dance, I tell you—we weren't able to talk like this."

"Ah, yes, a Scottish country dance."

"Did someone mention Scottish?"

"Caithren!" Surprised, Kendra turned and threw her arms around her sister-in-law. "What are you doing here?"

"We've only stopped in London for a few days before heading for Cainewood. Jase is insisting I see Dr. Willis."

Kendra frowned when a dancer had the nerve to bump into their happy little reunion. "The King's physician?"

"The very same." Cait sighed. "Just what I need— a man poking and prodding me. Wheesht!" she added as a broad-reared matron backed into her. "I've delivered a dozen bairns; I think I know what I'm doing."

"Shall we?" Trick asked, motioning them off the busy dance floor. "What's this all about?"

Kendra tried to look baffled. "Did I forget to tell you that Caithren is with child?"

"Aye, it seems you did." With a knowing smile, he turned to Cait. "Congratulations."

"Was Jason angry?" Kendra asked.

"Would ye believe I convinced him I didn't know?" Concealed by a lovely rose-colored gown with a silver-embroidered stomacher, Cait's stomach still looked flat. She grinned. "The truth is he's not quite sure, and in any case, his main concern was getting back to England before the weather set in."

"So what *was* his reaction, then?"

"I'm thrilled." Appearing from out of nowhere, Jason bent to give Kendra a kiss. "How are you doing?" he asked in her ear.

Dressed in dark green and looking wonderfully familiar, he made her wonder why she'd been so angry with him. "I'm happy," she admitted.

"I'm so glad." He had the good grace not to look smug, although she knew full well he would lord it over her in the future. He turned to his wife. "You didn't fool me for a minute, you know. I was just too pleased to make a fuss . . . although now the excitement's worn off a bit, I've a mind to make you pay for that deception."

She raised a brow. "I cannot wait."

The stern look Kendra was more accustomed to settled on his features. "Your health could have been at risk. And the babe's as well."

"I've never felt healthier in my life." Cait slipped an arm around his waist, leaning in and gazing up at him with a brilliant, calculated smile. "You're not really angry, are ye?"

His answer was an indulgent sigh. "So what are *you* doing here?" he asked Trick.

"I have something that belongs to Charles. Long story," he added when Cait went to ask. "I'm sure Kendra will enjoy the telling."

Kendra grinned. "He only says that hoping I'll make him out a hero."

"I cannot wait to hear," Caithren said, snagging her by the arm. "Shall we repair to the garden?"

The music stopped, and dancers started jostling past. His obligations over, King Charles caught Trick's gaze and sent him a significant nod.

"I'm afraid your talk will have to wait," he said. "I believe I've just been summoned home to Caldwell House."

"We'll talk tomorrow, then, Kendra." Cait dropped her arm and took Jason's. "And my husband will dance with me instead."

"Nothing energetic," he warned. "You will stick to the minuet."

"Ye see what I have to put up with?" she asked Kendra with a roll of her eyes. "Michty me, you'd think I was an invalid."

Chapter Twenty-four

At Caldwell House later that night, Trick watched as Charles swirled Madeira in his glass and then took an appreciative sip. "Amazing."

"The wine?"

The King's lips curved beneath his thin black mustache. " 'Tis admirable quality, to be sure. But then, your late father dealt only in the best."

Trick agreed with a curt nod. The best, yes. The best wine, the best fabrics, the best furnishings, the best books. His gaze wandered to the leather-bound tomes lining the walls in this, the most impressive study in all of London. He doubted the man had ever cracked open even one of them.

"However, 'twas your gift I was referring to." Charles set down the glass and reached into the chest, pulling out a solid-gold dish and turning its heavy weight thoughtfully in his hands. "To think my own father's treasure has resurfaced after all these years."

"Only to end up where it was said to be in the first place." Pensively, Trick played with the lock in his hands—the one he'd hacked off in the King's presence.

"Od's fish—that was none of your doing. 'Tis

pleased I am that you recovered what you did, and I'd be pleased as well to see you keep a part of it."

"I couldn't." He'd lost most of it already, no matter that Charles refused to place blame.

"I insist." He handed Trick the plate. "Here. As a memento, if nothing else."

"I . . . I appreciate the offer, but I really don't want to keep this." The dish had to be worth a small fortune, and Charles needed it far more than he did.

"There must be something here that strikes your fancy." He set down the plate and raised a jeweled goblet. "This. Or something else."

"No, really, I—"

"What is this?" Metal servingware clanked as Charles reached into the bottom and brought out the small ivory casket. His black eyes glittering, he lifted the unlocked lid and extracted the short necklace of large pearls. Raising it with one hand, he flicked a finger to set the giant teardrop pearl swinging. "There is a painting of my mother wearing this," he murmured.

"Henrietta Maria will be happy to have it back. 'Twill look lovely on her."

The King looked up. "Yes, it will," he said softly. "I thank you." He fished out the sapphire-and-diamond necklace that Kendra had held up earlier. "If you'll not take something for yourself, then take this for your new wife."

Suddenly inspired, Trick reached for the box, setting it in his lap to extricate a long strand of pearls from the tangle. "This," he said. "If you insist I take something, this is what I'd like."

Charles frowned at it. "Those pearls are ordinary.

And the clasp only amber. That is likely the least valuable item in the entire chest."

" 'Tis the one I want." Trick's tone left no room for doubt.

"You shall have it then, with my thanks." The King shut the casket with a bang and set it atop the gold and silver that crowded the trunk. He reached for his wineglass again, his long fingers worrying the stem. "How goes the mission?"

"Very well, but for the interruption." The pearls made soft clicking sounds as Trick shifted them in his hands, thinking about Kendra asleep in the late duke's gaudy orange bed upstairs. He hoped to wake her soon and set her mind at ease, once and for all. "I have some descriptions that I was preparing to give to Pendregast when I was called away to Scotland."

"Excellent." The King sipped. "I assume, being away, you haven't heard the latest news."

"News?" A tiny chill crept up Trick's spine. Or mayhap the chamber was a bit cold.

"There's been a reward posted for the mysterious Black Highwayman."

"Bloody hell." He could only hope his leads would pan out, and he'd have no need to pose as the highwayman again. "No one has connected him to me, so I don't expect I have anything to worry about."

"No one?"

"Just my wife. And her family." Damn. "I haven't told them the purpose for the disguise—"

"Good. Let us keep it that way."

Broadsides were likely plastered all over the kingdom, advertising the reward. Kendra would see them and worry herself sick. "I would like to tell only my wife—"

"If the job is almost complete, there is no sense involving anyone else."

"Just her—"

"I've never known a woman who could keep her mouth shut." Charles pinned him with his jet-black gaze. "Have you?"

Once Trick would have agreed, but now he knew he'd been wrong. His wife had kept Cait's secret, and she hadn't told her brothers about his supposed financial trouble or him continuing as a highwayman, either. "Kendra's not like that."

"I'm happy your marriage agrees with you, Amberley. But I trust no woman to stay quiet, not even your wife. And I'm trusting *you* to respect my wish for silence. Your loyalty will pay dividends. Your disloyalty . . ."

The unspoken words hung in the air. There it was, that veiled threat to withhold the pardon.

"I'm sorry, Amberley," Charles added with a sympathy that Trick knew was honest. Part of the charm that made the King so popular with the people. But under that genuine kindness hid a streak of determination that was every bit as integral to the man's personality. "I cannot afford to have it bandied about that the King is condoning robbery, no matter the reason or how deserving the victims. They are my subjects, nonetheless."

"But—"

"I'm asking you, as your monarch and your friend, to keep this wholly to yourself."

Trick mentally threw up his hands. Opposing the monarchy went against everything he believed in.

And although he'd started this mission out of patriotism for King and country, he needed to finish it for his marriage. For Kendra, and for the children he hoped they would have. Even now, an heir might be growing in her womb, and that son deserved Amberley.

He sighed. "Of course."

"Go back to Sussex and arrange to meet with Pendregast. Fear not, for I've been thinking since I heard the news, and I've a plan to wrap this up. I owe you a debt for solving this little problem, and I'll not see you or the Chases implicated in any way."

With a sinking heart, Trick listened to the plan. Despite his intentions otherwise, the deceptions would continue. For a man did not put his wife before his sovereign.

Not a wise one, in any case.

Kendra woke to a husky whisper in her ear. "I have a present for you, *leannan*." Her head was lifted, and something cool and heavy slid down about her neck.

Sleepily she reached for it, her fingers meeting a strand of smooth, hard orbs that could only be pearls. Her eyes flew open. "Has it an amber clasp?"

"But of course." Standing over her stark naked, her husband smiled. Dear God, he looked gorgeous, every muscle outlined in the low light of the fire. "Charles tried to give me a solid-gold platter as a reward, but I would have none of it."

She ran her tongue over her teeth, thinking of that tiny chip in his. "Well, are you going to come down here and let me thank you?"

She sighed as he joined her beneath the coverlet

and settled his warm body beside hers, then laughed when he reached for the hem of her chemise and tried to pull it off, needing to draw it through the necklace to accomplish his goal. With a grin, she grabbed the far end of the long strand and slipped it over his head, roping him close. "I've got you," she said.

"You certainly have." His mouth met hers for a long kiss, and she melted happily into his embrace. No matter how many hundreds of times he did this, she still thrilled like it was the first. A shiver of wanting rippled through her as she thought of all the times ahead. A flush heated her skin, warming the pearls that draped heavily on her neck. When he rolled the two of them to their sides, the strand tangled between them, and she reached to pull it off.

"I'll take those, *leannan*." He held out his hand. And she gave them over, expecting him to drop them to the night table, as she had been about to do. But instead, he just held the long rope in the air.

"They're beautiful," she said, watching them swing gently, firelight dancing off the gleaming round surfaces.

"Not half as beautiful as you." She'd never thought of herself as beautiful, and she swallowed hard as he brought the pearls under the covers and started drawing them over her body. Slowly. "Do you know how much I care for you, lass?"

Breathlessly caught in his gaze, she felt each individual pearl, an entire long row of them, skim her sensitive skin. "How much?" she whispered.

"Enough to make me question my loyalties."

Loyalties? Though she didn't quite understand, she could tell that admission was wrenched from somewhere deep inside him, and it softened the pain of not hearing the words she'd so desperately hoped he'd been about to say.

I love you.

She should tell him first, she thought, feeling light-headed as the pearls continued their sensual assault on her body. Over her arms, her back, her legs, her hip, her side, making soft little clicks as they went. Up until they trailed her breasts, hitching as they caught on a nipple. A shiver lanced through her. She should tell him first.

But she couldn't. Because he was still holding back.

Not here, though. Not now. He arranged the pearls around her breasts and leaned away. "Lovely," he murmured.

She mustered a weak smile. "I don't think that's the way they're meant to be worn. Rather scandalous, do you not think?"

"At King Charles's Court? Not a soul would even take notice." But he drew them off and bunched them in one hand, meeting her lips for a desperate kiss.

There was something about him tonight . . . something about the way his tongue swept her mouth, the way his hands worshipped her body, the way he molded his flesh to match every curve of hers. Something. Something that made her feel, even though he was more of a man than she'd known existed, that somewhere inside lurked a little lost boy. Waiting to get hurt.

So she was gentle tonight, and he was gentle in return, running the bunched pearls over her skin in a heavenly, softly clicking massage. Guided by his hand, they rolled between her breasts and over a hip

and down to her thighs. Her own hands smoothed
his skin, soothing, everywhere she could reach. She
sighed into his mouth, and his tongue stroked hers,
more softly than she could remember, so cherishing
that tears welled in her eyes and threatened to slip
between her closed lids.

"Open for me, *leannan*." A thick, velvet-edged
whisper, his voice sent a gust of desire shuddering
through her. And because she wanted to please him,
she did what he asked, parting her legs until she lay
there, flat on the bed, wantonly open and ready.
Then gasped when he drew the pearls, that long,
long strand, agonizingly slowly between them.

She felt every one distinctly, felt herself moisten as
they slipped. She wanted him, there, filling her where
she ached. "Oh, God, Trick."

"Hush," he murmured, nuzzling her throat. He
suckled her breasts, her nipples rising to hard points
that he circled with his tongue. And still down
below, the pearls continued their exquisite trail along
where she wanted him, deep inside.

This was torment, but oh, so sweet, each individual
pearl driving her to distraction. "I cannot stand this,
Trick. 'Tis too much." She reached for his free hand,
clenching it hard in hers.

"I cannot stand it, either," he grated out, and he
yanked the pearls away, coming over her to join their
bodies together.

Her rush of relief lasted mere seconds before a new
sense of urgency overwhelmed her. She wrapped
him with her legs, her fingers threading in his hair,
little sounds escaping her throat as his hips drove
every thought but him from her mind. She rocked
against him, wanting him closer, closer, hearing his

breath ragged in her ear. Her heart pounded against his as her hands worked down his back and lower to pull him closer still. If only she could climb the last of that wall and finally make them one.

Then, for one split second of infinity, they *were* one.

A long time later, Trick felt beneath the coverlet for the pearls, smiling when he found and snagged them. Drawing them out, he held them to his nose, breathing deep of her sweet scent before he dangled them above her head. "D'ye like these, *leannan*?"

"In more ways than I could have imagined." Her smile, soft and achingly erotic, lit his heart. "But Trick—"

"Aye?"

"I mostly like them because we can sell them."

His fingers tightened around them. "No, lass. They're for you."

She grabbed them from his hands, cradling them against her breasts. "They would feed the children for a decade, you said. No longer will you have to be a highwayman. I was going to beg you to stop anyway, Trick—I cannot stand the thought of you being hurt or caught in the act." If her smile had lit his heart, her words melted it. " 'Tis bad of me, I know, but you're much more important than the children. To me. The most important thing in my life."

She looked pained at that guilty admission, but not as pained as he felt inside. That she could put him above everything else . . . If only he hadn't the obligations that kept him from doing the same.

If only.

"Do you see the gift that Charles has given us?" She held it up. "We no longer have to choose between your safety and the children's welfare." Looking half-wistful, half-thrilled, she brought the pearls to her lips. "I will sell them tomorrow. And I have other ideas as well, for how we can help more children. This—this gift—will get us started." ·

Her enthusiasm was more than he could bear. Soon he could bring her to the docks, show her whichever of his ships were in port, tell her that he could support all the orphanages she wanted. Soon this would be over, and he vowed to himself he would be honest with his wife for the rest of his life. He would never make another promise that would be this hard to keep.

"You're not selling them tomorrow," he told her, peeling her fingers from the pearls. He lifted the strand and slipped it back over her head. "We're going home tomorrow. And I promise you, the children won't starve."

Chapter Twenty-five

Back at Amberley the next day, Trick barely took time to drop off their luggage before cleaning up and readying to leave. Stunned, Kendra stood in their bedchamber watching. "I have a job I must take care of," he told her, not quite meeting her eyes.

"A job?" Although he was standing close, she felt as if he'd physically pulled away. "Are you going out to play the highwayman again? I told you—"

"No. I am finished with that."

And he wasn't wearing black, either—he had dressed in a simple brown suit with a white shirt and cravat. She should have noticed that. Her usually sharp powers of observation were dulled by disappointment.

Just last night, she'd felt so emotionally attached. She'd thought that with everything they'd shared in Scotland and since, things would be different now.

But no matter that his hair had been cut and his eyes were unshielded—he was hiding from her again.

She backed away to sit on the gaudy red bed, her fingers going to the pearls around her neck. "Do you not need the money for the children?"

"No," he said, even more slowly than usual. "I

told you last night, the children will be taken care of."

"How?" Her head swirled with confusion. "Did Charles give you more than the pearls, then?"

He stared at her for a long moment. "You could say that," he said at last, and heaved a long sigh. A new determination lit his eyes as he moved closer. "The truth is, I have more than enough money to fund the orphanage without resorting to robbery. You have no cause to worry on that account."

The truth, he'd said. "I don't understand."

"My father's—the duke's—smuggling operation . . . when he died, I took those ships and used them to begin an importing business. Legitimate. I have nine ships now and a warehouse filled with goods from across the globe that are sold all over the country. I can well afford to support the children and anything else your heart desires."

As though she'd been physically hit, Kendra found it hard to draw breath. "Then why did you tell me you needed to do the robberies in order to fund the orphanage?"

"I never said that, Kendra."

"But you didn't correct me when I assumed it, either. A lie of omission is a lie, nonetheless." Everything she'd thought she'd gained seemed to be slipping away. She struggled to keep a hint of hysteria from her voice. "This makes no sense. Why is it, then, that you played the highwayman? For your own amusement, as you once said? When you knew it worried me, and my brothers had asked you to stop?"

"No, not for my amusement." Taking both her hands, he drew her to stand before him, his gaze filled with silent apology. "I'm sorry, *leannan*, but there are things I cannot tell you."

"Why?"

"I just cannot. You'll have to trust me." His knuckles skimmed her cheek. "Once you promised that you'd trust me. Has that changed?"

Her memory flashed on that day in the dungeon, and she blushed hot. But that had been in Scotland, where they'd spent every day, almost every minute, together. Where he hadn't kept secrets, so far as she could tell, and where they'd grown close and learned to be easy with one another.

Yet literally the moment they'd stepped foot in Amberley, everything had gone back to the way it was before they left. She'd thought she'd gotten through to him—that his wall was almost down— but obviously not. Not here. How could they have any kind of marriage when he insisted on holding back?

She wished they had never come home.

"I'm trying to trust you," she told him. "But 'tis very hard."

" 'Tis hard for me, too. You must believe that, lass. Just let me finish what I have to do." And with one kiss, so heartfelt it left her reeling, he was out the door.

It hadn't quite been a lie. Charles *had* given him more than the pearls—he'd given him orders not to tell his own wife what he was about. Bloody obstinate man. Though Trick never thought he'd be cursing his king, he did so all the way to the cottage to pick up his papers.

From there he traveled two villages over to meet

the contact Charles had arranged for, a man going by the absurd name of Zephaniah Pendregast and posing as a Puritan. On the ride, Trick switched from cursing Charles to railing at himself. What an idiot he'd been to tell Kendra about his shipping company.

He'd thought it would help to come clean with as much of the truth as he could, to relieve her mind where the children were concerned, at least. But he'd gravely miscalculated. He'd seen the doubt and confusion come into her eyes, and it had made him sick inside.

He had no experience with being in love, and he was doing it all wrong.

The foundations they'd built in Scotland were crumbling out from under him. He could only hope that this mission would come to an end before those foundations eroded entirely. That there would still be enough left upon which to rebuild trust. That his loyalty to the King wouldn't cost him his future.

Trick had sent a messenger before him, and Pendregast was waiting in back of the blacksmith's shop where Charles's men had arranged for his temporary employment.

"I hope 'tis damn good news you bring," Pendregast said, dropping his proper Puritan speech the moment they were out of earshot. He was tall and lean, dark-haired with a long, hollowed-out face. The blows of hammer on anvil rang in the background as they paced together into the fields behind the town's High Street shops. "I'm bloody bored in this swiving establishment."

" 'Tis sorry I am for the delay. I was called out of the country. In any case"—Trick pulled the roll of papers from his surcoat—"I have your descriptions."

They pored over the pages together, Pendregast asking questions and Trick answering as well as he could remember. "So do you know these men?" he finally asked.

"I've attended enough secret meetings to last a lifetime, I'll warrant you that. This description here"—Pendregast stabbed a finger at one of Trick's pages—"seems familiar. And one other. I'll ask around, see what I can find. I'll be in touch."

Trick walked him back to the smithy, where they shook hands. "I'll be glad to have this behind me."

"No more than I," Pendregast grated out through the fake smile he put on his face as he reentered the shop.

Knowing he'd have to leave Kendra home alone soon, Trick spent a tense couple of days tiptoeing around her, avoiding her hurt gaze while wracking his brain for a plausible explanation that wouldn't cause even more pain and distrust. Mostly he kept out of the house, acquainting himself with his estate—after all, he planned to be here more than he'd thought.

Life near the docks in London now held little appeal. He could correspond with his men from Amberley and make regular trips to check up on matters, bringing Kendra along with him. And, when he was a bit older, mayhap Niall would come along as well. Having discovered a family, Trick found himself entertaining grand ideas. Expanding his business to include ships based in Scotland was just the start.

Each night, he came home after Kendra was in bed, when darkness saved him from meeting her eyes. In those wee hours, he tried to tell her with his body what he couldn't say with words. And if her blissful sighs were laced with a touch of disillusionment, he could only remind himself that things would be better soon.

A terse message finally arrived: *Meet me at seven a.m. Saturday at the home of John Garrick. Z.P.*

John Garrick? Trick wondered. Was he working for Charles, too? Well, at least it would give him a solid excuse to spend the weekend away. Kendra might not question him going off for a card party at Garrick's—a house party her own brothers regularly attended. With any luck, she would accept that.

Apparently, however, luck was not on his side.

"So soon?" she asked when he found her going over menus in the kitchen. Dejection dulled her light-green eyes as she led him into the butler's pantry, then, finding it occupied by two maids polishing silver, all the way into the deserted two-story dining room. One foot tapping on the black-and-white checkered marble floor, she stared up at the wood-and-plasterwork ceiling, studying the painted scenes there as though they might hold the answers to her problem.

Him.

"We've been home less than a week," she said.

As she lowered her gaze to meet his, he shifted on his feet. "The card weekends are a long-standing tradition. 'Tis been months since the last one, ever since our marriage. The men have been awaiting my return."

She ran a fingertip along the carved and gilded mantel. The old duke had really outdone himself gussying up this chamber. "Trick, I'm . . ." His heart hurting, he watched her draw a deep breath. "I feel like I've lost you since we returned home."

"I'm right here." He forced a smile.

"You've been out and about doing God knows what. Can we not spend this weekend together? Should our relationship not come before a card game?"

" 'Tis already planned," he said, wishing he could find a way to make her feel as loved and secure as she deserved. He wanted that more than he wanted to breathe.

But that could only happen when this was finished. He was so close. He would send a messenger to King Charles immediately, letting him know that the mission was about to be concluded and it was time for the final plans to be set into motion.

The next morning found him leaving his sweet wife abed with a gentle kiss to her forehead, struggling not to give in when faced with her disappointed sigh. If a tinge of unease stayed lodged in his gut, he determined to ignore it. These counterfeiters were undermining the economy, threatening the very foundations of the monarchy. He had a job to do for his country, promises he'd made to his king.

An hour later, he arrived at Garrick's estate to find Pendregast waiting on the road, he and his horse hidden behind a hedge that concealed them from the mansion. "What gives?" Trick asked, reining in Chaucer. "Why are you not inside?"

"We cannot just walk in and make an arrest. We need some damning evidence first. Have you any ideas how to gain entry?"

"We might try knocking on the door." Trick peeked through the hedge. "Is Garrick in on this or not? How many men has Charles roped into this operation?"

"Just we two. Garrick is the suspect."

"John Garrick? A counterfeiter?" Trick jerked upright at the thought, and Chaucer danced beneath him. "Are you certain?"

"No. He could be just another link in the chain. But that description you gave me that sounded familiar? I asked around, found the man, and followed him for two-and-a-half days, until finally he led me here. Was in and out in five minutes. Then I hid for a while, and another man arrived. Didn't match any of your notes, but he was in and out in five minutes, too."

"So if Garrick isn't doing it himself . . ."

"I'm assuming he's at least involved in the distribution. But we need proof."

Trick's mind reeled, remembering Garrick's preachiness, his edginess, the way he always seemed to be snooping around. A closet Parliamentarian?

Damn. It could very well be. That would teach him to move into an area and start blindly socializing with the neighbors. He could have brought Garrick and the others to the cottage someday. They could have run across his props.

Damn.

"We need an excuse to get in," Pendregast said. "He has too many servants to just wait until he leaves. People are always around."

"I can gain us entry. I know him. And he owes me a meal."

"Pardon?"

Trick patted his stomach. "Breakfast."

*   *   *

"Mrs. Kendra? Were you not going to tell us about Clytie?"

With a sigh, Kendra flipped the page in the wonderful book of lesser-known myths she'd discovered in Amberley's double-leveled library. At least she'd thought it was wonderful last month when she found it. Today, reading from it, it didn't seem so wonderful at all.

Once she'd thought that attaining her dream, the orphanage, would be enough. But she'd been wrong. Working with the children was fulfilling, but it didn't fill the hole in her heart that had opened when Trick left her this morning.

Dragging her attention back to the children, she smiled at their rapt expressions.

"Clytie loved the Sun-god—"

"Apollo?" Andrew asked.

"Good memory," she said, trying not to sound annoyed at the interruption. Every little thing seemed to annoy her these past few days. "But for this story we think of him as the Sun-god. You see, he found nothing to love in Clytie, and so she pined away, sitting on the ground out-of-doors where she could watch him. And she would turn her face, following him with her eyes as he journeyed over the sky. And so gazing, she found herself changed into the sunflower, which ever turns toward the sun."

"Did ever he love her?" a chestnut-haired girl asked.

Kendra met her big brown eyes. "No." She sighed. "Clytie loved him with all her heart, but he could never return her feelings."

Just like Trick. Her feelings toward him had changed, but she was afraid his hadn't. The lies had started all over again, and so had the unexplained separations. No man could love a woman and treat her like that.

Was she destined, like Clytie, to follow him with her eyes all her life? Never succeeding in claiming his heart?

"Mrs. Kendra?"

She snapped the book shut. No use mooning about for these couple of days he'd be gone. He'd asked her to trust him, and she would do just that until she could force an explanation. They'd come too far for her to let her marriage go without a fight.

Susanna wandered over to tug on her skirt. "Are we not going to finish the lesson?"

"Tomorrow, maybe." Feeling better already, she smiled. "For now, let's play blindman's buff."

Chapter Twenty-six

"Lord Garrick is not yet awake," a stiff-necked butler told Trick.

"Well, then, wake him up." Without waiting to be invited, Trick stepped into the sprawling, dark manor house and motioned Pendregast to follow. "Tell him the Duke of Amberley is here to collect on a debt."

"With all due respect, Your Grace—"

"Yes, I am due respect. I believe I will wait in the dining room until I receive it." With a jerk of his head to Pendregast, he started wandering in the direction he figured a dining room might be. Sputtering, the butler marched up the stairs.

The third room he looked into had a dining table, and he promptly dropped into a dull mustard-upholstered chair. The rest of the chamber was no less drab. He'd seen no evidence of the remodeling Garrick had claimed as his reason not to host the house party, though the place was sorely in need of it.

Of course, the last thing a counterfeiter needed was strangers working on his house.

"Forgot about this." Pendregast took a folded note from his pocket. " 'Twas sent by special messenger to me this morning. To give to you."

Trick broke the red seal and unfolded it. A letter from King Charles—he'd have recognized his distinctive hand even without the "Your loving friend, Charles R." at the bottom. The King wrote with good news that all was set, the plan to culminate sometime Monday evening.

Damn. "A day or two," Charles had told him with his usual blithe attitude when describing the plan last week. It hadn't occurred to Trick to question that—he'd latched on to the convenient card party excuse, never considering the arrangements might prove too complicated to be carried out over a weekend.

Damn, damn, damn.

He couldn't even go home and try to explain to Kendra. The King's men were already waiting for him to arrive.

"Is something amiss?" Pendregast asked.

"Yes. No." He shook his head to clear it. "I just need to get a note off to my wife. I saw a desk in the sitting room next door—could I trouble you to fetch me quill and paper?"

While he waited, he composed the note in his head. Yet another half-truth. The web his marriage hung suspended on was getting more and more tangled.

He had it written by the time Garrick stomped into the room, hastily dressed and bleary-eyed.

"What is this about a debt, Amberley?"

"I seem to remember you showing up unexpectedly at my home, right in time for supper." Folding the paper, Trick plastered on a smile. "I just happened to be riding by this morning and noticed it was time for breakfast."

"What?"

"And you brought friends as well, did you not? This is my friend, um, Harold"—he slanted Pendregast a quick glance—"Gaunt. Sir Harold Gaunt."

"Pleased to meet you, Lord Garrick," Pendregast said.

Garrick gave him a curt nod before turning back to Trick. "The friends I brought were your friends, too."

"And so they were." Trick shrugged and held up the note. "Can I trouble you to have one of your staff run this to Amberley House? 'Tis rather urgent." He licked his lips. "What are you serving this morning?"

When Compton met Kendra at Amberley House's door with his silver tray in hand, her stomach knotted.

Received an urgent message from my shipping company's manager, the note read. *Following the weekend, must go to London for a day. Be back Monday evening or Tuesday. Will explain later. My love, T.*

Her legs felt leaden as she trudged up the stairs. London. Without her again. Did he truly even own a shipping company? Or had he made that up as an excuse to run off to his mistress?

Arriving in her bedchamber, she leaned against the door and took a calming breath. Surely her imagination was running wild. As usual, she was jumping to conclusions. *My love, T.* One finger traced the words. He'd asked her to trust him. She had to believe him.

But three long, empty days yawned ahead, and she didn't have to stay at home pining for him, either. She was no Clytie. If he could spend his weekend in the "traditional" way, playing cards with the men, she could keep her tradition with the women. In fact, Caithren was probably waiting for her, and no doubt Amy and Jewel would be at Cainewood, too. While the men did whatever it was men did, they could have themselves a party of their own.

Decision made, she packed a bag and headed for the stables. In no time at all she was barreling toward Cainewood, trying to enjoy the wind in her hair as she coaxed Pandora to go even faster. The miles sped by, the landscape becoming comfortingly familiar. Amy and Cait would help her put this all into perspective. Surely their marriages had gone through rocky times as well, but they were both clearly happy.

She thundered over the wooden drawbridge, slid off Pandora, and ran toward Cainewood's familiar double front doors.

A startled butler opened one of them. "Lady Kendra! I mean . . . welcome, Your Grace. What brings you here to Cainewood?"

"I wish to visit with Lady Cainewood. And—" Words failed her when she glimpsed her twin over the man's shoulder, pacing upstairs with a contemplative look on his face and a beaker filled with bluish fluid in his hands. "Ford?" she called, stepping inside. "Why are you not at the party?"

"Kendra?" He blinked, looked down at the door, then disappeared for a moment. Reappearing at the top of the stairs empty-handed, he ran down to catch her in a hug.

"What party?" he asked, pulling back. "Am I missing a party? Damn. Are there pretty women there, too?"

She frowned. "The card weekend, or whatever it is you men call it. Why are you not with the others?"

"There have been no card weekends since your marriage. They were always at Amberley—did you not know that?" Wrapping an arm around her shoulders, he drew her down the corridor toward the drawing room. "What made you think there was a house party this weekend?"

Once in the chamber, she dropped into a salmon-colored chair. Familiar, but not nearly as comforting as she'd hoped. "Trick. He told me he was leaving to play cards with the men, and he'd be back after the weekend. Then he changed it to say Monday night or Tuesday." She bit the inside of her cheek. "Are you sure there's no party?"

"As sure as I can be. I can tell you Jason isn't playing cards, or Colin that I know of, either."

You'll have to trust me. Once you promised that you'd trust me. Has that changed?

A lump rose in her throat as she hid her face in her hands. "I'm a fool then, aren't I? Over and over I believe what he tells me, but he always turns out to be hiding something."

"Perhaps he has a good reason." Ford sat in a matching chair, reaching to pull one hand from her face and hold it between his. "I cannot imagine—"

"No." She leapt up, breaking the contact. Overwhelming sadness turned to bitter anger instead. "There is no good reason to deceive your spouse." Admitting there were things he couldn't tell her was not the same as telling her an outright lie.

He'd lied to her from the beginning, before they were even married, starting by withholding the fact that he was a duke. Whatever had made her believe he'd change now? He'd implied that he needed to play the highwayman for the sake of the children, then turned around and claimed he owned a prosperous shipping firm. Which one of those facts was true?

My love, T. Another lie. A man who loved his wife wouldn't treat her like this. Wouldn't say he was going one place and end up another.

"He's in London with his mistress." She gritted her teeth, pacing the patterned black-and-salmon carpet. "That's why he was in such a hurry to return from Scotland. And afterward, to leave me at Amberley so he could go back to London alone."

And he'd made such a fuss out of telling her how he felt about infidelity. Over and over! The nerve of him, deliberately lulling her into false security with his trumped-up moral standards.

"Men talk, Kendra, and I've heard nothing of a mistress in London."

She looked away from the concern in Ford's deep-blue eyes. "You're my brother. He wouldn't tell you about something like that."

"For God's sake, you've been wed less than three months." The concern was gone from his voice, replaced by an impatience that set her teeth on edge. "The last card party was before you even met the man, and I heard nothing of a mistress then. Yet there you go, as usual, leaping to conclusions. Wait to hear what Trick has to say for himself, will you? I cannot believe we misjudged the man so keenly."

She crossed her arms. "Well, you did." She stared at a portrait of some stern, long-dead ancestor. Another controlling man, no doubt. Her brothers had misjudged Trick completely and pushed her into this marriage. 'Twas their fault she was hurting now.

Their fault she had fallen in love.

Dear God. She turned away, bringing her hands to her cheeks. In love—in love with a man who could never return it. Never trust her, never open up and share his life. She'd tried and tried to be the sort of wife he wanted, to no avail. She'd tried to listen, to trust him like he'd asked, only to be slapped with this bald-faced lie.

"Kendra." Ford drew her gaze. "You need to re-consider this in logical terms. I am sure Trick has an explanation."

She'd come here for her family's love and support, and here her own twin was siding with Trick. Tears threatened, but she wouldn't let them fall. Had Ford not listened to a word she'd said?

Well, of course not—he was a man. "This is your fault—yours and Jason's and Colin's. You stuck me with this lying adulterer of a husband. Where is Cait?"

"Upstairs, I think. These days she's usually taking a nap. But Kendra—"

She was already out of the room.

Garrick's kitchen had clearly been unprepared for breakfast guests. Engaging in desultory small talk with their reluctant host, Trick and Pendregast waited a good hour before an aging maid brought a tray of meat pottage and coffee. Two trips later, the table was also laden with spiced bread, caraway-seeded biscuits, fruited wheatmeal griddle cakes, and currant buns.

Sweets. Kendra would love this breakfast, Trick thought, wincing at the resulting stab of guilt.

The three of them ate until the butler arrived in the doorway. "A visitor, my lord."

Garrick blotted his flabby lips, then stood and patted his more flabby belly. "Enjoy your breakfast, gentlemen. I shall return posthaste."

"Five minutes, I'm guessing," Pendregast said when the man had left.

"I'm going to follow him. If he returns before I do, tell him I was in need of a chamber pot." Trick rose and peeked into the corridor. Thankfully, it was deserted. He slipped out and flattened himself against the wall, moving along until he almost reached the front door.

Having already closed it, Garrick was leading a short man down the other wing of the house. Trick waited, watching, until he saw them enter a room. Then he hurried after them and listened through the door.

There was a scraping sound, something heavy sliding open and then shut. Hearing no voices, he cracked open the door and took a look.

A study. Empty, just as he had thought. He ducked inside and hid himself in the kneehole of an aging oak desk. The grating noise came again, and he bent his head to see between the desk's claw-footed legs. A section of bookshelves disappeared, then slid back into place as he watched.

Garrick set something down on the desk above Trick's head. "Very well. But I don't want to see you for another month. Send someone else in the meantime—we cannot risk having the same men travel the roads all the time. Not until that black-guard is caught."

"Yes, my lord."

"I will see you out."

When the door closed behind them, Trick scooted from the cubby. A pewter candlestick now sat on the desk, and Garrick had not bothered to extinguish the taper. How convenient.

Trick felt around the bookcase for a handle, a button . . . ah, there it was. A latch. Throwing it, he was able to push the shelves behind the ones adjacent.

He grabbed the candle and held it up to illuminate the windowless space beyond. A fair-sized room, if bare of luxuries. Atop a table sat three crucibles, a melting pan, dies, shears, and other equipment Trick didn't recognize. But the coins scattered over the surface were familiar indeed, as were the bars of base metal.

He'd seen all he needed to see.

A couple of minutes later, he strolled back into the dining room, adjusting his breeches conspicuously. "Nice place you have here, Garrick." He aimed a discreet nod at Pendregast.

Garrick grunted. "I'm due for renovations."

"So you've said."

Pendregast pulled out a pocket watch. "Damn, I've forgotten an appointment. Garrick, my thanks for the fine food and company. Amberley, I'll stop by to see you later."

More senseless chitchat that lasted an hour, then longer. God's blood, Trick thought, would this never end? What the hell was taking Pendregast so long?

Garrick grew restless, pacing the chamber but unable to politely escape while Trick kept eating and engaging him in conversation. Trick wondered if he could cram in another morsel of food without vomiting, but supposed the meal might hold him for the long ordeal ahead. Although this had been almost too easy, he knew the next few days would be much harder.

But with any luck, by Monday night he'd be joining Kendra in their bed. For the rest of his life, if he had any say in the matter. And no more secrets.

Finally, the butler announced another arrival.

Trick followed Garrick to the door. "Sir Harold," Garrick said, finding Pendregast on the other side. "Have you forgotten something?"

"I'm afraid so." A balding man with a scar across his cheek stepped from around the corner. "The sheriff."

Chapter Twenty-seven

"**K**endra! Cait! Open up!"

Kendra scurried into the far corner of the bedchamber while Caithren made her way to the door and opened it a crack. "Your sister doesn't want to talk to ye," she told Jason. "Or Ford, either."

"Oh, for God's sake. Tell her it's dinnertime, and we've strawberry tarts for dessert."

Trust a man to think food would solve his problems, Kendra thought. Most especially a Chase man. Well, he wasn't going to coax her by tempting her sweet tooth. "Tell him I'm not hungry," she called to Cait. "Tell him I'm not going to eat until the absurd marriage he arranged is annulled."

"She's not hungry," Cait started. "She's—"

"Forget it." Jason stuck his boot in the doorway when Caithren would have shut it. "Tell her I'll be here when she's ready to talk. Tell her that until then she can starve for all I care. Tell her Cook is baking cherry pies for supper." He paused for a breath. "Are you coming down for dinner, then?"

"Nay. I believe I will stay here with Kendra."

"Women." Following the single terse word, Kendra heard his boots pound down the corridor.

Cait closed the door. "Cherry pies later, Kendra."

"Oh, my. I suppose I will have to save some room." She went back to her old dressing table, where a veritable feast was laid out, delivered by Cait's loyal maid, Dulcie. Sitting down, she stabbed her spoon into her second strawberry tart. "I believe I will skip the sallet and asparagus, then."

"Ye didn't mean that about an annulment, did ye?"

"I know not what I mean." She knew she and Trick had come too far to go back to their old lives, but she was too mad at his deceptions to think straight. "If I were you, Cait, I wouldn't believe a word I said right now."

Not about Trick and not about her brothers, either. After all she'd been through in Scotland, coming to love Trick and deciding her brothers had been right after all, her blaming them made no sense. But then, her emotions rarely did.

Cait took a bite of roast beef. "Your anger certainly hasn't affected your appetite. For sweets, anyway."

"Nothing ever does." She licked strawberry juice off her lips, looking at Trick's amber bracelet where it lay on the table's marble surface. Her wrist felt empty without it.

Her heart felt empty without him.

She turned to Cait. "Have you ever been this angry at Jason?"

"Dinna ask. There have been times, especially when we first met, that I'd have been happy to see the back of him forever. But we always worked it out."

"But you never suspected he was cheating on you."

"Nay, never that. I ken the man well enough to feel certain that has never happened."

"I thought I was coming to know Trick, too." No wonder Eros, the God of Love, was often portrayed wearing a blindfold. Love was truly blind.

"There could be another explanation, Kendra. Although I remember a time ye wouldn't have cared if he cheated." Cait sipped from her cup of wine, regarding her over the rim. "Things have been getting better for ye, then?"

"Things?"

"Ye know . . . in the bedchamber." Kendra felt her face heat, and Caithren laughed. "I can see that they have."

She couldn't stand to think about that now, let alone talk about it, not when she wondered if she'd ever feel that close to him again. "How was your visit home?" she asked Cait instead. "Is your cousin Cameron doing well? And Clarice and little Mary?"

Cait grinned. "Clarice is with child, too. And Cameron walks around all day with a smile on his face."

"I can imagine." Would she ever have children now? 'Twas clear enough Trick would never commit to the sort of marriage she'd dreamed of all her life, but could she learn to live with less? Could she accept only that part of him he was capable of giving? "I'm so happy for them—"

A knock on the door interrupted, and Cait went to answer.

"Are you finished, my lady?" Soft-spoken, her maid entered and began gathering dishes. She refilled their cups with the dregs of a bottle of wine, then smiled, revealing small, child-like teeth. "Would you like another bottle now, milady? I can ask John to fetch one from the cellars." John Foster was one of Cainewood's footmen and Dulcie's latest *amour*.

"Thank ye, that would be nice." Cait set a decimated tart on the tray. "How is Foster today, Dulcie?"

"Oh, fine, milady. He's had a half-day off and been into the village to visit with his mother. Would you know, he came back with interesting news."

Kendra drained her cup. She hoped this Foster fellow would fetch a new bottle soon. She needed more wine if she was going to decide whether to give up on the love of her life. "What news is that?"

"Word has it that the Black Highwayman has been caught and arrested at last. Hauled off to London this very morning to be tried."

"Tried?" Kendra's cup clunked to the marble-topped dressing table. "When will he be tried?"

Dulcie's gray eyes filled with confusion. "Monday, Your Grace. Say . . . are you all right?"

Kendra woke in her old bed at Cainewood with two of her brothers hanging over her. Wondering how she'd gotten there, she blinked at the mint-green canopy above their heads. Had she fainted? She had never fainted before in her life. Trick would pay for this.

Then she remembered, and an aching hollowness opened in her heart. No, Trick wouldn't pay for this. Trick would be dead.

She struggled to sit, looking around to make sure no one but family was in the chamber. "Did you hear?" she asked, her vow of silence forgotten. Her brothers, after all, were not the villains in this tragedy, no matter how much she wanted to blame them.

She needed them, and they were here for her, as they always were.

"Aye, they've heard," Cait said softly. "I told them."

Kendra's stomach felt leaden, and tears threatened to leak from her eyes. "How can this have happened now?" One tear did leak, running hot down her cheek. "He promised he was finished playing that game."

Jason's eyes were compassionate, but his mouth was set in a grim line. "I warned him."

"He must have gone out and done it, anyway. Stubborn fool." And more fool she, for believing him when he said he would stop. She sat and swung her feet off the bed. "I must go to him."

Ford put a hand on her arm. "I thought you wanted to be rid of him?"

"I thought so, too," she said, her voice rising in a wail. Her earlier anger seemed to have vanished, replaced with a fear that clawed at her insides. "But I never wanted to see him dead!"

Jason sat beside her and gathered her into his arms, patting her back as she sobbed against his shirtfront, wetting his shoulder. "Perhaps he'll be acquitted."

Accused criminals were rarely acquitted, but she clung to that thin thread of hope. "I must go see the trial. Take me to the trial."

"Think, Kendra." Ford crouched by the bed, looking up at her, his bright-blue eyes filled with the calm reason that seemed to evade her but come to him so easily. "Why would the Chases go to the trial of a common criminal? What will you tell those who ask? Especially if you look . . . distraught."

God, he was right. As things stood, no one connected the Duke of Amberley with the Black Highwayman, but if anyone discovered she'd been
married to the notorious outlaw, her reputation
would be in tatters, along with that of the rest of
her family.

But this was Trick. No matter how angry she was
at his falsehoods and deceptions, she had to go to
him. Had to see what was to become of the lying,
cheating rogue she had lost her heart to.

"I'll wear a disguise," she said. "But I'm going."

Never in her life had Kendra thought she'd find
herself outside the Justice Hall at the Old Bailey.
After almost two days spent in a sleepless fog of
wrenching misery, endless tears, anger, and self-
doubt, she'd thought that actually getting here and
seeing this trial through would be something of a
relief. But she knew now that nothing could be further from the truth.

The courtyard viewing gallery was mobbed with
Londoners hoping to get a glimpse of the notorious
accused, and even more people stood outside the
spike-topped iron fence. Wearing Dulcie's gray skirt
and plain blouse, with her telltale red hair stuffed
under a mobcap, Kendra grasped Ford's hand and
pulled him through the masses toward the front.

A light rain was falling, making the spectators—
no polite crowd to begin with—even more surly.
"Whyever do they make us stand outside?" she
grumbled, dodging a sharp elbow as she made her
way to the three-walled open courtroom.

Ford pushed back the straw hat he'd borrowed
from a stableman. "It reduces the risk of prisoners

infecting the spectators with gaol fever," he explained in his usual matter-of-fact manner.

She returned a tradesman's dirty glare with one of her own, tugging her sleeve down to cover her amber bracelet as she pushed her way to the rail. "Oh, God," she breathed, her heart clenching when she reached the front. She gripped the rail with both hands to keep her knees from buckling under her. "Oh, God, there he is."

Staring at Trick, she slowly jockeyed herself over to the right, nearer to where he sat in the enclosed dock, chained to eleven other men.

He was wearing black velvet and the long brown periwig that hopefully would keep any spectators from recognizing him as the Duke of Amberley. But the wig was a tangled mess, the usually immaculate black suit all rumpled, and he looked more exhausted than she'd ever seen him. His head was bowed, and his hands hung limply between his spread knees. A guard reached a pike through the bars to prod him to stand when the red-robed judge walked in, followed by jury members who shuffled to two long benches.

The dock's door swung open with an ominous creak, and the prisoners began making their way to the bar, their chains clanking as they dragged on one another. Watching Trick, Kendra felt as though her heart might burst. Literally pulled along by the others, he stumbled and had to be righted. Dark blood crusted his wrists beneath the iron cuffs. A sheen of sweat slicked his features, and he seemed to be having trouble just drawing breath.

He was ill.

She pressed against the rail as though she could

reach him. So close, maybe ten feet away, but oh, so far with the law between them. So very, very far. And ill.

"Dear God," she whispered to Ford. "Can he have caught the gaol fever already?"

"Hush." Her twin's eyes filled with sympathy as he peeled one of her hands from the rail, lacing it with his. " 'Tis starting."

The prisoners' names were called one by one, and they identified themselves by raising a hand. The charges were read in Latin before each of the accused pleaded either guilty or not guilty.

"But they cannot even understand with what they've been charged!" Kendra whispered in horrified protest. With unbelievable swiftness, witnesses were brought forward and evidence was presented by the prosecution. Prisoners were not allowed counsel. Of the eleven men brought to trial before Trick, one was acquitted when no witnesses appeared. The other ten were all sentenced to death, for felonies ranging from stealing an orange, to setting fire to an outhouse, to murdering a neighbor.

By the time Trick's turn arrived, Kendra had lost all hope. Tears swam in her eyes, and her body felt like a single, heavy mass of dread.

"The Black Highwayman," the clerk read, and the crowd hissed gleeful disapproval. They had saved the best for last. When Trick failed to raise his hand, the prisoner next to him did it for him. "What be your name?" the clerk demanded.

Trick stared. A long silence stretched.

"What be your name?"

He hung his head, looking too weak to lift it. Too weak to answer.

A speculative murmur rose from the onlookers. The guard prodded Trick with his pike, and Trick stumbled to his knees, taking the prisoners on either side down with him. With a rattle of chains, they hoisted him back up.

"Black Highwayman, what be your name?"

Inside her, Kendra was screaming. He was too ill to defend himself, could they not see it? Could they not wait for another day?

"Black Highwayman, *what* be your name?"

"Can you not see he's ill?" she called out. A gasp of disapproval rose from the crowd, and the clerk glared in her direction. Trick's gaze snapped to meet hers.

Recognition lit his eyes. But from where Kendra stood, they looked black, not golden. Dilated and dark, filled with regret and defeat.

She had lost her amber highwayman already.

The clerk tried another tack. "Black Highwayman, what do you plead?"

Trick's gaze was still locked on hers. One hand reached into his pocket, and he slowly drew out a piece of paper, crumpling it in his fist. Something was written upon it in black ink, but much too far away to see.

"The press!" The crowd began to chant. "The press! The press!"

"What is that?" Kendra asked, afraid she didn't want to know.

"They call it *peine forte et dure*," Ford whispered. "Prisoners who refuse to plead are stripped and laid on their backs, a wooden plank placed upon them and piled with stones."

"Stones?" 'Twas even worse than she'd imagined.

Salty blood flowed into her mouth, and she realized she was chewing the inside of her cheek.

"Yes, stones." Ford's fingers tightened around hers. "Three hundred pounds or more. And they add another fifty pounds every half hour until the man agrees to plead."

"The press! The press! The press!"

They couldn't. They couldn't do that to an ill man. How could this mob demand such a thing? What kind of barbarous riffraff were they?

"The press! The press! The press!"

"Silence!" The clerk's bellow rattled the very air, and the chant abruptly cut off. Soft rain pattered in the sudden stillness as he looked to the man in red robes.

"Guilty," the judge declared, doubtlessly thinking his decision merciful since the prisoner was too weak to plead. Ford's hand squeezed Kendra's so tight, 'twas a wonder her bones didn't snap. But though he succeeded in quelling her outcry, inside, every fiber of her being was howling. Trick had been spared the press, but she had no doubt what the sentence for a highwayman would be when she'd seen another man sent to the gallows for stealing a piece of fruit.

"Death by hanging." The judge banged his gavel. "Tomorrow at noon."

Trick's gaze stayed on hers, his eyes imploring. His mouth moved, but no words came out. Her fingers worried the amber bracelet, and she could see in his face that he noticed. A single tear welled and rolled down his cheek, making the tears in her own eyes flow faster. Suddenly he looked away and started scraping with a fingernail at one of the crusty scabs on his wrist.

Another group of accused prisoners were brought clanking into the dock, and Trick's line started moving out. She watched in a haze of pain as he drew a red-tipped finger across the crumpled paper in his other hand.

"He's writing something," she whispered in horror to Ford. "He's trying to write something. *In blood.*"

His hand with the paper shaking, he reached it toward her as he was dragged by. She pressed against the rail, straining to get closer, their fingers almost touching. She moaned when he was jerked back, the look in his eyes anguished but unreadable.

Seconds later, he was tugged from the chamber and out of sight.

"He's ill," she sobbed, tears running freely down her face to mix with the miserable cold rain. "He was trying to tell me something, wasn't he?"

"He was too weak." Ford wiped her cheeks. "There's nothing you can do about it now."

"He tried to give me a message in *blood*." Her eyes burned and her heart was cracking. The man had only preyed on Puritans—the real criminals in her eyes—and for the good of orphan children. No matter that he was a liar and an adulterer, he didn't deserve to die.

She leaned far over the rail and shouted to the guard who was closing the gate. "Where are they being taken?"

"Newgate," the man said as the iron bars banged shut.

Chapter Twenty-eight

"Kendra, you cannot go to Newgate." At the Chase town house in Lincoln's Inn Fields, Jason pushed her onto the drawing room's burgundy brocade couch and handed her a large goblet of Rhenish wine. " 'Tis a hellhouse. And there's nothing you can do for him, anyway."

"I must see him." Maybe she could sneak him out. At least she could say good-bye. "I'm going." She set down the wine and rose.

He took her by the shoulders, his bright-green gaze determined. "You cannot go."

Equally determined, she wrenched from his grasp. "You cannot stop me."

"We'll go to King Charles," Ford said.

She whirled to him. "What?"

"We'll go to Charles and ask for a pardon."

Hope fluttered in her chest. "Could . . . could that work?"

He shrugged. " 'Tis certainly within his power. I saw him pardon Swift Nicks."

"Who?" Her legs felt weak, and she dropped back onto the couch.

"The infamous highwayman, Jack Nevison." Ford started pacing. "Early one morn he robbed a fellow in Kent who turned out to be an acquaintance and threatened to turn him in. To give himself an alibi, he rode for York, arriving the same evening—''

"Impossible," she burst out, never mind that she didn't care to hear this since it had nothing to do with Trick. The ride to York took at least four days, more likely a week.

"Apparently not impossible when his life was at risk. He had friends in the taverns all along the Great North Road who supplied him with a fresh horse every hour. When he arrived in the town that evening, he hurried to the bowling green, in time to play a game of bowls with the mayor and other city functionaries. When he was brought to trial later, no less than six dignitaries could honestly swear he'd been in York that day, not Kent."

"Then Charles had no need to pardon him."

"But he had past crimes. The tale made the London rounds, and when Charles heard it, he commanded Nevison to Court to tell the story himself. The King laughed until tears came to his eyes and then dismissed him with a signed and sealed pardon for all his prior misdeeds. I will never forget it. So you can see that Charles can be prevailed upon in the right circumstances."

"Regardless of whether our merry monarch might be swayed by a bit of humor," Kendra said, "you have no knee-slapping story to tell him. There is nothing funny about Trick's situation."

"True," Jason admitted. "But perhaps when he hears only Puritans were robbed, 'twill soften his heart."

"Possible," Ford said. "And let us not forget he knows and likes Trick as the Duke of Amberley."

"And Trick just brought him all that treasure." Kendra grasped at a wisp of hope. "But are you really willing to bring all of this up? Admit that my husband and the Black Highwayman are one and the same?"

"We will do whatever it takes," Jason said. "Considering the alternative, I hardly think Trick will care that the Caldwell name is tarnished."

"And *our* name?" She cared not a whit for their reputation compared to Trick's life, but he was her husband, not theirs.

Yet their expressions told her, unquestionably, that they felt the same. And melted whatever resentment was left in her heart.

"Thank you," she said softly, knowing they were right. Not only about this, but about how she always jumped to conclusions without giving them the benefit of the doubt. "I know you married me to Trick with only good intentions, and I shouldn't have blamed you for his lies." She drew a calming breath. "I'm sorry I got angry. 'Twill not happen again, I promise."

Jason released a choked laugh. "Of course it will happen again. We're family."

Ford's blue eyes twinkled. "Besides, those times when you storm off not speaking to us are the only peace and quiet we get around here."

"We're your brothers," Jason said, "and we'll always be here for you to lean on."

"And abuse," Ford added with a smile. "That's part of our being family, too."

Once she had told Trick something similar. Her eyes flooded at the memory. "But I'm going to try to do better, anyway. I love you both."

"We never doubted it," Jason told her, turning serious once more as he faced his brother. "Shall we go ask for that pardon?"

" 'Twill not hurt to ask," she sighed. No matter that the Chases and Trick were all intimates of Charles, she had little confidence they'd get him to pardon another infamous highwayman. One prank on that order made for a rollicking good story—he might feel that twice would make him look like a man who had no care for his subjects' welfare. Appearances counted in politics.

Besides, the King might not even be at Whitehall for all they knew.

But they had to try. She started to rise. "Let us go ask now. I have my doubts that this will work, but the sooner we find out, the better. Trick is ill."

"You're staying here." The gentle, forgiving smile on Jason's face disappeared as he pushed her down to the couch and shoved the wine back into her hands. "Women are rarely granted audiences, as you're well aware, unless they take place in the Royal Bedchamber. Just sit tight, and we'll be back before you know it."

When her brothers left, Kendra was still wearing her disguise, and she was still determined to see Trick. Having heard that gaolers were fond of bribes, she pocketed some coins and slipped out into Lincoln's Inn Fields to hail a hackney cab.

On the bumpy ride to Newgate, she wondered what she could say to him. Though she was still furious at his lies and infidelity, a man at death's door deserved some peace of mind.

Then the cab jolted and she heard his voice.

I'm sorry, leannan, but there are things I cannot tell you. You'll have to trust me. Once you promised you'd trust me . . .

A surge of panic overwhelmed her.

Could it be she'd misjudged her husband as badly as she had her brothers? Had she jumped to conclusions there, too?

Her heart raced as all the memories rushed back. The way he'd been slowly revealing himself; the hushed, earnest words; her conviction that he always wanted to do right.

Do you know how much I care for you, lass? Enough to make me question my loyalties.

What had he meant by those words? What if he really did have an explanation for all that had gone on? He'd been trying to tell her something at the trial and been cheated of his chance.

My love, T.

Dear God, she loved him, too.

She could have been wrong. As she'd been many times before, she could have been so, so wrong. And now it might be too late.

Her brothers had to get that pardon. They just had to. And if they failed . . .

She would go to the King herself. The hanging wasn't scheduled until noon tomorrow, so she had all night. She didn't care if she had to go into the Royal Bedchamber. Hell, she would even sleep with Charles if it meant he'd pardon Trick. She was willing to do whatever it took to save her husband from the noose.

But that was for later, after she heard back from Jason and Ford. For now, she just wanted to get into that gaol. She just wanted to see Trick and wrap him

into her arms and tell him she was sorry, so sorry . . .
As the cab rattled to a halt, she unclenched her fists
and hurried to get out.

Newgate Prison had burned in the Great Fire two
years earlier and was only partially rebuilt. The new
entrance was magnificently decorated. Four figures
represented Liberty, Peace, Security, and Plenty, but
behind the impressive facade, the gaol itself remained as miserable as Kendra had always heard.

After she paid a man at the gate, it creaked open
to admit her to what seemed a dark pit of squalor.
Her footsteps echoed in a stone corridor still blackened from the fire. Noxious odors of slops, rotten
food, and unwashed bodies made her gag before she
stepped into the relatively luxurious keeper's house.

"Walter Cowday," a hard, graying man introduced
himself. "Who you here to see?"

"The Black Highwayman."

He raised a grizzled brow and held out a hand.
Her heart pounding, she put a silver coin in it, and
then another and another. When he remained silent,
she added the one she had of gold. She clenched her
hand around her few remaining coins; she'd never
imagined it would cost this much.

"He went straight to the condemned hold. Lucky
bastard don't have to wait. Tyburn Fair day tomorrow." When she failed to show the proper excitement
for the public holiday that an execution meant, he
pocketed the money and motioned for her to follow
him back to the corridor. He lifted a hatch door and
pointed down. "There you go. If you've more silver,
a guard will point the way."

Holding her cumbersome skirts in one hand, she
descended a ladder and dropped to a damp stone

floor. Bleak gray cells lined both sides of another corridor, moisture trickling down their walls. Each looked about eight feet by six, furnished with a wooden bench and a Bible. The iron candlesticks, one per hold bolted to the stone, apparently were saved for night. The only light came filtered though a tiny window high in each cell, covered by heavy iron bars.

She swallowed hard and started searching down the corridor. 'Twas cold and dark, and she stumbled more than once. Men hooted at her, and chains clanked as they stuck their arms through the bars and grabbed at her in the blackness. Tears pricked her eyelids.

Trick was nowhere to be found.

"Who goes there?"

She couldn't remember ever being as relieved when a uniformed guard appeared in the corridor holding a burning torch. Blessed light.

"I'm looking for the Black Highwayman."

Wordlessly, he held out a hand, and she gladly filled it with the last of her silver. Yet he made no move to show her the way.

Through heartache and fear, indignation rose. "Well, where is he?" she demanded.

"Doctor took him."

Once again, hope fluttered in her breast. Maybe they'd noticed he was ill and brought him to an infirmary. Perhaps they'd let him recover and retry his case. 'Twas possible the pardon would be unnecessary, after all.

"He's not here?" she asked.

The man shook his head.

'Twas like pulling teeth to get answers from the

cur, and this after she'd paid. Impatience and worry combined to make her jaw tighten and her words sound shrewish. "Where did the doctor take him to, then?"

"The graveyard, mistress."

Chapter Twenty-nine

"The graveyard?" A wave of apprehension swamped her. Her chest felt as though it might burst, and her breath came in short, shallow pants. She couldn't have heard the guard right. "The graveyard? Are you sure? What happened?"

The uniformed man shrugged.

"Tell me what happened! I paid you, damn it!"

She rarely used such language, but it could be effective. He blinked and took a small step back. "He was ill when he came in, ye see. A doctor went in to examine him, came out, and said he was dead. Of the plague."

"The plague?" She knew it could kill swiftly, but she'd seen Trick only hours ago. Ill, but very much alive.

And he'd wanted to tell her something.

"Are you sure?"

"Well, I will own up I didn't go in there. One don't mess with the plague, mistress."

"Did you see him at all?"

"Aye, through the bars from a safe distance. He was dead, all right. Blue spots all over 'im, and he was stiff as a long-trapped rat. Within an hour he was put in a coffin and carried out. I imagine he was buried just as quick."

She sank to the sticky stones, not caring that she sat in filth shared with bugs and rats. Her lids slid closed against the tears that welled, poised to fall. Trick was dead. Dead and buried. Along with his lies and his deceptions, his soft words and cherishing kisses.

And she was dead inside.

It was over, and she had no emotion left in her.

"Mistress?" The guard shook her shoulder. "Mistress, ye cannot just sit here."

She opened her eyes and took a deep breath. No, she could not just sit here. The man reached down a hand, and she let him help her up.

Her brothers. She needed to get to her brothers. Hopefully they had not made fools of themselves already by asking the King for a highwayman's pardon. And she needed to lean on them, too. To let them take her home. They would order up a bath, and she would wash off the incredible stink of Newgate. Then she would sleep and escape this nightmare her life had turned into.

She'd no money left for a hackney, but when she tearfully asked a driver to take her to Whitehall Palace and promised to see he got paid, he agreed.

The gatekeeper at Whitehall was not about to let a servant girl in.

"I'm Kendra Chase, the Marquess of Cainewood's sister."

"Sure you are." Dressed in red livery, the man looked her over with patent disbelief. "And I'm King Charles himself."

"I mean . . ." Drawing a shuddering breath, she

closed her eyes, opened them, tried again. "I'm the Duchess of Amberley."

"Kendra!"

The voice, heavy and seductive, came from an open window overhead. She'd forgotten Lady Castlemaine's suite was over Holbein's Gate. Although both of them had spent the Commonwealth years with King Charles's exiled Court, Barbara, the King's longtime mistress, had never been her favorite woman. But now was not the time to be choosy.

"Barbara!" she called up. "My brothers are here, and this gentleman refuses to let me in."

"Dolt," Barbara said. Her titian head disappeared from the window, and a minute later she was standing on the other side of the scrolled wrought-iron gate.

Kendra felt like a guttersnipe next to Barbara's lush, fashionable form, but she couldn't dredge up enough energy to feel properly chagrined. She was so tired.

"Let her in, you clodpoll," Barbara said. She'd never been known for her tact. The gate swung open. "I know just where your brothers are." Before Kendra knew it, she was following Barbara down the maze of halls that traversed Whitehall's two thousand rooms. "And your husband along with them."

"What?" She stopped in her tracks, her heart leaping with relief—until she realized Barbara had to be mistaken.

"You're married to Amberley, are you not?" Barbara pouted as she took Kendra's arm and hurried her along. "And I wasn't invited to the wedding. You know how I like a good party."

"We didn't have much of a wedding," she said

woodenly. Trick wasn't here—he was dead in the
ground in a graveyard near Newgate.

The woman threw open a magnificent carved and
gilded door. Beyond lay a splendid sitting room in
shades of gold and black. A fire blazed on a marble
hearth. King Charles sat in a tufted velvet chair, his
head thrown back in laughter. Jason sat in another,
laughing right along with him.

And reclining on a black satin daybed, a smile
curving his lips and a cheroot in one hand, sat Patrick Iain Caldwell.

The bastard wasn't dead.

If she'd had a pistol at her disposal, she'd have
rectified that.

She bolted past Barbara and retraced her steps
through the palace and outside. The hackney was
still waiting, and when a hysterical woman begged
the driver to take her to a town house, he wasn't
about to disagree.

She hadn't known it was possible to feel such deep
hurt. No matter Trick's reasons, that he could let her
go through all that, allow her to think he was *dead* . . .

'Twas the most unforgivable betrayal she could
imagine. He would never, ever measure up to even
the lowest of her expectations. She couldn't live with
such a man—couldn't live with herself if she accepted such a marriage. Such a lack of basic caring
and commitment.

Cold anger. 'Twas the safest emotion to feel, the
one—the only one—that would protect her from
being ripped apart.

She was going to her house, not Trick's. Caldwell
House had never felt like hers, and it never would,

any more than Amberley or Duncraven had. When the hackney pulled up in front of the house in Lincoln's Inn Fields, she couldn't wait to get inside.

As always, Goodwin opened the door. "A bath, please, Goodwin. And pay the hackney driver, if you will." Leaving him openmouthed, she barged past, heading for the wide, curving staircase and the comfort of her feminine chamber upstairs. A chamber no man had ever slept in.

Ford was waiting in the entry, seated in one of two matching brocade chairs. "Kendra."

Not wanting to, she stopped and turned.

His blue gaze swept her costumed form. "When we arrived at Whitehall and learned from King Charles what had happened, Jason sent me back immediately to let you know your husband was well and would soon be free. But you weren't here."

His voice betokened both vexation and distress, but she didn't have it in her to express sorrow for causing him worry. Not now. She had no space left for any more emotions now.

"I sent six servants out looking—"

Turning away from his accusatory eyes, she climbed the graceful stairs, one foot in front of the other, just as she always had.

Her chamber was the same as always, too. A green oasis of familiarity. Nothing in her life had been familiar lately—not her feelings and not her surroundings. Here, in her old room, she could flip back the calendar to last June, when she'd been an innocent virgin going on about her boring life. Here, in her old room, she could call for a bath and wash away not only the stink of Newgate, but all her confusing emotions. The first blush of love and the subsequent

hurt. The incredible joy of fulfillment, the disappointment and disillusion. All of it—the ups and the
downs, and the downs and the ups, and the final
descent into that pit of despair. She'd never appreci-
ated how wonderful her old, predictable life had
been.

When the bath was prepared, she peeled off Dulcie's clothes and sank into the steaming water right
up to her chin, ready to recover that lovely, boring
life. Who needed a husband? Especially one who felt
so little for her that he would lie to escape her and
then let her think he was dead and laugh it off like
the world's best joke.

She knew when it was time to give up.

With shaking fingers, she unfastened the clasp on
the amber bracelet and let it fall to the carpeted floor.
Then she tugged off the plain gold band. When she
dropped it, it rolled a few inches from the carpet
onto polished wood before landing flat with a tiny
plop. Until now, since that fateful day in Cainewood's little chapel, it had never left her hand.

She hardly noticed her tears dripping into the
lavender-scented water. Just as she hardly noticed
the knock at the door until it opened.

"Kendra."

The expression on Trick's face was achingly apologetic, but she'd been through that before. He
wouldn't fool her ever again.

Sinking deeper into the water, she dashed the tears
from her cheeks and narrowed her eyes. "Who invited you in here?"

Still dressed in rumpled black velvet and looking
more than a little unsteady, he quietly shut the door

behind him. His gaze flicked to the gold and amber, then back to her. "You didn't complain the last time I walked in on your bath."

Despite all the anger and hurt, she blushed to remember. "That was before I left you," she said. "That was a lifetime ago, when I was still blind and innocent."

He walked over, and, wordlessly, handed her a crumpled sheet of paper.

Tearing her gaze from him, she unfolded it with wet, shaky hands. The five words were barely legible, thick swashes of rusty red-brown.

DON'T WORRY JUST AN ACT

Leaning close, he turned the paper over in her hands, and her heart turned over along with it. He straightened while she read the words in black ink— the writing she hadn't been able to make out at the trial.

When love on my sweet wife's wings
Comes to hover within my walls
If I turn it away with untruths and deceit
'Tis myself I must blame for the fall.

Trust must be earned then earned again
Ere forgiveness can overcome sorrows
Yesterday's errors wiped from the slate
May leave room for joyful tomorrows.

Stone walls do not a prison make
Nor iron bars well-turned

While I bear hope, mayhap forlorn
My love will be returned.

Poetry written in prison. Reassurance written in blood.

Tears flooded her eyes, blurring her vision. Instead of her mint-green chamber, what she saw was the damp, crowded courtyard outside the open courtroom of the Old Bailey. Instead of the soft swish of water, what she heard was the jeering crowd. And she remembered Trick's stricken face as he tried to reach her, first with words and then with this very same note—and the expression in his eyes when he failed to succeed.

"Why?" she asked, finally ready to listen. "Why all the lies?"

He stayed riveted in place. "Before I ever met you," he said slowly, "I made a promise to King Charles. I thought that promise, to my sovereign, was more important than my wife. I was wrong. And if I've lost you because of that mistake, I will never forgive myself."

Oh, God, he was getting to her. Could she allow herself to feel this again? "What was this promise?"

"I was never really a highwayman, Kendra. 'Twas naught but a ruse to find some counterfeiters who were bedeviling the country's economy. Emptying the King's purse and undermining his credibility. I was part of his scheme to uncover it."

"Just as I guessed, only I never completed the connection."

He nodded. "And I'd sworn not to tell a soul. I never considered that the Black Highwayman might become a wanted man. When it happened, Charles devised a plan to get rid of him, so I could live my life as the duke without anyone ever suspecting that the highwayman and I were one and the same. He arranged for the arrest and the public trial. And he had a doctor drug me to make me look ill, and that same doctor visit later and paint blue spots on my body, then declare me dead and carry me away. I suggested we use black nightshade."

"Dwale." The fever, the slowed breathing, the weakness, the dilated eyes. She should have realized. "It killed your mother, Trick. It could have killed you."

"Weeks of it killed my mother, and my father recovered, after all. 'Twas one dose. A calculated risk, and at least I knew what I was getting into."

" 'Twas a perfect plan," she admitted. "Brilliant."

"Not perfect. Because Charles still refused to let me tell you. And I was foolish enough to believe we could pull this off over a couple of days when I could give you another excuse to be gone, and you'd never find out."

"But I did."

"Aye." He took a step closer, then swayed. "I was wrong, *leannan*. I trusted you even if Charles didn't, and I should have told you everything, no matter that he ordered me not to. I was wrong to think you'd never find out, and I was wrong to lie to you about what I was doing. But most of all, I was wrong to think any promise to a king, or the King himself, is more important than you. Nothing is more important than you."

Disregarding Royal orders was considered much worse than highway robbery. *Punishable by hanging*, she heard herself whisper deep in a dungeon in Scot-

land. *Punishable by hanging, drawing, quartering . . .*
"Nothing is more important? Not even treason?"

"Nothing. I knew it—I knew it while I sat in that prison awaiting trial, wondering where you were and whether rumors had reached your ears to cause you torment. And then when I saw you standing at that rail . . ." His eyes mirrored the anguish she'd seen in them that moment.

"But by then," he continued, " 'twas too late. I was too weak, too drugged." He swayed again. "I still am, it seems. They told me I wasn't recovered enough to come home yet, but, like you, I didn't listen. Like you, I couldn't listen, not when my love was at stake." He risked a tiny grin, that chipped tooth just peeking through a tentative smile. It cracked her heart.

She had been wrong, too. He'd asked her to trust him, said there were things he couldn't tell her. But she hadn't listened. She wanted to say she understood, but her throat closed with emotion.

She looked down at the page in her hand, the dear words blurring through fresh tears. In his own blood, he'd tried to tell her not to worry. And he'd written a poem for her, admitting his love, promising to earn her trust, asking for forgiveness.

Poetry. He'd shared himself, just as she'd hoped for all along. His wall had finally come down, or maybe she'd managed to scale it.

He came forward and took the paper from her trembling hands, setting it aside.

Then he stepped right into the water.

"Your boots!" she gasped.

In the big tub, he knelt at her feet. "I own a shipping line and a warehouse stacked with imported goods from all over the world. I can buy a hundred pairs of boots." His voice was thick and unsteady, his amber eyes so intense, they seemed to spear her to her very soul.

He reached beneath the water to take her hands in his. "Do you not understand, *leannan*? I can buy almost anything—anything, that is, except your love."

"You have it," she whispered.

Epilogue

Six years later

Kendra ran down Amberley's marble front steps, then, waiting for Trick, paused and looked back at the house. She smiled at the incongruous stone lintel over the elegant double front doors—a long, decidedly unelegant rock with symbols chiseled into it: the letters KC and PC, a ship, a heart, and a date. 1668.

"What is that?" she'd asked Trick the day she first came home from the orphanage to see it.

He'd blinked. "Do you not remember Falkland? And the marriage lintels?"

"Well, yes. But this isn't a weaver's cottage in Scotland—it's a mansion in Sussex. And this house wasn't built in 1668."

"Mayhap it wasn't," he'd told her, pulling her toward him for a kiss. "But that was the year it became a home."

Remembering now, the same warmth filled her heart that had filled it then. She fingered the stones on her amber bracelet, knowing with a certainty that she'd never take it off again.

Trick finally sauntered out, displaying none of her own impatience.

"Hurry, Trick, or Cait's babe will be born before we get there."

"Slow down, or *our* babe will be born too early." Walking her over to the caleche, he smiled and ran a possessive hand over the slight bulge of her stomach. "Besides, we were there already. 'Twas you insisted we leave everyone and come back home to get the gift you forgot."

" 'Twas *you* insisted on the hour we just spent in the bedchamber." Grinning as he climbed up beside her, she leaned to give him a quick kiss.

With a hand on the back of her neck, he held her close, his lips meeting hers in a much longer, warmer caress. His mouth opened, his tongue circling hers, sending a wild swirl of excitement spiraling through her. Her senses reeled, and the soft, paper-wrapped package in her hands slipped to the caleche's boards.

He broke off and, with a low laugh, reached to snag it and set it back on her lap. "D'ye want to go back upstairs, *leannan*?"

"Oh, yes," she sighed, then shook her head. "But no."

"Women." He shook his own head, bright gold in the sun, and lifted the caleche's reins.

"Drive fast," she urged, and then, "Faster," until they were racing toward Cainewood at an alarming speed, considering her delicate state. "I want to be there with Cait when the babe greets the world."

But as she was hurrying up Cainewood's carved stone staircase, the thready cry of a newborn split the air. She paused with her hand on the gray marble rail.

Trick squeezed her around the shoulders. "Sorry we're late, lass, but do you not think our little interlude was worth it? We so rarely have time to ourselves these days."

"I suppose." She gave him a mock pout. "Let us go meet the child."

The door to Jason and Caithren's chamber was wide open, the room crammed with cooing Chases. Cait reclined like a queen in the cobalt-curtained bed, a squalling infant in her arms.

"For me?" she asked with a smile, indicating the gift in Kendra's hands. "Or the babe?"

"Both." Kendra handed it to her. "Though really it's from your cousin Cameron. I wrote asking him to send it. Then he wouldn't accept my money." Looking around the noisy chamber while Caithren opened the package, she spotted Jason and Colin, but not her twin. "Is Ford not here yet?"

Jason sat beside Cait. "He sent a message from Lakefield House that they would be a bit late," he said, helping his wife unfold a green and blue plaid blanket. "Seems to think he's on the verge of some discovery."

"Turning iron into gold? He always wanted to be Midas." Kendra laughed, moving closer as a grinning Cait wrapped her child in the Leslie tartan. Like magic, the babe quieted.

Swathed in its mother's clan colors, the child looked so precious and content. Feeling her heart melt with tenderness, Kendra ran a fingertip along its downy cheek. "Everything went well?" she asked Cait while smiling down at the newborn. " 'Tis healthy? And you're fine?"

"Aye. Everything went perfectly."

The baby grasped her finger with tiny fingers of its own. Such a miracle. Beneath the new blanket, 'twas swaddled in white, not blue or pink. She looked up. "Well, what is it?"

Cait gave a happy sigh. "A lad."

"*Another* boy?"

That made three. The Chase family had multiplied in the six years since Kendra and Trick were wed.

Cait's two older sons were bouncing on the canopied bed. Thankfully the babe didn't seem to mind the wild ride.

The rest of the chamber was no more calm. Amy and Colin's two boys were racing around the room, chasing Kendra and Trick's two giggling daughters and gleefully careening off the tapestried walls. The oldest of the cousins at seven, Jewel was a bit more sedate. Of course that was because she was busy at the moment, serenading the new arrival with a lullaby—at the top of her lungs.

One of Kendra's young daughters rammed into her knees, the result of a hopeless attempt to escape her pursuing cousins. As she lifted the girl into her arms, Trick moved close. "Chaos, as always," he whispered.

"Yes," she said, turning to him. "But a happy chaos, don't you think?"

He grinned and took her mouth in a kiss, right there in front of her brothers and everyone, like that first kiss in Cainewood's chapel so many years before.

And this kiss left her every bit as shaken.

A glorious thing, true love was, she thought as she pulled back with a smile, their daughter wriggling between them. Once, long ago, she'd promised he would find true love, and she'd followed through, had she not?

A Chase promise was not given lightly.

Author's Note

King Charles's baggage ferry really did go down in the Firth of Forth that fated summer of 1633, although—so far as I know!—nobody had substituted rocks for the treasure. Interestingly, the sinking wasn't common knowledge until the early 1990s. Apparently embarrassed by the loss, Charles did his best to keep it quiet, and it was centuries before a historian noticed a footnote and began to look into it. Since then, three accounts have been found that make mention of the sinking. But although all the writers were contemporary to the incident, none of them were actually present, and therefore, little is known about what actually lies at the bottom of the Firth of Forth. We know that one of two wooden ferries went down, carrying a portion of the King's household property, but which possessions were aboard remains to be seen. It is assumed to be mostly kitchen goods—a Royal "kitchen" consisting mainly of silver and gold serving pieces—but this is only a guess based on accountings of replacement items that were ordered in the months afterward.

The search for the shipwreck began soon after discovery of its existence, but progress has been slow, because conditions in the Forth—frigid, choppy water, strong tides, poor visibility—severely limit diving opportunities. Early on, an American team searched for several summers, but their efforts proved unsuccessful. Following two years of inactivity, the project resumed, this time under a nonprofit group formed for the purpose, Burntisland Heritage Trust. The search is being carried out in accordance with strict archaeological guidelines, and Historic Scotland is responsible for assuring that these standards are met and maintained. As of this writing, the Trust's divers have targeted an area and laid a control survey line, and their next step is to sweep search from that.

If you're interested in following the progress, news is posted regularly on the Trust's Web site at www.kingcharles-wrex.co.uk. You can also find a link on my Web site at www.laurenroyal.com. The world waits with bated breath to see what will rise from the Firth of Forth. . . . Here's hoping they don't find chests filled with rocks!

As for the highwayman Jack Nevison (nicknamed Swift Nicks by King Charles II himself), the story Ford told of his ride from London to York was true, as well as the tale of his Court visit and pardon from Charles. But alas, not one to learn from his mistakes, the notorious robber continued his life of crime. His escapes from prison were legendary, including the stunt I borrowed where a doctor friend painted him with blue spots and declared him dead. In 1685, he was caught for the last time in York. Brought to a hasty trial before he could devise an escape, he pleaded the King's most gracious pardon, which he claimed covered subsequent as well as prior misdeeds. Not surprisingly, the court dismissed his defense, and at the ripe old age of forty-six, Swift Nicks found himself hanged.

The homes in my stories are usually inspired by real-life places, and this book is no exception. Though in a different geographic location, Amberley House and its beautiful gardens were loosely modeled on Hatfield House in Hertfordshire, England. The original palace, built in 1497 by the Bishop of Ely, was the childhood and young-adult home of the first Queen Elizabeth. Two portraits of her can be viewed in the home today, along with some of her clothing and letters.

Elizabeth's successor, James I, did not care for Hatfield as a home, preferring Theobalds, the residence of Robert Cecil, first Earl of Salisbury. He proposed an exchange, and the Cecils agreed. In 1608, the earl tore down most of the palace and began building the present house in what was then a modern style, at a cost of over £38,000, a staggering amount of money in those times. Though first designed by Robert Lyminge, the plans were modified by others, including, it is thought, young Inigo Jones. This is the house that you can visit today, and the one Kendra saw when she first rode up that long drive.

From the seventeenth century until present day, Hatfield House has served as both a social and political center, hosting luminaries from royalty on down. Well worth a visit, the magnificent house is open for tours from March through October, and most of the gardens are open year-round.

Duncraven Castle was invented when I stayed at Borthwick Castle, twin towers located just south of Edinburgh in Scotland (although, once again, I took the liberty of moving it). Built in 1430 by the first

Lord Borthwick, whose sepulchre can still be seen with that of his Lady in the old village church, its virtually impregnable stone walls sheltered Mary Queen of Scots in her last days of freedom. When a force of some thousand men surrounded the castle, her husband, Bothwell, escaped, leaving Mary behind under the protection of the Borthwicks. Disguised as a page boy, Mary then climbed through a window in the Great Hall, lowered herself by rope to the ground below, and set off through the gate and across the glen in search of her husband. The stuff of romance novels, isn't it? But sadly, their reunion was a short one, and the tragic Queen never again knew real freedom.

Nearly a century later, Borthwick Castle was besieged by the forces of Oliver Cromwell, whose letter demanding surrender—the same one read by Trick in my story—hangs framed in today's Great Hall. Weathered and nobly scarred, Borthwick still stands hundreds of years later. Sir Walter Scott described Borthwick as by far the finest example of the Scottish castles which consist of a single "donjon," or keep. So it was, and so it still is, now run as a bed and breakfast. Do treat yourself with a stay there if ever you get a chance. After a delicious gourmet dinner, you may sit before the immense fireplace, sipping spirits while the caretakers regale you with stories of ghosts and legends. And when you climb the winding staircase to your chamber, don't be surprised if you find yourself looking over your shoulder. . . .

If you'd like to see pictures of these places and others in my books, please visit my Web site at www.laurenroyal.com. There you may also enter a contest, sign up for my newsletter, and find recipes for some of the seventeenth-century foods that Kendra and Trick ate in this story. My favorite is the Tarte of Spinage (otherwise known as spinach pie), but I adore reader mail, so I hope you will write and tell me which one *you* like the best!